The Best
AMERICAN
SHORT
STORIES
1989

The Best AMERICAN SHORT STORIES 1989

Selected from
U.S. and Canadian Magazines
by MARGARET ATWOOD
with SHANNON RAVENEL

With an Introduction by Margaret Atwood

HOUGHTON MIFFLIN COMPANY BOSTON

Shannon Ravenel is grateful to Shanon Woods and to Johanna Wood, both of whom provided able assistance and valuable consultation.

ISSN 0067-6233
ISBN 0-395-47097-8
ISBN 0-395-47098-6 (PBK.)

Printed in the United States of America

M 10 9 8 7 6 5 4 3

Contents

Publisher's Note

The *Best American Short Stories* series was started in 1915 under the editorship of Edward J. O'Brien. Its title reflects the optimism of a time when people assumed that an objective "best" could be identified, even in fields not measured in physical terms.

Martha Foley took over as editor of the series in 1942. With her husband, Whit Burnett, she had edited *Story* magazine since 1931, and in later years she taught creative writing at Columbia School of Journalism. When Miss Foley died in 1977, at the age of eighty, she was at work on what would have been her thirty-seventh volume of *The Best American Short Stories*.

Beginning with the 1978 edition, Houghton Mifflin introduced a new editorial arrangement for the anthology. Inviting a different writer or critic to edit each new annual volume would provide a variety of viewpoints to enliven the series and broaden its scope. *Best American Short Stories* has thus become a series of informed but differing opinions that gains credibility from its very diversity.

Also beginning with the 1978 volume, the guest editors have worked with the series editor, Shannon Ravenel, who during each calendar year reads as many qualifying short stories as she can get hold of, makes a preliminary selection of 120 stories for the guest editor's consideration, and compiles the "100 Other Distinguished Stories," a listing that has always been an important feature of these volumes.

In the twelve years that have passed since then, there has

been growing interest in the short story, and the form itself has grown. The range of approaches and techniques and stances it attracts is ever broader. And so is its audience. In response to this anthology's increasingly enthusiastic readership, the 1987 volume introduced a new feature. Each of the authors of the twenty stories selected by the guest editor is invited to describe briefly how his or her story came to be written. The contributors have accepted what is clearly a challenging assignment, and their short essays appear at the back of the volume in the "Contributors' Notes" section.

The stories chosen for this year's anthology were originally published in magazines issued between January 1988 and January 1989. The qualifications for selection are: (1) original publication in nationally distributed American or Canadian periodicals; (2) publication in English by writers who are American or Canadian; and (3) publication *as* short stories (novel excerpts are not knowingly considered by the editors). A list of the magazines consulted by Ms. Ravenel appears at the back of this volume. Other publications wishing to make sure that their contributors are considered for the series should include Ms. Ravenel on their subscription list (P.O. Box 3176, University City, Missouri 63130).

Introduction:
Reading Blind

WHENEVER I'm asked to talk about what constitutes a "good" story, or what makes one well-written story "better" than another, I begin to feel very uncomfortable. Once you start making lists or devising rules for stories, or for any other kind of writing, some writer will be sure to happen along and casually break every abstract rule you or anyone else has ever thought up, and take your breath away in the process. The word *should* is a dangerous one to use when speaking of writing. It's a kind of challenge to the deviousness and inventiveness and audacity and perversity of the creative spirit. Sooner or later, anyone who has been too free with it will be liable to end up wearing it like a dunce's cap. We don't judge good stories by the application to them of some set of external measurements, as we judge giant pumpkins at the Fall Fair. We judge them by the way they strike us. And that will depend on a great many subjective imponderables, which we lump together under the general heading of taste.

All of which may explain why, when I sat down to read through the large heap of stories from which I was to select for this collection, I did so with misgiving. There were so many stories to choose from, and all of them, as they say, publishable. I knew this because they had already been published. Over the course of the previous year, the indefatigable and devoted series editor, Shannon Ravenel, had read every short story in every known magazine, large or small, famous or obscure, in both the United States and Canada — a total of over two thousand stories. Of these she had chosen a hundred and twenty, from which I was to pick twenty. But how was I to do this? What would be my criteria, if any? How would I be able to tell the best from the merely better? How would I *know*?

I had elected to read these stories "blind," which meant that Shannon Ravenel had inked out the names of the authors. I had no idea, in advance, how these small black oblongs would transform the act of editing from a judicious task to a gleeful pleasure. Reading through these authorless manuscripts was like playing hooky: with a hundred strokes of a black marker, I had been freed from the weight of authorial reputation. I didn't have to pay any attention to who ought to be in because of his or her general worthiness or previous critical hosannas. I didn't have to worry about who might feel slighted if not included. That weighing, measuring, calculating side of me — and even the most scrupulously disinterested editor has one — had been safely locked away, leaving me to wallow among the ownerless pages unencumbered. Picking up each new story was like a child's game of Fish. You never knew what you would get: it might be a piece of plastic or it might be something wonderful, a gift, a treasure.

In addition to remaining ignorant about authorial worth, I could disregard any considerations about territory. I had no way of knowing, for instance, whether a story with a female narrator was by a female author, whether one with a male narrator was by a man; whether a story about a Chinese immigrant was by a writer with a Chinese background, whether one about a nineteenth-century Canadian poet was by a Canadian. I've recently heard it argued that writers should tell stories only from a point of view that is their own, or that of a group to which they themselves belong. Writing from the point of view of someone "other" is a form of poaching, the appropriation of material you haven't earned and to which you have no right. Men, for instance, should not write as women; although it's less frequently said that women should not write as men.

This view is understandable but, in the end, self-defeating. Not only does it condemn as thieves and imposters such writers as George Eliot, James Joyce, Emily Brontë, and William Faulkner, and, incidentally, a number of the writers in this book; it is also inhibiting to the imagination in a fundamental way. It's only a short step from saying we can't write from the point of view of an "other" to saying we can't read that way either, and from there to the position that no one can really understand anyone else, so we might as well stop trying. Follow this line of reasoning to its logical conclusion, and we would all be stuck with reading nothing but our own work, over and over; which would be my personal idea of hell. Surely the delight and the wonder come not from who tells the story but from what the story tells, and how.

Reading blind is an intriguing metaphor. When you read blind, you see everything but the author. He or she may be visible intermittently, as a trick of style, a locale about which nobody else is likely to write, a characteristic twist of the plot; but apart from such clues he is incognito. You're stranded with the voice of the story.

The Voice of the Story, the Story as Voice

> In the houses of the people who knew us we were asked to come in and sit, given cold water or lemonade; and while we sat there being refreshed, the people continued their conversations or went about their chores. Little by little we began to piece a story together, a secret, terrible, awful story.
> Toni Morrison, *The Bluest Eye*

> It is only the story that can continue beyond the war and the warrior. . . . It is only the story . . . that saves our progeny from blundering like blind beggars into the spikes of the cactus fence. The story is our escort; without it, we are blind. Does the blind man own his escort? No, neither do we the story; rather it is the story that owns us.
> Chinua Achebe, *Anthills of the Savannah*

How do we learn our notions of what a story is? What sets "a story" apart from mere background noise, the wash of syllables that surrounds us and flows through us and is forgotten every day? What makes a good story a unified whole, something complete and satisfying in itself? What makes it significant speech? In other words, what qualities was I searching for, perhaps without knowing it, as I read diligently through my pile of tear-sheets?

I've spoken of "the voice of the story," which has become a sort of catchall phrase; but by it I intend something more specific: a speaking voice, like the singing voice in music, that moves not across space, across the page, but through time. Surely every written story is, in the final analysis, a score for voice. Those little black marks on the page mean nothing without their re-translation into sound. Even when we read silently, we read with the ear, unless we are reading bank statements.

Perhaps, by abolishing the Victorian practice of family reading and by removing from our school curricula those old standbys, the set memory piece and the recitation, we've deprived both writers and readers of something essential to stories. We've led them to believe that prose comes in visual blocks, not in rhythms and cadences; that its texture should be flat because a page is flat; that written emotion should not be immediate, like a drumbeat, but more remote, like a painted landscape: something to be contemplated. But understatement can be overdone, plainsong can get too plain. When I asked a group of young writers, earlier this year, how many of them ever read their own work aloud, not one of them said she did.

I'm not arguing for the abolition of the eye, merely for the reinstatement of the voice, and for an appreciation of the way it carries the listener along with it at the pace of the story. (Incidentally, reading aloud disallows cheating; when you're reading aloud, you can't skip ahead.)

Our first stories come to us through the air. We hear voices.

Children in oral societies grow up within a web of stories; but so do all children. We listen before we can read. Some of our listening is more like listening in, to the calamitous or seductive voices of the adult world, on the radio or the television or in our daily lives. Often it's an overhearing of things we aren't supposed to hear, eavesdropping on scandalous gossip or family secrets. From all these scraps of voices, from the whispers and shouts that surround us, even from the ominous silences, the unfilled gaps in meaning, we patch together for ourselves an order of events, a plot or plots; these, then, are the things that happen, these are the people they happen to, this is the forbidden knowledge.

We have all been little pitchers with big ears, shooed out of the kitchen when the unspoken is being spoken, and we have probably all been tale-bearers, blurters at the dinner table, unwitting violators of adult rules of censorship. Perhaps this is what writers are: those who never kicked the habit. We remained tale-bearers. We learned to keep our eyes open, but not to keep our mouths shut.

If we're lucky, we may also be given stories meant for our ears, stories intended for us. These may be children's Bible stories, tidied up and simplified and with the vicious bits left out. They may be fairy tales, similarly sugared, although if we are very lucky it will be the straight stuff in both instances, with the slaughters, thunderbolts, and red-hot shoes left in. In any case, these tales will have deliberate, molded shapes, unlike the stories we have patched together for ourselves. They will contain mountains, deserts, talking donkeys, dragons; and, unlike the kitchen stories, they will have definite endings. We are likely to accept these stories as being on the same level of reality as the kitchen stories. It's only when we are older that we are taught to regard one kind of story as real and the other kind as mere invention. This is about the same time we're taught to believe that dentists are useful, and writers are not.

Traditionally, both the kitchen gossips and the readers-out-loud have been mothers or grandmothers, native languages have been mother tongues, and the kinds of stories that are told to children have been called nursery tales or old wives' tales. It struck me as no great coincidence when I learned recently that, when a great number of prominent writers were asked to write about the family member who had had the greatest influence on their literary careers, almost all of them, male as well as female, had picked their mothers. Perhaps this reflects the extent to which North American children have been deprived of their grandfathers, those other great repositories of story; perhaps it will come to change if men come to share in early child care, and we will have old husbands' tales. But as things are, language, including the language of our earliest-learned stories, is a verbal matrix, not a verbal patrix.

I used to wonder why — as seems to be the case — so many more male writers chose to write from a female point of view than the other way around. (In this collection, for instance, male authors with female narrators outnumber the reverse four to one.) But possibly the prevailing gender of the earliest storytelling voice has something to do with it.

Two kinds of stories we first encounter — the shaped tale, the overheard impromptu narrative we piece together — form our idea of what a story is and color the expectations we bring to stories later. Perhaps it's from the collisions between these two kinds of stories — what is often called "real life" (and which writers greedily think of as their "material") and what is sometimes dismissed as "mere literature" or "the kinds of things that happen only in stories" — that original and living writing is generated. A writer with nothing but a formal sense will produce dead work, but so will one whose only excuse for what is on the page is that it really happened. Anyone who has been trapped in a bus beside a nonstop talker graced with no narrative skill or sense of timing can testify to that. Or, as Raymond Chandler says in "The Simple Art of Murder":

> All language begins with speech, and the speech of common men at that, but when it develops to the point of becoming a literary medium it only looks like speech.

Expressing yourself is not nearly enough. You must express the story.

The Uncertainty Principle

All of which gets me no closer to an explanation of why I chose one story over another, twenty stories over the remaining hundred. The uncertainty principle, as it applies to writing, might be stated: *You can say why a story is bad, but it's much harder to say why it's good.* Determining quality in fiction may be as hard as determining the reason for the happiness in families, only in reverse. The old saying has it that happy families are all happy in the same way, but each unhappy family is unique. In fiction, however, excellence resides in divergence, or how else could we be surprised? Hence the trickiness of the formulations.

Here is what I did. I sat on the floor, spread out the stories, and read through them in no particular order. I put each completed story into a "yes" pile, a "no" pile, and a "maybe" pile. By the time I'd gone through them once, I had about twenty-five stories in "yes," an equal number in "no," and the rest in "maybe."

Here things got harder. The first fourteen yes stories were instant choices: I knew I wouldn't change my mind about them. After that there were gradations, yeses shading to maybes, maybes that could easily be on the low end of yes. To make the final choices, I was forced to be more conscious and deliberate. I went back over my fourteen instant yes stories and tried to figure out what, if anything, they had in common.

They were widely different in content, in tone, in setting, in narrative strategy. Some were funny, others melancholy, others contemplative, others downright sad, yet others violent. Some went over ground that, Lord knows, had been gone over before: the breakdown, the breakup, love and death. Collectively they did not represent any school of writing or propound any common philosophy. I was beginning to feel stupid and lacking in standards. Was I to be thrown back on that old crutch of the Creative Writing Seminar, *It worked for me?*

Perhaps, I thought, my criteria are very simple-minded. Perhaps all I want from a good story is what children want when they listen to tales both told and overheard — which turns out to be a good deal.

They want their attention held, and so do I. I always read to the end, out of some puritanical, and adult, sense of duty owed; but if I start to fidget and skip pages, and wonder if conscience demands I go back and read the middle, it's a sign that the story has lost me, or I have lost it.

They want to feel they are in safe hands, that they can trust the teller. With children this may mean simply that they know the speaker will not betray them by closing the book in the middle, or mixing up the heroes and the villains. With adult readers it's more complicated than that, and involves many dimensions, but there's the same element of keeping faith. Faith must be kept with the language — even if the story is funny, its language must be taken seriously — with the concrete details of locale, mannerism, clothing; with the shape of the story itself. A good story may tease, as long as this activity is foreplay and not used as an end in itself. If there's a promise held out, it must be honored. Whatever is hidden behind the curtain must be revealed at last, and it must be at one and the same time completely unexpected and inevitable. It's in this last respect that the story (as distinct from the novel) comes closest to resembling two of its oral predecessors, the riddle and the joke. Both, or all three, require the same mystifying buildup, the same surprising twist, the same impeccable sense of timing. If we guess the riddle at once, or if we can't guess it because the answer makes no sense — if we see the joke coming, or if the point is lost because the teller gets it muddled — there is failure. Stories can fail in the same way.

But anyone who has ever told, or tried to tell, a story to children will know that there is one thing without which none of the rest is any good. Young children have little sense of dutifulness or of delaying anticipation. They are longing to hear a story, but only if you are longing to tell one. They will not put up with your lassitude or boredom: if you want their full attention, you must give them yours. You must hold them with your glittering eye or suffer the pinches and whispering. You need the Ancient Mariner element, the Scheherazade element: a sense of urgency. *This is the story I must tell; this is the story you must hear.*

Urgency does not mean frenzy. The story can be a quiet story, a story about dismay or missed chances or a wordless revelation. But it must be urgently told. It must be told with as much intentness as if the teller's life depended on it. And, if you are a writer, so it does, because your life as the writer of each particular story is only as long, and as good, as the story itself. Most of those who hear it or read it will never know you, but they will know the story. Their act of listening is its reincarnation.

Is all this too much to ask? Not really; because many stories, many of these stories, do it superbly.

Down to Specifics

But they do it in a multiplicity of ways. When I was reading through the stories, someone asked me, "Is there a trend?" There is no trend. There are only twenty strong, exciting, and unique stories.

I didn't think anyone could ever write a story about taking drugs in the sixties that would hold my attention for more than five minutes, but Michael Cunningham does it brilliantly in "White Angel" — because the narrator is a young boy, "the most criminally advanced nine-year-old in my fourth-grade class," who is being initiated into almost everything by his adored sixteen-year-old brother. The sensual richness of this story is impressive; so is the way it shifts from out-of-control feverishness and hilarity, as the two brothers scramble their brains with acid against a background of Leave-It-to-Beaver Cleveland domesticity ("We slipped the tabs into our mouths at breakfast, while our mother paused over the bacon"), to the nearly unbearable poignancy of its tragic ending.

Another story that blindsided me by taking an unlikely subject and turning it inside out was "The Flowers of Boredom." Who could hope to write with any conviction or panache about working as a paper-shuffler for a defense contractor? But Rick DeMarinis does. The visionary glimpse of cosmic horror at the end is come by honestly, step by step, through dailiness and small disgusts. This story is one of those truly original collisions between delicately handled form and banal but alarming content that leaves you aghast and slightly battered.

"Hell lay about them in their infancy," Graham Greene remarks in *The Lawless Roads,* and this is the tone of Barbara Gowdy's "Disneyland." If "The Flowers of Boredom" views the military enterprise as a giant, superhuman pattern, "Disneyland" squints at it through Groucho Marx glasses gone rotten. The controlling figure is a domineering father obsessed with his early-sixties fallout shelter. He and his mania would be ludicrous, almost a parody, viewed from a safe distance; but the distance is not safe. This man is seen from beneath by his children, who are forced to play platoon to his drill sergeant in the smelly, dark, tyrannical, and terrifying hell in which he has imprisoned them. The sense of claustrophobia and entrapment are intense.

There are several other fine stories that concern themselves with the terrors, and sometimes the delights, of childhood and with the powerlessness of children caught under the gigantic, heedless feet of the adult world. Mark Richard's "Strays," with its two poor-white boys abandoned by their runaway mother and rescued, after a fashion, by their rogue gambler of an uncle, is one fine example. Its deadpan delivery of the squalid and the grotesque reminds us that everything that happens to children is accepted as normal by them; or if not exactly normal, unalterable. For them, reality and enchantment are the same thing, and they are held in thrall.

Dale Ray Phillips's "What Men Love For" contains another child who is under a spell, that cast by his fragile, manic-depressive mother. Against the various rituals she uses to keep herself stuck together, and those the boy himself is in the process of inventing for his own preservation, there's the magic of his father — a magic of luck, risk, hope, and chance embodied in the motorcycle he drives too fast.

"The Boy on the Train," by Arthur Robinson, is a wonderful, warped memoir of sorts. Instead of being about one childhood, it's really about two. Two children grow up to be fathers, two fathers misunderstand their sons, and two sons bedevil their fathers in niggling, embarrassing, or nauseating ways designed to get right under their skin: "In prepubescence, Edward gazed at his face in the mirror a great deal and studied the effects he could get with it. Once he discovered that a strip of toothpaste artfully placed just below a nostril produced an effect that could easily turn his father's queasy stomach. The result was more than he could have hoped for." The beautiful way this story turns around on itself, loops back, plays variations on three generations, is a delight to follow.

Two of these stories have an almost fablelike simplicity and structure. One of them is M. T. Sharif's "The Letter Writer," whose hapless protagonist, Haji, is arrested during the Iranian revolution because he is suspected of being the brother of a supposed spy and can't prove he isn't. But the authorities can't prove he is, and since he won't confess and they can't convict him, he is given a make-work job: covering up the bare arms,

legs, heads, and necks of women pictured in Western magazines
by drawing clothes on them with pen and ink. Earlier, a passing
dervish had prophesied that Haji would end up living in a palace, attended by concubines and servants. The manner in which
this fate is actually fulfilled is reminiscent of both Kafka and the
tradition of the ironic Eastern tale.

Harriet Doerr's "Edie: A Life" has the plain charm of a sam-
pler. It violates almost every rule I have ever heard about the
construction of short stories. It doesn't concentrate, for instance, on an in-depth study of character, or on a short period
of time, a single incident that focuses a life. Instead it gives the
entire life, in miniature as it were, complete and rounded and
unexplained as an apple.

Other stories persuade us and move us in other ways. Larry
Brown, in "Kubuku Rides (This Is It)," gives his sad story of an
alcoholic wife its edge and drive through the immediacy and
vigor of his language, as does Blanche McCrary Boyd in her
uneasily uproarious "The Black Hand Girl." (The hand, which
is a man's, gets black by being sprained in a panty girdle. Read
on.) Douglas Glover, in "Why I Decide to Kill Myself and Other
Jokes," also draws on the mordant, self-deprecating humor of
women. There's a murder with a hammer, a rescue from the
snow, an attempted rescue with a skillet. There's a Chinese
woman, in David Wong Louie's "Displacement," who is trying
to make the best of America, and a native Indian woman, in
Linda Hogan's "Aunt Moon's Young Man," who is also trying
to make the best of it. There's a left-wing mother whose son
rebels by taking up religion. But these are just hints. To get the
real story, you have to read the story, as always.

I must admit that, although I was reading blind, I did guess
the identities of three of the authors. Bharati Mukherjee's "The
Management of Grief" wasn't even a guess, as I had read it
before and it had stayed with me. It's a finely tuned, acutely felt
story about an Indian immigrant wife's reactions when the plane
carrying her husband and sons is blown up over the Irish Sea
by terrorists. The sleepwalking intensity with which she gropes
her way through the emotional debris scattered by these sense-
less deaths and eventually makes a mystic sense out of them for
herself is sparely but unsparingly rendered.

When I read "The Concert Party," I guessed that it was either

by Mavis Gallant or by a male writer doing a very good imitation
of her. Who else would, or could, write so convincingly and with
such interest about a hopeless nerd from Saskatchewan bun-
gling around loose in France in the early fifties? The story did
turn out to be by Mavis Gallant, leaving me to admire once again
her deftness with a full canvas, her skill at interweaving the fates
of her characters, her sharp eye for the details of small pompos-
ities, and her camera work, if it may be called that. Watch the
way she shifts, at the end, from closeup to long shot:

> Remembering Edie at the split second when she came to a decision,
> I can find it in me to envy them. The rest of us were born knowing
> better, which means we were stuck. When I finally looked away from
> her it was at another pool of candlelight, and the glowing, blooming
> children. I wonder now if there was anything about us for the chil-
> dren to remember, if they ever later on reminded one another:
> There was that long table of English-speaking people, still in bud.

I think I would recognize an Alice Munro story in Braille,
even though I don't read Braille. The strength and distinctive-
ness of her voice will always give her away. "Meneseteung" is,
for my money, one of Alice Munro's best and, in the manner of
its telling, quirkiest stories yet. It purports to be about a minor
sentimental "poetess" — the word, here, is appropriate — living
in a small, raw, cowpat-strewn, treeless nineteenth-century
town, which is a far cry from our idyllic notions of a golden past
as the poet's sugary verses are from real life. Our sweet picture
of bygone days is destroyed, and, in the process, our concep-
tions of how a story should proceed. Similarly, the poet herself
disintegrates in the harsh and multiple presence of the vivid life
that surrounds her and that finally proves too huge and real for
her. Or does it? Does she disintegrate or integrate? Does crossing the borders of convention lead toward insanity or sanity?
"She doesn't mistake that for reality, and neither does she mistake anything else for reality," we are told when the crocheted
roses on the tablecloth began to float, "and that is how she knows
that she is sane."

The last word is not the poet's, however, but the nameless
narrator's, the "I" who has been searching for the poet, or

scraps of her, through time. These last words could be an epi-
graph for this collection of stories, or for the act of writing itself:

> People are curious. A few people are. They will be driven to find
> things out, even trivial things. They will put things together, knowing
> all along that they may be mistaken. You see them going around with
> notebooks, scraping the dirt off gravestones, reading microfilm, just
> in the hope of seeing this trickle in time, making a connection, res-
> cuing one thing from the rubbish.

I thank all the authors in this book for the pleasure their
stories have given me, and for what they added to my own sense
of what a story is, and can be.

From listening to the stories of others, we learn to tell our
own.

MARGARET ATWOOD

The Best
AMERICAN
SHORT
STORIES
1989

CHARLES BAXTER

Fenstad's Mother

FROM THE ATLANTIC

ON SUNDAY MORNING after Communion Fenstad drove across town to visit his mother. Behind the wheel, he exhaled with his hand flat in front of his mouth to determine if the wine on his breath could be detected. He didn't think so. Fenstad's mother was a lifelong social progressive who was amused by her son's churchgoing, and, wine or no wine, she could guess where he had been. She had spent her life in the company of rebels and deviationists, and she recognized all their styles.

Passing a frozen pond in the city park, Fenstad slowed down to watch the skaters, many of whom he knew by name and skating style. From a distance they were dots of color ready for flight, frictionless. To express grief on skates seemed almost impossible, and Fenstad liked that. He parked his car on a residential block and took out his skates from the back seat, where he kept them all winter. With his fingertips he touched the wooden blade guards, thinking of the time. He checked his watch; he had fifteen minutes.

Out on the ice, still wearing his churchy Sunday-morning suit, tie, and overcoat, but now circling the outside edge of the pond with his bare hands in his overcoat pockets, Fenstad admired the overcast sky and luxuriated in the brittle cold. He was active and alert in winter but felt sleepy throughout the summer. He passed a little girl in a pink jacket, pushing a tiny chair over the ice. He waved to his friend Ann, an off-duty cop, practicing her twirls. He waved to other friends. Without exception they waved back. As usual, he was impressed by the way skates improved human character.

Twenty minutes later, in the doorway of her apartment, his mother said, "Your cheeks are red." She glanced down at his trousers, damp with melted snow. "You've been skating." She kissed him on the cheek and turned to walk into her living room. "Skating after church? Isn't that some sort of error?"

"It's just happiness," Fenstad said. Quickly he checked her apartment for any signs of memory loss or depression. He found none and immediately felt relief. The apartment smelled of soap and Lysol, the signs of an old woman who wouldn't tolerate nonsense. Out on her coffee table, as usual, were the letters she was writing to her congressman and to political dictators around the globe. Fenstad's mother pleaded for enlightened behavior and berated the dictators for their bad political habits.

She grasped the arm of the sofa and let herself down slowly. Only then did she smile. "How's your soul, Harry?" she asked. "What's the news?"

He smiled back and smoothed his hair. Martin Luther King's eyes locked into his from the framed picture on the wall opposite him. In the picture King was shaking hands with Fenstad's mother, the two of them surrounded by smiling faces. "My soul's okay, Ma," he said. "It's a hard project. I'm always working on it." He reached down for a chocolate-chunk cookie from a box on top of the television. "Who brought you these?"

"Your daughter Sharon. She came to see me on Friday." Fenstad's mother tilted her head at him. "You *want* to be a good person, but she's the real article. Goodness comes to her without any effort at all. She says you have a new girlfriend. A pharmacist this time. Susan, is it?" Fenstad nodded. "Harry, why does your generation always have to find the right person? Why can't you learn to live with the wrong person? Sooner or later everyone's wrong. Love isn't the most important thing, Harry, far from it. Why can't you see that? I still don't comprehend why you couldn't live with Eleanor." Eleanor was Fenstad's exwife. They had been divorced for a decade, but Fenstad's mother hoped for a reconciliation.

"Come on, Ma," Fenstad said. "Over and done with, gone and gone." He took another cookie.

"You live with somebody so that you're living with *somebody,* and then you go out and do the work of the world. I don't understand all this pickiness about lovers. In a pinch anybody'll do, Harry, believe me."

On the side table was a picture of her late husband, Fenstad's mild, middle-of-the-road father. Fenstad glanced at the picture and let the silence hang between them before asking, "How are you, Ma?"

"I'm all right." She leaned back in the sofa, whose springs made a strange, almost human groan. "I want to get out. I spend too much time in this place in January. You should expand my horizons. Take me somewhere."

"Come to my composition class," Fenstad said. "I'll pick you up at dinnertime on Tuesday. Eat early."

"They'll notice me," she said, squinting. "I'm too old."

"I'll introduce you," her son said. "You'll fit right in."

Fenstad wrote brochures in the publicity department of a computer company during the day, and taught an extension English-composition class at the downtown campus of the state university two nights a week. He didn't need the money; he taught the class because he liked teaching strangers and because he enjoyed the sense of hope that classrooms held for him. This hopefulness and didacticism he had picked up from his mother.

On Tuesday night she was standing at the door of the retirement apartment building, dressed in a dark blue overcoat — her best. Her stylishness was belied slightly by a pair of old fuzzy red earmuffs. Inside the car Fenstad noticed that she had put on perfume, unusual for her. Leaning back, she gazed out contentedly at the nighttime lights.

"Who's in this group of students?" she asked. "Working-class people, I hope. Those are the ones you should be teaching. Anything else is just a career."

"Oh, they work, all right." He looked at his mother and saw, as they passed under a streetlight, a combination of sadness and delicacy in her face. Her usual mask of tough optimism seemed to be deserting her. He braked at a red light and said, "I have a hairdresser and a garage mechanic and a housewife, a Mrs. Nelson, and three guys who're sanitation workers. Plenty of others. One guy you'll really like is a young black man with glasses who sits in the back row and reads *Workers' Vanguard* and Bakunin during class. He's brilliant. I don't know why he didn't test out of this class. His name's York Follette, and he's —"

"I want to meet him," she said quickly. She scowled at the moonlit snow. "A man with ideas. People like that have gone out of my life." She looked over at her son. "What I hate about being my age is how *nice* everyone tries to be. I was never nice, but now everybody is pelting me with sugar cubes." She opened her window an inch and let the cold air blow over her, ruffling her stiff gray hair.

When they arrived at the school, snow had started to fall, and at the other end of the parking lot a police car's flashing light beamed long crimson rays through the dense flakes. Fenstad's mother walked deliberately toward the door, shaking her head mistrustfully at the building and the police. Approaching the steps, she took her son's hand. "I liked the columns on the old buildings," she said, "the old university buildings, I mean. I liked Greek Revival better than this Modernist-bunker stuff." Inside, she blinked in the light at the smooth, waxed linoleum floors and cement-block walls. She held up her hand to shade her eyes. Fenstad took her elbow to guide her over the snow melting in puddles in the entryway. "I never asked you what you're teaching tonight."

"Logic," Fenstad said.

"Ah." She smiled and nodded. "Dialectics!"

"Not quite. Just logic."

She shrugged. She was looking at the clumps of students standing in the glare of the hallway, drinking coffee from paper cups and smoking cigarettes in the general conversational din. She wasn't used to such noise: she stopped in the middle of the corridor underneath a wall clock and stared happily in no particular direction. With her eyes shut she breathed in the close air, smelling of wet overcoats and smoke, and Fenstad remembered how much his mother had always liked smoke-filled rooms, where ideas fought each other, and where some of those ideas died.

"Come on," he said, taking her hand again. Inside Fenstad's classroom six people sat in the angular postures of pre-boredom. York Follette was already in the back row, his copy of

Workers' Vanguard shielding his face. Fenstad's mother headed straight for him and sat down in the desk next to his. Fenstad saw them shake hands, and in two minutes they were talking in low, rushed murmurs. He saw York Follette laugh quietly and nod. What was it that blacks saw and appreciated in his mother? They had always liked her — written to her, called her, checked up on her — and Fenstad wondered if they recognized something in his mother that he himself had never been able to see.

At 7:35 most of the students had arrived and were talking to each other vigorously, as if they didn't want Fenstad to start and thought they could delay him. He stared at them, and when they wouldn't quiet down, he made himself rigid and said, "Good evening. We have a guest tonight." Immediately the class grew silent. He held his arm out straight, indicating with a flick of his hand the old woman in the back row. "My mother," he said. "Clara Fenstad." For the first time all semester his students appeared to be paying attention: they turned around collectively and looked at Fenstad's mother, who smiled and waved. A few of the students began to applaud; others joined in. The applause was quiet but apparently genuine. Fenstad's mother brought herself slowly to her feet and made a suggestion of a bow. Two of the students sitting in front of her turned around and began to talk to her. At the front of the class Fenstad started his lecture on logic, but his mother wouldn't quiet down. This was a class for adults. They were free to do as they liked.

Lowering his head and facing the blackboard, Fenstad reviewed problems in logic, following point by point the outline set down by the textbook: *post hoc* fallacies, false authorities, begging the question, circular reasoning, *ad hominem* arguments, all the rest. Explaining these problems, his back turned, he heard sighs of boredom, boldly expressed. Occasionally he glanced at the back of the room. His mother was watching him carefully, and her face was expressing all the complexity of dismay. Dismay radiated from her. Her disappointment wasn't personal, because his mother didn't think that people as individuals were at fault for what they did. As usual, her disappointed hope was located in history and in the way people agreed with already existing histories.

She was angry with him for collaborating with grammar. She

would call it unconsciously installed authority. Then she would
find other names for it.

"All right," he said loudly, trying to make eye contact with
someone in the room besides his mother, "let's try some exam-
ples. Can anyone tell me what, if anything, is wrong with the
following sentence? 'I, like most people, have a unique problem.' "

The three sanitation workers, in the third row, began to
laugh. Fenstad caught himself glowering and singled out the
middle one.

"Yes, it is funny, isn't it?"

The man in the middle smirked and looked at the floor. "I
was just thinking of my unique problem."

"Right," Fenstad said. "But what's wrong with saying, 'I, like
most people, have a unique problem'?"

"Solving it?" This was Mrs. Nelson, who sat by the window so
that she could gaze at the tree outside, lit by a streetlight. All
through class she looked at the tree as if it were a lover.

"Solving what?"

"Solving the problem you have. What is the problem?"

"That's actually not what I'm getting at," Fenstad said. "Although it's a good *related* point. I'm asking what might be wrong
logically with that sentence."

"It depends," Harold Ronson said. He worked in a service
station and sometimes came to class wearing his work shirt with
his name tag, HAROLD, stitched into it. "It depends on what your
problem is. You haven't told us your problem."

"No," Fenstad said, "my problem is *not* the problem." He
thought of Alice in Wonderland and felt, physically, as if he
himself were getting small. "Let's try this again. What might be
wrong with saying that most people have a unique problem?"

"You shouldn't be so critical," Timothy Melville said. "You
should look on the bright side, if possible."

"What?"

"He's right," Mrs. Nelson said. "Most people have unique
problems, but many people do their best to help themselves,
such as taking night classes or working at meditation."

"No doubt that's true," Fenstad said. "But why can't most
people have a unique problem?"

"Oh, I disagree," Mrs. Nelson said, still looking at her tree. Fenstad glanced at it and saw that it was crested with snow. It *was* beautiful. No wonder she looked at it. "I believe that most people do have unique problems. They just shouldn't talk about them all the time."

"Can anyone," Fenstad asked, looking at the back wall and hoping to see something there that was not wall, "can anyone give me an example of a unique problem?"

"Divorce," Barb Kjellerud said. She sat near the door and knitted during class. She answered questions without looking up. "Divorce is unique."

"No, it isn't!" Fenstad said, failing in the crucial moment to control his voice. He and his mother exchanged glances. In his mother's face for a split second was the history of her compassionate, ambivalent attention to him. "Divorce is not unique." He waited to calm himself. "It's everywhere. Now try again. Give me a unique problem."

Silence. "This is a trick question," Arlene Hubbly said. "I'm sure it's a trick question."

"Not necessarily. Does anyone know what *unique* means?"

"One of a kind," York Follette said, gazing at Fenstad with dry amusement. Sometimes he took pity on Fenstad and helped him out of jams. Fenstad's mother smiled and nodded.

"Right," Fenstad crowed, racing toward the blackboard as if he were about to write something. "So let's try again. Give me a unique problem."

"You give *us* a unique problem," one of the sanitation workers said. Fenstad didn't know whether he'd been given a statement or a command. He decided to treat it as a command.

"All right," he said. He stopped and looked down at his shoes. Maybe it *was* a trick question. He thought for ten seconds. Problem after problem presented itself to him. He thought of poverty, of the assaults on the earth, of the awful complexities of love. "I can't think of one," Fenstad said. His hands went into his pockets.

"That's because problems aren't personal," Fenstad's mother said from the back of the room. "They're collective." She waited while several students in the class sat up and nodded. "And people must work together on their solutions." She talked for

another two minutes, taking the subject out of logic and putting
it neatly in politics, where she knew it belonged.

The snow had stopped by the time the class was over. Fenstad
took his mother's arm and escorted her to the car. After letting
her down on the passenger side and starting the engine, he
began to clear the front windshield. He didn't have a scraper
and had forgotten his gloves, so he was using his bare hands.
When he brushed the snow away on his mother's side, she
looked out at him, surprised, a terribly aged Sleeping Beauty
awakened against her will.

Once the car had warmed up, she was in a gruff mood and
repositioned herself under the seat belt while making quiet but
aggressive remarks. The sight of the new snow didn't seem to
calm her. "Logic," she said at last. "That wasn't logic. Those are
just rhetorical tactics. It's filler and drudgery."

"I don't want to discuss it now."

"All right. I'm sorry. Let's talk about something more pleasant."

They rode together in silence. Then she began to shake her
head. "Don't take me home," she said. "I want to have a spot of
tea somewhere before I go back. A nice place where they serve
tea, all right?"

He parked outside an all-night restaurant with huge front
plate-glass windows; it was called Country Bob's. He held his
mother's elbow from the car to the door. At the door, looking
back to make sure that he had turned off his headlights, he saw
his tracks and his mother's in the snow. His were separate footprints, but hers formed two long lines.

Inside, at the table, she sipped her tea and gazed at her son
for a long time. "Thanks for the adventure, Harry. I do appreciate it. What're you doing in class next week? Oh, I remember.
How-to papers. That should be interesting."

"Want to come?"

"Very much. I'll keep quiet next time, if you want me to."

Fenstad shook his head. "It's okay. It's fun having you along.
You can say whatever you want. The students loved you. I knew
you'd be a sensation, and you were. They'd probably rather
have you teaching the class than me."

He noticed that his mother was watching something going on behind him, and Fenstad turned around in the booth so that he could see what it was. At first all he saw was a woman, a young woman with long hair wet from snow and hanging in clumps, talking in the aisle to two young men, both of whom were nodding at her. Then she moved on to the next table. She spoke softly. Fenstad couldn't hear her words, but he saw the solitary customer to whom she was speaking shake his head once, keeping his eyes down. Then the woman saw Fenstad and his mother. In a moment she was standing in front of them.

She wore two green plaid flannel shirts and a thin torn jacket. Like Fenstad, she wore no gloves. Her jeans were patched, and she gave off a strong smell, something like hay, Fenstad thought, mixed with tar and sweat. He looked down at her feet and saw that she was wearing penny loafers with no socks. Coins, old pennies, were in both shoes; the leather was wet and cracked. He looked in the woman's face. Under a hat that seemed to collapse on either side of her head, the woman's face was thin and chalk-white except for the fatigue lines under her eyes. The eyes themselves were bright blue, beautiful, and crazy. To Fenstad, she looked desperate, percolating slightly with insanity, and he was about to say so to his mother when the woman bent down toward him and said, "Mister, can you spare any money?"

Involuntarily, Fenstad looked toward the kitchen, hoping that the manager would spot this person and take her away. When he looked back again, his mother was taking her blue coat off, wriggling in the booth to free her arms from the sleeves. Stopping and starting again, she appeared to be stuck inside the coat; then she lifted herself up, trying to stand, and with a quick, quiet groan slipped the coat off. She reached down and folded the coat over and held it toward the woman. "Here," she said. "Here's my coat. Take it before my son stops me."

"Mother, you can't." Fenstad reached forward to grab the coat, but his mother pulled it away from him

When Fenstad looked back at the woman, her mouth was open, showing several gray teeth. Her hands were outstretched, and he understood, after a moment, that this was a posture of refusal, a gesture saying no, and that the woman wasn't used to it and did it awkwardly. Fenstad's mother was standing and trying to push the coat toward the woman, not toward her hands but lower, at waist level, and she was saying, "Here, here, here, here." The sound, like a human birdcall, frightened Fenstad, and he stood up quickly, reached for his wallet, and removed the first two bills he could find, two twenties. He grabbed the woman's chapped, ungloved left hand.

"Take these," he said, putting the two bills in her icy palm, "for the love of God, and please go."

He was close to her face. Tonight he would pray for her. For a moment the woman's expression was vacant. His mother was still pushing the coat at her, and the woman was unsteadily bracing herself. The woman's mouth was open, and her stagnant-water breath washed over him. "I know you," she said. "You're my little baby cousin."

"Go away, please," Fenstad said. He pushed at her. She turned, clutching his money. He reached around to put his hands on his mother's shoulders. "Ma," he said, "she's gone now. Mother, sit down. I gave her money for a coat." His mother fell down on her side of the booth, and her blue coat rolled over on the bench beside her, showing the label and the shiny inner lining. When he looked up, the woman who had been begging had disappeared, though he could still smell her odor, an essence of wretchedness.

"Excuse me, Harry," his mother said. "I have to go to the bathroom."

She rose and walked toward the front of the restaurant, turned a corner, and was out of sight. Fenstad sat and tried to collect himself. When the waiter came, a boy with an earring and red hair in a flattop, Fenstad just shook his head and said, "More tea." He realized that his mother hadn't taken off her earmuffs, and the image of his mother in the ladies' room with her earmuffs on gave him a fit of uneasiness. After getting up from the booth and following the path that his mother had taken, he stood outside the ladies' room door and, when no one came in or out, he knocked. He waited for a decent interval. Still hearing no answer, he opened the door.

His mother was standing with her arms down on either side of the first sink. She was holding herself there, her eyes following the hot water as it poured from the tap around the bright porcelain sink down into the drain, and she looked furious. Fenstad touched her and she snapped toward him.

"Your logic!" she said.

He opened the door for her and helped her back to the booth. The second cup of tea had been served, and Fenstad's mother sipped it in silence. They did not converse. When she had finished, she said, "All right. I do feel better now. Let's go."

At the curb in front of her apartment building he leaned forward and kissed her on the cheek. "Pick me up next Tuesday," she said. "I want to go back to that class." He nodded. He watched as she made her way past the security guard at the front desk; then he put his car into drive and started home.

That night he skated in the dark for an hour with his friend Susan, the pharmacist. She was an excellent skater; they had met on the ice. She kept late hours and, like Fenstad, enjoyed skating at night. She listened attentively to his story about his mother and the woman in the restaurant. To his great relief she recommended no course of action. She listened. She didn't believe in giving advice, even when asked.

The following Tuesday, Fenstad's mother was again in the back row next to York Follette. One of the fluorescent lights overhead was flickering, which gave the room, Fenstad thought, a sinister quality, like a debtors' prison or a refuge for the homeless. He'd been thinking about such people for the entire week. For seven days now he had caught whiffs of the woman's breath in the air, and one morning, Friday, he thought he caught a touch of the rotten-celery smell on his own breath, after a particularly difficult sales meeting.

Tonight was how-to night. The students were expected to stand at the front of the class and read their papers, instructing their peers and answering questions if necessary. Starting off, and reading her paper in a frightened monotone, Mrs. Nelson told the class how to bake a cheese soufflé. Arlene Hubbly's paper was about mushroom hunting. Fenstad was put off by the introduction. "The advantage to mushrooms," Arlene Hubbly read, "is that they are delicious. The disadvantage to mushrooms is that they can make you sick, even die." But then she

explained how to recognize the common shaggymane by its cy-
lindrical cap and dark tufts; she drew a model on the board.
She warned the class against the *Clitocybe illudens*, the Jack-o'-
Lantern. "Never eat a mushroom like this one or *any* mushroom
that glows in the dark. Take heed!" she said, fixing her gaze on
the class. Fenstad saw his mother taking rapid notes. Harold
Ronson, the mechanic, reading his own prose painfully and
slowly, told the class how to get rust spots out of their automobiles. Again Fenstad noticed his mother taking notes. York Follette told the class about the proper procedures for laying down
attic insulation and how to know when enough was enough, so
that a homeowner wouldn't be robbed blind, as he put it, by the
salesmen, in whose ranks he had once counted himself.

Barb Kjellerud had brought along a cassette player, and told
the class that her hobby was ballroom dancing; she would instruct them in the basic waltz. She pushed the play button on
the tape machine, and *Tales from the Vienna Woods* came booming
out. To the accompaniment of the music she read her paper,
illustrating, as she went, how the steps were to be performed.
She danced alone in front of them, doing so with flair. Her
blond hair swayed as she danced, Fenstad noticed. She looked a
bit like a contestant in a beauty contest who had too much personality to win. She explained to the men the necessity of leading. Someone had to lead, she said, and tradition had given this
responsibility to the male. Fenstad heard his mother snicker.

When Barb Kjellerud asked for volunteers, Fenstad's mother
raised her hand. She said she knew how to waltz and would help
out. At the front of the class she made a counterclockwise motion with her hand, and for the next minute, sitting at the back
of the room, Fenstad watched his mother and one of the sanitation workers waltzing under the flickering fluorescent lights.

"What a wonderful class," Fenstad's mother said on the way
home. "I hope you're paying attention to what they tell you."

Fenstad nodded. "Tea?" he asked.

She shook her head. "Where're you going after you drop me
off?"

"Skating," he said. "I usually go skating. I have a date."

"With the pharmacist? In the dark?"

"We both like it, Ma." As he drove, he made an all-purpose gesture. "The moon and the stars," he said simply.

When he left her off, he felt unsettled. He considered, as a point of courtesy, staying with her a few minutes, but by the time he had this idea he was already away from the building and was headed down the street.

He and Susan were out on the ice together, skating in large circles, when Susan pointed to a solitary figure sitting on a park bench near the lake's edge. The sky had cleared; the moon gave everything a cold, fine-edged clarity. When Fenstad followed the line of Susan's finger, he saw at once that the figure on the bench was his mother. He realized it simply because of the way she sat there, drawn into herself, attentive even in the winter dark. He skated through the uncleared snow over the ice until he was standing close enough to speak to her. "Mother," he said, "what are you doing here?"

She was bundled up, a thick woolen cap drawn over her head, and two scarves covering much of her face. He could see little other than the two lenses of her glasses facing him in the dark. "I wanted to see you two," she told him. "I thought you'd look happy, and you did. I like to watch happiness. I always have."

"How can you see us? We're so far away."

"That's how I saw you."

This made no sense to him, so he asked, "How'd you get here?"

"I took a cab. That part was easy."

"Aren't you freezing?"

"I don't know. I don't know if I'm freezing or not."

He and Susan took her back to her apartment as soon as they could get their boots on. In the car Mrs. Fenstad insisted on asking Susan what kind of safety procedures were used to ensure that drugs weren't smuggled out of pharmacies and sold illegally, but she didn't appear to listen to the answer, and by the time they reached her building, she seemed to be falling asleep. They helped her up to her apartment. Susan thought that they should give her a warm bath before putting her into bed, and, together, they did. She did not protest. She didn't even seem to notice them as they guided her in and out of the bathtub.

Fenstad feared that his mother would catch some lung infection, and it turned out to be bronchitis, which kept her in her apartment for the first three weeks of February, until her cough went down. Fenstad came by every other day to see how she was, and one Tuesday, after work, he went up to her floor and heard piano music: an old recording, which sounded much played, of the brightest and fastest jazz piano he had ever heard — music of superhuman brilliance. He swung open the door to her apartment and saw York Follette sitting near his mother's bed. On the bedside table was a small tape player, from which the music poured into the room.

Fenstad's mother was leaning back against the pillow, smiling, her eyes closed.

Follette turned toward Fenstad. He had been talking softly. He motioned toward the tape machine and said, "Art Tatum. It's a cut called 'Battery Bounce.' Your mother's never heard it."

"Jazz, Harry," Fenstad's mother said, her eyes still closed, not needing to see her son. "York is explaining to me about Art Tatum and jazz. Next week he's going to try something more progressive on me." Now his mother opened her eyes. "Have you ever heard such music before, Harry?"

They were both looking at him. "No," he said, "I never heard anything like it."

"This is my unique problem, Harry." Fenstad's mother coughed and then waited to recover her breath. "I never heard enough jazz." She smiled. "What glimpses!" she said at last.

After she recovered, he often found her listening to the tape machine that York Follette had given her. She liked to hear the Oscar Peterson Trio as the sun set and the lights of evening came on. She now often mentioned glimpses. Back at home, every night, Fenstad spoke about his mother in his prayers of remembrance and thanksgiving, even though he knew she would disapprove.

MADISON SMARTT BELL

Customs of the Country

FROM HARPER'S MAGAZINE

I DON'T REMEMBER much about that place anymore. It was nothing but somewhere I came to put in some pretty bad time, though that was not what I had planned on when I went there. I had it in mind to improve things, but I don't think you could fairly claim that's what I did. So that's one reason I might just as soon forget about it. And I didn't stay there all that long, not more than about nine months or so, about the same time, come to think, that the child I was there to try to get back had lived inside my body.

It was a cluster-housing thing a little ways north out of town from Roanoke, on a two-lane road that crossed the railroad cut and went about a mile farther up through the woods. The buildings looked something like a motel, a little raw still, though they weren't new. My apartment was no more than a place that would barely look all right and yet cost me little enough so I had something left over to give the lawyer. There was fresh paint on the walls and the trim in the kitchen and bathroom was in fair shape. And it was real quiet mostly, except that the man next door used to beat up his wife a couple of times a week. The place was soundproof enough I couldn't usually hear talk but I could hear yelling plain as day and when he got going good he would slam her bang into our common wall. If she hit in just the right spot it would send my pots and pans flying off the pegboard where I'd hung them above the stove.

Not that it mattered to me that the pots fell down, except for the noise and the time it took to pick them up again. Living

alone like I was, I didn't have the heart to do much cooking and
if I did fix myself something I mostly used an old iron skillet
that hung there on the same wall. All the others I only had out
for show. The whole apartment was done about the same way,
made into something I kept spotless and didn't much care to
use. I wore my hands out scrubbing everything clean and then
saw to it that it stayed that way. I sewed slipcovers for that
threadbare batch of Goodwill furniture I'd put in the place, and
I hung curtains and found some sunshiny posters to tack on the
walls, and I never cared a damn about any of it. It was an act,
and I wasn't putting it on for me or for Davey, but for all the
other people I expected to come to see it and judge it. And
however good I could get it looking, it never felt quite right.

I felt even less at home there than I did at my job, which was
waitressing three snake-bends of the counter at the Truckstops
of America out at the I-81 interchange. The supervisor was a
man named Tim that used to know my husband Patrick from
before we had the trouble. He was nice about letting me take
my phone calls there and giving me time off to see the lawyer,
and in most other ways he was a decent man to work for, except
that now and then he would have a tantrum over something or
other and try to scream the walls down. Still, it never went
beyond yelling, and he always acted sorry once he got through.
The other waitress on my shift was an older lady named Prissy,
and I liked her all right in spite of the name.

We were both on a swing shift that rolled over every ten days,
which was the main thing I didn't like about that job. The six-
to-two I hated the worst because it would have me getting back
to my apartment building around three in the morning, not the
time it looked its best. It was the kind of place where at that time
of night I could expect to find the deputies out there looking
for somebody, or else some other kind of trouble. I never got to
know the neighbors any too well, but a lot of them were pretty
sorry — small-time criminals, dope dealers and thieves, none of
them much good at whatever it was they did. There was one
check forger that I knew of, and a man who would break into
the other apartments looking for whiskey. One thing and another, along that line.

The man next door, the one that beat up his wife, didn't do

crimes or work either that I ever heard. He just seemed to lay around the place, maybe drawing some kind of welfare. There wasn't a whole lot of him, he was just a stringy little man, hair and mustache a dishwater-brown, cheap green tattoos running up his arms. Maybe he was stronger than he looked, but I did wonder how come his wife would take it from him, since she was about a head taller and must have outweighed him an easy ten pounds. I might have thought she was whipping on him — stranger things have been known to go on — but she was the one that seemed like she might break out crying if you looked at her crooked. She was a big fine-looking girl with a lovely shape, and long brown hair real smooth and straight and shiny. I guess she was too hammered down most of the time to pay much attention to how she dressed, but still she had pretty brown eyes, big and long-lashed and soft, sort of like a cow's eyes, except I never saw a cow that looked that miserable.

At first I thought maybe I might make a friend of her, she was about the only one around there I felt like I might want to. Our paths crossed pretty frequent, either around the apartment building or in the Kwik Sack back toward town, where I'd find her running the register some days. But she was shy of me, shy of anybody I suppose. She would flinch if you did so much as say hello. So after a while I quit trying. She'd get hers about twice a week, maybe other times I wasn't around to hear it happen. It's a wonder all the things you can learn to ignore, and after a month or so I was that accustomed I barely noticed when they would start in. I would just wait till I thought they were good and through, and then get up and hang those pans back on the wall where they were supposed to go. And all the while I would just be thinking about some other thing, like what might be going on with my Davey.

The place where he had been fostered out was not all that far away, just about ten or twelve miles up the road, out there in the farm country. The people were named Baker. I never got to first names with them, just called them Mr. and Mrs. They were older than me, both just into their forties, and they didn't have any children of their own. The place was only a small farm but Mr. Baker grew tobacco on the most of it and I'm told he made it a paying thing. Mrs. Baker kept a milk cow or two and

she grew a garden and canned in the old-time way. Thrifty
people. They were real sweet to Davey and he seemed to like
being with them pretty well. He had been staying there almost
the whole two years, which was lucky too, since most children
usually got moved around a whole lot more than that.

And that was the trouble, like the lawyer explained to me, it
was just too good. Davey was doing too well out there. He'd
made out better in the first grade than anybody would have
thought. So nobody really felt like he needed to be moved. The
worst of it was the Bakers had got to like him well enough they
were saying they wanted to adopt him if they could. Well, it
would have been hard enough for me without that coming into
it.

Even though he was so close, I didn't go out to see Davey near
as much as I would have liked to. The lawyer kept telling me it
wasn't a good idea to look like I was pressing too hard. Better
take it easy till all the evaluations came in and we had our court
date and all. Still, I would call and go on out there maybe a little
more than once a month, most usually on the weekends, since
that seemed to suit the Bakers better. They never acted like it
was any trouble, and they were always pleasant to me, or polite
might be a better word yet. The way it sometimes seemed they
didn't trust me did bother me a little. I would have liked to take
him out to the movies a time or two, but I could see plain
enough the Bakers wouldn't have been easy about me having
him off their place.

But I can't remember us having a bad time, any of those times
I went. He was always happy to see me, though he'd be quiet
when we were in the house, with Mrs. Baker hovering. So I
would get us outside quick as ever I could and, once we were
out, we would just play like both of us were children. There was
an open pasture, a creek with a patch of woods, a hay barn
where we would play hide-and-go-seek. I don't know what all
else we did, silly things mostly. That was how I could get near
him the easiest, he didn't get a whole lot of playing in, way out
there. The Bakers weren't what you would call playful and there
weren't any other children living near. So that was the thing I
could give him that was all mine to give. When the weather was
good we would stay outside together most all the day and he

would just wear me out. But over the winter those visits seemed to get shorter and shorter, like the days.

Davey called me Momma still, but I suppose he had come to think your mother was something more like a big sister or just some kind of a friend. Mrs. Baker was the one doing for him all the time. I don't know just what he remembered from before, or if he remembered any of the bad part. He would always mind me but he never acted scared around me, and if anybody says he did they lie. But I never really did get to know what he had going on in the back of his mind about the past. At first I worried the Bakers might have been talking against me, but after I had seen a little more of them I knew they wouldn't have done anything like that, wouldn't have thought it right. So I expect whatever Davey knew about that other time he remembered on his own. He never mentioned Patrick hardly and I think he really had forgotten about him. Thinking back I guess he never saw that much of Patrick even when we were all living together. But Davey had Patrick's mark all over him, the same eyes and the same red hair.

Patrick had thick wavy hair the shade of an Irish setter's, and a big rolling mustache the same color. Maybe that was his best feature, but he was a good-looking man altogether, still is I suppose, though the prison haircut don't suit him. If he ever had much of a thought in his head I suspect he had knocked it clean out with dope, yet he was always fun to be around. I wasn't but seventeen when I married him and I didn't have any better sense myself. Right to the end I never thought anything much was the matter, all his vices looked so small to me. He was good-tempered almost all the time, and good with Davey when he did notice him. Never once did he raise his hand to either one of us. In little ways he was unreliable, late, not showing up at all, gone out of the house for days sometimes. Hindsight shows me he ran with other women, but I managed not to know anything about that at the time. He had not quite finished high school and the best job he could hold was being an orderly down at the hospital, but he made a good deal of extra money stealing pills out of there and selling them on the street.

That was something else I didn't allow myself to think on much back then. Patrick never told me a lot about it anyhow,

always acted real mysterious about whatever he was up to in that
line. He would disappear on one of his trips and come back with
a whole mess of money, and I would spend up my share and be
glad I had it too. I never thought much about where it was
coming from, the money or the pills either one. He used to keep
all manner of pills around the house, Valium and ludes and a
lot of different kinds of speed, and we both took what we felt
like whenever we felt in the mood. But what Patrick made the
most on was Dilaudid. I used to take it without ever knowing
what it really was, but once everything fell in on us I found out
it was a bad thing, bad as heroin they said, and not much different, and it was what they gave Patrick most of his time for.

I truly was surprised to find out that it was the strongest dope
we had, because I never really even felt like it made you all that
high. You would just take one and kick back on a long slow
stroke and whatever trouble you might have, it would not be
able to find you. It came on like nothing but it was the hardest
habit to lose, and I was a long time shaking it. I might be thinking about it yet if I would let myself, and there were times, all
through the winter I spent in that apartment, I'd catch myself
remembering the feeling.

You couldn't call it a real bad winter, there wasn't much snow
or anything, but I was cold just about all the time, except when
I was at work. All I had in the apartment was some electric
baseboard heaters, and they cost too much for me to leave them
running very long at a stretch. I'd keep it just warm enough so
I couldn't see my breath, and spend my time in a hot bathtub or
under a big pile of blankets on the bed. Or else I would just be
cold.

There was some kind of strange quietness about that place all
during the cold weather. If the phone rang it would make me
jump. Didn't seem like there was any TV or radio ever playing
next door. The only sound coming out of there was Susan getting beat up once in a while. That was her name, a sweet name,
I think. I found it out from hearing him say it, which he used
to do almost every time before he started on her. "Su-*san*," he'd
call out, loud enough I could hear him through the wall. He'd
do it a time or two, he might have been calling her to him, and

I suppose she went. After that would come a bad silence that reminded you of a snake being somewhere around. Then a few minutes' worth of hitting sounds and then the big slam as she hit the wall, and the clatter of my pots falling on the floor. He'd throw her at the wall maybe once or twice, usually when he was about to get through. By the time the pots had quit spinning on the floor it would be real quiet over there again, and the next time I saw Susan she'd be walking in that ginger way people have when they're hiding a hurt, and if I said hello to her she'd give a little jump and look away.

After a while I quit paying it much mind, it didn't feel any different to me than hearing the news on the radio. All their carrying on was not any more to me than a bump in the rut I had worked myself into, going back and forth from the job, cleaning that apartment till it hurt, calling up the lawyer about once a week to find out what was happening, which never was much. He was forever trying to get our case before some particular doctor or social worker or judge who'd be more apt to help us than another, so he said. I would call him up from the TOA, all eager to hear what news he had, and every time it was another delay. In the beginning I used to talk it all over with Tim or Prissy after I hung up, but after a while I got out of the mood to discuss it. I kept ahead making those calls but every one of them just wore out my hope a little more, like a drip of water wearing down a stone. And little by little I got in the habit of thinking that nothing really was going to change.

Somehow or other that winter passed by, with me going from one phone call to the next, going out to wait on that TOA counter, coming home to shiver and hold hands with myself and lie awake all through the night, or the day, depending what shift I was on. It was springtime, well into warm weather, before anything really happened at all. That was when the lawyer called *me*, for a change, and told me he had some people lined up to see me at last.

Well, I was all ready for them to come visit, come see how I'd fixed up my house and all the rest of my business to get set for having Davey back with me again. But as it turned out, nobody seemed to feel like they were called on to make that trip. "I don't think that will be necessary" was what one of them said, I don't recall which. They both talked about the same, in voices that sounded like filling out forms.

So all I had to do was drive downtown a couple of times and see them in their offices. That child psychologist was the first and I doubt he kept me more than half an hour. I couldn't tell the point of most of the questions he asked. My second trip I saw the social worker, who turned out to be a black lady once I got down there, though I never could have told it over the phone. Her voice sounded like it was coming out of the TV. She looked me in the eye while she was asking her questions, but I couldn't tell a thing about what she thought. It wasn't till I was back in the apartment that I understood she must have already had her mind made up.

That came to me in a sort of a flash, while I was standing in the kitchen washing out a cup. Soon as I walked back in the door I saw my coffee mug left over from breakfast, and I kicked myself for letting it sit out. I was giving it a hard scrub with a scouring pad when I realized it didn't matter anymore. I might just as well have dropped it on the floor and got what kick I could out of watching it smash, because it wasn't going to make any difference to anybody now. But all the same I rinsed it and set it in the drainer, careful as if it was an eggshell. Then I stepped backward out of the kitchen and took a long look around that cold shabby place and thought it might be for the best that nobody was coming. How could I have expected it to fool anybody else when it wasn't even good enough to fool me? A lonesomeness came over me, I felt like I was floating all alone in the middle of cold air, and then I began to remember some things I would just as soon have not.

No, I never did like to think about this part, but I have had to think about it time and again, with never a break for a long, long time, because I needed to get to understand it at least well enough to believe it never would ever happen anymore. And I had come to believe that, in the end. If I hadn't, I never would have come back at all. I had found a way to trust myself again, though it took me a full two years to do it, and though of course it still didn't mean that anybody else would trust me.

What had happened was that Patrick went off on one of his mystery trips and stayed gone a deal longer than usual. Two nights away, I was used to that, but on the third I did start to wonder. He normally would have called at least, if he was going to be gone that long of a stretch. But I didn't hear a peep until about halfway through the fourth day. And it wasn't Patrick himself that called, but one of those public-assistance lawyers from downtown.

Seemed like the night before Patrick had got himself stopped on the interstate loop down there. The troopers said he was driving like a blind man, and he was so messed up on whiskey and ludes I suppose he must have been pretty near blind at that. Well, maybe he would have just lost his license or something like that, only that the backseat of the car was loaded up with all he had lately stole out of the hospital.

So it was bad. It was so bad my mind just could not contain it, and every hour it seemed to be getting worse. I spent the next couple of days running back and forth between the jail and that lawyer, and I had to haul Davey along with me wherever I went. He was too little for school and I couldn't find anybody to take him right then, though all that running around made him awful cranky. Patrick was just grim, he would barely speak. He already knew pretty well for sure that he'd be going to prison. The lawyer had told him there wasn't no use in getting a bonds-man, he might just as well stay on in there and start pulling his time. I don't know how much he really saved himself that way, though, since what they ended up giving him was twenty-five years.

That was when all my troubles found me, quick. Two days after Patrick got arrested, I came down real sick with something. I thought at first it was a bad cold or the flu. My nose kept running and I felt so wore out I couldn't hardly get up off the bed and yet at the same time I felt real restless, like all my nerves had been scraped bare. Well, I didn't really connect it up to the fact that I'd popped the last pill in the house a couple of days before. What was really the matter was me coming off that Dilaudid, but I didn't have any notion of that at the time.

I was laying there in bed not able to get up and about ready to jump right out of my skin at the same time when Davey got the drawer underneath the stove open. Of course he was getting restless himself with all that had been going on, and me not able to pay him much mind. All our pots and pans were down in that drawer then, and he began to take them out one at a time and throw them on the floor. It made a hell of a racket, and the shape I was in, I felt like he must be doing it on purpose to devil me. I called out to him and asked him to quit. Nice at first: "You stop that, now, Davey. Momma don't feel good." But he kept right ahead. All he wanted was to have my attention, I know, but my mind wasn't working right just then. I knew I should get up and just go lead him away from there, but I couldn't seem to get myself to move. I had a picture of myself doing the right thing, but I just wasn't doing it. I was still lying there calling to him to quit and he was still banging those pots around and before long I was screaming at him outright, and starting to cry at the same time. But he never stopped a minute. I guess I had scared him some already and he was just locked into doing it, or maybe he wanted to drown me out. Every time he flung a pot it felt like I was getting shot at. And the next thing I knew I got myself in the kitchen someway and I was snatching him up off the floor.

To this day I don't remember doing it, though I have tried and tried. I thought if I could call it back then maybe I could root it out of myself and be shed of it for good and all. But all I ever knew was one minute I was grabbing a hold of him and the next he was laying on the far side of the room with his right leg folded up funny where it was broke, not even crying, just looking surprised. And I knew that it had to be me that threw him over there because as sure as hell is real there was nobody else around that could have done it.

I drove him to the hospital myself. I laid him straight on the front seat beside me and drove with one hand all the way so I could hold on to him with the other. He was real quiet and real brave the whole time, never cried the least bit, just kept a tight hold on my hand with his. Well, after a while, we got there and they ran him off somewhere to get his leg set and pretty soon the doctor came back out and asked me how it had happened.

It was the same hospital where Patrick had worked and I even knew that doctor a little bit. Not that being connected to Patrick would have done me a whole lot of good around there at that time. Still, I have often thought since then that things might have come out better for me and Davey both if I just could have

lied to that man, but I was not up to telling a lie that anybody
would be apt to believe. All I could do was start to scream and
jabber like a crazy person, and it ended up I stayed in that
hospital quite a few days myself. They took me for a junkie and
I guess I really was one too, though I hadn't known it till that
very day. And I never saw Davey again for a whole two years,
not till the first time they let me go out to the Bakers'.

Sometimes you don't get but one mistake, if the one you pick is
bad enough. Do as much as step in the road one time without
looking, and your life could be over with then and there. But
during those two years I taught myself to believe that this mistake of mine could be wiped out, that if I struggled hard enough
with myself and the world I could make it like it never had been.

Three weeks went by after I went to see that social worker,
and I didn't have any idea what was happening, or if anything
was. Didn't call anybody, I expect I was afraid to. Then one day
the phone rang for me out there at the TOA. It was the lawyer
and I could tell right off from the sound of his voice I wasn't
going to care for his news. Well, he told me all the evaluations
had come in now, sure enough, and they weren't running in
our favor. They weren't against *me*, he made sure to say that, it
was more like they were *for* the Bakers. And his judgment was
it wouldn't pay me anything if we went on to court. It looked
like the Bakers would get Davey for good anyhow, and they
were likely to be easier about visitation if there wasn't any big
tussle. But if I drug them into court, then we would have to
start going back over that whole case history —

That was the word he used, *case history*, and it was around
about there that I hung up. I went walking stiff-legged back
across to the counter and just let myself sort of drop on a stool.
Prissy had been covering my station while I was on the phone
and she came right over to me then.

"What is it?" she said. I guess she could tell it was something
by the look on my face.

"I lost him," I said.

"Oh, hon, you know I'm so sorry," she said. She reached out
for my hand but I snatched it back. I know she meant it well but
I just was not in the mood to be touched.

"There's no forgiveness," I said. I felt bitter about it. It had been a hard road for me to come as near forgiving myself as I ever could. And Davey forgave me, I really knew that, I could tell it in the way he acted when we were together. And if us two could do it, I didn't feel like it ought to be anybody else's business but ours. Tim walked up then and Prissy whispered something to him, and then he took a step nearer to me.

"I'm sorry," he told me.

"Not like I am," I said. "You don't know the meaning of the word."

"Go ahead and take off the rest of your shift if you feel like it," he said. "I'll wait on these tables myself, need be."

"I don't know it would make any difference," I said.

"Better take it easy on yourself," he said. "No use in taking it so hard. You're just going to have to get used to it."

"Is that a fact?" I said. And I lit myself a cigarette and turned my face away. We had been pretty busy, it was lunchtime, and the people were getting restless seeing all of us standing around there not doing a whole lot about bringing them their food. Somebody called out something to Tim, I didn't hear just what it was, but it set off one of his temper fits.

"Go on and get out of here if that's how you feel," he said. He was getting red in the face and waving his arms around to include everybody there in what he was saying. "Go on and clear out of here, every last one of you, and we don't care if you never come back. There's not one of you couldn't stand to miss a meal anyhow. Take a look at yourselves, you're all fat as hogs . . ."

It seemed like he might be going to keep it up a good while, and he had already said I could leave, so I hung up my apron and got my purse and I left. It was the first time he ever blew up at the customers that way, it had always been me or Prissy or one of the cooks. I never did find out what came of it all because I never went back to that place again.

I drove home in such a poison mood I barely knew I was driving a car or that there were any others on the road. I was ripe to get killed or kill somebody, and I wouldn't have cared much either way. I kept thinking about what Tim had said about having to get used to it. It came to me that I was used to it already, I really hadn't been all that surprised. That's what I'd been doing all those months, just gradually getting used to losing my child forever.

When I got back to the apartment I just fell in a chair and sat there staring across at the kitchen wall. It was in my mind to pack my traps and leave that place, but I hadn't yet figured out where I could go. I sat there a good while, I guess. The door was ajar from me not paying attention, but it wasn't cold enough out to make any difference. If I turned my head that way I could see a slice of the parking lot. I saw Susan drive up and park and come limping toward the building with an armload of groceries. Because of the angle I couldn't see her go into their apartment but I heard the door open and shut and after that it was quiet as a tomb. I kept on sitting there thinking about how used to everything I had got. There must have been generous numbers of other people too, I thought, who had got themselves accustomed to all kinds of things. Some were used to taking the pain and the rest were used to serving it up. About half of the world was screaming in misery, and it wasn't anything but a habit.

When I started to hear the hitting sounds come toward me through the wall, a smile came on my face like it was cut there with a knife. I'd been expecting it, you see, and the mood I was in I felt satisfied to see what I had expected was going to happen. So I listened a little more carefully than I'd been inclined to do before. It was *hit hit hit* going along together with a groan and a hiss of the wind being knocked out of her. I had to strain pretty hard to hear that breathing part, and I could hear him grunt too, when he got in a good one. There was about three minutes of that with some little breaks, and then a longer pause. When she hit the wall it was the hardest she had yet, I think. It brought down every last one of my pots at one time, including that big iron skillet that was the only one I ever used.

It was the first time they'd managed to knock that skillet down, and I was so impressed that I went over and stood looking down at it like I needed to make sure it was a real thing. I stared at the skillet so long it went out of focus and started looking more like a big black hole in the floor. That's when it dawned on me that this was one thing I didn't really have to keep on being used to.

It took three or four knocks before he came to the door, but that didn't worry me at all. I had faith, I knew he was going to come. I meant to stay right there till he did. When he came, he opened the door wide and stood there with his arms folded and his face all stiff with his secrets. It was fairly dark behind him, they had all the curtains drawn. I had that skillet held out in front of me in both my hands, like maybe I had come over to borrow a little hot grease or something. It was so heavy it kept wanting to dip down toward the floor like a water witch's rod. When I saw he wasn't expecting anything, I twisted the skillet back over my shoulder like baseball players do their bats, and I hit him bang across the face as hard as I knew how. He went down and out at the same time and fetched up on his back clear in the middle of the room.

Then I went in after him, with the skillet cocked and ready in case he made to get up. But he didn't look like there was a whole lot of fight left in him right then. He was awake, at least partly awake, but his nose was just spouting blood and it seemed like I'd knocked out a few of his teeth. I wish I could tell you I was sorry or glad, but I didn't feel much of anything really, just that high lonesome whistle in the blood I used to get when I took all that Dilaudid. Susan was sitting on the floor against the wall, leaning down on her knees and sniveling. Her eyes were red but she didn't have any bruises where they showed. He never did hit her on the face, that was the kind he was. There was a big crack coming down the wall behind her and I remember thinking it probably wouldn't be too much longer before it worked through to my side.

"I'm going to pack and drive over to Norfolk," I told her. I hadn't thought of it before but once it came out my mouth I knew it was what I would do. "You can ride along with me if you want to. With your looks you could make enough money serving drinks to the sailors to buy that Kwik Sack and blow it up."

She didn't say anything, just raised her head up and stared at me kind of bug-eyed. And after a minute I turned around and went out. It didn't take me any time at all to get ready. All I had was a suitcase and a couple of boxes of other stuff. The sheets and blankets I just pulled off the bed and stuffed in the trunk all in one big wad. I didn't care a damn about that furniture, I would have lit it on fire on a dare.

When I was done I stuck my head back into the other apartment. The door was still open like I had left it. What was she doing but kneeling down over that son of a bitch and trying to clean off his face with a washrag. I noticed he was making a funny sound when he breathed, and his nose was still bleeding pretty quick, so I thought maybe I had broke it. Well, I can't say that worried me much.

"Come on now if you're coming, girl," I said. She looked up at me, not telling me one word, just giving me a stare out of those big cow eyes of hers like I was the one had been beating on her that whole winter through. And I saw then that they were both of them stuck in their groove and that she would not be the one to step out of it. So I pulled back out of the doorway and went on down the steps to my car.

I was speeding on the road to Norfolk, doing seventy, seventy-five. I'd have liked to gone faster if the car had been up to it. I can't say I felt sorry for busting that guy, though I didn't enjoy the thought of it either. I just didn't know what difference it had made, and chances were it had made none at all. Kind of a funny thing, when you thought about it that way. It was the second time in my life I'd hurt somebody bad, and the other time I hadn't meant to do it at all. This time I'd known what I was doing for sure, but I still didn't know what I'd done.

ROBERT BOSWELL

Living to Be a Hundred

FROM THE IOWA REVIEW

IT'S FAIR TO SAY that our house was not in order. Furniture from the living room filled the kitchen. Chairs inverted on chairs surrounded the dining table. A long tan couch, stripped of its cushions, blocked the hall. In our bedroom, beside the dresser, a wooden coffee table stood upright like a basset hound begging for scraps.

On our knees in the emptied living room, we pieced together carpet remnants. I aligned a wide strip of tape, bending low to hold it, my shirt wrinkling against my back like molting skin. Harvis applied heat with Linda's travel iron while she held the odd-shaped pieces together. We inched across the floor, inhaling the odors of scorched glue, new carpet, our own sweating bodies. An oscillating fan vibrated against the wall every fifteen seconds, the air from it blocked by Mix, our sleeping golden retriever.

"This is not the way I thought it would work," Linda said. She pressed against the upside down carpet — material rough and woven like a gunny sack. In the crush of hands, her fingers lay on top of mine, our wedding rings grating. "It's going so slowly." Drops of sweat glistened at the base of her neck and on her chest, the straps of her white blouse turning gray with it. Her hair, gathered in a bun behind her head, had ends like the teeth of a comb, and even they drooped in the heat. "It's going to take forever." Her voice sounded desperate, with an edge that suggested she was about to cry. Ordinarily, Linda was the handy one around the house — fixing the clock radio when the numbers quit rolling, building a box to cover Kitty's litter bed — but putting a carpet together had been my idea. For weeks Harvis and I had collected remnants from the construction site where we worked.

"Maybe we should take a break," I said.

The fan rattled against the wall. Linda shook her head until the noise stopped. "The house is such a mess. We can't quit now." She was twenty-eight, with a sweetly freckled face and hair as blond as running water. We'd met in college, an archaeology class, which had been my major. She'd studied art history. We had been married seven years and put up with a lot of lousy jobs and bad apartments, but the past couple of years it had become harder because we couldn't see an end to it.

"Damn." Harvis shook his hand in the air. "Burned my pinkie." A bubble of glue coagulated on a finger as thick as a wiener. He put his hands on his knees and straightened his back. Beads of perspiration shone on his forehead. "We won't finish today," he said. "That's clear enough."

The dog groaned at this remark, which made us laugh, and, just like that, we changed our moods and worked happily again.

Linda bought and sold used clothing at a hip secondhand store. Before I got the job working construction, I had been a short-order cook, and before that, a cashier at a convenience market. I was thirty-two. Construction paid best and it wasn't so killing. You know what I mean, killing? The past couple of years had been tough, but I had begun to think things were looking up.

Linda started talking about a woman who had come into the store carrying a black fingertip coat and wanting another just like it. "We don't stock many coats this time of year. I knew I couldn't help her." She ran her hand across the base of her neck as she spoke, wiping the sweat onto her jeans.

Harvis leaned against the iron. "What'd she want with a coat like the one she already had?"

Linda nodded. "That's what I wanted to know."

It seemed obvious to me. "Someone had told her what a nice coat it was, and she wanted to make a gift of one just like it."

"Women don't do that," Harvis said. "They never want anyone to have the same clothes."

"I asked her." Linda pushed a new piece of carpet toward me, leaning low. I could see down her blouse. We slept in the same bed every night, but the sight of her breasts at that moment pleased me as it would a teenager. Harvis was looking too. "She wanted to get rid of the coat but couldn't bear to do it until she had another like it. She said she just felt like a change."

I laughed. "Sounds like a nut." I cut another strip of tape. The dog groaned again and rolled onto his back.

"She didn't look like one," Linda said. "She looked very normal."

"You can't tell a nut by its shell." Harvis smiled at his joke. Then he jerked his hand away from the iron. "Life is too much," he said and stuck his thumb in his mouth.

"Let me iron for a while." I pushed him out of the way. "You aren't going to have any fingers left."

"I'm going to make some iced tea." Linda smiled as she stood. We were all happy, even Harvis with his burned fingers.

I shoved the scraps we hadn't used into a corner, making a path from the front door to the kitchen. There was no point in returning furniture. We were only half finished. The theater down the street offered a discount in the afternoon, and we had decided to get out of the heat and away from the mess. Harvis showered first, then took Mix on a walk.

"That was almost fun," Linda said, her back to the shower nozzle, water spraying off her head in all directions. "It was almost awful, too." Her teeth were as white as porcelain.

"It'll be nice once we're through," I said. "And we could never afford it otherwise."

"You don't have to convince me." She rubbed soap on my chest. A year earlier, after a Sunday of sweating and only half finishing, we would have been angry with one another. We would have blamed and accused. Linda ran the bar of soap across my stomach, down my thighs, and kissed me.

"Harvis is a good friend," she said, soaping me now between my legs, and kissing me again, so that the only way I had to agree was to nod.

"We can save Harvis a seat." Linda stood in the hall, tucking a purple T-shirt into a pair of khaki shorts. The couch separated us. She combed her wet hair with her fingers. "I can't stand this."

Kitty was in her box, wailing. She was an old cat, one Linda had been given for her fifteenth birthday. Over the course of the past year almost everything had become painful for her. Linda had built the box to reduce odor, but it had become the container for such yowls of anguish that each time the cat entered we were afraid she would not come out.

Linda crawled across the couch, and just as we opened the front door, the wailing stopped. Kitty padded across the room and out to the porch, where she leaped to the railing, stretched, and closed her eyes. Linda rubbed the cat's belly. "Lazy Kitty," she said, then stepped down from the porch and to the hibiscus bush, which was in bloom. The flowers were red and long, shaped like the end of a bugle. She put one behind her ear, giggling.

Down the hill, Harvis approached, hands in his pockets, Mix loping beside him, leash trailing the ground. Harvis saw this as a way of getting around the leash law. He liked circumventing rules. While we watched, Mix abruptly lifted his head and darted into the street. A yellow cat streaked across the pavement to a utility pole. Mix, as usual, arrived late, barking and standing on his hind legs. The cat climbed straight up the pole.

"That's why there's a leash law." Linda called out so that Harvis could hear.

He had already grabbed the dog by the collar and pulled him away. "Mix wouldn't hurt anything."

"You better hurry," I said. "We'll miss the start of the movie."

Then everyone was in motion. Harvis and Mix ran to the house while Linda and I walked toward the pole. "Hey, cat," Linda called. "You can come down now." The cat looked at us but kept climbing. "Here, kitty," she said. "Here, kitty, kitty." The yellow cat reached the transformer box and stepped onto it.

"Maybe she needs to turn around," I said, but Linda kept calling. Meanwhile, Kitty had jumped down from the porch railing and obediently trotted down the hill.

"Did you think I was calling you?" Linda said. She retrieved Kitty and began walking back to the house, passing Harvis, who had bolted out of the door to catch us.

"You're going the wrong way," he said.

At that moment, high above me — a loud electric snap. I spun, raising my arms. The yellow cat paused in midair, three feet above the transformer box, before beginning her fall to the asphalt. She bounced once, then lay still.

Linda screamed. She looked at me in disbelief, as if it were I who had fallen. "God," she said, her voice squeaking, and ran into the house. Harvis stood on the pavement like a statue, hands suspended above his waist, legs spread as if he were about to run.

Here's what I couldn't decide: Should I go to the cat or to my wife? The cat surely was dead. My wife was crying. What comfort can you give the dead? I wish that was all there was to my decision, but there was also this: I didn't want to touch a thing so newly dead.

Linda knelt on a pile of carpet scraps, crying, stroking Kitty. "How could that happen? How bad is it hurt?"

"It's dead. The shock killed it." I dropped to one knee and touched her back. "Or maybe the fall."

"I should have kept Mix on the leash." Harvis stood by the door, hands in his pockets.

"It was a freak thing," I said. "We should get a trash bag. We shouldn't leave it out there."

"A box," Linda said, leaving me, stepping over another mound of carpet and then onto the couch, ducking her head as she crossed into the hall. She returned with a cardboard box from our bedroom closet.

From the porch, Linda watched Harvis and me walk back down the street, but the cat was gone. "Jesus," I said and knelt as if it were still there. A tiny square of blood marked the asphalt. "I was sure it was dead."

"It must be in terrible pain," Harvis said.

"They hide," Linda called as she ran toward us. "When they're hurt or something's wrong, they find a place to hide."

We searched under cars and porch steps, beneath an old tub in a neighbor's yard, inside a tipped garbage can. I lifted a sheet of plywood that leaned against the side of an adobe house. A black and white cat stared at me, nothing like the one who had fallen. We searched separately until dark, and we returned separately, Linda several steps ahead, arms crossed as if against a chill, and I thought what little it took to throw your life off, to turn it upside down.

"Castellani," Johansson said to me. "Tella truth. You think any of these punks they got fighting today could stand up to Joe Louis? Or Ezzard Charles? Ingemar Johansson? Tella truth, what you think?"

We sat together for lunch in what little shade the skeletal building offered — Johansson, Lernic, Harvis, and I. There used to be more of us, but this was a desert town and it dried out in the summer, everyone going away, out of the heat. Then Graham was fired for drinking and Iglesia deported. The apartments were almost completed. Our crew stayed small.

"I don't follow boxing," I said and finished off the sandwich I'd thrown together before leaving for work. It had been a bad night, Linda and I with no place to sit but the bed, nothing to do but the carpet, and neither of us willing to work on that. Harvis had gone home, but I'd wished that he'd stayed for a while. Sometimes he made it easier for us to be together. Linda, I'm pretty sure, had felt the same.

"They couldn't hold Ingemar's mouthpiece," Johansson said. "He's practically a relative of yours truly, more or less, like we'd be cousins if he lived around here." Johansson was in charge of us, a red-faced little man who wore long-sleeve plaid shirts rolled to the elbows. "And he could punch. You ever seen those films of him whupping Patterson? Tella truth, you ever seen such a punch? On my father's side, we all been fighters."

Johansson and Lernic sat on the tailgate of a company truck. Harvis and I reclined against concrete, the foundation for the apartments. Dry-wallers worked down the site from us, where we'd been the week before. At the far end were painters and carpet layers. Eventually it would be a big complex. The pool was already in.

"I like to watch girls fight," Lernic said. "They don't have rules for that." His face was big, sloppy; his skin, the color and texture of angel food cake. "Rip those clothes, Mama. Yank that hair. Bite that tit." He laughed and leaned back on his elbows. "Harvis was a boxer, I bet. Big and dumb enough. Fag enough. You a boxer, Harvis?"

"Fuck off," Harvis said.

"Scratch you like a girl, I bet." Lernic laughed again. "Big old nothing Harvis rip at your shirt. 'Let me at them titties. Let me at them titties.' " Lernic waggled his fingers at Johansson's shirt, then leaned back again. "Bite this, Harvis." He gripped the crotch of his pants.

I stood and nudged Harvis on the shoulder. "Let's walk off lunch. We've got fifteen minutes."

"He don't mean nothing," Johansson said. "Tell them you don't mean nothing, Lernic. It's his way of being funny."

Lernic's hand was still at his crotch. "Watch your step, Castellani. That big fag'll cornhole you in the behind."

"That's redundant," I said, walking away. "Like saying Lernic the dumbass."

"There you go," Johansson said. "Everybody's got a way of being funny."

"That guy makes me crazy," Harvis said, throwing his thumb over his shoulder when we'd walked far enough away.

"Screw Lernic," I said. "You let assholes get to you and your life is shit."

"I'm supposed to act like he doesn't exist?"

"He's a pathetic boob."

"You've got Linda," Harvis said. "You can say that stuff. I've got to take boobs seriously. I could wind up one. Hell, I could be one already. You've got Linda. You can let the rest go."

"So, you've got me *and* Linda," I said.

"See?" Harvis put one of his big fingers square in my chest. "That's just the kind of thing you say to a pathetic boob. See there?"

After lunch I took off my shirt. That was one of the things I liked about the job. I could take off my shirt and work on the high boards, stepping from scaffolding to beam. And the smell of lumber. The pull and give of my muscles. The paycheck.

I had planned to be an archaeologist, although I know now I might as well have planned to be an astronaut. "You can be whatever you want," my mother had told me, "whatever you put your heart into." A good-natured lie. I could not be an archaeologist, not and make enough money to eat.

Our plan, Linda's and mine, had been for her to go to grad-

uate school to become a librarian. It wasn't exactly what she'd
wanted, but it sounded all right to her. Then she'd get a job
and I'd study archaeology again, give it a shot. That was why
we'd moved here, near a university. There was nothing wrong
with our plan, but we couldn't make it work. At first we
needed Linda's income to get by. Then we bought a television
on time. We went to the movies. Sometimes we went out and
ate steak. We didn't sell out our dreams — we siphoned them
off.

Construction was better than cooking burgers, a lot better,
but once, years ago, I went as a student on a dig in Mexico, and
with a whisk and an airbrush, I uncovered a clay jar, a carved
spoon, the curved line of a jawbone. I studied people by looking
at what had endured. At the ruins of Palenque, I climbed to the
opening in the temple, then descended dark stairs, turned a
narrow corner, and there was the sepulchral slab, covering the
body of an ancient priest. What I felt was wonder, and no matter
how many nails I pounded or boards I sawed, I could not claim
wonder at seeing a building become. There were some who
could; I was not among them. My life hadn't worked out the
way I'd planned.

"Johansson." Lernic yelled although Johansson was only a few
feet away.

I looked down at them. Lernic, on his knees, marked a sheet
of plywood. Johansson and Harvis unloaded lumber from the
truck.

"You see that show on TV last night?" Lernic said. "I almost
forgot. You see it?"

"My television gets nothing but static these days. Lot like you,
Mr. Lernic." Johansson backed away from the truck with an
armload of two-by-fours. Harvis lifted the other end.

"It was educational, Mr. Johansson. And you could have used
it to save one of your employees — Mr. Harvis. You do have a
Mr. Harvis working for you?" He quit marking the plywood and
stared at Johansson, as if Harvis weren't there. I could see it all
from the second-story scaffolding.

"Go to fucking hell," Harvis said.

"Lay off," Johansson said.

"I got something to tell you, goddamn it." Lernic stood and

faced Harvis. "This guy on TV said you can die from screwing nothing but your hand, and here I am trying to save your worthless life, and you got no gratitude."

Harvis dropped his end of the lumber. The boards rattled against the tailgate. "You fuck," he said and stepped toward him.

Lernic picked up the circular saw and revved it once. "Come on, meat. Come get carved."

"Put that down," Johansson said. "Quit being funny. You want a keep your job, you put that down."

Lernic turned his head from Harvis to Johansson and back to Harvis. For an instant, none of us moved.

I lifted the hammer from my belt and let it drop near Lernic's feet. He jumped, then smiled up at me. "Huh," he grunted, put down the saw, and went back to work.

I couldn't hate Lernic, although I wanted to. There had been a day, only a couple of weeks back, when Harvis was down with the flu and staying at our house because his cooler was out and he had no television. I had gone home at lunch break to have a bowl of soup with him and was ten minutes late getting back. I didn't want Lernic to have anything else to throw at Harvis, so I said it was Linda who was sick.

Johansson let it go, but Lernic, of course, didn't.

"You pussy-whipped bastard. Worst case I've ever seen," he said. He'd met Linda when she used to take me to work, before I knew Harvis well enough to ride with him.

That same afternoon Johansson told us about a book he'd like to write, *The Life and Legend of Ingemar Johansson*. "I got the first sentence. That's the hardest part. You listen a this," he said. "Every man has a day in his life when nobody can defeat him, and that day for Ingemar Johansson happened when he was fighting for the heavyweight championship of the world." He beamed. "You read that sentence, who's gonna be able to stop? I figure I write about that whole idea, how everybody gets one day when they're the best. Ingemar, he got his day when he had the big fight. That's a difference between a great man and one a us."

"Shit," Lernic said.

"No," Johansson said. "Really, what you think? Most people,

they get their day, they probably sleep through it or lay around
drunk. A Johansson don't. He gets the fight of his life."

Lernic snorted. "You're not related to any champion, and you
know it."

"We got the same name."

"A name don't mean shit."

"Name's as good as anything. Tella truth, if they'd been a
Ingemar Lernic who whupped Joe Frazier, say. You'd be proud
as two peacocks."

"The only guy could have beaten Frazier was just what beat
him: another big, dumb nigger. I'm going to be proud because
I got the same name as a big, dumb nigger?" Lernic hammered
against a board three times, as if in answer to his question.

"Names mean a lot," Johansson said. "Castellani, tella truth.
If there was a Ingemar Castellani, you'd be as proud as two
peacocks."

"You never called anybody a nigger when Graham worked
here," I said to Lernic.

"So? He was a nigger. You think I'm stupid?" He raised the
hammer to pound the board again. There were no nails in the
board.

"Names must mean something," I said.

"You see there." Johansson waggled a knobby finger. "Now
that's settled. We got work to do."

Johansson walked away, but Lernic put his hand on my shoulder. "Your wife is pretty," he said. He looked at me as if I should
understand something. "I know all about it." He squeezed my
shoulder slightly, then looked at Johansson's back for a second.
"The hardest thing for a man is to be a man and still keep a
woman." He dropped his hand to the head of his hammer,
which rode in his carpenter's belt. "I just thought I'd say that."

"Yeah," I said. "Okay."

He lifted the hammer to eye level, staring at it self-con-
sciously. For an instant I saw it as an archaeologist might
hundreds of years from now, how the blunt black head and
sweeping rear prongs resembled the head of a dragon.

"We got work to do," Lernic said, and since then, I couldn't
hate him, much as I tried.

*

Harvis and I arrived at the house before Linda. The living room, the mess of carpet and tape, and the kitchen, the tangle of chairs around Kitty's box, kept us from entering. We sat on the front porch, stalling, until she arrived.

"We can't seem to face it," I said as she walked up the porch steps.

She shielded her eyes with her hands and looked in the window. "This is a test." She spoke somberly, her lips inches from the glass. "A trial of some sort." Linda believed in God, not a man with a gray beard, but a force that gave reason to being. "If we can get through this, it'll mean something."

"If we get through this, it'll mean there is no intelligent life on this planet," I said.

Harvis shook his big head. "If we get through this, it'll mean we'll live to be a hundred."

Linda turned from the window. She wasn't smiling. "Let's go somewhere and have a beer," she said.

Harvis chucked his thumb toward the window. "I left some in the refrigerator."

"I know that." She stepped from the porch and we followed.

We had pepperoni pizza with extra sauce and drank beer by the pitcher. Harvis told us how he used to be a mugger. "It's the truth," he said. "For about a week. I wasn't any good at it." I wanted to know what made him do it. Linda wanted to know what made him quit.

"I was broke and living in this little dump in Chicago, and my head was all turned around every which way, and I couldn't get a job, and I couldn't think straight, and I'd see these women by themselves or with little kids, and they all had purses, and all I had to do was go and yank it away and run off, and there it was." Harvis, when he drank, rambled.

"You were a purse snatcher," Linda said. "That's not the same as a mugger."

"Whatever you call it, it was low, and I felt mean about it, but I couldn't get turned around the right way until one day I was out in the park and along comes a young woman carrying a bundle with both arms and a big purse hanging from her elbow, one of those hippie bags, and I figured she wouldn't have much money, but I could just run by and grab the purse and keep on running, and I didn't need all that much money — you see, I

was all turned around in my head, but I wasn't greedy." He took
an enormous drink from his glass, filled it again, and took another big drink. He emptied the pitcher, then tapped it against
the table, holding it as if it were a mug, tapping it as if it were a
gavel.

"I ran right up to her, and I had my hand out to rip off her
purse, and just then she turned to me, and stared right at me,
and she said, 'I need to find the hospital. My baby has died.'"
He brought the pitcher down again, breaking it, the handle
remaining in his hand, the pitcher falling into his lap. His palm
began to bleed. "My head wasn't on straight, and I didn't know
what was up, and I didn't know what was down, and that little
baby was no bigger than a football, and I wanted to do something good for that woman, and you know, I couldn't think of
anything, except taking her to the hospital, which is what I did."

Linda reached into his lap and retrieved the pitcher. She
kissed him on the forehead and on the cheek.

Each night we found a reason not to work on the carpet, or we
worked for half an hour, then sat next to the fan and drank
beer and talked. Friday morning, I stepped out of the shower,
and Linda lay over the arm of the couch in the hall, crying. I
tried to lift her to me, but she didn't want to be held. "We'll
finish this tomorrow," I said, "if it takes all day and night." She
just crawled across the couch.

After work, Harvis drove me to the florist, then dropped me
off at the secondhand store, where I waited in our car until
Linda was free. We went out to eat, then drove to a motel.

What I'm saying is I knew there was real danger. I was trying
to ward it off.

The motel room was a pastel yellow. A painting of the ocean
at night hung above our bed. The air conditioner, which lined
the wall beneath the window, hummed and chortled like a
friendly drunk. We crawled under the sheets and watched a
movie on television. A red-headed woman walked briskly down
a city street, wearing a red blouse, red skirt, red shoes. She
practically skipped. Linda put her hand on my chest. "How can
we afford this?" It was the first thing either of us had said for a
long time.

"We needed to get out of the house." I spoke softly and

touched her hair. "We can fix it tomorrow. Tonight we needed to get out."

"We could have stayed with Harvis," she said. "We didn't have to spend all this money."

"This is better," I said.

The woman, in an office now, lifted her red blouse over her head, untied her red skirt, and she was naked. It startled me, like going to a friend's house and a stranger answers the door.

"This must be cable." Linda leaned forward in the bed. "Do you think she's pretty?"

"I don't know," I said, although she was obviously very pretty.

"She is," Linda said. The woman walked around the office in high heels. A man behind a desk smoked a cigar as he watched her. "Why do you think Harvis can't get a girlfriend?"

"I don't know that he can't. He just doesn't. He's shy around women."

Linda crossed her arms across her breasts. We were naked, and I had been hoping we would make love. "He's not shy around me," she said.

"He knows you."

The woman stepped behind the desk and began undressing the man.

"Are they going to show everything?" Linda said. "Are they going to do it? Is this that kind of movie?"

We watched the man and woman make love. The camera moved in close and then backed away.

"They're really doing it." Linda raised herself to her knees and watched. I ran my hand along her leg, but she took it in her palms, patted it gently just the way she pats Mix, then placed it back at my side. "You know who would enjoy this?" she said. "You know what would be fun?"

"That's not a good idea," I said.

"I'll just call and tell him about it." She had already moved toward the phone. "We haven't seen him all day."

"I worked with him eight hours. He took me to the florist. He drove me to the store." She had begun to dial. I reached between her arms and stopped the call.

Linda dropped the receiver and walked to the window. She

peeked through the curtains. "Oh," she said softly, and I thought she said something more.

"Come back to bed." I sat on the edge.

She faced me, my beautiful wife, naked, almost crying. "Let me do what I want."

"I've been with him all day. I don't want to see Harvis." Before I could say anything else, she opened the door and stepped outside. *Jealous?*

The night was warm. Cicadas rattled. The sky dark, as if blackened by fire. She stood with her back to me in the parking lot. I dragged along the bedspread and threw it over both of us. Her fingers locked around my neck, elbows at my chest. We rested forehead to forehead. "Did you feed Mix?" she whispered. "Did you put something out for Kitty?"

"Harvis said he'd take care of it. He wanted to walk Mix."

Tears appeared on her lashes. "I'm all turned around inside," she said. Whether she knew she was echoing Harvis, I'm not sure. "I want to run through this parking lot naked. I want to scream and wake up everyone. I want to hit you. I want this off of me." She yanked the bedspread down. "I want to stand in the middle of the street and shout the meanest things I can think of. I want to leave you." She tried to pull away from me, but I had a good grip around her waist.

"We'll go back inside." I jerked her even closer. "You can call anyone you want."

She shook her head once, sharply. But she came with me and turned off the television and turned off the lights and lay near me in the dark until she could sleep.

We woke early and drove home. Harvis got there at eight, work time. He had Mix with him. "You let this dog sleep in bed with you? He's a bed hog. Almost nuzzled me to the floor."

"You want coffee?" I said.

"Yeah." He petted Mix and looked at Linda. "He farts too."

She laughed and pointed at me. "He won't let him on our bed."

"I don't blame him," Harvis said. "There's too much dog in this dog."

By ten it was sweltering. We worked steadily, switching jobs,

crawling across the floor. Linda and I were in shorts; our knees
and elbows burned. We had used all the big scraps, and now
pieced together the small ones, which took longer and accomplished less.

"Maybe we don't have enough to make it," Linda said. She
sounded hopeful.

"We've got plenty," Harvis said.

"We've got enough for the hall, too," I added, but she didn't
laugh.

We ate lunch on the porch, sitting on the rough, sun-dried
planks, our backs against the railing. The odor of hibiscus, normally sweet, smelled like smoke, as if cooked by the sun.

"This is good." Harvis waved his egg salad sandwich, his arm
brilliant with sweat.

"Oh yeah?" Linda said. "You must have something different
from mine. Let me have a bite."

"No way," he said.

She grabbed his arm and tried to wrestle it toward her. "A
bite. A bite," she said, laughing, pressing her cheek against his
bicep.

"Forget it," he said.

She leaned into him hard and pulled on his slick arm.

"I'll get it." I tried to sound conspiratorial. Before I could
snatch the sandwich she threw herself on top of Harvis and dug
her face into the smashed sandwich. Egg salad covered her
mouth and cheeks, the bridge of her nose. "Delicious," she said,
lifting her head. She wiped off her chin and offered me the
finger. When I parted my lips, she pressed her finger deep into
my mouth.

At two-thirty Harvis and I crept across the couch to the bedroom and searched through drawers until I found PE shorts
that fit him. His jeans had become unbearable. We crawled back
and worked bare chested. "Cheats," Linda said when we took
off our shirts. She pulled off her shoes and socks, then wiped
her face with the tail of her T-shirt. Her bare stomach startled
me as the television had the night before. She saw my face,
looked to Harvis, who had his nose in the carpet, then lifted the

T-shirt higher, wiping her forehead and exposing her white breasts.

My heart beat against my chest like a paddle.

By three, we knew we would not finish before dark, probably not even if we worked well into the night. A screech came from the kitchen, from Kitty's box, a scale of pain.

"I can't stand it," Linda said. She ran to the couch, ducked low, and disappeared down the hall.

"I'm a fool," I said. A rash had begun on my chest. The cat's cry flattened, then lifted again.

"Give me some more tape," Harvis said.

We heard the shower begin. We fitted more carpet and ironed. When Linda stepped off the couch, she had on a clean white T-shirt and the bottom half of her black bikini. Her wet breasts showed through the shirt like the mounds of a relief map.

We worked as if under water, each movement deliberate and unreal. Harvis pointed at my rash and put his shirt back on, but I knew and Linda knew it was to hide his erection. He turned his back to us to button the shirt. I looked at Linda and shook my head. It was the wrong thing to do.

She touched Harvis's thigh. He was on his knees facing away, hands still at his buttons. "Linda," I whispered, as if she would hear and not Harvis. She touched his thigh above the knee, lightly, then moved up his leg. He stared at the wall. Her fingers reached the bottom of the PE shorts, ran along the narrow hem. For an instant, none of us moved.

I wish I could say that I yanked her hand away or that I burst into tears, but there was a trembling inside me, a vacillation of spirit. Some part of me wanted to see her fingers continue their climb up his leg, and that part kept the rest of me silent for the long seconds that followed, until Linda pulled her hand away.

We worked another twenty minutes. "I'll make iced tea," Linda said, almost a whisper, but she did not go to the kitchen. She crawled onto the couch and down the hall.

Harvis stood and stared at the doorway where she had just vanished. "I've never wanted anything so bad in my life," he said, then wiped the sweat from his face. I stood and he put his arm around me. "Do something," he said. "Do something fast."

He hugged me for an instant. I felt his erection against my hip. He picked up his jeans and left.

I waited for her, expecting her to appear in just the T-shirt. Or less. When she stepped off the couch, she was wearing an old pair of trousers and a blue workshirt. Her eyes were red, her face mottled.

"Harvis had to go," I said.

"Oh." She looked at her pants. "I've been crying."

"It's been tough today."

She nodded. "Do you think we should quit or stick it out?"

My heart pounded again. "I can do a lot myself, if you're tired."

She shook her head and knelt beside me to return to the hard work.

Near dawn, we glued the final fragment into place and flipped the carpet side up, a difficult maneuver, then inched it into the corners, pushing and pulling, flattening. We lay side by side on the carpet we'd made. She put her head against my shoulder.

"We should have bought a mat to go beneath it," she said. "It looks so good. How long will it last without a mat? A year? Two years?"

"It could last a long time," I said.

She rose and turned off the light, then lay beside me again in the dark. "This was a test."

"No, it wasn't." I closed my eyes. "This was just one of those things."

"Oh, is that what this was?" She whispered this in my ear, laughing gently. "I want to sleep here tonight."

I nodded, and our long fatigue settled us one against the other, letting us sleep.

Almost a month later, Harvis and I were asked to work a Saturday for time and a half pay. The smallness of our crew had permitted the dry-wallers to catch up.

Johansson refused on principle. "They don't want this thing built," he told us. "They just want us to fry out there. I worked construction thirty years. I don't gotta take this. My kid could do better than this. Tella truth, boys, you ever seen such a mess?"

I worked the high boards, pounding a tenpenny nail through a two-by-four into a four-by-four column. I had taken my shirt off. The rash was gone.

Harvis and Lernic hammered beneath me. Hung over, Lernic had been quiet the first hour, but once he started, he talked as if it was all that kept him standing. He talked as if his life depended on it.

"How far up your ass do you shove this hammer every night, Harvis? I'm taking a scientific survey. Three inches? Six inches? I suppose it depends on which end goes in first."

Harvis handled him by being mute, which seemed to push Lernic on. I tried to speak for him, but it did no good. Maybe Johansson could have stopped it. He had the power to fire.

We would quit at noon, I thought. We'd go home and eat with Linda and not return. At ten-twenty, I stepped from the scaffolding to the crossbeams. Below me, between my legs, were the two of them, Harvis, like me, hitting a nail, Lernic looking up.

"Castellani," Lernic said, "settle something for me. That wife of yours, Linda?"

I stared at him and nodded.

"She do fags like Harvis here, or —"

Harvis's hammer swung away from its board, a backhanded swing of the dragon-head hammer, the blood from Lernic's forehead a sudden hibiscus bloom. His knees gave simultaneously, and he fell to them, and then to the cement, where his body began quivering, and the life shook out of him.

The nail I'd been hammering still stuck out half an inch. My arm swelled with the next swing. That was my position in it: Would I hit the nail while Lernic bled beneath me?

I did not.

"Give me an a hour," Harvis said. "I can get to Mexico."

"I'll try," I said.

"Life's too much." He unbuckled his carpenter's belt, letting it fall, the hammer still in his hand.

I nodded, clinging now to the column, arms tight around it.

"Explain to Linda," he said. "Make her understand. As best you can."

I said, "Check his pulse, Harvis."

Harvis shook his head. "He's dead."

"Check it, Harvis."

"I don't want to touch the bastard."

"We have to make sure he's dead," I said. "He could still be alive."

Harvis knelt over Lernic, his knee in the red puddle. He raised his hammer high.

"No!" I yelled it.

Harvis threw the hammer past me. I ducked, but it missed me by a few feet.

"Some things you don't ask," he said, and he ran to his car.

I stayed up there a while. Lernic's blood made a big pool. I had to be careful getting down.

The police kept me a couple of hours. Johansson was called. He put on a coat and tie and drove over, his hair greased flat against his head and perfectly parted, a gesture of respect, I guess, for the dead or for the police. "The deceased was a no good who liked to cause trouble," he said. "He was asking for something like this all a his life." They wanted to know where Harvis might run. I told them he'd lived in Chicago, that he might have family there, or friends. It wasn't exactly a lie. They didn't hassle me too much. They believed me when I said that I was on the high boards when it happened.

I walked home.

I could tell you about the walk, the alleys I deliberately took, the broken glass and rotting fruit, the sweating magazines peeking out of the trash lids. I could tell you how, when I finally came down to earth, I tried to pinpoint the moment my life had turned wrong, and how I came to decide that I never should have married Linda, that I should have struggled to pursue my obsessions, that I had been made a coward by love.

I would make my life over, I decided. I would let Linda leave me.

I could tell you about my plans, grand ones and petty ones, but when I came out of the alley near our house, I saw Linda in the afternoon sun. She was in the grass on her hands and knees. Her hair was thrown over her head to dry, the way women for generations have dried their hair, a position as timeless as the curve of bone. The back of her neck was white and smooth, an exposed and vulnerable swatch. A thing of wonder.

BLANCHE McCRARY BOYD

The Black Hand Girl

FROM VOICE LITERARY SUPPLEMENT

MY MOTHER hadn't wanted me to go to Harvard Summer School because of the Boston Strangler. "I just hate to think of you like that," she kept saying, "with your face all purple and your tongue hanging out. Why can't you be a normal girl and get a tan?"

The Dean at Duke University probably had not wanted me to go to Harvard either. At Duke I was viewed as a troublemaker, partly because of hypnosis.

When I was in high school I had learned to hypnotize people by accident. "Look deep into my eyes," I said to my cousin Sister-Girl one night when we'd been watching an evil hypnotist in a B movie on television. I said this with great conviction, and Sister-Girl looked at me in great fun. Then something peculiar happened: Sister-Girl seemed to drift toward my eyes. "I'm going to count to five," I whispered, "and when I get to five you'll be in a deep trance." I whispered because I was afraid. There was a current between us as certain as the electricity in a doorbell I'd once touched.

Sister-Girl's eyelids fluttered. She was a sweet, lumpish girl everyone loved. I counted to five and her eyes closed. "Can you bark?" I asked.

"Yes," she said.

"Will you do it?"

"Yes."

"Be a dog, then. Bark."

Her eyes remained closed, but Sister-Girl's lips pulled back from her teeth. She began to make little yipping noises. I recognized our neighbor's Pomeranian.

I counted backward from five and Sister-Girl woke up. "I don't think we ought to tell Momma or Aunt Rose about this," I said.

During my senior year in high school I developed a different technique, no longer hypnotizing through eye contact, which scared me too much, but with a lighted cigarette in a semi-dark room. My favorite trick remained making people bark. Sometimes I asked, after they were barking, "What kind of dog are you?" The answer might be, "I'm a German shepherd," or "I'm a Lhasa apso." I knew I shouldn't be doing hypnosis, especially at parties, but at Duke it made me popular and feared.

College caused me authority problems. There were rules against women wearing pants to classes or to the dining room, and rules against wearing curlers in public; there was even a "suggestion" against women smoking cigarettes standing up. Soon there was a new regulation concerning hypnosis.

The Dean's note came right after second semester began. For my audience I wore a madras wraparound skirt, a Gant button-down shirt, and a cardigan that had leather patches on the elbows. I even wore a panty girdle and hose. The Dean would see that I was a normal, healthy sorority girl, not a troublemaker.

Dean Pottle was at least forty years old. Her hair was brown and she was wearing a brown tailored suit. Her skin was pocked, as if she'd once had acne. She was smoking a cigarette and seemed quite friendly as she invited me to sit down across from her.

"Ellen," she said comfortingly, "we have had a report that you went to Dr. Hillyer's class in the medical school wearing nothing but a bathing suit and carrying a bottle of champagne on a silver tray."

I tried to think of how best to reply. "I'm not in the medical school," I said, "so I didn't think the regular rules would apply. Anyway, it was Dr. Hillyer's birthday, and some of his students asked me to deliver the champagne. It seemed harmless enough. I would never have agreed to do it if I'd known the class was at eight-thirty in the morning, I can assure you of that."

When the Dean said nothing, I continued with less confi-

dence. "I wore my trench coat over my bathing suit until I got
to the door of the classroom, and I put it right back on as soon
as I gave him the champagne."

Her eyes seemed less affable. "The same trench coat you've
been wearing to your regular classes?"

I nodded.

"Is it true you've been wearing your trench coat to classes with
nothing under it?"

"It certainly is not true, Dean Pottle. I wear a slip and a bra. I
even wear hose."

"Ellen, you do know about the dress code, don't you?"

"I'm within the dress code, Dean Pottle. It just says you can't
wear pants, it doesn't say you have to wear skirts. Also, a slip is
a kind of skirt, isn't it?"

The Dean was trying to look stern, but I began to suspect she
might like me. "Do you think of yourself as an unusual girl?"

I nodded miserably. "Listen, Dean Pottle, would you mind if
I smoked too? I'm very nervous."

"Go ahead. You have a tendency to bend the rules a bit, don't
you think, Ellen?"

I lit a Winston. "I don't know."

"Let's start with the hypnosis."

"There was no rule against hypnosis."

The Dean took a final meditative drag on her own cigarette
and crushed it out in a brown glass ashtray.

"Anyway, there's not much to it," I said. "To hypnosis. I saw
it on TV one night. I say corny stuff like 'Look only at the tip of
my cigarette, your eyelids are getting heavy.' Most people are
just dying to go into a trance."

The Dean was staring at the smoke curling from my cigarette.
"Hello?"

With effort she looked up at me. When she didn't speak I
continued, "I tell them, look at the glowing ember of the cigarette. Let your mind relax."

The Dean looked back at my cigarette. She seemed like a nice
enough person. She probably thought the rules were dumb too.

"Your eyelids will close by themselves."

Her eyelids lowered quietly, like dancers bowing.

I counted slowly to ten. "That's good. You're feeling very
good. Just rest now."

A manila folder with my name on it was lying on her desk. In it were my college application, my board scores, and a hand-written report on the hypnosis incidents. The conclusion said I had difficulty accepting discipline and was on academic proba-tion for poor grades.

I replaced the folder and said in my most soothing voice, "When you wake up, you'll feel great. You won't have any mem-ory of this trance. No memory of it at all. You'll think Ellen Burns is a nice, interesting girl with no problems. Nod your head if you understand me."

The Dean nodded.

I was curious to know what kind of dog she might be, but someone could walk in, and I wanted to put this unexpected opportunity to use. Several acquaintances of mine were going to Harvard for the summer.

"When you wake up, I'm going to ask you about recommend-ing me for Harvard Summer School, and you're going to think that's a wonderful idea, in spite of my academic record. You'll say that Harvard is going to help me with my authority prob-lems. Do you understand?"

She nodded again.

I counted slowly backwards from ten to one, then said, "Wake up now."

The Dean's eyes opened. "I feel great. You're a wonderful girl, Ellen, with no serious problems."

I put out my cigarette in her brown glass ashtray. "Dean Pot-tle, I wanted to ask you about Harvard Summer School."

I had made several unsuccessful attempts to lose my virginity at Duke, and Harvard had begun to seem like a possible solution.

My roommate at Duke was named Darlene. Darlene was an angular, good-looking girl with sharp cheekbones and black hair cut in a smooth pageboy that swayed when she moved.

She had been coaching me on the loss of my virginity. In high school I had read an article that said sperm could swim right through your underpants, so whenever I got close to inter-course with a boy, I imagined microscopic tadpoles swimming desperately through cotton fibers the size of the columns at Stonehenge. And I was distracted by other thoughts: germs swim back and forth between mouths; the tongue is a muscle and disappears down the back of the throat, so what is it attached to?

"I want to be normal," I kept saying to Darlene. "I want to lose my normal virginity. Normally."

"I'll fix you up with Don. He doesn't have any experience either. You can learn together."

"Darlene, how could that be a good idea?"

"Trust me, it's a good idea."

Darlene arranged for Don to take me to dinner at a restaurant called Chicken in the Rough. The restaurant's logo was a long-legged chicken in a tam-o'-shanter swinging a golf club. Sitting in one of the dark red booths, I felt as if I were in a dentist's waiting room.

Don was a melancholy boy with dark, dramatic looks. His thick black eyebrows moved when he chewed. When he bit into a chicken leg I pointed at the tiny string of meat hanging from the bone. "That's a ligament. In the fourth grade they told us that you could see what ligaments were when you ate fried chicken."

He looked uncertain.

"I only eat white meat," I said.

"Why are you telling me this?"

"Once the top of my mouth started getting loose. I could move the skin with my tongue. So I went to the dentist and said, 'The roof of my mouth is rotting off. I have some terrible disease.' He looked in my mouth and said, 'Do you eat soup?' So I said of course I eat soup. 'Do you drink coffee?' Yes I drink coffee. 'Well, you're drinking it too hot.' I was kind of disappointed, you know? I thought I had some rare disease."

Don put down his chicken leg. "I don't know what Darlene said to you, but we don't have to do anything. We really don't."

"Could we drink some beer?" I said.

So, while the fried chicken and fried potatoes congealed in their grease and the salad wilted in its pool of dressing, Don and I drank a pitcher of beer, and I began to relax. Don was a good enough looking boy, although he lacked the wildness I found compelling in Darlene's boyfriend, who had taken the mike away from the singer of a black blues band at a fraternity party and sung a version of "Put Your Head on My Shoulder" called "Put Your Legs Round My Shoulders."

Don had been raised by his grandmother in Greensboro, North Carolina. When he graduated he wanted to be a newspaper reporter in a small Southern town. His grandmother's lifelong wish was to meet Lawrence Welk, and someday Don hoped to arrange that for her.

"I have to go to the bathroom," I said.

In the bathroom I confronted the most serious obstacle to the loss of my virginity: under my skirt I was wearing a panty girdle. I hadn't meant to wear the girdle, but when I was dressing, I kept hearing my mother's voice saying *Any woman looks better in a girdle*, so I'd put it on experimentally, and it felt so secure, so bracing, I'd left it on. Now I didn't know what to do about it. I considered taking it off, but it was too bulky for the pocket of my trench coat.

What I did have in the pocket of my trench coat was a Norform vaginal suppository that Darlene had given me to insert "just before intercourse." It was supposed to lubricate me, a word which made me feel like a car. But when was "just before intercourse"? After I peed, I inserted the suppository and pulled the girdle back into place, feeling deeply relieved: the girdle meant I couldn't make love, but the suppository meant I sincerely wanted to.

On the way out of Chicken in the Rough I stopped at the bar in the front room and downed a double shot of bourbon, neat. "I never met anybody like you," Don said.

"I'm just normal," I said, feeling a rush of love for the shot glass. "I'm normal for me. Really."

The November night was inky blue, the air clean and brisk. Don put his arm around me as we walked. The bourbon warmed my blood and the Norform melting made me feel odd. I stopped Don on the street and kissed him on the mouth the way I thought someone in a movie might kiss.

Soon we were in the dormitory parking lot, leaning against a stranger's empty car, still kissing cinematically. Then we were in the back seat of the same car, half lying down. Just when the kissing was getting boring, Don put his hand up my skirt. I had never had anyone's hand up my skirt before.

His fingers moved tentatively up my legs. "My God, what's this?" he said, encountering the girdle.

I wanted to explain, but I felt too dizzy.

His hand wandered around the flesh of my thigh, then moved inward and upward. The dissolved Norform was all over the crotch of the girdle. "My God, you're wet," he said.

I tried to hold still.

"Okay," he mumbled, sliding two fingers awkwardly up the leg of the panty girdle. When he touched me something flashed in my head, and my hips pushed hard against his hand.

"Oh my God, oh my God," he said, pulling his hand free.

"I'll take it off," I said. "No problem. No problem, really."

Don was still crouched over his hand. His fingers glistened in the darkness. A lump appeared behind his knuckle and swelled while I watched.

"It's . . . it's growing," I said.

"It's sprained," he said.

Don's hand was not sprained, but he had broken a blood vessel behind his knuckle. Overnight the blood spread under his skin, turning it puffy and greenish. By the end of the week his hand had turned black, with a dark red palm.

Apparently Don told no one about the girdle, perhaps out of kindness, perhaps to save face, but he did admit to Darlene's boyfriend that his injury was "sort of sexual."

"*Sort of* sexual," Darlene's boyfriend kept saying to her. "*Sort of* sexual."

I became famous almost overnight. Boys I had never heard of called me, and Don followed me to several classes. "We'll try it again. We've got to try it again." He looked vulnerable, stunned by love, extending his black hand.

I never wanted to see Don again in my whole life, so when my mother telephoned and said, "Why don't you fly home this weekend and get measured for your hand-sewn human hair wig?" I felt relieved at the chance to leave school.

My mother met me at the airport in Charleston, just before midnight on a Friday. She was wearing purple toreador pants, a gold lamé shirt, gold lamé slippers, a stroller-length mink coat, and large dark glasses. "I don't want anyone to *recognize* me," she whispered, looking uneasily around the deserted airport. "That's why I have on these *glasses*."

For two years my mother had been addicted to diet pills. "*Ambars*," she would say in a singsongy voice, "I was a different person before I found *Ambars!* The *am* stands for amphetamine and the *bar* stands for barbiturate! The amphetamine speeds you *up*, and the barbiturate slows you *down!* You don't have any *ap*petite, but you're not *ner*vous!"

Before my mother had found diet pills, she did not speak in italics and exclamations, and she was not wiry and loud. Before she found diet pills, she was heavy and depressed. Now she liked to scrub the tiles in the bathroom with a toothbrush, and she had fired the maid because she said it felt so good to push the vacuum cleaner around and polish the silverware herself. She liked to get down between the tines of the forks. "It takes *patience*," she said. "I have lots of *patience!*"

Her arms vibrated as she embraced me. "Doesn't it look real?" she whispered. "Isn't it *astounding?*" She patted her French twist.

Her hair was so smoothly arranged that no false scalp showed, but the elegant twist looked odd: my mother's real hair is naturally curly.

The next day I was staring at myself in the beautician's mirror. "Thank you, Momma." Like Momma's wig, Aunt Rose's wig, and Sister-Girl's wig, mine was set in a French twist.

The four of us were standing around the beauty parlor. We had a monolithic look, like a gang. "The French Twist Gang," Sister-Girl said quietly, meeting my eyes in the mirror.

Sister-Girl had become large and statuesque, a natural blonde with a sweet smile and a quiet manner. A year older than me, she had declined college graciously, as if she were not hungry for dessert.

Her mother, Rose, was my mother's sister. "We all look alike in these wigs," Rose said, "but I'm the inflated version." Rose didn't care for the diet pills because they made her heart hurt.

Rose was built square, "like a refrigerator," she said cheerfully, and she wheezed almost all the time. "There's just not much room for air in there," Sister-Girl had once remarked.

After my wig fitting, we all went shopping, and I bought a garter belt. "I'm not wearing girdles anymore, Momma," I said. "Don't ask. I'm just not, no matter what."

The wig not only changed how I looked, it changed how I felt about myself. When I got back to school, boys stopped pursuing me. Perhaps they no longer recognized the black hand girl. I abandoned not only the hypnosis but parties, and my study habits improved. By the time I went to Harvard Summer School, I had been taken off academic probation. Dean Pottle thought it was her confidence in me that had "turned me around."

At Harvard Summer School I met the man I would eventually marry. On a sticky Saturday night in a drugstore in Harvard Square I was buying a new copy of *Peyton Place* because the pages of my copy were falling out. Nicky Sommers was buying a book called *Thinking About the Unthinkable,* which I assumed was pornographic. It turned out to be about nuclear war.

My copy of *Peyton Place* was worn out because, in the long afternoons in my apartment in the Back Bay, while my room-mate, Dottie Plant, was out waitressing, I had discovered masturbation.

When I was wearing the wig, I dressed like a Duke sorority girl and studied calmly, but when I was not wearing the wig a certain wildness seemed to overtake me. So I wore my French twist almost every day and I was making very good grades. Dean Pottle was going to be proud.

My wig got gummy with dirt, and I had to give it up for six days to have it professionally cleaned. Without the wig I began to wear white lipstick. I combed my hair out straight, drank Scotch on the rocks while I studied, and imagined I was a beatnik like the ones I'd seen in *Time* magazine. I was at Harvard and no one in the South need ever know I was behaving this way.

Sexually, I began to experiment. I read the sex scenes in *Peyton Place* and drifted into them like hypnosis, my old teddy bear clutched tight between my legs. I felt bad about my teddy bear, who was not holding up well under this assault, but as long as I didn't touch myself directly, I was sure I couldn't be doing anything wrong. Then, one afternoon when it was too hot in the apartment to wear a lot of clothes, the situation got out of hand, so to speak. I bled and it wasn't my period. The word masturbation came to me. I realized I had deflowered myself.

I was getting my wig back on Monday. On Saturday night, since I was ruined anyway, I went to a drugstore in Harvard Square in my white lipstick, my black jersey and tight black jeans, to buy a new copy of *Peyton Place*. I was standing furtively behind the paperback rack when this greasy, stringy-haired boy in Levi's that looked like they hadn't been washed in weeks said to me, "Are you from down home?" He had an unmistakable southern drawl.

I didn't answer, of course. My mother's warning about the Boston Strangler had made a vivid impression on me, so vivid, in fact, that when I tried to swear off *Peyton Place*, fantasies about the Boston Strangler had drifted in to replace them.

"Southerners look different," the boy continued. I looked at him out of the corner of my eye. "We walk different, or something."

It seemed unlikely that the Boston Strangler was a Southerner, so I looked him full in the face. "Where are you from?"

"Texas." He had a nice smile and crooked teeth.

"Texas isn't the South," I said. "Texas is the West."

If I hadn't agreed to go drink beer with Nicky Sommers, I wouldn't have told him funny stories about Sister-Girl and Aunt Rose, and if he hadn't laughed so much at my stories, I wouldn't have drunk so much, I wouldn't have ended up back at my apartment with him. When he kissed me I put his hands on my throat. "Squeeze just a little bit," I said. "I want to see how it feels." If Dottie Plant had been home, I wouldn't have ended up on the sofa with him, and if he hadn't been lying with his skinny hip jammed against my tight black jeans, I wouldn't have drifted into *Peyton Place*.

Your nipples are as hard as diamonds, the irresistible man in *Peyton Place* had whispered.

Do it to me, the woman whispered back.

Nicky unbuttoned my shirt and cupped his whole hand over my breast.

"Diamonds!" I shouted, and we both began to shudder. I was extremely embarrassed and shut my eyes tight.

"Hey," Nicky kept saying, "hey," only it wasn't as if he expected an answer.

I was breathing like I'd been running.

"Wow," Nicky whispered. "You had an orgasm."

"I certainly did not." I was trying not to cry.

"Wow. I never gave a girl an orgasm. Hey. Wow."

When Nicky arrived at my apartment for our first real date on Monday night, he had cut his hair and shaved so close his jaw looked raw and scraped. We were going to dinner at a restaurant where, Nicky had promised, the menu would be written in French.

Nicky was wearing a suit and tie, and on his feet were grown-up, lace-up men's shoes. In his hand was a bouquet of daisies.

I had picked up my wig from the cleaners. I was wearing a blue dress, a garter belt, hose and high heels.

"Your hair looks great that way," Nicky said.

We stared dumbly at each other, like people who have fallen in love.

LARRY BROWN

Kubuku Rides (This Is It)

FROM THE GREENSBORO REVIEW

ANGEL HEAR the back door slam. It Alan, in from work. She start
to hide the glass and then she don't hide the glass, he got a nose
like a bloodhound and gonna smell it anyway, so she just keep
sitting on the couch. She going to act like nothing happening,
like everything cool. Little boy in the yard playing, he don't
know nothing. He think Mama in here watching Andy Griffith.
Cooking supper. She better now anyway. Just wine, beer, no
whiskey no vodka. No gin. She getting well, she gonna make it.
He have to be patient with her. She trying. He no rose garden
himself anyway.

She start to get up and then she don't, it better if she stay
down like nothing going on. She nervous, though. She know he
looking, trying to catch her messing up. He watch her like a
hawk, like somebody with eyes in the back of they head. He
don't miss much. He come into the room and he see her. She
smile, try to, but it wrong, she know it wrong, she guilty. He see
it. He been out loading lumber or something all day long, he
tired and ready for supper. But ain't no supper yet. She know
all this and ain't said nothing. She scared to speak because she
so guilty. But she mad over having to *feel* guilty, because some
of this guilt *his* fault. Not all his fault. But some of it. Maybe
half. Maybe less. This thing been going on a while. This thing
nothing new.

"Hey honey," she say.

"I done unloaded two tons of two-by-fours today," he say.

"You poor baby," she say. "Come on and have a little drink
with Mama." That the wrong thing to say.

"What?" he say. "You drinkin' again? I done told you and told you and told you."

"It's just wine," she say.

"Well, woman, how many you done had?"

"This just my first one," she say, but she lying. She done had five and ain't even took nothing out the deep freeze. Wind up having a turkey potpie or something. Something don't nobody want. She can't cook while she trying to figure out what to do. Don't know what to do. Ain't gonna drink nothing at all when she get up. Worries all day about drinking, then in the evening she done worried so much over *not* drinking she starts *in* drinking. She in one of them vicious circles. She done even thought about doing away with herself, but she hate to leave her husband and her little boy alone in the world. Probably mess her little boy up for the rest of his life. She don't want to die anyway. Angel ain't but about thirty years old. She still good-looking, too. And love her husband like God love Jesus. Ain't no answer, that's it.

"Where that bottle?" he say.

Now she gonna act like she don't know what he talking about. "What bottle?" she say.

"Hell, woman. Bottle you drinkin' from. What you mean what bottle?"

She scared now, frightened of his wrath. He don't usually go off. But he go off on her drinking in a minute. He put up with anything but her drinking.

"It's in the fridge," she say.

He run in there. She hear him open the door. He going to bust it in a million pieces. She get up and go after him, wobbly. She grabbing for doors and stuff, trying to get in there. He done took her money away, she can't have no more. He don't let her write no checks. He holding the bottle up where she can see it good. The contents of that bottle done trashed.

He say: "First glass my ass."

"Oh, Alan," she say. "That a old bottle."

"Old bottle? That what you say, old bottle?"

"I found it," she say.

"Lyin'!" he say.

She shake her head no no no no no. She wanting that last drink because everything else hid.

"What you mean goin' out buyin' some more?" he say. He got veins standing up in his neck. He mad, he madder than she ever seen him.

"Oh, Alan, please," she say. She hate herself begging like this. She ready to get down on her knees if she have to, though.

"I found it," she say.

"You been to the liquor store. Come on, now," he say. "You been to the liquor store, ain't you?"

Angel start to say something, start to scream something, but she see Randy come in from the front yard. He stop behind his daddy. Mama fixing to get down on the floor for that bottle. Daddy yelling stuff. Ain't no good time to come in. He eight year old but he know what going on. He tiptoe back out.

"Don't pour it out," she say. "Just let me finish it and I'll quit. Start supper," she say.

"Lie to me," he say. "Lie to me and take money and promise. How many times you promised?"

She go to him. He put the bottle behind his back, saying, "Don't, now, baby." He moaning, like.

"Alan *please*," she say. She put one arm around his waist and try for that bottle. He stronger than her. It ain't fair! They stumble around in the kitchen. She trying for the bottle, he heading for the sink, she trying to get it. Done done this before. Ain't no fun no more.

He say: "I done told you what I's goin' to do."

She say: "Just let me finish it, Alan. Don't make me beg," she say. Ain't no way she hold him, he too strong. Lift weights three days a week. Runs. Got muscles like concrete. Know how to box but don't never hit her. She done hit him plenty with her little drunk fists, ain't hurt him, though. He turn away and start taking the cap off the bottle. She grab for it. She got both hands on it. He trying to pull it away. She panting. He pulling the bottle away, down in the sink so he can pour it out. They going to break it. Somebody going to get cut. May be him, may be her. Don't matter who. They tugging, back and forth, up and down. Ain't nobody in they right mind.

"Let go!" she say. She know Randy hearing it. He done run away once. Ain't enough for her. Ought to be but ain't.

He jerk it away and it hit the side of the sink and break. Blood gushing out of his hand. Mixing with the wine. Blood and wine all over the sink. Don't look good. Look bad. Look like maybe somebody have to kill theirself before it all get over with. Can't keep on like this. Done gone on too long.

"Godomightydamn," he say. Done sliced his hand wide open. It bad, she don't know how bad. Angel don't want to see. She run back to the living room for the rest of that glass. She don't drink it, he'll get it. She grab it. Pour it down. Two inches of wine. Then it all gone. She throw the glass into the mirror and everything break. Alan yell something in the kitchen and she run back in there and look. He got a bloody towel wrap around his hand. Done unloaded two tons of wood today and hospital bill gonna be more than he made. Won't take fifteen minutes. Emergency room robbery take longer than plain robbery but don't require no gun.

He shout: "This is it!" He crying and he don't cry. "Can't stand it! Sick of it!"

She sick too. He won't leave her alone. He love her. He done cut his hand wide open because of this love. He crying, little boy terrified. He run off again, somebody liable to snatch him up and they never see him again. Ought to be enough but ain't. Ain't never enough.

She flashing back now. She done had a wreck a few weeks ago. She done went out with some friends of hern, Betty and Glynnis and Sue. She done bought clothes for Randy and towels for her mama and cowboy boots for Alan. Pretty ones. Rhino's hide and hippo's toes. She working then, she still have a job then. It a Saturday. Randy and Alan at Randy's Little League game. She think she going over later, but she never make it. She get drunk instead.

They gone have just one little drink, her and Betty and Sue and them. One little drink ain't gone hurt nothing or nobody. Betty telling about her divorce and new men she checking out. She don't give no details, though. They drinking a light white wine but Angel having a double 151 and Coke. She ain't messing around. This a few weeks ago, she ain't got time for no wine. And she drink hers off real quick and order and get another one before they even get they wines down. She think maybe

they won't even notice she done had two, they all so busy listening to Betty telling about these wimps she messing with. But it
ain't even interesting and they notice right away. Angel going
to the game, though. She definitely going to the game. She done
promised everybody in the country. Time done come where she
have to be straight. She got to quit breaking these promises. She
got to quit all this lying and conniving.

Then before long they start talking about leaving. She ask
them to stay, say Please, ya'll just stay and have one more. But
naw, they got to go. Glynnis, she claim she got this hot date
tonight. She talk like she got a hot date every night. Betty got
this new man she going out with and she got to roll her hair and
stuff. But Sue now is true. Angel done went to high school with
her. They was in school together back when they was wearing
hot pants and stuff. This like a old relationship. But Sue know
what going on. She just hate to say anything. She just hate to
bring it out in the wide open. She got to say something, though.
She wait till the rest of them go and then she speak up.

She say: "I thought you goin' to the ball game, girl." She look
at her watch.

"Yeah," Angel say. "Honey, I'm goin'. I wouldn't miss it for
the world. But first I got to have me some more 151 and Coke."

Sue know she lying. She done lied to everybody about everything. This thing a problem can't keep quiet. She done had
troubles at work. She done called in late, and sick, done called
in and lied like a dog about her physical condition with these
hungovers.

Now Angel hurting. She know Sue know the truth but too
good to nag. She know Sue one good person she can depend on
the rest of her life, but she know too Sue ain't putting up with
her killing herself in her midst. She know Sue gone say something, but Sue don't say nothing until she finish her second
wine. This after Angel ask her to have a third wine. Somebody
got to stop her. She keep on, she be asking to stay for a eighth
and a ninth wine. She be asking to stay till the place close down.

So Sue say: "You gone miss that ball game, girl."

She say she already late. She motion for another drink. Sue
reach over and put her hand over Angel's glass and say: "Don't
do that, girl."

"Late already," she say. "One more won't make no difference."

She know that her speech and stuff is messed up, which is
embarrassing, but the barmaid, she bring the drink. And Sue
reach out, put her hand over the glass and say: "Don't you give
her that shit, woman."

Girl back up and say: *"Ma'am?"* Real nice like.

"Don't you give her that," say Sue.

Girl say "Yes'm, but ma'am, she order it, ma'am."

Girl look at Angel.

"Thank you, hon," she say. She reach and take the drink and
give the girl some money. Then she tip her a dollar and the girl
walk away. Angel grab this drink and slosh some of it out on
her. She know it but she can't help it. She don't know what went
wrong. She shopping and going to the ball game and now this
done happened again. She ain't making no ball game. Ball game
done shot to hell. She be in perhaps two three in the morning.

Sue now, she tired of this.

"When you goin' to admit it?" she say.

"Admit what?"

"Girl, *you* know. Layin' drunk. Runnin' around here drinkin'
every night. Stayin' out."

She say: "I don't know what you talkin' about," like she huffy.
She drinking every day. Even Sunday. Especially Sunday. Sunday the worst because ain't nothing open. She don't hit the
liquor store Saturday night she climbing the walls Sunday afternoon. She done even got drunk and listened to the services on
TV Sunday morning and got all depressed and passed out before dinnertime. Then Alan and Randy have to eat them turkey
potpies again.

"Alan and Randy don't understand me," she say.

"They love you," Sue say.

"And I love them," she say.

"Listen now," Sue tell her, "you gonna lose that baby and that
man if you don't stop this messin' around."

"Ain't gonna do that no such of a thing," she say, but she
know Sue right. She still pouring that rum down, she ain't
slacked off. She just have to deny the truth because old truth
hurt too much to face.

Sue get up, she got tears in her eye and stuff, she dabbing
with Kleenexes. Can't nobody talk sense to this fool.

"Yes you will," she say, and she leave. She ain't gone hang
around and watch this self-destruction. Woman done turned
into a time bomb ticking. She got to get away from here, so she
run out the door. She booking home. Everybody looking.

Angel all alone now. She order two more singles and drink
both of them. But she shitfaced time she drink that last one, she
done been in the booth an hour and a half. Which has done
caused some men to think about hitting on her, they done seen
them thin legs and stuff she got. This one wimp done even come
over to the table, he just assume she lonesome and want some
male company, he think he gonna come over like he Robert
Goulet or somebody and just invite himself to sit down. He done
seen her wedding ring, but he thinking, Man, this woman horny
or something, she wouldn't be sitting here all by her lonesome.
And this fool almost sit down in the booth with her, he gonna
buy her a drink, talk some trash to her, when he really thinking
is he gonna get her in some motel room and take her panties
off. But she done recognized his act, she ain't having nothing to
do with this fool. She tell him off right quick. Of course he get
huffy and leave. That's fine. Ain't asked that fool to sit down
with her anyway.

Now she done decided she don't want to have another drink
in this place. Old depression setting in. People coming in now
to eat seafood with they families, little kids and stuff, grandma-
mas, she don't need to be hanging around in here no more.
Waiters looking at her. She know they wanting her to leave
before she give their place a bad name. Plus she taking up room
in this booth where some family wanting to eat some filet catfish.
She know all this stuff. She know she better leave before they
ask her to. She done had embarrassment enough, don't need
no more.

Ain't eat nothing yet. Don't want nothing to eat. Don't even
eat at home much. Done lost weight, breasts done come down,
was fine and full, legs even done got skinny. She know Alan
notice it when she undress. She don't even weigh what she
weigh on they wedding night when she give herself to Alan. She
know he worried sick about her. He get her in the bed and
squeeze her so tight he hurt her, but she don't say Let go.

She trying to walk straight when she go out to her car, but she look like somebody afflicted. Bumping into hoods and stuff. She done late already. Ball game over. It after six and Randy and Alan already home by now. Ain't no way she going home right now. She ain't gonna face them crying faces. And, too, she go home, Alan ain't letting her drink another drop. So she decide to get her a bottle and just ride around a while. She gonna ride around and sober up, then she gonna go home. And she need to do this anyway because this give her time to think something up like say the car tore up or something, why she late.

Only thing, she done gone in the liquor store so many times she ashamed to. She see these same people and she know they thinking: Damn, this woman done been in here four times this week. Drinking like a fish. She don't like to look in they eyes. So she hunt her up anther store on the other side of town. She don't want to get too drunk, so she just get a sixer of beers and some schnapps. She going to ride around, cruise a little and sober up. That what she thinking.

She driving okay. Hitting them beers occasionally, hitting that peach schnapps every few minutes because it so good and ain't but 48 proof. It so weak it ain't gonna make her drunk. Not no half-pint. She ain't gonna ride around but a hour. Then she gonna go home.

She afraid to take a drink when anybody behind her. She thinking the police gonna see her and throw them blue lights on her. Then she be in jail calling Alan to come bail her out. Which he already done twice before. She don't want to stay in town. She gonna drive out on the lake road. They not as much traffic out there. So she go off out there, on this blacktop road. She gonna ride out to the boat landing. Ain't nobody out there, it too cold to fish. She curve around through the woods three or four miles. She done finished one of them beers and throwed the bottle out the window. She get her another one and drink some more of that schnapps. That stuff go down so easy and so hard to stop on. Usually when she open a half-pint, she throw the cap far as she can.

Angel weaving a little, but she ain't drunk. She just a little tired. She wishing she home in the bed right now. She know they gonna have a big argument when she get home. She dreading that. Alan, he have to fix supper for Randy, and his mama

ain't taught him nothing about cooking. Only thing he know
how to do is warm up a TV dinner, and Randy just sull up when
he have to eat one of them. She wishing now she'd just gone on
home. Wouldn't have been so bad then. Going to be worse now,
much worser than if she'd just gone on home after them double
151s. Way it is, though. Get started, can't stop. Take that first
drink, she ain't gonna stop till she pass out or run out. She don't
know what it is. She ain't even understand it herself. Didn't start
out like this. Didn't use to be this way. Use to be a beer once in
a while, little wine at New Year's. Things just get out of hand.
Don't mean to be this way. Just can't help it. Alan used to would
drink a little beer on weekends and it done turned him flat
against it. He don't even want to be around nobody drinking
now. Somebody offer him a drink now he tell em to get it out
of his face. He done even lost some of his friends over this thing.

Angel get down to the boat ramp, ain't a soul there. Windy
out there, water dark, scare her to death just to see it. What
would it be to be out in them waves, them black waves closing
over your head, ain't nobody around to hear you screaming.
Coat be water-logged and pulling you down. Hurt just a little
and that's all. Just a brief pain. Be dead then, won't know nothing. Won't have no hurts. Easy way out. They get over it eventually. Could make it look like an accident. Drive her car right
off in the water, everybody think it a mistake. Just a tragedy,
that's all, a unfortunate thing. Don't want to hurt nobody. What
so wrong with her life she do the things she do? Killing her baby
and her man little at a time. And her ownself. But have to have
it. Thinking things when she drinking she wouldn't think at all
when she not drinking. But now she drinking all the time, and
she thinking same way all the time.

She drink some more beer and schnapps, and then she pass
out or go to sleep, she don't know which. Same thing. Sleeping
she don't have to think no more. Ain't no hurting when she
sleeping. Sleeping good, but can't sleep forever. Somebody
done woke her up, knocking on the glass. Some boy out there.
High school boy. Truck parked beside, some more kids in it.
She scared at first, think something bad. But they look all right.
Don't look mean or nothing. Just look worried. She get up and
roll her window down just a little, just crack it.

"Ma'am?" this boy say. "You all right, ma'am?"

"Yes," she say. "Fine, thank you."

"Seen you settin' here," he say. "Thought your car tore up maybe."

"No," Angel say. "Just sleepy," she say. "Leavin' now," she say, and she roll the window up. She turn the lights on, car still running, ain't even shut it off. Out in the middle of nowhere asleep, ain't locked the door. Somebody walk up and slit her throat, she not even know it. She crazy. She got to get home. She done been asleep no telling how long.

She afraid they gonna follow her out. They do. She can't stand for nobody to get behind her like that. Make her nervous. She decide she gonna speed up and leave them behind. She get up to about sixty-five. She start to pull away. She sobered up a little while she asleep. Be okay to get another one of them beers out the sack now. Beer sack down in the floor. Have to lean over and take her eyes off the road just a second to get that beer, no problem.

Her face hit the windshield, the seat slam her up. Too quick. Lights shining up against a tree. Don't even know what happened. Windshield broke all to pieces. Smoke coming out the hood. She wiping her face. Interior light on, she got blood all over her hands. Face bleeding. She look in the rearview mirror, she don't know her own self. Look like something in a monster movie. She screaming now. Face cut all to pieces. She black out again. She come to, she out on the ground. People helping her up. She screaming I'm ruint I'm ruint. Lights in her eyes, legs moving in front of her. Kids talking. One of them say she just drive right off the road into that tree. She don't believe it. Road move or something. Tree jump out in front of her. She a good driver. She drive too good for something like this.

Cost three thousand dollars to fix the car this time. Don't even drive right no more. Alan say the frame bent. Alan say it won't never drive right no more. And ain't even paid for. She don't know about no frame. She just know it jerk going down the road.

She in the hospital a while. She don't remember exactly, three or four days. They done had to sew her face up. People see them scars even through thick makeup the rest of her life. She bruised so bad she don't get out the bed for a week. Alan keep saying they lucky she ain't dead. He keep praising God his wife ain't dead. She know she just gonna have to go through it again now sometime, till a worse one happen. Police done come and talked to her. She lie her way out of it, though. Can't prove nothing. Alan keep saying we lucky.

Ain't lucky. Boss call, want to know when she coming back to work. She hem and haw. Done missed all them Mondays. She can't give no definite answer. He clear his throat. Maybe he should find somebody else for her position since she so vague. Well yessir, she say. Yessir, if you think that the best thing.

Alan awful quiet after this happen. He just sit and stare. She touch him out on the porch, he just draw away. Like her hand a bad thing to feel on him. This go on about a week. Then he come home from work one evening and she sitting in the living room with a glass of wine in her hand.

He back now from having his hand sewed up. He sitting in the kitchen drinking coffee, he done bought some cigarettes and he smoking one after another. Done been quit two years, say it the hardest thing he ever done. He say never stop wanting one, that he have to brace himself every day. Now he done started back. She know: This what she done to him.

Angel not drinking anything. Don't mean she don't have nothing. Just can't have it right now. He awake now. Later he be asleep. He think the house clean. House ain't clean. Lots of places to hide things, you want to hide them bad enough. Ain't like Easter eggs, like Christmas presents. Like life and death.

Wouldn't never think on her wedding night it ever be like this. She in the living room by herself, he in the kitchen by himself. TV on, she ain't watching it, some fool on Johnny Carson telling stuff ain't even funny. She ain't got the sound on. Ain't hear nothing, ain't see nothing. She hear him like choke in there once in a while. Randy in the bed asleep. Want so bad to get up and go in there and tell Alan, Baby I promise I will quit. Again. But ain't no use in saying it, she don't mean it. Just words. Don't mean nothing. Done lost trust anyway. Lose trust, a man and wife, done lost everything. Even if she quit now, stay quit, he always be looking over that shoulder, he always be smelling her breath. Lost his trust she won't never get it back.

He come in there where she at finally. He been crying, she tell it by looking at him. He not hurting for himself, he not hurting for his hand. He cut off his hand and throw it away she ask him to. He hurting for her. She know all this, don't nobody have to tell her. Why it don't do no good to talk to her. She know it all already.

"Baby," he say, "I goin' to bed. Had a long day today."

His face look like he about sixty years old. He thirty-one. Weigh 165 and bench press 290. "You comin'?" he say.

She want to. Morning be soon enough to drink something else. He be gone to work, Randy be gone to school. House be quiet by 7:30. She do what she want to then. Whole day be hers to do what she want to. Things be better tomorrow maybe. She cook them something good for supper, she make them a good old pie and have ice cream. She get better. They know she trying. She just weak, she just need some time. This thing not something you throw off like a cold. This thing deep, this thing beat more good people than her.

Angel say, "Not just yet, baby. I goin' to sit in here in the livin' room a while. I so sorry you cut yo han," she say.

"You want to move?" he say. "Another state? Another country? You say the word I quit my job tomorrow. Don't matter. Just a job," he say.

"Don't want to move," she say. She trembling.

"Don't matter what people thinks," he say.

She think he going to come over and get down on the floor and hug her knees and cry, but he don't. He look like he holding back to keep from doing that. And she glad he don't. He do that, she make them promises again. She promise anything if he just stop.

"Okay," he say. "I goin' to bed now." He look beat.

He go. She by herself. It real quiet now. Hear anything. Hear walls pop, hear mice move. They eating something in the cabinet, she need to set some traps.

Time go by so slow. She know he in there listening. He listen for any step she make, which room she move into, which furniture she reach for. She have to wait. It risky now. He think she in here drinking, they gonna have it all over again. One time a night enough. Smart thing is go to bed. Get next to him. That what he want. Ought to be what she want. Use to be she did.

Thirty minutes a long time like this. She holding her breath
when she go in there to look at him. He just a lump in the dark.
Can't tell if he sleeping or not. Could be laying there looking at
her. Too dark to tell. He probably asleep, though. He tired, he
give out. He work so hard for them.

Tomorrow be better. Tomorrow she have to try harder.
She know she can do it, she got will power. Just need a little
time. They have to be patient with her. Ain't built Rome in a
day. And she gonna be so good in the future, it ain't gonna
hurt nothing to have a few cold beers tonight. Ain't drinking
no whiskey now. Liquor store done closed anyway. Big Star
still open. She just run down get some beer and then run right
back. Don't need to drink what she got hid anyway. Probably
won't need none later, she gonna quit anyway, but just in
case.

She know where the checkbook laying. She ain't making no
noise. If he awake he ain't saying nothing. If he awake he'd be
done said something. He won't know she ever been gone. Won't
miss no three-dollar check no way. Put it in with groceries sometime.

Side door squeak every time. Don't never notice it in daytime.
Squeak like hell at night. Porch light on. He always leave it on
if she going to be out. Ain't no need to turn it off. She be back
in ten minutes. He never know she gone. Car in the driveway.
It raining. A little.

Ain't cold. Don't need no coat.

She get in, ease the door to. Trying to be quiet. He so tired,
he need his rest. She look at the bedroom window when she
turn the key. And the light come on in there.

Caught now. Wasn't even asleep. Trying to just catch her on
purpose. Laying in there in the dark just making out like he
asleep. Don't trust her. Won't never trust her. It like he making
her slip around. Damn him anyway.

Ain't nothing to do but talk to him. He standing on the step
in his underwear. She put it in reverse and back on up. She stop
beside him and roll down the window. She hate to. Neighbors
gonna see him out here in his underwear. What he think he
doing anyway, can't leave her alone. Treat her like some baby
he can't take his eye off of for five minutes.

"I just goin' to the store," she say. "I be right back."

"Don't care for you goin' to the store," he say. "Long as you come back. You comin' back?"

He got his arms wrapped around him, he shivering in the night air. He look like he been asleep.

"I just goin' after some cigarettes," she say. "I be back in ten minutes. Go on back to bed. I be right back. I promise."

He step off the porch and come next the car. He hugging himself and shaking, barefooted. Standing in the driveway getting wet.

"I won't say nothin' about you drinkin' if you just do it at home," he say. "Go git you somethin' to drink. But come back home," he say. "Please," he say.

It hit her now, this enough. This enough to stop anything, anybody, every thing. He done give up.

"Baby," he say, "know you ain't gone stop. Done said all I can say. Just don't get out on the road drinkin'. Don't care about the car. Just don't hurt yoself."

"I done told you I be back in ten minutes," she say. "I be *back* in ten minutes."

Something cross his face. Can't tell rain from tears in this. But what he shivering from she don't think is cold.

"Okay, baby," he say, "okay," and he turn away. She relieved. Now maybe won't be no argument. Now maybe won't be no dread. She telling the truth anyway. Ain't going nowhere but Big Star. Be back in ten minutes. All this fussing for nothing. Neighbors probably looking out the windows.

He go up on the porch and put his hand on the door. He watching her back out the driveway, she watching him standing there half-naked. All this foolishness over a little trip to Big Star. She shake her head while she backing out the driveway. It almost like he ain't even expecting her to come back. She almost laugh at this. Ain't nothing even open this late but bars, and she *ain't* going to none of them, no ma'am. She see him watch her again, and then she see him step inside. What he need to do. Go on back to bed, get him some rest. He got to go to work in the morning. All she got to do is sleep.

She turn the wipers on to see better. The porch light shining out there, yellow light showing rain, it slanting down hard. It

shine on the driveway and on Randy's bicycle and on they bar-
becue grill setting there getting wet. It make her feel good to
know this all hers, that she always got this to come back to. This
light show her home, this warm place she own that mean everything to her. This light, it always on for her. That what she
thinking when it go out.

FREDERICK BUSCH

Ralph the Duck

FROM THE QUARTERLY

I WOKE UP at 5:25 because the dog was vomiting. I carried seventy-five pounds of heaving golden retriever to the door and poured him onto the silver, moonlit snow. "Good boy," I said, because he'd done his only trick. Outside, he retched, and I went back up, passing the sofa on which Fanny lay. I tiptoed with enough weight on my toes to let her know how considerate I was while she was deserting me. She blinked her eyes. I swear I heard her blink her eyes. Whenever I tell her that I hear her blink her eyes, she tells me I'm lying; but I can hear the damp slap of lash after I have made her weep.

In bed and warm again, noting the red digital numbers (5:29) and certain that I wouldn't sleep, I didn't. I read a book about men who kill each other for pay or for their honor. I forget which, and so did they. It was 5:45, the alarm would buzz at 6:00, and I would make a pot of coffee and start the woodstove; I would call Fanny and pour her coffee into her mug; I would apologize, because I always did, and then she would forgive me if I hadn't been too awful — I didn't think I'd been that bad — and we would stagger through the day, exhausted but pretty sure we were all right, and we'd sleep that night, probably after sex, and then we'd waken in the same bed to the alarm at 6:00, or to the dog, if he'd returned to the frozen deer carcass he'd been eating in the forest on our land. He loved what made him sick. The alarm went off, I got into jeans and woolen socks and a sweatshirt, and I went downstairs to let the dog in. He'd be hungry, of course.

I was the oldest college student in America, I thought. But of course I wasn't. There were always ancient women with parchment for skin who graduated at seventy-nine from places like Barnard and the University of Georgia. I was only forty-two, and I hardly qualified as a student. I patrolled the college at night in a Bronco with a leaky exhaust system, and I went from room to room in the classroom buildings, kicking out students who were studying or humping in chairs — they'd do it *anywhere* — and answering emergency calls with my little blue light winking on top of the truck. I didn't carry a gun or a billy, but I had a flashlight that took six batteries and I'd used it twice on some of my overprivileged northeastern playboy part-time classmates. On Tuesdays and Thursdays, I would waken at 6:00 with my wife, and I'd do my homework, and work around the house, and go to school at 11:30 to sit there for an hour and a half while thirty-five stomachs growled with hunger and boredom and this guy gave instruction about books. Because I was on the staff, the college let me take a course for nothing every term. I was getting educated, in a kind of slow-motion way — it would take me something like fifteen or sixteen years to graduate, and I would no doubt get an F in gym and have to repeat — and there were times when I respected myself for it. Fanny did, and that was fair incentive.

I am not unintelligent. *You are not an unintelligent writer*, my professor wrote on my paper about Nathaniel Hawthorne. We had to read short stories, I and the other students, and then we had to write little essays about them. I told how I saw Kafka and Hawthorne in a similar light, and I was not unintelligent, he said. He ran into me at dusk one time, when I answered a call about a dead battery and found out it was him. I jumped his Buick from the Bronco's battery, and he was looking me over, I could tell, while I clamped onto the terminals and cranked it up. He was a tall, handsome guy who never wore a suit. He wore khakis and sweaters, loafers or sneaks, and he was always talking to the female students with the brightest hair and best builds. But he couldn't get a Buick going on an ice-cold night, and he didn't know enough to look for cells starting to go bad. I told him he would probably have to get a new battery, and he looked me over the way men sometimes do with other men who fix their cars for them.

"Vietnam?"

I said, "Too old."

"Not at the beginning. Not if you were an advisor. So-called. Or one of the Phoenix Project fellas?"

I was wearing a watch cap made of navy wool and an old Marine fatigue jacket. Slick characters on the order of my professor like it if you're a killer, or at least a one-time middleweight fighter. I smiled like I knew something. "Take it easy," I said, and I went back to the truck to swing around the cemetery at the top of the campus. They'd been known to screw in down-filled sleeping bags on horizontal stones up there, and the dean of students didn't want anybody dying of frostbite while joined at the hip to a matriculating fellow resident of our northeastern camp for the overindulged.

He blinked his high beams at me as I went.

"You are not an unintelligent driver," I said.

Fanny had left me a bowl of something made with sausages and sauerkraut and potatoes, and the dog hadn't eaten too much more than his fair share. He watched me eat his leftovers and then make myself a king-sized drink composed of sourmash whiskey and ice. In our back room, which is on the northern end of the house, and cold for sitting in that close to dawn, I sat and watched the texture of the sky change. It was going to snow, and I wanted to see the storm come up the valley. I woke up that way, sitting in the rocker with its loose right arm, holding a watery drink and thinking right away of the girl I'd convinced to go back inside. She'd been standing outside her dormitory, looking up at a window that was dark in the midst of all those lighted panes — they never turned a light off and often let the faucets run half the night — and crying onto her bathrobe. She was barefoot in shoepacs, the brown ones so many of them wore unlaced, and for all I know, she was naked under the robe. She was beautiful, I thought, and she was somebody's redheaded daughter, standing in a quadrangle how many miles from home and weeping.

"He doesn't love anyone," the kid told me. "He doesn't love his wife — I mean his ex-wife. And he doesn't love the ex-wife before that, or the one before that. And you know what? He doesn't love me. I don't know anyone who *does!*"

"It isn't your fault if he isn't smart enough to love you," I said, steering her toward the truck.

She stopped. She turned. "You know him?"

I couldn't help it. I hugged her hard, and she let me, and then she stepped back, and of course I let her go. "Don't you *touch* me! Is this sexual harassment? Do you know the rules? Isn't this sexual harassment?"

"I'm sorry," I said at the door to the truck. "But I think I have to be able to give you a grade before it counts as harassment."

She got in. I told her we were driving to the dean of students' house. She smelled like marijuana and something very sweet, maybe one of those coffee-with-cream liqueurs you don't buy unless you hate to drink.

As the heat of the truck struck her, she started going kind of clay-gray-green, and I reached across her to open the window.

"You touched my breast!" she said.

"It's the smallest one I've touched all night, I'm afraid."

She leaned out the window and gave her rendition of my dog.

But in my rocker, waking up, at whatever time in the morning in my silent house, I thought of her as someone's child. Which made me think of ours, of course. I went for more ice, and I started on a wet breakfast. At the door of the dean of students' house, she'd turned her chalky face to me and asked, "What grade would you give me, then?"

It was a week composed of two teachers locked out of their offices late at night, a Toyota with a flat and no spare, an attempted rape on a senior girl walking home from the library, a major fight outside a fraternity house (broken wrist and significant concussion), and variations on breaking-and-entering. I was scolded by the director of nonacademic services for embracing a student who was drunk; I told him to keep his job, but he called me back because I was right to hug her, he said, and also wrong, but what the hell, and he'd promised to admonish me, and now he had, and would I please stay. I thought of the fringe benefits — graduation in only sixteen years — so I went back to work.

My professor assigned a story called "A Rose for Emily," and I wrote him a paper about the mechanics of corpse fucking, and how, since she clearly couldn't screw her dead boyfriend, she was keeping his rotten body in bed because she truly loved him. I called the paper "True Love." He gave me a B and wrote *see me, pls.* In his office after class, his feet up on his desk, he trimmed a cigar with a giant folding knife he kept in his drawer.

"You've got to clean the hole out," he said, "or they don't draw."

"I don't smoke," I said.

"Bad habit. Real *habit,* though. I started in smoking 'em in Georgia, in the service. My CO smoked 'em. We collaborated on a brothel inspection one time, and we ended up smoking these with a couple of women —" He waggled his eyebrows at me, now that his malehood had been established.

"Were the women smoking them, too?"

He snorted laughter through his nose, while the greasy smoke came curling off his thin, dry lips. "They were pretty smoky, I'll tell ya!" Then he propped up his feet — he was wearing cowboy boots that day — and he sat forward. "It's a little hard to explain. But — hell. You just don't say *fuck* when you write an essay for a college prof. Okay?" Like a scoutmaster with a kid he'd caught in the outhouse jerking off: "All right? You don't wanna do that."

"Did it shock you?"

"Fuck, no, it didn't shock me. I just told you. It violates certain proprieties."

"But if I'm writing it to you, like a letter —"

"You're writing it for posterity. For some mythical reader someplace, not just me. You're making a *statement.*"

"Right. My statement said how hard it must be for a woman to fuck with a corpse."

"And a point worth making. I said so. Here."

"But you said I shouldn't say it."

"No. Listen. Just because you're talking about fucking, you don't have to say *fuck.* Does that make it any clearer?"

"No."

"I wish you'd lied to me just now," he said.

I nodded. I did, too.

"Where'd you do your service?" he asked.

"Baltimore. Baltimore, Maryland."

"What's in Baltimore?"

"Railroads. I worked with freight runs of army matériel. I killed a couple of bums on the rod with my bare hands, though."

He snorted again, but I could see how disappointed he was. He'd been banking on my having been a murderer. Interesting guy in one of my classes, he must have told some terrific woman at an overpriced meal: I just *know* the guy was a rubout specialist in 'Nam, he had to have said. I figured I should come to work wearing my fatigue jacket and a red bandanna tied around my head, say "man" to him a couple of times, hang a fist in the air for grief and solidarity, and look terribly worn, exhausted by experiences he was fairly certain that he envied me. His dungarees were ironed, I noticed.

On Saturday, we went back to the campus, because Fanny wanted to see a movie called *The Seven Samurai*. I fell alseep, and I'm afraid I snored. She let me sleep until the auditorium was almost empty. Then she kissed me awake. "Who was screaming in my dream?" I asked her.

"Kurosawa," she said.

"Who?"

"Ask your professor friend."

I looked around, but he wasn't there. "Not an unweird man," I said.

We went home and cleaned up after the dog and put him out. We drank a little Spanish brandy and went upstairs and made love. I was fairly premature, you might say, but one way and another, by the time we fell asleep, we were glad to be there with each other, and glad that it was Sunday coming up the valley toward us, and nobody with it. The dog was howling at another dog someplace, or at the moon, or maybe just at his moon-thrown shadow on the snow. I did not strangle him when I opened the back door, and he limped happily past me and stumbled up the stairs. I followed him into our bedroom and groaned for just being satisfied as I got into bed.

You'll notice I didn't say "fuck."

He stopped me in the hall after class on a Thursday and asked me, How's it goin'? — just one of the kickers drinking sour beer and eating pickled eggs and watching the tube in a country bar.

How's it goin'? I nodded. I wanted a grade from the man, and I did want to learn about expressing myself. I nodded and made what I thought was a smile. He'd let his mustache grow out and his hair grow longer. He was starting to wear dark shirts with lighter ties. I thought he looked like someone in *The Godfather*. He still wore those light little loafers or his high-heeled cowboy boots. His corduroy pants looked baggy. I guess he wanted them to look that way. He motioned me to the wall of the hallway, and he looked up and said, 'How about the Baltimore stuff?"

I said, "Yeah?"

"Was that really true?" He was almost blinking, he wanted so much for me to be a damaged war vet just looking for a tower to climb into and start firing from. The college didn't have a tower you could get up into, though I'd once spent an ugly hour chasing a drunken ATO down from the roof of the observatory. "You were just clocking through boxcars in Baltimore?"

I said, "Nah."

"I thought so!" He gave a kind of sigh.

"I killed people," I said.

"You know, I could have sworn you did," he said.

I nodded, and he nodded back.

I'd made him so happy.

The assignment was to write something to influence somebody. He called it Rhetoric and Persuasion. We read an essay by George Orwell and *A Modest Proposal* by Jonathan Swift. I liked the Orwell better, but I wasn't comfortable with it. He talked about "niggers," and I felt him saying it two ways.

I wrote "Ralph the Duck."

> Once upon a time, there was a duck named Ralph who didn't have any feathers on either wing. So when the cold wind blew, Ralph said, Brr, and shivered and shook.
>
> What's the matter? Ralph's mommy asked.
>
> I'm *cold*, Ralph said.
>
> Oh, the mommy said. Here. I'll keep you warm.
>
> So she spread her big, feathery fingers and hugged Ralph tight, and when the cold wind blew, Ralph was warm and snuggly, and fell fast asleep.

The next Thursday, he was wearing canvas pants and hiking boots. He mentioned kind of casually to some of the girls in the class how whenever there was a storm he wore his Lake District walking outfit. He had a big, hairy sweater on. I kept waiting for him to make a noise like a mountain goat. But the girls seemed to like it. His boots made a creaky squeak on the linoleum of the hall when he caught up with me after class.

"As I told you," he said, "it isn't unappealing. It's just — not a college theme."

"Right," I said. "Okay. You want me to do it over?"

"No," he said. "Not at all. But the D will remain your grade. I'll read something else if you want to write it."

"This'll be fine," I said.

"Did you understand the assignment?"

"Write something to influence someone — Rhetoric and Persuasion."

We were at his office door and the redheaded kid who had gotten sick in my truck was waiting for him. She looked at me like one of us was in the wrong place, which struck me as accurate enough. He was interested in getting into his office with the redhead, but he remembered to turn around and flash me a grin he seemed to think he was known for.

Instead of going on shift a few hours after class, the way I'm supposed to, I told my supervisor I was sick, and I went home. Fanny was frightened when I came in, because I don't get sick and I don't miss work. She looked at my face and she grew sad. I kissed her hello and went upstairs, to change. I always used to change my clothes when I was a kid as soon as I came home from school. I put on jeans and a flannel shirt and thick wool socks, and I made myself a dark drink of sourmash. Fanny poured herself some wine and came into the cold northern room a few minutes later. I was sitting in the rocker, looking over the valley. The wind was lining up a lot of rows of cloud, so that the sky looked like a baked trout when you lift the skin off. "It'll snow," I said to her.

She sat on the old sofa and waited. After a while, she said, "I wonder why they always call it a mackerel sky."

"Good eating, mackerel," I said.

Fanny said, "Shit! You're never that laconic unless you feel crazy. What's wrong? Who'd you punch out at the playground?"

"We had to write a composition," I said.

"Did he like it?"

"He gave me a D."

"Well, you're familiar enough with D's. I never saw you get this low over a grade."

"I wrote about Ralph the duck."

She said, "You did?" She said, "Baby." She came over and stood beside the rocker and leaned into me and hugged my head and neck. "Baby," she said. "Baby."

It was the worst of the winter's storms, and one of the worst in years. That afternoon they closed the college, which they almost never do. But the roads were jammed with snow over ice, and now it was freezing rain on top of that, and the only people working at the school that night were the operator who took emergency calls and me. Everyone else had gone home except the students, and most of them were inside. The ones who weren't were drunk, and I kept on sending them in and telling them to act like grownups. A number of them said they were, and I really couldn't argue. I had the bright beams on, the defroster set high, the little blue light winking, and a thermos of sourmash and coffee that I sipped from every time I had to get out of the truck or every time I realized how cold all that wetness was out there.

About eight o'clock, as the rain was turning back to snow and the cold was worse, the roads impossible, just as I was done helping a county sander on the edge of the campus pull a panel truck out of a snowbank, I got an emergency call from the college operator. We had a student missing. The roommates thought the kid was headed for the quarry. This meant I had to get the Bronco up on a narrow road above the campus, above the old cemetery, into all kinds of woods and rough track that I figured would be choked with ice and snow. Any kid up there would really have to want to be there, and I couldn't go in on foot, because you'd only want to be there on account of drugs, booze, or craziness, and either way I'd be needing blankets and heat, and then a fast ride down to the hospital in town. So I dropped into four-wheel drive to get me up the hill above the campus, bucking snow and sliding on ice, putting all the heater's warmth up onto the windshield, because I couldn't see much more than swarming snow. My feet were still cold from the tow job, and it didn't seem to matter that I had on heavy socks and insulated boots I'd coated with waterproofing. I shivered, and I thought of Ralph the duck.

I had to grind the rest of the way from the cemetery in four-wheel low, and in spite of the cold, I was smoking my gearbox by the time I was close enough to the quarry — they really did take a lot of the rocks for the campus buildings from there — to see I'd have to make my way on foot to where she was. It was a kind of scooped-out shape, maybe four or five stories high, where she stood — well, wobbled is more like it. She was as chalky as she'd been the last time, and her red hair didn't catch the light anymore. It just lay on her like something that had died on top of her head. She was in a white nightgown that was plastered to her body. She had her arms crossed as if she wanted to be warm. She swayed, kind of, in front of the big, dark, scooped-out rock face, where the trees and brush had been cleared for trucks and earth movers. She looked tiny against all the darkness. From where I stood, I could see the snow driving down in front of the lights I'd left on, but I couldn't see it near her. All it looked like around her was dark. She was shaking with the cold, and she was crying.

I had a blanket with me, and I shoved it down the front of my coat to keep it dry for her, and because I was so cold. I waved. I stood in the lights and I waved. I don't know what she saw — a big shadow, maybe. I surely didn't reassure her, because when she saw me she backed up until she was near the face of the quarry. She couldn't go any farther, anyway.

I called, "Hello! I brought a blanket. Are you cold? I thought you might want a blanket."

Her roommates had told the operator about pills, so I didn't bring her the coffee laced with mash. I figured I didn't have all that much time, anyway, to get her down and pumped out. The booze with whatever pills she'd taken would make her die that much faster.

I hated that word. Die. It made me furious with her. I heard myself seething when I breathed. I pulled my scarf and collar up above my mouth. I didn't want her to see how close I might come to wanting to kill her because she wanted to die.

I called, "Remember me?"

I was closer now. I could see the purple mottling of her skin. I didn't know if it was cold or dying. It probably didn't matter much to distinguish between them right now, I thought. That made me smile. I felt the smile, and I pulled the scarf down so she could look at it. She didn't seem awfully reassured.

"You're the sexual harassment guy," she said. She said it very slowly. Her lips were clumsy. It was like looking at a ventriloquist's dummy.

"I gave you an A," I said.

"When?"

"It's a joke," I said. "You don't want me making jokes. You want me to give you a nice warm blanket, though. And then you want me to take you home."

She leaned against the rock face when I approached. I pulled the blanket out, then zipped my jacket back up. The snow had stopped, I realized, and that wasn't really a very good sign. It felt as if an arctic cold was descending in its place. I held the blanket out to her, but she only looked at it.

"You'll just have to turn me in," I said. "I'm gonna hug you again."

She screamed, "No more! I don't want any more hugs!"

But she kept her arms on her chest, and I wrapped the blanket around her and stuffed a piece into each of her tight, small fists. I didn't know what to do for her feet. Finally, I got down on my haunches in front of her. She crouched down, too, protecting herself.

"No," I said. "No. You're fine."

I took off the woolen mittens I'd been wearing. Mittens kept you warmer than gloves because they trap your hand's heat around the fingers and palms at once. Fanny had knitted them for me. I put a mitten as far onto each of her feet as I could. She let me. She was going to collapse, I thought.

"Now let's go home," I said. "Let's get you better."

With her funny, stiff lips, she said, "I've been very self-indulgent and weird, and I'm sorry. But I'd really like to die." She sounded so reasonable that I found myself nodding in agreement as she spoke.

"You can't just die," I said.

"Aren't I dying already? I took all of them and then" — she giggled like a child, which of course is what she was — "I borrowed different ones from other people's rooms. See, this isn't some teenage cry like for *help*. Understand? I'm seriously interested in death and I have to like stay out here a little longer and fall asleep. All right?"

"You can't do that," I said. "You ever hear of Vietnam?"

"I saw that movie," she said. "With the opera in it. *Apocalypse?* Whatever."

"I was there!" I said. "I killed people! I helped to kill them! And when they die, you see their bones later on. You dream about their bones and blood on the ends of the splintered ones, and this kind of mucous stuff coming out of their eyes. You probably heard of guys having dreams like that, didn't you? Whacked-out Vietnam vets? That's me, see? So I'm telling you, I know about dead people and their eyeballs and everything falling out. And people keep dreaming about the dead people they knew, see? You can't make people dream about you like that! It isn't fair!"

"You dream about me?" She was ready to go. She was ready to fall down, and I was going to lift her up and get her to the truck.

"I will," I said. "If you die."

"I want you to," she said. Her lips were hardly moving now. Her eyes were closed. "I want you all to."

I dropped my shoulder and put it into her waist and picked her up and carried her down to the Bronco. She was talking, but not a lot, and her voice leaked down my back. I jammed her into the truck and wrapped the blanket around her better and then put another one down around her feet. I strapped her in with the seat belt. She was shaking, and her eyes were closed and her mouth open. She was breathing. I checked that twice, once when I strapped her in and then again when I strapped myself in and backed up hard into a sapling and took it down. I got us into first gear, held the clutch in, leaned over to listen for breathing, heard it — shallow panting, like a kid asleep on your lap for a nap — and then I put the gear in and howled down the hillside on what I thought might be the road.

We passed the cemetery. I told her that was a good sign. She didn't respond. I found myself panting, too, as if we were breathing for each other. It made me dizzy, but I couldn't stop. We passed the highest dorm, and I dropped the truck into four-wheel high. The cab smelled like burned oil and hot metal. We were past the chapel now, and the observatory, the president's house, then the bookstore. I had the blue light winking and the V-6 roaring, and I drove on the edge of out-of-control, sensing the skids just before I slid into them and getting back out of them as I needed to. I took a little fender off once, and a bit of the corner of a classroom building, but I worked us back on course, and all I needed to do now was negotiate the sharp turn around the administration building, past the library, then floor it for the sraight run to the town's main street and then the hospital.

I was panting into the mike, and the operator kept saying, "Say again?"

I made myself slow down some, and I said we'd need stomach pumping, and to get the names of the pills from her friends in the dorm, and I'd be there in less than five minutes or we were crumpled up someplace and dead.

"Roger," the radio said. "Roger all that."

My throat tightened and tears came into my eyes. They were helping us, they'd told me: Roger.

I said to the girl, whose head was slumped and whose face looked too blue all through its whiteness. "You know, I had a girl once. My wife, Fanny. She and I had a small girl one time."

I reached over and touched her cheek.

It was cold.

The truck swerved, and I got my hands on the wheel.

I came to the campus gates doing fifty on the ice and snow, smoking the engine, grinding the clutch, and I bounced off a wrought-iron fence to give me the curve going left that I needed. On a pool table, it would have been a bank shot worth applause. The town cop picked me up and got out ahead of me and let the street have all the lights and noise it could want. We banged up to the emergency room entrance and I was out and at the other door before the cop on duty, Elmo St. John, could loosen his seat belt. I loosened hers, and I carried her into the lobby of the ER. They had a gurney, and doctors, and they took

her away from me. I tried to talk to them, but they made me sit
down and do my shaking on a dirty sofa decorated with drawings of little spinning wheels. Somebody brought me hot coffee,
I think it was Elmo, but I couldn't hold it.

"They won't," he kept saying to me. "They won't."

"What?"

"You just been sitting there for a minute and a half like St.
Vitus dancing, telling me, 'Don't let her die. Don't let her die.' "

"Oh."

"You all *right?*"

"How about the kid?"

"They'll tell us soon."

"She better be all right."

"That's right."

"She — somebody's gonna have to tell me plenty if she isn't."

"That's right."

"She better not die this time," I guess I said.

Fanny came downstairs to see where I was. I was at the northern
windows, looking through the mullions down the valley to the
faint red line along the mounds and little peaks of the ridge
beyond the valley. The sun was going to come up, and I was
looking for it.

Fanny stood behind me. I could hear her. I could smell her
hair and the sleep on her. The crimson line widened, and I
squinted at it. I heard the dog limp in behind her, catching up.
He panted and I knew why his panting sounded familiar. She
put her hands on my shoulders and arms. I made muscles to
impress her with, and then I let them go, and let my head drop
down until my chin was on my chest.

"I didn't think you'd be able to sleep after that," Fanny said.

"I brought enough adrenaline home to run a football team."

"But you hate being a hero, huh? You're hiding in here because somebody's going to call, or come over, and want to talk
to you — her parents for shooting sure, sooner or later. Or is
that supposed to be part of the service up at the playground?
Saving their suicidal daughters. Almost dying to find them in
the woods and driving too fast for *any* weather, much less what
we had last night. Getting their babies home. The bastards." She

was crying. I knew she was going to be. I could hear the soft sound of her lashes. She sniffed, and I could feel her arm move as she felt for the tissues on the coffee table.

"I have them over here," I said. "On the windowsill."

"Yes." She blew her nose, and the dog thumped his tail. He seemed to think it one of Fanny's finer tricks, and he had wagged for her for thirteen years whenever she'd done it. "Well, you're going to have to talk to them," she said.

"I will," I said. "I will." The sun was in our sky now, climbing. We had built the room so we could watch it climb. "I think that jackass with the smile, my prof? She showed up a lot at his office the last few weeks. He called her 'my advisee,' you know? The way those guys sound about what they're achieving by getting up and shaving and going to work and saying the same thing every day. Every year. Well, she was his advisee, I bet. He was shoving home the old advice."

"She'll be okay," Fanny said. "Her parents will take her home and love her up and get her some help." Fanny began to cry again, then she stopped. She blew her nose, and the dog's tail thumped. She kept a hand between my shoulder and my neck. "So tell me what you'll tell a waiting world. How'd you talk her out?"

"Well, I didn't, really. I got up close and picked her up and carried her, is all."

"You didn't say *anything*?"

"Sure, I did. Kid's standing in the snow outside of a lot of pills, you're gonna say something."

"So what'd you *say*?"

"I told her stories," I said. "I did Rhetoric and Persuasion."

Fanny said, "Go in early on Thursday, you go in half an hour early, you get that guy to jack up your grade."

MICHAEL CUNNINGHAM

White Angel

FROM THE NEW YORKER

WE LIVED THEN in Cleveland, in the middle of everything. It was the sixties — our radios sang out love all day long. This of course is history. It was before the city of Cleveland went broke, before its river caught fire. We were four. My mother and father, Carlton, and me. Carlton turned sixteen the year I turned nine. Between us were several brothers and sisters, weak flames quenched in our mother's womb. We are not a fruitful or many-branched line. Our family name is Morrow.

Our father was a high school music teacher. Our mother taught children called "exceptional," which meant that some could name the day Christmas would fall in the year 2000 but couldn't remember to take down their pants when they peed. We lived in a tract called Woodlawn — neat one- and two-story houses painted optimisic colors. The tract bordered a cemetery. Behind our back yard was a gully choked with brush and, beyond that, the field of smooth, polished stones. I grew up with the cemetery and didn't mind it. It could be beautiful. A single stone angel, small-breasted and determined, rose amid the more conservative markers close to our house. Farther away, in a richer section, miniature mosques and Parthenons spoke silently to Cleveland of man's enduring accomplishments. Carlton and I played in the cemetery as children and, with a little more age, smoked joints and drank Southern Comfort there. I was, thanks to Carlton, the most criminally advanced nine-year-old in my fourth-grade class. I was going places. I made no move without his counsel.

Here is Carlton several months before his death, in an hour so alive with snow that earth and sky are identically white. He labors among the markers, and I run after, stung by snow, following the light of his red knitted cap. Carlton's hair is pulled back into a ponytail, neat and economical, a perfect pine cone of hair. He is thrifty, in his way.

We have taken hits of acid with our breakfast juice. Or, rather, Carlton has taken a hit, and I, in consideration of my youth, have been allowed half. This acid is called windowpane. It is for clarity of vision, as Vicks is for decongestion of the nose. Our parents are at work, earning the daily bread. We have come out into the cold so that the house, when we reenter it, will shock us with its warmth and righteousness. Carlton believes in shocks.

"I think I'm coming on to it," I call out. Carlton has on his buckskin jacket, which is worn down to the shine. On the back, across his shoulder blades, his girlfriend has stitched an electric blue eye. As we walk I speak into the eye. "I think I feel something," I say.

"Too soon," Carlton calls back. "Stay loose, Frisco. You'll know when the time comes."

I am excited and terrified. We are into serious stuff. Carlton has done acid half a dozen times before, but I am new at it. We slipped the tabs into our mouths at breakfast, while our mother paused over the bacon. Carlton likes taking risks.

Snow collects in the engraved letters on the headstones. I lean into the wind, trying to decide whether everything around me seems strange because of the drug or just because everything truly is strange. Three weeks earlier, a family across town had been sitting at home, watching television, when a single-engine plane fell on them. Snow swirls around us, seeming to fall up as well as down.

Carlton leads the way to our spot, the pillared entrance to a society tomb. This tomb is a palace. Stone cherubs cluster on the peaked roof, with their stunted, frozen wings and matrons' faces. Under the roof is a veranda, backed by cast-iron doors that lead to the house of the dead proper. In summer this veranda is cool. In winter it blocks the wind. We keep a bottle of Southern Comfort here.

Carlton finds the bottle, unscrews the cap, and takes a good, long draw. He is studded with snowflakes. He hands me the bottle, and I take a more conservative drink. Even in winter, the tomb smells mossy. Dead leaves and a yellow M&M's wrapper, worried by the wind, scrape on the marble floor.

"Are you scared?" Carlton asks me.

I nod. I never think of lying to him.

"Don't be, man," he says. "Fear will screw you right up. Drugs can't hurt you if you feel no fear."

I nod.

We stand sheltered, passing the bottle. I lean into Carlton's certainty as if it gave off heat.

"We can do acid all the time at Woodstock," I say.

"Right on. Woodstock Nation. Yow!"

"Do people really *live* there?" I ask.

"Man, you've got to stop asking that. The concert's over, but people are still there. It's a new nation. Have faith."

I nod again, satisfied. There is a different country for us to live in. I am already a new person, renamed Frisco. My old name was Robert.

"We'll do acid all the time," I say.

"You better believe we will." Carlton's face, surrounded by snow and marble, is lit. His eyes are vivid as neon. Something in them tells me he can see the future, a ghost that hovers over everybody's head. In Carlton's future we all get released from our jobs and schooling. Awaiting us all, and soon, is a bright, perfect simplicity. A life among the trees by the river.

"How are you feeling, man?" he asks me.

"Great," I tell him, and it is purely the truth. Doves clatter up out of a bare tree and turn at the same instant, transforming themselves from steel to silver in snow-blown light. I know then that the drug is working. Everything before me has become suddenly, radiantly itself. How could Carlton have known this was about to happen? "Oh," I whisper. His hand settles on my shoulder.

"Stay loose, Frisco," he says. "There's not a thing in this pretty world to be afraid of. I'm here."

I am not afraid. I am astonished. I had not realized until this moment how real everything is. A twig lies on the marble at my feet, bearing a cluster of hard brown berries. The broken-off end is raw, white, fleshy. Trees are alive.

"I'm here," Carlton says again, and he is.

Hours later, we are sprawled on the sofa in front of the television, ordinary as Wally and the Beav. Our mother makes dinner in the kitchen. A pot lid clangs. We are undercover agents. I am trying to conceal my amazement.

Our father is building a grandfather clock from a kit. He wants to have something to leave us, something for us to pass along. We can hear him in the basement, sawing and pounding. I know what is laid out on his sawhorses — a long, raw wooden box, onto which he glues fancy moldings. A pearl of sweat meanders down his forehead as he works. Tonight I discovered my ability to see every room of the house at once, to know every single thing that goes on. A mouse nibbles inside the wall. Electrical wires curl behind the plaster, hidden and patient as snakes.

"Sh-h-h," I say to Carlton, who has not said anything. He is watching television through his splayed fingers. Gunshots ping. Bullets raise chalk dust on a concrete wall. I have no idea what we are watching.

"Boys?" our mother calls from the kitchen. I can, with my new ears, hear her slap hamburger into patties. "Set the table like good citizens," she calls.

"O.K., Ma," Carlton replies, in a gorgeous imitation of normality. Our father hammers in the basement. I can feel Carlton's heart ticking. He pats my hand, to assure me that everything's perfect.

We set the table, fork knife spoon, paper napkins triangled to one side. We know the moves cold. After we are done I pause to notice the dining room wallpaper: a golden farm, backed by mountains. Cows graze, autumn trees cast golden shade. This scene repeats itelf three times, on three walls. "Zap," Carlton whispers. "Zzzzzoom."

"Did we do it right?" I ask him.

"We did everything perfect, little son. How are you doing in there, anyway?" He raps lightly on my head.

"Perfect, I guess." I am staring at the wallpaper as if I were thinking of stepping into it.

"You guess. You guess? You and I are going to other planets, man. Come over here."

"Where?"

"Here. Come here." He leads me to the window. Outside, snow skitters under the street lamps. Ranch-style houses hoard their warmth but bleed light into the gathering snow.

"You and I are going to fly, man," Carlton whispers, close to my ear. He opens the window. Snow blows in, sparking on the carpet. "Fly," he says, and we do. For a moment we strain up and out, the black night wind blowing in our faces — we raise ourselves up off the cocoa-colored deep-pile wool-and-polyester carpet by a sliver of an inch. I swear it to this day. Sweet glory. The secret of flight is this: You have to do it immediately, before your body realizes it is defying the laws.

We both know we have taken momentary leave of the earth. It does not strike either of us as remarkable, any more than does the fact that airplanes sometimes fall from the sky, or that we have always lived in Ohio and will soon leave for a new nation. We settle back down. Carlton touches my shoulder.

"You wait, Frisco," he says. "Miracles are happening. Goddam miracles."

I nod. He pulls down the window, which reseals itself with a sucking sound. Our own faces look back at us from the cold, dark glass. Behind us, our mother drops the hamburgers into the skillet. Our father bends to his work under a hooded light bulb, preparing the long box into which he will lay clockwork, pendulum, a face. A plane drones by overhead, invisible in the clouds. I glance nervously at Carlton. He smiles his assurance and squeezes the back of my neck.

March. After the thaw. I am walking through the cemetery, thinking about my endless life. One of the beauties of living in Cleveland is that any direction feels like progress. I've memorized the map. We are by my calculations 350 miles shy of Woodstock, New York. On this raw new day I am walking east, to the place where Carlton and I keep our bottle. I am going to have an early nip, to celebrate my bright future.

When I get to our spot I hear low moans coming from behind the tomb. I freeze, considering my options. The sound is a long,

drawn-out agony with a whip at the end, a final high C, something like "ooooooOw." A wolf's cry run backward. What decides me on investigation rather than flight is the need to create
a story. In the stories Carlton likes best, people always do the
foolish, risky thing. I find I can reach decisions this way — by
thinking of myself as a character in a story told by Carlton.

I creep around the side of the monument, cautious as a
badger, pressed up close to the marble. I peer over a cherub's
girlish shoulder. What I find is Carlton on the ground with his
girlfriend, in a jumble of clothes and bare flesh. Carlton's jacket,
the one with the embroidered eye, is draped over the stone,
keeping watch.

I hunch behind the statue. I can see the girl's naked arms,
and the familiar bones of Carlton's spine. The two of them
moan together in the brown winter grass. Though I can't make
out the girl's expression, Carlton's face is twisted and grimacing,
the cords of his neck pulled tight. I had never thought the
experience might be painful. I watch, trying to learn. I hold on
to the cherub's cold wings.

It isn't long before Carlton catches sight of me. His eyes rove
briefly, ecstatically skyward, and what do they light on but his
brother's small head, sticking up next to a cherub's. We lock
eyes and spend a moment in mutual decision. The girl keeps on
clutching at Carlton's skinny back. He decides to smile at me.
He decides to wink.

I am out of there so fast I tear up divots. I dodge among the
stones, jump the gully, clear the fence into the swing-set-and-
picnic-table sanctity of the back yard. Something about that
wink. My heart beats fast as a sparrow's.

I go into the kitchen and find our mother washing fruit. She
asks what's going on. I tell her nothing is. Nothing at all.

She sighs over an apple's imperfection. The curtains sport
blue teapots. Our mother works the apple with a scrub brush.
She believes they come coated with poison.

"Where's Carlton?" she asks.

"Don't know," I tell her.

"Bobby?"

"Huh?"

"What exactly is going on?"

"Nothing," I say. My heart works itself up to a hummingbird's rate, more buzz than beat.

"I think something is. Will you answer a question?"

"O.K."

"Is your brother taking drugs?"

I relax a bit. It's only drugs. I know why she is asking. Lately police cars have been cruising past our house like sharks. They pause, take note, glide on. Some neighborhood crackdown. Carlton is famous in these parts.

"No," I tell her.

She faces me with the brush in one hand, an apple in the other. "You wouldn't lie to me, would you?" She knows something is up. Her nerves run through this house. She can feel dust settling on the tabletops, milk starting to turn in the refrigerator.

"No," I say.

"Something's going on," she sighs. She is a small, efficient woman who looks at things as if they gave off a painful light. She grew up on a farm in Wisconsin and spent her girlhood tying up bean rows, worrying over the sun and rain. She is still trying to overcome her habit of modest expectations.

I leave the kitchen, pretending sudden interest in the cat. Our mother follows, holding her brush. She means to scrub the truth out of me. I follow the cat, his erect black tail and pink anus.

"Don't walk away when I'm talking to you," our mother says.

I keep walking, to see how far I'll get, calling "Kittykittykitty." In the front hall, our father's homemade clock chimes the half hour. I make for the clock. I get as far as the rubber plant before she collars me.

"I told you not to walk away," she says, and cuffs me a good one with the brush. She catches me on the ear and sets it ringing. The cat is out of there quick as a quarter note.

I stand for a minute, to let her know I've received the message. Then I resume walking. She hits me again, this time on the back of the head, hard enough to make me see colors. "Will you *stop*?" she screams. Still, I keep walking. Our house runs west to east. With every step I get closer to Yasgur's farm.

*

Carlton comes home whistling. Our mother treats him like a guest who's overstayed. He doesn't care. He is lost in optimism. He pats her cheek and calls her "Professor." He treats her as if she were harmless, and so she is.

She never hits Carlton. She suffers him the way farm girls suffer a thieving crow, with a grudge so old it borders on reverence. She gives him a scrubbed apple and tells him what she'll do if he tracks mud on the carpet.

I am waiting in our room. He brings the smell of the cemetery with him — its old snow and wet pine needles. He rolls his eyes at me, takes a crunch of his apple. "What's happening, Frisco?" he says.

I have arranged myself loosely on my bed, trying to pull a Dylan riff out of my harmonica. I have always figured I can bluff my way into wisdom. I offer Carlton a dignified nod.

He drops onto his own bed. I can see a crushed crocus stuck to the black rubber sole of his boot.

"Well, Frisco," he says. "Today you are a man."

I nod again. Is that all there is to it?

"*Yow*," Carlton says. He laughs, pleased with himself and the world. "That was so perfect."

I pick out what I can of "Blowin' in the Wind."

Carlton says, "Man, when I saw you out there spying on us I thought to myself, *Yes*. Now *I'm* really here. You know what I'm saying?" He waves his apple core.

"Uh-huh," I say.

"Frisco, that was the first time her and I ever did it. I mean, we'd talked. But when we finally got down to it, there you were. My brother. Like you *knew*."

I nod, and this time for real. What happened was an adventure we had together. All right. The story is beginning to make sense.

"Aw, Frisco," Carlton says. "I'm gonna find you a girl, too. You're nine. You been a virgin too long."

"Really?" I say.

"*Man*. We'll find you a woman from the sixth grade, somebody with a little experience. We'll get stoned and all make out under the trees in the boneyard. I want to be present at your deflowering, man. You're gonna need a brother there."

I am about to ask, as casually as I can manage, about the relationship between love and bodily pain, when our mother's voice cuts into the room. "You did it," she screams. "You tracked mud all over the rug."

A family entanglement follows. Our mother brings our father, who comes and stands in the doorway with her, taking in evidence. He is a formerly handsome man. His face has been worn down by too much patience. He has lately taken up some sporty touches — a goatee, a pair of calfskin boots.

Our mother points out the trail of muddy half-moons that lead from the door to Carlton's bed. Dangling over the end of the bed are the culprits themselves, voluptuously muddy, with Carlton's criminal feet still in them.

"You see?" she says. "You see what he thinks of me?"

Our father, a reasonable man, suggests that Carlton clean it up. Our mother finds that too small a gesture. She wants Carlton not to have done it in the first place. "I don't ask for much," she says. "I don't ask where he goes. I don't ask why the police are suddenly so interested in our house. I ask that he not track mud all over the floor. That's all." She squints in the glare of her own outrage.

"Better clean it right up," our father says to Carlton.

"And that's it?" our mother says. "He cleans up the mess and all is forgiven?"

"Well, what do you want him to do? Lick it up?"

"I want some consideration," she says, turning helplessly to me. "That's what I want."

I shrug, at a loss. I sympathize with our mother but am not on her team.

"All right," she says. "I just won't bother cleaning the house anymore. I'll let you men handle it. I'll sit and watch television and throw my candy wrappers on the floor."

She starts out, cutting the air like a blade. On the way she picks up a jar of pencils, looks at it, and tosses the pencils on the floor. They fall like fortune-telling sticks, in pairs and crisscrosses.

Our father goes after her, calling her name. Her name is Isabel. We can hear them making their way across the house, our father calling "Isabel, Isabel, Isabel," while our mother, pleased with the way the pencils looked, dumps more things onto the floor.

"I hope she doesn't break the TV," I say.

"She'll do what she needs to do," Carlton says.

"I hate her," I say. I am not certain about that. I want to test the sound of it, to see if it's true.

"She's got more balls than any of us, Frisco," he says. "Better watch what you say about her."

I keep quiet. Soon I get up and start gathering pencils, because I prefer that to lying around and trying to follow the shifting lines of allegiance. Carlton goes for a sponge and starts in on the mud.

"You get shit on the carpet, you clean it up," he says. "Simple."

The time for all my questions about love has passed, and I am not so unhip as to force a subject. I know it will come up again. I make a neat bouquet of pencils. Our mother rages through the house.

Later, after she has thrown enough and we three have picked it all up, I lie on my bed thinking things over. Carlton is on the phone to his girlfriend, talking low. Our mother, becalmed but still dangerous, cooks dinner. She sings as she cooks, some slow forties number that must have been all over the jukes when her first husband's plane went down in the Pacific. Our father plays his clarinet in the basement. That is where he goes to practice, down among his woodworking tools, the neatly hung hammers and awls that throw oversized shadows in the light of the single bulb. If I put my ear to the floor, I can hear him, pulling a long, low tomcat moan out of that horn. There is some strange comfort in pressing my ear to the carpet and hearing our father's music leaking up through the floorboards. Lying down, with my ear to the floor, I join in on my harmonica.

That spring our parents have a party to celebrate the sun's return. It has been a long, bitter winter, and now the first wild daisies are poking up on the lawns and among the graves.

Our parents' parties are mannerly affairs. Their friends, schoolteachers all, bring wine jugs and guitars. They are Ohio hip. Though they hold jobs and meet mortgages, they think of themselves as independent spirits on a spying mission. They have agreed to impersonate teachers until they write their novels, finish their dissertations, or just save up enough money to set themselves free.

Carlton and I are the lackeys. We take coats, fetch drinks. We have done this at every party since we were small, trading on our precocity, doing a brother act. We know the moves. A big, lipsticked woman who has devoted her maidenhood to ninth-grade math calls me Mr. Right. An assistant vice principal in a Russian fur hat asks us both whether we expect to vote Democratic or Socialist. By sneaking sips I manage to get myself semi-crocked.

The reliability of the evening is derailed halfway through, however, by a half dozen of Carlton's friends. They rap on the door and I go for it, anxious as a carnival sharp to see who will step up next and swallow the illusion that I'm a kindly, sober nine-year-old child. I'm expecting callow adults, and what do I find but a pack of young outlaws, big-booted and wild-haired. Carlton's girlfriend stands in front, in an outfit made up almost entirely of fringe.

"Hi, Bobby," she says confidently. She comes from New York, and is more than just locally smart.

"Hi," I say. I let them all in despite a retrograde urge to lock the door and phone the police. Three are girls, four boys. They pass me in a cloud of dope smoke and sly-eyed greeting.

What they do is invade the party. Carlton is standing on the far side of the rumpus room, picking the next album, and his girl cuts straight through the crowd to his side. She has the bones and the loose, liquid moves some people consider beautiful. She walks through that room as if she'd been sent to teach the whole party a lesson.

Carlton's face tips me off that this was planned. Our mother demands to know what's going on here. She is wearing a long, dark red dress that doesn't interfere with her shoulders. When she dresses up, you can see what it is about her, or what it was. She is the source of Carlton's beauty. I have our father's face.

Carlton does some quick talking. Though it is against our mother's better judgment, the invaders are suffered to stay. One of them, an Eddie Haskell for all his leather and hair, tells her she is looking good. She is willing to hear it.

So the outlaws, house-sanctioned, start to mingle. I work my way over to Carlton's side, the side unoccupied by his girlfriend. I would like to say something ironic and wised-up, something that will band Carlton and me against every other person in the room. I can feel the shape of the comment I have in mind, but, being a tipsy nine-year-old, can't get my mouth around it. What I say is "Shit, man."

Carlton's girl laughs. I would like to tell her what I have figured out about her, but I am nine, and three-quarters gone on Tom Collinses. Even sober, I can only imagine a sharp-tongued wit.

"Hang on, Frisco," Carlton tells me. "This could turn into a real party."

I can tell by the light in his eyes what is going down. He has arranged a blind date between our parents' friends and his own. It's a Woodstock move — he is plotting a future in which young and old have business together. I agree to hang on, and go to the kitchen, hoping to sneak a few knocks of gin.

There I find our father leaning up against the refrigerator. A line of butterfly-shaped magnets hovers around his head. "Are you enjoying this party?" he asks, touching his goatee. He is still getting used to being a man with a beard.

"Uh-huh."

"I am, too," he says sadly. He never meant to be a high school music teacher. The money question caught up with him.

"What do you think of this music?" he asks. Carlton has put the Stones on the turntable. Mick Jagger sings "19th Nervous Breakdown." Our father gestures in an openhanded way that takes in the room, the party, the whole house — everything the music touches.

"I like it," I say.

"So do I." He stirs his drink with his finger, and sucks on the finger.

"I *love* it," I say, too loud. Something about our father leads me to raise my voice. I want to grab handfuls of music out of the air and stuff them into my mouth.

"I'm not sure I could say I love it," he says. "I'm not sure if I could say that, no. I would say I'm friendly to its intentions. I would say that if this is the direction music is going in, I won't stand in its way."

"Uh-huh," I say. I am already anxious to get back to the party but don't want to hurt his feelings. If he senses he's being avoided, he can fall into fits of apology more terrifying than our mother's rages.

"I think I may have been too rigid with my students," our father says. "Maybe over the summer you boys could teach me a few things about the music young people are listening to these days."

"Sure," I say loudly. We spend a minute waiting for the next thing to say.

"You boys are happy, aren't you?" he asks. "Are you enjoying this party?"

"We're having a great time," I say.

"I thought you were. I am, too."

I have by this time gotten myself to within jumping distance of the door. I call out, "Well, goodbye," and dive back into the party.

Something has happened in my absence. The party has started to roll. Call it an accident of history and the weather. Carlton's friends are on decent behavior, and our parents' friends have decided to give up some of their wine-and-folk-song propriety to see what they can learn. Carlton is dancing with a vice principal's wife. Carlton's friend Frank, with his ancient-child face and I.Q. in the low sixties, dances with our mother. I see that our father has followed me out of the kitchen. He positions himself at the party's edge; I leap into its center. I invite the fuchsia-lipped math teacher to dance. She is only too happy. She is big and graceful as a parade float, and I steer her effortlessly out into the middle of everything. My mother, who is known around school for Sicilian discipline, dances freely, which is news to everybody. There is no getting around her beauty.

The night rises higher and higher. A wildness sets in. Carlton throws new music on the turntable — Janis Joplin, the Doors, the Dead. The future shines for everyone, rich with the possibility of more nights exactly like this. Even our father is pressed into dancing, which he does like a flightless bird, all flapping arms and potbelly. Still, he dances. Our mother has a kiss for him.

Finally I nod out on the sofa, blissful under the drinks. I am dreaming of flight when our mother comes and touches my shoulder. I smile up into her flushed, smiling face.

"It's hours past your bedtime," she says, all velvet motherliness. I nod. I can't dispute the fact.

She keeps on nudging my shoulder. I am a moment or two apprehending the fact that she actually wants me to leave the party and go to bed. "No," I tell her.

"Yes," she smiles.

"No," I say cordially, experimentally. This new mother can dance, and flirt. Who knows what else she might allow?

"Yes." The velvet motherliness leaves her voice. She means business of the usual kind. I get myself off the sofa and I run to Carlton for protection. He is laughing with his girl, a sweaty question mark of hair plastered to his forehead. I plow into him so hard he nearly goes over.

"Whoa, Frisco," he says. He takes me up under the arms and swings me a half turn. Our mother plucks me out of his hands and sets me down, with a good, farm-style hold on the back of my neck.

"Say good night, Bobby," she says. She adds, for the benefit of Carlton's girl, "He should have been in bed before this party started."

"*No*," I holler. I try to twist loose, but our mother has a grip that could crack walnuts.

Carlton's girl tosses her hair and says, "Good night, baby." She smiles a victor's smile. She smooths the stray hair off Carlton's forehead.

"*No*," I scream again. Something about the way she touches his hair. Our mother calls our father, who comes and scoops me up and starts out of the room with me, holding me like a live bomb. Before I go, I lock eyes with Carlton. He shrugs and says, "Night, man." Our father hustles me out. I do not take it bravely. I leave flailing, too furious to cry, dribbling a thread of spittle.

Later I lie alone on my narrow bed, feeling the music hum in the coiled springs. Life is cracking open right there in our house. People are changing. By tomorrow, no one will be quite the same. How can they let me miss it? I dream up revenge against our parents, and worse for Carlton. He is the one who could have saved me. He could have banded with me against them. What I can't forgive is his shrug, his mild-eyed "Night, man." He has joined the adults. He has made himself bigger and taken size from me. As the Doors thump "Strange Days," I hope something awful happens to him. I say so to myself.

Around midnight, dim-witted Frank announces he has seen a flying saucer hovering over the back yard. I can hear his deep, excited voice all the way in my room. He says it is like a blinking, luminous cloud. I hear half the party struggling out through the sliding glass door in a disorganized whooping knot. By that time everyone is so delirious a flying saucer would be just what was expected. That much celebration would logically attract an answering happiness from across the stars.

I get out of bed and sneak down the hall. I will not miss alien visitors for anyone, not even at the cost of our mother's wrath or our father's disappointment. I stop at the end of the hallway, though, embarrassed to be in pajamas. If there really are aliens, they will think I am the lowest member of the house. While I hesitate over whether to go back to my room to change, people start coming back inside, talking about a trick of the mist and an airplane. People resume their dancing.

Carlton must have jumped the back fence. He must have wanted to be there alone, singular, in case they decided to take somebody with them. A few nights later I will go out and stand where he could have been standing. On the far side of the gully, now a river swollen with melted snow, the cemetery will gleam like a lost city. The moon will be full. I will hang around just as Carlton must have, hypnotized by the silver light on the stones, the white angel raising her arms across the river.

According to our parents the mystery is why he ran back to the house full tilt. Something in the graveyard may have scared him, he may have needed to break its spell, but I think it's more likely that when he came back to himself he just couldn't wait to return to the music and the people, the noisy disorder of continuing life.

Somebody has shut the sliding glass door. Carlton's girlfriend looks lazily out, touching base with her own reflection. I look, too. Carlton is running toward the house. I hesitate. Then I figure he can bump his nose. It will be a good joke on him. I let him keep coming. His girlfriend sees him through her own reflection, starts to scream a warning just as Carlton hits the glass.

It is an explosion. Triangles of glass fly brightly through the room. I think that for him, it must be more surprising than painful, like hitting water from a great height. He stands blinking for a moment. The whole party stops, stares, getting its bearings. Bob Dylan sings "Just Like a Woman." Carlton reaches up curiously to take out the shard of glass that is stuck in his neck, and that is when the blood starts. It shoots out of him. Our mother screams. Carlton steps forward into his girlfriend's arms and the two of them fall together. Our mother throws herself down on top of him and the girl. People shout their accident wisdom. Don't lift him. Call an ambulance. I watch from the hallway. Carlton's blood spurts, soaking into the carpet, spattering people's clothes. Our mother and father both try to plug the wound with their hands, but the blood just shoots between their fingers. Carlton looks more puzzled than anything, as if he can't quite follow this turn of events. "It's all right," our father tells him, trying to stop the blood. "It's all right, just don't move, it's all right." Carlton nods, and holds our father's hand. His eyes take on an astonished light. Our mother screams, "Is anybody *doing* anything?" What comes out of Carlton grows darker, almost black. I watch. Our father tries to get a hold on Carlton's neck while Carlton keeps trying to take his hand. Our mother's hair is matted with blood. It runs down her face. Carlton's girl holds him to her breasts, touches his hair, whispers in his ear.

He is gone by the time the ambulance gets there. You can see the life drain out of him. When his face goes slack our mother wails. A part of her flies wailing through the house, where it will wail and rage forever. I feel our mother pass through me on her way out. She covers Carlton's body with her own.

He is buried in the cemetery out back. Years have passed — we are living in the future, and it has turned out differently from what we'd planned. Our mother has established her life of separateness behind the guest room door. Our father mutters his greetings to the door as he passes.

One April night, almost a year to the day after Carlton's accident, I hear cautious footsteps shuffling across the living room floor after midnight. I run out eagerly, thinking of ghosts, but find only our father in moth-colored pajamas. He looks unsteadily at the dark air in front of him.

"Hi, Dad," I say from the doorway.

He looks in my direction. "Yes?"

"It's me. Bobby."

"Oh, Bobby," he says. "What are you doing up, young man?"

"Nothing," I tell him. "Dad?"

"Yes, son."

"Maybe you better come back to bed. O.K.?"

"Maybe I had," he says. "I just came out here for a drink of water, but I seem to have gotten turned around in the darkness. Yes, maybe I better had."

I take his hand and lead him down the hall to his room. The grandfather clock chimes the quarter hour.

"Sorry," our father says.

I get him into bed. "There," I say. "O.K.?"

"Perfect. Could not be better."

"O.K. Good night."

"Good night. Bobby?"

"Uh-huh?"

"Why don't you stay a minute?" he says. "We could have ourselves a talk, you and me. How would that be?"

"O.K.," I say. I sit on the edge of his mattress. His bedside clock ticks off the minutes.

I can hear the low rasp of his breathing. Around our house, the Ohio night chirps and buzzes. The small gray finger of Carlton's stone pokes up among the others, within sight of the angel's white eyes. Above us, airplanes and satellites sparkle. People are flying even now toward New York or California, to take up lives of risk and invention.

I stay until our father has worked his way into a muttering sleep.

Carlton's girlfriend moved to Denver with her family a month before. I never learned what it was she'd whispered to him. Though she'd kept her head admirably during the accident, she lost it afterward. She cried so hard at the funeral that she had to be taken away by her mother — an older, redder-haired version of her. She started seeing a psychiatrist three times a week. Everyone, including my parents, talked about how hard it was for her, to have held a dying boy in her arms at that age. I'm grateful to her for holding my brother while he died, but I never once heard her mention the fact that though she had been through something terrible, at least she was still alive and going places. At least she had protected herself by trying to warn him. I can appreciate the intricacies of her pain. But as long as she was in Cleveland, I could never look her straight in the face. I couldn't talk about the wounds she suffered. I can't even write her name.

RICK DeMARINIS

The Flowers of Boredom

FROM THE ANTIOCH REVIEW

He would gladly make the earth a shambles and swallow the world in
a yawn.
    Baudelaire, "Au Lecteur"

LAMAR SITS in his office near the end of the day, looking out at
the bent heads of the sixteen men who work for him. The men
appear to be engrossed in a new manual that reviews company
policy concerning the cost-effectiveness of redundant systems
intended to upgrade product reliability. The product is a vital
part for a proposed new Mach 3.0 bomber that carries the in-
formal in-house designation Big Buck. Big Buck will probably
never be produced, or, if it is, it will most likely be awarded to a
company headquartered in Texas, one-time home of the vice
president. Favors, like hard currency, are always paid back in
Washington. The deck is stacked, as usual, and Lamar's company, Locust Airframes, Inc., is close to the bottom of this one.
Still, this going-through-the-motions is necessary, and profitable
in itself, since the buyer — in this case the Air Force — picks up
the tabs for these ritual dances the defense industry puts on.
Lamar's sixteen men are part of the dance, recently hired to
fatten the payroll roster of Advanced Proposals Engineering
(APE), the section of Locust Airframes whose mission is to bid
for contracts. Lamar himself is a new man insofar as he has
been promoted from the rank of reliability engineer step III to
full-fledged manager. This has involved a change of ID badge
color from tepid aqua to radiant orange, an upgraded ward-

robe, modifications in demeanor, and a tidy jump in salary and benefits. Job security, of course, is still tied to the shifting sands of Department of Defense wants and desires, which are always creatures of the latest Red Threat scenario and not necessarily a realistic response to the international situation. Lamar has been around long enough to know better — thirteen years now — but he's impressed by his good fortune anyway. He now has his own secretary instead of having to share a pool typist. She is a new employee also, and has eyes for him already. Eyes, that is, for management. Power, Lamar knows, is one of the more dependable aphrodisiacs. Lamar encourages a protective cynicism in himself, but he's only human and knows he would be stupid to look this splendid gift horse in the mouth.

The window in his office is one-way glass, allowing Lamar to observe his sixteen men while cloaked in smoky invisibility. The situation, Lamar muses, is analogous to that of a god, looking down from a screen of clouds at the unhappy mortals below who believe with touching urgency that their frenetic schemes and counterschemes are extensions of conscious ideals. The god maintains this illusion in order to hold the level of human unhappiness constant. He ensures that the noblest projects of those he rules become the *means* of their unhappiness. *Lamar, Lamar,* Lamar thinks, chiding himself for such bloated fantasies, *where do you get such ideas?* He has a partial memory of where such ideas come from — a walk in the dark with a fallen angel — but no, that's literature, something he read years ago in college. In any case, the fantasy is benign, since Lamar has genuine sympathy for his men. He knows, for instance, that he is also being monitored by middle management — carefully jealous men who are halfway up the corporate ladder and do not intend to be bumped by an ambitious underling who doesn't know the rules of climbing. *We are all in the same boat, friends,* Lamar thinks as he looks out at the round-shouldered men. *It's just that I'm on a higher deck than you.*

Lamar sees that one of his new men is hiding his near baldness with wings of yellowish-white hair stretched over his dome from the thriving area above his right ear. The man is in his fifties and is lucky to have been hired at all. This is likely to be the last job he will ever have in the defense industry. After the contract has been let to the Texas company the ax will fall and the sixteen men, along with Lamar himself, will be sent scrambling for other positions within the company. The bald man in his fifties will be cut loose. Age isn't his only albatross. His relatively high salary makes his tenure an impossibility during the austere period following a lost contract. And his chances outside the defense industry are nil. Companies that are connected to legitimate free-enterprise adventures, such as IBM, AT&T, or the small but highly efficient consulting firms, want no part of men who have spent their adult lives in the defense industry. Men such as Lamar's bald man are not what the want ads refer to as "self-starters." Their ponderous, insouciant demeanor makes the personnel interviewers shake their heads in smiling dismay.

The bald man, Lamar knows, has been in the defense industry since the 1950s. B.S. in electrical engineering from Fresno or San Jose State, but has by now forgotten most of his elementary calculus and differential equations. He is what is known in the business as a "Warm Body." The Air Force, before letting a contract, likes to see a company have enough self-confidence to maintain a large, well-paid work force. This results in extreme overhiring in the months before a big contract is about to come down. Lamar has been raised to management to preside over sixteen Warm Bodies. He doesn't mind — it's the system. But only the middle-aged bald man *knows* he is a Warm Body. The others are naive kids, a few years out of college, though the more intelligent ones are becoming restless. They glance, blindly, from time to time at the smoked glass of Lamar's office as if to ask, "Isn't there anything for me to *do?*" Sometimes the blind glance is sharply suspicious — premature inklings of what the bald man knows.

The bald man cannot do real work, anyway. No one expects him to. He, and the others like him, have made their homes through the decades of cold war in such places as Boeing, Lockheed, North American, or McDonnell Douglas, where they grew dim and paunchy reading turgid manuals while dreaming of overseas travel, golf, or a resurrected sexual urge. If such a man is approaching old age and has given up on the vigorous pastimes, it's possible that the simplest pleasures, such as good strong bowel movements or freedom from stiff joints, occupy his reverie. He is terrorized now and again by the streaky pains in his pectorals and arm, sudden sieges of caffeine-instigated vertigo, or shortness of breath. He is probably well past caring about his wife's slow evolution toward complete and self-sufficient indifference. Lamar is not without compassion for the bald man, who was born without ambition, though he once had all the appetites ambition serves. Now he just wants to stay comfortably alive.

Lamar is sympathetic because he knows that he is not substantially different from the bald man. They are brothers in the same tribe. Lamar's single advantage, he believes, is that he knew — and *liked* — the rules of the game when he first hired in, thirteen years ago. He seems to have been born with an instinctive grasp of what the system liked to see in a new man. Early in his career he learned how to appear innovative and energetic while at the same time assuring his superiors that these alarming qualities were empty of substance. And though he was ambitious, he understood the politics of ambition: never frighten the man immediately above you on the ladder; he is in an excellent position to stomp on your head.

It's a Byzantine institution, the defense industry, with its own rules, rituals, and arcana that confuse and frustrate the uninitiated. And yet it manages to produce weapons of ever-increasing sophistication. That some of these weapons do not work is beside the point, a quibble rooted in a fundamental misunderstanding of the mission of the defense industry, which is, simply, to keep itself well nourished with cost-plus money, to increase steadily in manpower and physical plant, and to reveal itself to the gullible citizenry as an economic savior as well as a vital necessity in a dangerous world. In any case, most of the weapons *do* work, eventually, if not after the first production run of operational units. As long as the fabulous deep pocket of cost-plus money is reachable, the missiles will find their targets, the bombers will get off the ground, and the submarines will float. Lamar's Reliability Section is the arm of Locust Airframes that devotes itself to the creation of documents that further this notion. Reliability achieved through redundant components is costly, but as the number of additional back-up systems in-

creases on a given piece of equipment, the theoretical failure
rate dwindles steadily toward the infinitesimal. It's as if men
were equipped with one or two extra hearts, or had fresh, sup-
ple arteries ready to back up their old, cholesterol-choked ones
should they fail. Reliability is the dream of immortality transferred to electronics, hydraulics, and structural mechanics.

With nothing much to do himself, Lamar now studies the
stiffening necks of the younger men in his section. They are
primed for significant action. They are bright, hard-working,
and very well trained. The system will blunt their keen appetites
for real work and discourage their desire to understand their
jobs better by gaining an overview of the entire operation of
Locust Airframes, from design to production. Only a chosen
few have such indispensable omniscience. And these few are
never seen by men such as Lamar's. Soon, the better of these
young engineers will become deeply frustrated and resign.
Though Lamar is not old — not quite forty — the sight of the
young engineers makes him feel a fatigue rightfully belonging
to a man twenty years older. It's their clear-eyed visionary look,
the look that tells you they believe in what they are doing and
that it makes a real difference to the geopolitical future of the
planet. They haven't understood yet that boredom is the soil in
which they must grow, if they are to stay on. The soil of boredom is gray, which is the color of the walls, the desks, and the
carpeting. Lamar has thrived in this gray soil, a hardy survivor,
like mesquite or wild rose. These moments of spiritual fatigue
are few. And though he prefers to wear gray suits, his neckties
are always bold. The effect is: Ambition Under Control.

Across the street from Advanced Proposals Engineering is a
topless bar called The Web. Lamar comes here every day after
work for a pick-me-up. The Web owes its existence to APE, its
clientele consisting of engineers, secretaries, and the occasional
manager. And spies. Lamar remembers a time here when two
thick-set men in three-piece suits handcuffed and searched a
man wearing an engineer's badge. "Spy," the bartender told
him. "The Feds have had their eyes on him for months. The
guy drank nothing but lime rickeys like it was summer in Ha-
vana. You can spot the type a mile off."

Lamar was required to watch a film, when he first was hired

by Locust, that warned about spies. "The pleasant chap occupying the desk next to yours might be an agent of the Communist conspiracy." The narrator was Ronald Reagan — a young, pre-office-holding Ronald Reagan — and the tone of the film was McCarthy-era serious. The statistics given were certified by the FBI. "There may be as many as four hundred spies in your plant. Think about it." Lamar thought about it but never saw much in the way of suspicious activity. He never saw much in the way of *any* kind of activity, except in the factory areas themselves. But in the vast office buildings all he saw was the interminable browsing through documents by men fighting a grass-roots existential conviction that a cancer of meaninglessness had taken root in their lives.

Once a pleasant man from Hungary, a refugee, was hauled away from the desk next to Lamar's by armed guards. It turned out the man had not been totally candid about his political affiliations when he hired into Locust. He'd been a member of the Communist party in Hungary, before the 1956 revolt, though he'd renounced it shortly afterward. But he left this chapter of his life off his personnel data sheet. The man had a name the other engineers joked about — Dumbalink Banjo Wits, something like that. Dumbalink was a fierce and outspoken anti-Communist and an American patriot, but was taken away in handcuffs and never heard from again. Lamar had liked Dumbalink Banjo Wits and had called Security with the intention of telling them that the Hungarian made most of the engineers in his section look like fellow travelers by comparison, but Security wasn't interested. "He fibbed," the bored Security man had told Lamar.

Lamar, lost in bourbon daydreams, hasn't noticed that someone has slipped into the booth and is sitting opposite him. It's his secretary, a tall, olive-skinned girl with hair so blond it hurts his eyes. Her name is Theresa Keyser but she has told him to please call her Terry. Lamar has fixed her age at twenty-nine, though her job application said twenty-five.

"So, this is where you disappear to," Terry says, smiling. Her blue eyes are intense and, it seems to Lamar, too confident.

"My second home," Lamar says, lifting his bourbon and winking.

"Meanwhile, dinner is in the oven in your *first* home."

Lamar is annoyed, but her smile is splendidly straightforward. It makes him believe that she is being aggressive out of nervousness. "Hell," he says, "*APE* is my first home," and she laughs the tension out of her voice and touches his hand.

"I'll have a gimlet," she says to him, though the barmaid, a topless girl with spiders tattooed on her breasts, has been waiting to take her order.

They have two drinks apiece, their conversation gradually changing from office talk to the more revealing narratives alcohol inspires. Lamar learns that Terry has been married and divorced twice and is now unattached. He doesn't try to characterize his own decade-long marriage beyond suggesting that his wife's interests and his own have diverged somewhat over the years. He tells her this in a joking, cavalier manner: his views of marriage are a mixture of fatalism and the always optimistic belief in renewable relationships. This is California, after all, the land of expected transformations. Terry laughs easily at his bittersweet jokes — maybe too easily — but Lamar appreciates it anyway. He likes her, sees that she is intelligent and that her expectations are sober and under control. He reaches across the table and touches her hand. She takes his wrist and applies brief but significant pressure. Her eyes, which had been bold, are now disturbingly vulnerable. *Jesus,* Lamar thinks, knowing that three bourbons and water have inflamed some old romantic notions, *here we go.*

The barmaid brings them two more drinks. "Compliments of the sport in the rubber sandals," she says, gesturing toward a man in a black suit seated at the bar. The man is watching TV — a game show — and is wearing white socks and lipstick-red sandals. He is a Howard Hughes look-alike, trying to create the impression of "renegade genius gone seedy." Even his stringy hair is long and unwashed. The man, sensing Lamar's peevish gaze, looks at him and waves his swizzle stick. His smile is a yellow leer. Lamar knows something about that leer, has seen it before, and is about to tell the barmaid to take the drinks away when Terry returns the man's swizzle-stick salute and says, "Thanks!" just like that, loud enough to make several heads turn toward their booth.

And then it hits Lamar that he knows the man in the rubber

sandals. He was a high-level procurement manager for Locust
a few years ago. Lamar, in fact, had worked for him when he
first hired into Locust. Then there was a big cutback and the
man was caught in the middle of an in-company war of attrition.
He lost out to men who were more adroit in making the company classify them as indispensable. "Voss," Lamar says, under
his breath. When Terry looks at him with raised eyebrows, he
says, "Randy Voss. Used to be a wheel. He was supposed to be
in line for company president. Crazy genius, they used to say.
He must have jumped when he should have ducked."

Lamar is a little rocky when they finally leave The Web. On
their way out the door they have to pass by Randy Voss. "De-
parting so soon?" Voss says to them. Up close his yellow leer is
a toxic stain. "The evening is still young, kids. Tell you what,
let's make a killer night of it. I'm still fat." He takes out his wallet
and taps the bar with it.

Terry starts to answer but Lamar takes her arm and pulls her
along. What she doesn't know is that the old ex-manager is a
degenerate who thinks it would be nice if the three of them
could get together in a downtown motel, in the wino district,
and play out some rank fantasy starring himself. Lamar has
heard all the Randy Voss stories. When the man had power the
stories had the glitter of outré high times. Now he's just flea
meat, another unremarkable scum bag.

It's almost dark outside. Terry takes Lamar's arm as they cross
the street to the Locust parking lot. "Are you going to come
over?" she asks, leaning toward him.

Lamar looks at his watch. "It's late," he says.

"Do you care?"

She lives in a fourplex, upstairs, the view of the ocean blocked
by a new high-rise condo that has been painted the slate-gray
color of the ocean under a winter overcast. "They know how to
break your heart, don't they?" Lamar says, mostly to himself.

Terry makes Lamar a bourbon and water and a gimlet for
herself. Lamar carries his drink in the palm of his hand as he
tours the small apartment. "You do this?" he asks, nodding at a
murky painting of a western scene.

"I'm afraid so," she says modestly. "I take art in night school."

"Nice."

"Do you like the condor?"

Lamar leans toward the painting which is hanging over the sofa. A bird — it looks like a crow to him — is suspended in midair above a lumpish roadkill on a desert highway.

"It's about to feast on that overripe deer," she explains.

Crow or condor, the bird seems incapable of flight. A stone bird with cast-iron wings. The deer is generic meat, a formless wedge of brown paint streaked with crimson.

"I call it The Angel of Death," Terry says. "But maybe that's too trite. I think I'll change it to Feast of Life. I don't know. I'm torn. What do you think?"

She is standing close to him. He can see her lungs move as she breathes, the rise and fall of her sweater. He begins to see her details: the small, nearly black mole just above her collarbone, the finely scented neck hair, the lovely cut of her lips and nostrils. He slips his arm around her and she looks up at him, lips parting for the kiss. He kisses her chilly lips, and then they both put down their drinks and kiss again, with heat.

"I vote for Feast," he says. "Feast of Life."

Lamar wakes from a dream frightened, unable to tell himself where he is. He is reasonably sure he is not home. The rumble of traffic outside is not familiar. His heart is beating light and fast, like an engine in too high a gear to have any power. His fear begins to escalate into panic. It's happened to him before. He has a method for calming himself down. He begins with his name, the color of his hair and eyes, the ghost-white scar on his left forearm. He makes a list of keystone events: the year he was born, the years he graduated high school and college; the year he got married, and the name of the town he and his wife had eloped to. In this way he gradually finds himself. He reaches over and touches the woman next to him. She makes a sound he does not recognize as she turns over to face him.

"Theresa Keyser," he says, not *addressing* but naming her.

"Are you still here?" she says, picking up her clock radio to study its dial. "Shouldn't you get home?"

His memory, set in motion by the emergency Lamar has declared, continues to fill him in: an image of the man he had forgotten about, the degenerate ex-manager, Randy Voss, comes to him unbidden. Voss is saying something to him. They are walking, ten or more years ago, near an assembly-and-checkout area of the plant. Missiles on huge transport vehicles are slipping slowly out of a black building. It is a rainy night. Voss is laughing — *crazily*, Lamar thinks. "Nobody knows jackshit," Voss is saying to Lamar. "If you are going to stay in this business, you've got to remember that. Something else, something besides men and machines gets all this fancy work done."

Lamar, watching the glistening missiles slide through the rain, thinks he understands what Voss is telling him. A missile, a bomber, a sub, they are all jigsaw puzzles, the pieces made all over the country. The men who make the individual pieces don't know — or need to know — the purpose of their work. The pieces are assembled by other bored functionaries who are also ignorant of the big picture.

"I see what you mean," Lamar says.

"No you don't. You really don't," Voss says. "What I am telling you is that there is a great dark . . . *consensus* . . . that sweeps things along to their inevitable conclusion. There is an intelligence behind it, but, believe me, it is not human. It is the intelligence of *soil*, the thing that lifts trees and flowers out of the ground. I am too astonished and thrilled to be frightened by it."

Lamar saw, even then, that Randy Voss was crazy, but what he had said made a lasting impression. And over the years he has come to adopt Voss's idea as his own. But it was something he was unable to talk about to anyone else, even his wife. How could you convince anyone that in this industry no single individual, or group of individuals, suspects the existence of a vital sub rosa mechanism that produces and deploys our beautifully elegant weapons? How could you *say* to someone that the process is holistic, that a headstrong organic magic is at work, or that a god presides?

HARRIET DOERR

Edie: A Life

IN THE MIDDLE of an April night in 1919, a plain woman named Edith Fisk, lifted from England to California on a tide of world peace, arrived at the Ransom house to raise five half-orphaned children.

A few hours later, at seven in the morning, this Edith, more widely called Edie, invited the three eldest to her room for tea. They were James, seven; Eliza, six; and Jenny, four. Being handed cups of tea, no matter how reduced by milk, made them believe that they had grown up overnight.

"Have some sugar," said Edie, and spooned it in. Moments later she said, "Have another cup." But her *h*'s went unspoken and became the first of hundreds, then thousands, which would accumulate in the corners of the house and thicken in the air like sighs.

In an adjoining room the twins, entirely responsible for their mother's death, had finished their bottles and fallen back into guiltless sleep. At the far end of the house, the widower, Thomas Ransom, who had spent the night aching for his truant wife, lay across his bed, half awake, half asleep, and dreaming.

The three children sat in silence at Edie's table. She had grizzled hair pulled up in a knot, heavy brows, high cheeks, and two long hairs in her chin. She was bony and flat, and looked starched, like the apron she had tied around her. Her teeth were large and white and even, her eyes an uncompromising blue.

She talked to the children as if they were her age, forty-one. "My father was an ostler," she told them, and they listened without comprehension. "My youngest brother died at Wipers," she said. "My nephew was gassed at Verdun."

These were places the children had never heard of. But all three of them, even Jenny, understood the word "die."

"Our mother died," said James.

Edie nodded.

"I was born, oldest of eight, in Atherleigh, a town in Devon. I've lived in five English counties," she told them, without saying what a county was. "And taken care of thirty children, a few of them best forgotten."

"Which ones?" said James.

But Edie only talked of her latest charges, the girls she had left to come to America.

"Lady Alice and Lady Anne," said Edie, and described two paragons of quietness and clean knees who lived in a castle in Kent.

Edie didn't say "castle," she said "big brick house." She didn't say "lake," she said "pond." But the children, dazzled by illustrations in *Cinderella* and *King Arthur,* assumed princesses. And after that, they assumed castle, tower, moat, lake, lily, swan.

Lady Alice was seven and Lady Anne was eight when last seen immaculately crayoning with their ankles crossed in their tower overlooking the lake.

Eliza touched Edie's arm. "What is 'gassed'?" she said.

Edie explained.

Jenny lifted her spoon for attention. "I saw Father cry," she said. "Twice."

"Oh, be quiet," said James.

With Edie, they could say anything.

After that morning, they would love tea forever, all their lives, in sitting rooms and restaurants, on terraces and balconies, at sidewalk cafés and whistle stops, even under awnings in the rain. They would drink it indiscriminately, careless of flavor, out of paper cups or Spode, with lemon, honey, milk, or cream, with spices or with rum.

*

Before Edie came to the Ransom house, signs of orphanhood were everywhere — in the twins' colic, in Eliza's aggravated impulse to pinch Jenny, in the state of James's sheets every morning. Their father, recognizing symptoms of grief, brought home wrapped packages in his overcoat pockets. He gave the children a Victrola and Harry Lauder records.

"Shall we read?" he would ask in the evening, and take Edward Lear from the shelf. "There was an Old Man with a beard," read Thomas Ransom, and he and his children listened solemnly to the unaccustomed voice speaking the familiar words.

While the twins baffled everyone by episodes of weight loss and angry tears, various efforts to please were directed toward the other three. The cook baked cakes and frosted their names into the icing. The sympathetic gardener packed them into his wheelbarrow and pushed them at high speeds down sloping paths. Two aunts, the dead mother's sisters, improvised weekly outings — to the ostrich farm, the alligator farm, the lion farm, to a picnic in the mountains, a shell hunt at the beach. These contrived entertainments failed. None substituted for what was needed: the reappearance at the piano or on the stairs of a young woman with freckles, green eyes, and a ribbon around her waist.

Edie came to rescue the Ransoms through the intervention of the aunts' English friend, Cissy. When hope for joy in any degree was almost lost, Cissy wrote and produced the remedy.

The aunts brought her letter to Thomas Ransom in his study on a February afternoon. Outside the window a young sycamore, planted by his wife last year, cast its sparse shadow on a patch of grass.

Cissy wrote that all her friends lost sons and brothers in the war and she was happy she had none to offer up. Wherever one went in London wounded veterans, wearing their military medals, were performing for money. She saw a legless man in uniform playing an accordion outside Harrods. Others, on Piccadilly, had harmonicas wired in front of their faces so they could play without hands. Blind men, dressed for parade, sang in the rain for theatre queues.

And the weather, wrote Cissy. Winter seemed to be a state of

life and not a season. How lucky one was to be living, untouched
by it all, in America, particularly California. Oh, to wake up to
sunshine every morning, to spend one's days warm and dry.

Now she arrived at the point of her letter. Did anyone they
knew want Edith Fisk, who had taken care of children for
twenty-five years and was personally known to Cissy? Edie intended to live near a cousin in Texas. California might be just
the place.

The reading of the letter ended.

"Who is Cissy?" said Thomas Ransom, unable to foresee that
within a dozen years he would marry her.

James, who had been listening at the door, heard only the
first part of the letter. Long before Cissy proposed Edie, he was
upstairs in his room, trying to attach a harmonica to his mouth
with kite string.

Edie was there within two months. The aunts and Thomas Ransom began to witness change.

Within weeks the teasing stopped. Within months the nighttime sheets stayed dry. The twins, male and identical, fattened
and pulled toys apart. Edie bestowed on each of the five equal
shares of attention and concern. She hung their drawings in her
room, even the ones of moles in traps and inhabited houses
burning to the ground. Samples of the twins' scribblings remained on permanent display. The children's pictures eventually occupied almost all one wall and surrounded a framed
photograph of Lady Alice and Lady Anne, two small, light-
haired girls sitting straight-backed on dappled ponies.

"Can we have ponies?" Eliza and Jenny asked their father, but
he had fallen in love with a woman named Trish and, distracted,
brought home a cage of canaries instead.

Edie and the Ransom children suited each other. It seemed
right to them all that she had come to braid hair, turn hems,
push swings, take walks; to apply iodine to cuts and embrace the
cry that followed, to pinch her fingers between the muddy rubber and the shoe. Edie stopped nightmares almost before they
started. At a child's first gasp she would be in the doorway,
uncombed and toothless, tying on her wrapper, a glass of water
in her hand.

The older children repaid this bounty with torments of their own devising. They would rush at her in a trio, shout, "We've 'idden your 'at in the 'all," and run shrieking with laughter, out of her sight. They crept into her room at night, found the pink gums and big white teeth where they lay floating in a mug and, in a frenzy of bad manners, hid them in a hat box or behind the books.

Edie never reported these lapses of deportment to Thomas Ransom. Instead she would invoke the names and virtues of Lady Alice and Lady Anne.

"They didn't talk like roustabouts," said Edie. "They slept like angels through the night."

Between spring and fall the nonsense ceased. Edie grew into the Ransoms' lives and was accepted there, like air and water and the food they ate. From the start, the children saw her as a refuge. Flounder as they might in the choppy sea where orphans and half-orphans drown, they trusted her to save them.

Later on, when their father emerged from mourning, Edie was the mast they clung to in a squall of stepmothers.

Within a period of ten years Thomas Ransom, grasping at the outer fringe of happiness, brought three wives in close succession to the matrimonial bed he first shared with the children's now sainted mother. He chose women he believed were like her, and it was true that all three, Trish, Irene, and Cissy, were small-boned and energetic. But they were brown-eyed and, on the whole, not musical.

The first to come was Trish, nineteen years old and porcelain-skinned. Before her arrival Thomas Ransom asked the children not to come knocking at his bedroom door day and night, as they had in the past. Once she was there, other things changed. The children heard him humming at his desk in the study. They noticed that he often left in midmorning, instead of at eight, for the office where he practiced law.

Eliza asked questions at early morning tea. "Why are they always in their room, with the door locked?"

And Jenny said, "Yes. Even before dinner."

"Don't you know anything?" said James.

Edie poured more pale tea. "Hold your cups properly. Don't

spill," she told them, and the lost *h* floated into the steam rising
from the pot.

Trish, at nineteen, was neither mother nor sister to the children.
Given their priorities of blood and birth and previous residence,
they inevitably outdistanced her. They knew to the oldest
steamer trunk and the latest cookie the contents of the attic and
larder. They walked oblivious across rugs stained with their
spilled ink. The hall banister shone with the years of their sliding. Long ago they had enlisted the cook and the gardener as
allies. Three of them remembered their mother. The other two
thought they did.

Trish said good morning at noon and drove off with friends.
Later she paused to say good night in a rustle of taffeta on
Thomas Ransom's arm as they left for a dinner or a dance.

James made computations. "She's nine years older than I am,"
he said, "and eighteen years younger than Father."

"He keeps staring at her," said Eliza.

"And kissing her hand," said Jenny.

Edie opened a door on a sliver of her past. "I knew a girl once
with curly red hair like that, in Atherleigh."

"What was her name?" James asked, as if for solid evidence.

Edie bit off her darning thread. She looked backward with
her inward eye. Finally she said, "Lily Stiles. The day I went
into service in Dorset, Lily went to work at the Rose and
Plough."

"The Rose and Plough," repeated Eliza. "What's that?"

"It's a pub," said Edie, and she explained what a public house
was. Immediately this establishment, with its gleaming bar and
its game of darts, was elevated in the children's minds to the
mysterious realm of Lady Alice and Lady Anne and set in place
a stone's throw from their castle.

At home, Trish's encounters with her husband's children were
brief. In passing, she waved to them all and patted the twins on
their dark heads. She saw more of the three eldest on those
Saturday afternoons when she took them, along with Edie, to
the movies.

Together they sat in the close, expectant dark of the Rivoli

Theatre, watched the shimmering curtains part, shivered to the organist's opening chords, and at the appearance of an image on the screen, cast off their everyday lives to be periled, rescued, rejected, and adored. They sat spellbound through the film, and when the words "The End" came on, rose depleted and blinking from their seats to face the hot sidewalk and full sun outside.

Trish selected the pictures, and though they occasionally included Fairbanks films and ones that starred the Gishes, these were not her favorites. She detested comedies. To avoid Harold Lloyd, they saw Rudolph Valentino in *The Sheik*. Rather than endure Buster Keaton, they went to *Gypsy Blood*, starring Alla Nazimova.

"I should speak to your father," Edie would say later on at home. But she never did. Instead, she only remarked at bedtime, "It's a nice change, going to the pictures."

Trish left at the end of two years, during which the children, according to individual predispositions, grew taller and developed the hands and feet and faces they would always keep. They learned more about words and numbers, they began to like oysters, they swam the Australian crawl. They survived crises. These included scarlet fever, which the twins contracted and recovered from, and James's near electrocution as a result of his tinkering with wires and sockets.

Eliza and Jenny, exposed to chicken pox on the same day, ran simultaneous fevers and began to scratch. Edie brought ice and invented games. She cleared the table between their beds and knotted a handkerchief into arms and legs and a smooth, round head. She made it face each invalid and bow.

"This is how my sister Frahnces likes to dahnce the fahncy dahnces," Edie said, and the knotted handkerchief waltzed and two-stepped back and forth across the table.

Mesmerized by each other, the twins made few demands. A mechanical walking bear occupied them for weeks, a wind-up train for months. They shared a rocking horse and crashed slowly into one another on tricycles.

James, at eleven, sat in headphones by the hour in front of a crystal radio set. Sometimes he invited Edie to scratch a chip of rock with wire and hear a human voice advance and recede in the distance.

"Where's he talking from?" Edie would ask, and James said, "Oak Bluff. Ten miles away."

Together they marveled.

The two aunts, after one of their frequent visits, tried to squeeze the children into categories. James is the experimenter, they agreed. Jenny, the romantic. The twins, at five, too young to pigeonhole. Eliza was the bookish one.

A single-minded child, she read while walking to school, in the car on mountain curves, on the train in tunnels, on her back on the beach at noon, in theatres under dimming lights, between the sheets by flashlight. Eliza saw all the world through thick lenses adjusted for fine print. On Saturdays, she would often desert her invited friend and choose to read by herself instead.

At these times Edie would approach the bewildered visitor. Would she like to feed the canaries? Climb into the tree house?

"We'll make tiaras," she told one abandoned guest and, taking Jenny along, led the way to the orange grove.

"We're brides," announced Jenny a few minutes later, and she and Eliza's friend, balancing circles of flowers on their heads, stalked in a barefoot procession of two through the trees.

That afternoon, Jenny, as though she had never seen it before, inquired about Edie's ring. "Are you engaged?"

"I was once," said Edie, and went on to expose another slit of her past. "To Alfred Trotter."

"Was he killed at Wipers?"

Edie shook her head. "The war came later. He worked for his father at the Rose and Plough."

In a field beyond the grove, Jenny saw a plough, ploughing roses.

"Why didn't you get married?"

Edie looked at her watch and said it was five o'clock. She brushed off her skirt and got to her feet. "I wasn't the only girl in Atherleigh."

Jenny, peering into the past, caught a glimpse of Lily Stiles behind the bar at the Rose and Plough.

After Trish left, two more years went by before the children's father brought home his third wife. This was Irene, come to transplant herself in Ransom ground. Behind her she trailed a wake of friends, men with beards and women in batik scarves, who sat about the porch with big hats between them and the sun. In a circle of wicker chairs, they discussed Cubism, Freud, Proust, and Schoenberg's twelve-tone row. They passed perfumed candies to the children.

Irene changed all the lampshades in the house from white paper to red silk, threw a Persian prayer rug over the piano, and gave the children incense sticks for Christmas. She recited poems translated from the Sanskrit and wore saris to the grocery store. In spite of efforts on both sides, Irene remained an envoy from a foreign land.

One autumn day, not long before the end of her tenure as Thomas Ransom's wife, she took Edie and all five children to a fortune teller at the county fair. A pale-eyed, wasted man sold them tickets outside Madame Zelma's tent and pointed to the curtained entrance. Crowding into the stale air of the interior, they gradually made out the fortune teller's veiled head and jeweled neck behind two lighted candelabra on a desk.

"Have a seat," said Madame.

All found places on a bench or hassocks, and rose, one by one, to approach the palmist as she beckoned them to a chair facing her.

Madame Zelma, starting with the eldest, pointed to Edie.

"I see children," said the fortune teller. She concentrated in silence for a moment. "You will cross the ocean. I see a handsome man."

Alfred Trotter, thought Jenny. Us.

Madame Zelma, having wound Edie's life backward from present to past, summoned Irene.

"I see a musical instrument," said Madame, as if she knew of Irene's guitar and the chords in minor keys that were its repertory. "Your flower is the poppy. Your fruit, the pear." The fortune teller leaned closer to Irene's hand. "Expect a change of residence soon."

Edie and the children listened.

And so the fortunes went, the three eldest's full of prizes and professions, talents and awards, happy marriages, big families, silver mines and fame.

By the time Madame Zelma reached the twins, she had little

left to predict. "Long lives," was all she told them. But what more could anyone divine from the trackless palms of seven-year-olds?

By the time Cissy, the next wife, came, James's voice had changed and his sisters had bobbed their hair. The twins had joined in painting an oversized panorama, titled *After the Earthquake*. Edie hung it on her wall.

Cissy, the children's last stepmother, traveled all the way from England, like Edie. Introduced by the aunts through a letter, Thomas Ransom met her in London, rode with her in Hyde Park, drove with her to Windsor for the day, then took her boating on the upper reaches of the Thames. They were married in a registry, she for the third, he for the fourth time, and spent their honeymoon on the Isle of Skye in a long, gray drizzle.

"I can hardly wait for California," said Cissy.

Once there, she lay about in the sun until she blistered. "Darling, bring my parasol, bring my gloves," she entreated whichever child was near.

"Are the hills always this brown?" she asked, splashing rose water on her throat. "Has that stream dried up for good?"

Cissy climbed mountain paths looking for wildflowers and came back with toyon and sage. Twice a week on her horse, Sweet William, she rode trails into the countryside, flushing up rattlesnakes instead of grouse.

On national holidays which celebrated American separation from Britain, Cissy felt in some way historically at fault. On the day before Thanksgiving, she strung cranberries silently at Edie's side. On the Fourth of July they sat together holding sparklers six thousand miles from the counties where their roots, still green, were sunk in English soil.

During the dry season of the year, from April to December, the children sometimes watched Cissy as she stood at a corner of the terrace, her head turning from east to west, her eyes searching the implacable blue sky. But for what? An English bird? The smell of fog?

By now the children were half grown or more, and old enough to recognize utter misery.

"Cissy didn't know what to expect," they told each other.

"She's homesick for the Sussex downs," said Edie, releasing the *h* into space.

"Are you homesick, too, for Atherleigh?" asked Eliza.

"I am not."

"You knew what to expect," said Jenny.

Edie said, "Almost."

The children discussed with her the final departure of each stepmother.

"Well, she's gone," said James, who was usually called to help carry out bags. "Maybe we'll have some peace."

After Cissy left, he made calculations. "Between the three of them, they had six husbands," he told the others.

"And father's had four wives," said one of the twins. "Six husbands and four wives make ten," said the other.

"Ten what?" said James.

"Poor souls," said Edie.

At last the children were as tall as they would ever be. The aunts could no longer say, "How are they ever to grow up?" For here they were, reasonably bright and reasonably healthy, survivors of a world war and a great depression, durable relics of their mother's premature and irreversible defection and their father's abrupt remarriages.

They had got through it all — the removal of tonsils, the straightening of teeth, the first night at camp, the first dance, the goodbyes waved from the rear platforms of trains that, like boats crossing the Styx, carried them away to college. This is not to say they were the same children they would have been if their mother had lived. They were not among the few who can suffer anything, loss or gain, without effect. But no one could point to a Ransom child's smile or frown or sleeping habits and reasonably comment, "No mother."

Edie stayed in the Ransom house until the twins left for college. By now, Eliza and Jenny were married, James married, divorced, and remarried. Edie went to all the graduations and weddings.

On these occasions the children hurried across playing fields and lawns to reach and embrace her.

"Edie!" they said. "You came!" They introduced their fellow

graduates and the persons they had married. "This is Edie. Edie, this is Bill, Terry, Peter, Joan," and were carried off in whirlwinds of friends.

As the Ransom house emptied of family, it began to expand. The bedrooms grew larger, the hall banister longer, the porch too wide for the wicker chairs. Edie took leave of the place for want of children in 1938. She was sixty years old.

She talked to Thomas Ransom in his study, where his first wife's portrait, painted in pastels, had been restored to its place on the wall facing his desk. Edie sat under the green-eyed young face, her unfaltering blue glance on her employer. Each tried to make the parting easy. It was clear, however, that they were dividing between them, top to bottom, a frail, towering structure of nineteen accumulated years, which was the time it had taken to turn five children, with their interminable questions, unfounded terrors, and destructive impulses, into mature adults who could vote, follow maps, make omelets, and reach an accord of sorts with life and death.

Thinking back over the intervening years, Thomas Ransom remembered Edie's cousin in Texas and inquired, only to find that Texas had been a disappointment, as had America itself. The cousin had returned to England twelve years ago.

"Would you like that?" he asked Edie. "To go back to England?"

She had grown used to California, she said. She had no one in Atherleigh. So, in the end, prompted by the look in his first wife's eyes, Thomas Ransom offered Edie a cottage and a pension to be hers for the rest of her life.

Edie's beach cottage was two blocks back from the sea and very small. On one wall she hung a few of the children's drawings, including the earthquake aftermath. Opposite them, by itself, she hung the framed photograph of Lady Alice and Lady Anne, fair and well-seated astride their ponies. Edie had become the repository of pets. The long-lived fish swam languidly in one corner of her sitting room, the last of the canaries molted in another.

Each Ransom child came to her house once for tea, pulling in to the curb next to a mailbox marked Edith Fisk.

"Edie, you live so far away!"

On their first Christmas apart, the children sent five cards, the next year four, then two for several years, then one, or sometimes none.

During the first September of Edie's retirement, England declared war on Germany. She knitted socks for the British troops and, on one occasion four years after she left it, returned briefly to the Ransom house. This was when the twins were killed in Europe a month apart at the age of twenty-four, one in a fighter plane over the Baltic, the other in a bomber over the Rhine. Two months later Thomas Ransom asked Edie to dispose of their things and she came back for a week to her old, now anonymous, room.

She was unprepared for the mass of articles to be dealt with. The older children had cleared away childhood possessions at the time of their marriages. But here were all the books the twins had ever read, from Dr. Doolittle to Hemingway, and all their entertainments, from a Ouija board to skis and swim fins. Years of their civilian trousers, coats, and shoes crowded the closets.

Edie first wrapped and packed the bulky objects, then folded into cartons the heaps of clothing, much of which she knew. A week was barely time enough to sort it all and reach decisions. Then, suddenly, as though it had been a matter of minutes, the boxes were packed and at the door. Edie marked each one with black crayon. Boys' Club, she printed, Children's Hospital, Red Cross, Veterans.

That afternoon, she stood for a moment with Thomas Ransom on the porch, the silent house behind them. The November air was cold and fresh, the sky cloudless.

"Lovely day," said Edie.

Thomas Ransom nodded, admiring the climate while his life thinned out.

If the three surviving children had written Edie during the years that followed, this is what she would have learned.

At thirty-five, James, instead of having become an electrical engineer or a master mechanic, was a junior partner in his father's law firm. Twice divorced and about to take a new wife, he had apparently learned nothing from Thomas Ransom, not even how to marry happily once. Each marriage had produced two children, four intended cures that failed. James's practice involved foreign corporations and he was often abroad. He moved from executive offices to board rooms and back, and made no attempt to diagnose his discontent. On vacations at home, he dismantled and reassembled heaters and fans, and wired every room of his house for sound.

Whenever he visited England, he tried, and failed, to find time to send Edie a card.

Eliza had been carried off from her research library by an archaeologist ten years older and three inches shorter than she. He took her first to Guatemala, then to Mexico, where they lived in a series of jungle huts in Chiapas and Yucatán. It was hard to find native help and the clothes Eliza washed often hung drying for days on the teeming underbrush. Her damp books, on shelves and still in boxes, began to mildew. She cooked food wrapped in leaves over a charcoal fire. On special days, like her birthday and Christmas, Eliza would stand under the thatch of her doorway and stare northwest through the rain and vegetation, in the direction of the house where she was born and first tasted tea.

Edie still lived in the house when Jenny, through a letter from her last stepmother, Cissy, met the Englishman she would marry. Thin as a pencil and pale as parchment, he had entered the local university as an exchange fellow. Jenny was immediately moved to take care of him, sew on his missing buttons, comb his sandy hair. His English speech enchanted her.

"Tell about boating at Henley," she urged him. "Tell about climbing the Trossachs. Explain cricket." And while he described these things as fully as his inherent reserve would allow, the inflections of another voice fell across his. Jenny heard "fahncy dahnces." She heard "poor souls."

"Have you ever been to Atherleigh in Devon?" she asked him.

"That's Hatherleigh," he said.

If Jenny had written Edie, she would have said, "I love Massachusetts, I love my house, I can make scones, come and see us."

*

On a spring afternoon in 1948, Thomas Ransom called his children together in the same study where the aunts had read Cissy's letter of lament and recommendation. The tree his wife planted thirty years ago towered in green leaf outside the window.

The children had gathered from the outposts of the world — James from Paris, Eliza from the Mayan tropics, Jenny from snowed-in Boston. When he summoned them, they had assumed a crisis involving their father. Now they sat uneasily under the portrait of their mother, a girl years younger than themselves. Thomas Ransom offered them tea and sherry. He looked through the window at the tree.

At last he presented his news. "Edie is dying," he said. "She is in the hospital with cancer," as if cancer were a friend Edie had always longed to share a room with.

They visited her on a shining April morning, much like the one when they first met. With their first gray hairs and new lines at their eyes, they waited a moment on the hospital steps.

James took charge. "We'll go in one by one," he said.

So, as if they had rehearsed together, each of them stood alone outside the door that had a sign, No Visitors; stood there while carts of half-eaten lunches or patients prepared for surgery were wheeled past; stood and collected their childhood until a nurse noticed and said, "Go in. She wants to see you." Then, one after another, they pushed the door open, went to the high narrow bed, and said, "Edie."

She may not have known they were there. She had started to be a skeleton. Her skull was pulling her eyes in. Once they had spoken her name, there was nothing more to say. Before leaving, they touched the familiar, unrecognizable hand of shoelaces and hair ribbons and knew it, for the first time, disengaged.

After their separate visits, they assembled again on the hospital steps. It was now they remembered Lady Alice and Lady Anne.

"Where was that castle?" Eliza asked.

"In Kent," said Jenny.

All at one time, they imagined the girls in their tower after tea. Below them, swans pulled lengthening reflections behind them across the smooth surface of the lake. Lady Alice sat at her rosewood desk, Lady Anne at hers. They were still seven and eight years old. They wrote on thick paper with mother-of-pearl pens dipped into ivory inkwells.

"Dear Edie," wrote Lady Alice.

"Dear Edie," wrote Lady Anne.

"I am sorry to hear you are ill," they both wrote.

Then, as if they were performing an exercise in penmanship, they copied "I am sorry" over and over in flowing script until they reached the bottom of the page. When there was no more room, they signed one letter, Alice, and the other letter, Anne.

In the midst of all this, Edie died.

MAVIS GALLANT

The Concert Party

FROM THE NEW YORKER

ONCE, LONG AGO, for just a few minutes I tried to pretend I was
Harry Lapwing. Not that I admired him or hoped to become a
minor Lapwing; in fact, my distaste was so overloaded that it
seemed to add weight to other troubles I was piling up then, at
twenty-five. I thought that if I could not keep my feelings cor-
dial I might at least try to flatten them out, and I remembered
advice my Aunt Elspeth had given me: "Put yourself in the
other fellow's place, Steve. It saves wear."

I was in the South of France, walking along a quay battered
by autumn waves, as low in mind as I was ever likely to be. My
marriage had dropped from a height. There weren't two pieces
left I could fit together. Lapwing wasn't to blame, yet I kept
wanting to hold him responsible for something. Why? I still
don't know. I said to myself, O.K., imagine your name is Harry
Lapwing. Harry Lapwing. You are a prairie Socialist, a William
Morris scholar. All your life this will make you appear boring
and dull. When you went to England in the late forties and said
you were Canadian, and Socialist, and working on aspects of
William Morris, people got a stiff, trapped look, as if you were
about to read them a poem. You had the same conversation
twenty-seven times, once for each year of your life:

"Which part of Canada are you from?"

"I was born in Manitoba."

"We have cousins in Victoria."

"I've never been out there."

"I believe it's quite pretty."

"I wouldn't know. Anyway, I haven't much eye."

One day, in France, at a shabby Mediterranean resort called Rivebelle (you had gone there because it was cheap) someone said, "I'd say you've got quite an eye — very much so," looking straight at Edie, your wife.

The speaker was a tall, slouched man with straight black hair, pale skin, and a limp. (It turned out that some kid at the beach had gouged him behind the knee with the point of a sunshade.) You met in the airless, shadowed salon of a Victorian villa, where an English novelist had invited everyone he could think of — friends and neighbors and strangers picked up in cafés — to hear a protégé of his playing Scriabin and Schubert through the hottest hours of the day.

You took one look at the ashy stranger and labeled him "the mooch." He had already said he was a playwright. No one had asked, but in those days, the late Truman era, travelers from North America felt bound to explain why they weren't back home and on the job. It seemed all right for a playwright to drift through Europe. You pictured him sitting in airports, taking down dialogue.

He had said, "What part of Canada are you from?"

You weren't expecting this, because he sounded as if he came from some part of Canada, too. He should have known before asking that your answer could be brief and direct or cautious and reserved; you might say, "That's hard to explain," or even "I'm not sure what you mean." You were so startled, in fact, that you missed four lines of the usual exchange and replied, "I wouldn't know. Anyway, I don't have much eye."

He said, "I'd say you've got quite an eye . . ." and then turned to Edie: "How about you?"

"Oh, I'm not from any part of anything," Edie said. "My people came from Poland."

Now, you have already told her not to say this without *also* mentioning that her father was big in cement. At that time Poland just meant Polack. Chopin was dead. History hadn't got round to John Paul II. She looked over your head at the big guy, the mooch. Fergus Bray was his name; the accent you had spotted but couldn't place was Cape Breton Island. So that he wasn't asking the usual empty question (empty because for most people virtually any answer was bound to be unrevealing) but making a social remark — the only social remark he will ever address to you.

You are not tall. Your head is large — not abnormally but remarkably. Once, at the beach, someone placed a child's life belt with an inflated toy sea horse on your head, and it sat there, like Cleopatra's diadem. Your wife laughed, with her mouth wide open, uncovering a few of the iron fillings they plugged kids' teeth with during the Depression. You said, "Ah, that's enough, Edie," but your voice lacked authority. The first time you ever heard a recording of your own voice, you couldn't figure out who that squeaker might be. Some showoff in London said you had a voice like H. G. Wells's — all but the accent. You have no objection to sounding like Wells. Your voice is the product of two or three generations of advanced university education, not made for bawling orders.

Today, nearly forty years later, no one would dare crown you with a sea-horse life belt or criticize your voice. You are Dr. Lapwing, recently retired as president of a prairie university called Osier, after having been for a long time the head of its English department. You still travel and publish. You have been presented to the Queen, and have lunched with a prime minister. He urged you to accept a cigar, and frowned with displeasure when you started to smoke.

To the Queen you said, ". . . and I also write books."

"Oh?" said Her Majesty. "And do you earn a great deal of money from writing books?"

You started to give your opinion of the academic publishing crisis, but there were a number of other persons waiting, and the Queen was obliged to turn away. You found this exchange dazzling. For ten minutes you became a monarchist, until you discovered that Her Majesty often asks the same question: "Do you earn a great deal of money with your poems, vaulting poles, copper mines, music scores?" The reason for the question must be that the answer cannot drag much beyond "Yes" or "No." "Do you like writing books?" might bring on a full paragraph, and there isn't time. You are proud that you tried to furnish a complete and truthful answer. You are once more antimonarchist, and will not be taken in a second time.

The subject of your studies is still William Morris. Your metaphor is "frontiers." You have published a number of volumes that elegantly combine your two preoccupations: *William Morris: Frontiers of Indifference. Continuity of a Frontier: The Young William Morris. Widening Frontiers: The Role of the Divine in William Morris. Secondary Transformations in William Morris: A Double Frontier.*

When you and Edie shook hands with the mooch for the first time, you were on a grant, pursuing your first Morris mirage. To be allowed to pursue anything for a year was a singular honor; grants were hard to come by. While you wrote and reflected, your books and papers spread over the kitchen table in the two-room dwelling you had rented in the oldest part of Rivebelle, your wife sat across from you, reading a novel. There was nowhere else for her to sit; the bedroom gave on a narrow medieval alley. You could not very well ask Edie to spend her life in the dark, or send her into the streets to be stared at by yokels. She didn't object to the staring, but it disturbed you. You couldn't concentrate, knowing that she was out there, alone, with men trying to guess what she looked like with her clothes off.

What was she reading? Not the thick, gray, cementlike Prix Goncourt novel you had chosen, had even cut the pages of, for her. You looked, and saw a French translation of *Forever Amber.* She had been taught to read French by nuns — another problem; she was too Polish Catholic for your enlightened friends, and too flighty about religion to count as a mystic. To intellectual Protestants, she seemed to be one more lapsed Catholic without guilt or conviction.

"You shouldn't be reading that. It's trash."

"It's not trash. It's a classic. The woman in the bookstore said so. It's published in a classics series."

"Maybe in France. Nowhere else in the civilized world."

"Well, it's their own business, isn't it? It's French."

"Edie, it's American. There was even a movie."

"When?"

"I don't know. Last year. Five years ago. It's the kind of movie I wouldn't be caught dead at."

"Neither would I," said Edie staunchly.

"Only the French would call that a classic."

"Then what are we doing here?"

"Have you forgotten London? The bedbugs?"

"At least there was a scale in the room."

Oh, yes; she used to scramble out of bed in London saying, "If you have the right kind of experience, it makes you lose weight." The great innocence of her, crouched on the scale; hands on her knees, trying to read the British system. The best you could think of to say was "You'll catch cold."

"What's a stone?" she would ask, frowning.

"I've already told you. It's either seven or eleven or fourteen pounds."

"Whatever it is, I haven't lost anything."

For no reason you knew, she suddenly stopped washing your nylon shirts in the kitchen sink and letting them drip in melancholy folds on *France-Soir*. You will never again see a French newspaper without imagining it blistered, as sallow in color as the shirts. The words "nylon shirt" will remind you of a French municipal-bonds scandal, a page-one story of the time. She ceased to shop, light the fire in the coal-and-wood stove (the only kind of stove in your French kitchen), cook anything decent, wash the plates, carry out the ashes and garbage. She came to bed late, when she thought you had gone to sleep, put out her cigarette at your request, and hung on to her book, her thumb between the pages, while you tried to make love to her.

One night, speaking of Fergus Bray, you said, "Could you sleep with a creep like him?"

"Who, the mooch? I might, if he'd let me smoke."

With this man she made a monkey of you, crossed one of your favorite figures of speech ("frontiers") and vanished into Franco's Spain. You, of course, will not set foot in Franco territory — not even to reclaim your lazy, commonplace, ignorant, Polack, lower-middle-class, gorgeous rose garden of a wife. Not for the moment.

I am twenty-seven, you say to yourself. She is nearly twenty-nine. When I am only thirty-eight, she will be pushing forty, and fat and apathetic. Those blond Slavs turn into pumpkins.

Well, she is gone. Look at it this way: you can work in peace, cross a few frontiers of your own, visit the places your political development requires — Latvia, Estonia, Poland. You join a French touring group, with a guide moonlighting from a celebrated language institute in Paris. (He doesn't know Polish, it turns out; Edie might have been useful.) You make your Eastern rounds, eyes keen for the cultural flowering some of your friends have described to you. You see quite a bit of the beet harvest in Silesia, and return by way of London. At Canada House, you sign a fraudulent statement declaring the loss of your passport, and receive a new one. The idea is to get rid of every trace of your Socialist visas. Nothing has changed in the past few weeks. Your wife is still in Madrid. You know, now, that she has an address on Calle de Hortaleza, and that Fergus Bray has a wife named Monica in Glace Bay, Nova Scotia.

Your new passport announces, as the old one did, that a Canadian citizen is a British subject. You object, once again, to the high-handed assumption that a citizen doesn't care what he is called. You would like to cross the words out with indelible ink, but the willful defacement of a piece of government property, following close on to a false statement made under oath, won't do your career any good should it come to light. Besides, you may need the Brits. Canada still refuses to recognize the Franco regime. There is no embassy, no consulate in Madrid, just a man in an office trying to sell Canadian wheat. What if Fergus Bray belts you on the nose, breaks your glasses? You can always ring the British doorbell and ask for justice and revenge.

You pocket the clean passport and embark on a train journey requiring three changes. In Madrid you find Edie bedraggled, worn out, ready to be rescued. She is barelegged, with canvas sandals tied on her feet. The mooch has pawned her wedding ring and sold her shoes in the flea market. You discover that she has been supporting the bastard — she who never found your generous grant enough for two, who used to go shopping with the francs you had carefully counted into her hand and return with nothing but a few tomatoes. Her beauty has coarsened, which gives you faith in abstract justice. You remind yourself that you are not groveling before this woman; you are taking her back, greasy hair, chapped skin, skinny legs, and all. Even the superb breasts seem lower and flatter, as well as you can tell under the cheap cotton dress she has on.

The mooch is out, prowling the city. "He does that a lot," she says.

You choose a clean, reasonable restaurant and buy her a meal.

With the first course (garlic soup) her beauty returns. While you talk, quietly, without a trace of rebuke, she goes on eating. She is listening, probably, but this steady gluttonous attention to food seems the equivalent of keeping her thumb between the pages of *Forever Amber*. Color floods her cheeks and forehead. She finishes a portion of stewed chicken, licks her fingers, sweeps back her tangled hair. She seems much as before — cheerful, patient, glowing, just a little distracted.

Already, men at other tables are starting to glance at her — not just the Latins, who will stare at anyone, but decent tourists, the good kind, Swedes, Swiss, whose own wives are clean, smart, have better table manners. These men are gazing at Edie the way the mooch did that first time, when she looked back at him over your head. You think of Susanna and the Elders. You can't tell her to cover up: the dress is a gunnysack, nothing shows. You tell yourself that something must be showing.

All this on a bowl of soup, a helping of chicken, two glasses of wine. "I'm sure I look terrible," she says. If she could, she would curl up on her chair and go to sleep. You cannot allow her to sleep, even in imagination. There is too much to discuss. She resists discussion. The two of you were apart, now you are back together. That seems to be all she wants to hear. She sighs, as if you were keeping her from something she craves (sleep?), and says, "It's all right, Harry. Whatever it is you've done, I forgive you. I'll never throw anything up to you. I've never held a grudge in my life."

In plain terms, this is not a recollection but the memory of one, riddled with mistakes of false time and with hindsight. When Lapwing lost and found his wife, the Queen was a princess, John Paul II was barely out of a seminary, and Lapwing was edging crabwise toward his William Morris oeuvre — for some reason, by way of a study of Saint Paul. Stories about the passport fraud and how Fergus Bray is supposed to have sold Edie's shoes had not begun to circulate. Lapwing's try at engaging Her Majesty in conversation — a favorite academic anecdote, perhaps of doubtful authenticity — was made some thirty years later.

Osier, when Lapwing started teaching, was a one-building

college, designed by a nostalgic Old Country architect to repro-
duce a Glasgow train shed. In the library hung a map of Ulster
and a photograph of Princess May of Teck on her wedding day;
on the shelves was a history of England, in fifteen volumes, but
none of Canada — or, indeed, of any part of North America.
There were bound copies of *Maclean's,* loose copies of *The Saturday Evening Post,* and a row of prewar British novels in brown,
plum, and deep blue bindings, reinforced with tape — the leg-
acy of an alumnus who had gone away to die in Bermuda. From
the front windows, Lapwing could see mud and a provincial
highway; from the back, a basketball court and the staff parking
lot. Visiting Soviet agricultural experts were always shown
round the lot, so that they could count the spoils of democracy.
Lapwing was the second Canadian-educated teacher ever to be
hired; the first, Miss Mary MacLeod, a brilliant Old Testament
scholar, taught Nutrition and Health. She and Lapwing shared
Kraft cheese sandwiches and subversive minority conversation.
After skinning alive the rest of the staff, Miss MacLeod would
remember Universal Vision and say it was probably better to
have a lot of Brits than a lot of Americans. Americans would
never last a winter up here. They were too rich and spoiled.

In the nineteen-sixties, a worldwide tide of euphoric prosper-
ity and love of country reached Osier, dislodging the British.
When the tide receded, it was discovered that their places had
been taken by teachers from Colorado, Wyoming, and Montana, who could stand the winters. By the seventies, Osier had
buried Nutrition and Health (Miss MacLeod was recycled into
Language Structure), invented a graduate-studies program, had
the grounds landscaped — with vast undulating lawns that,
owing to drought and the nature of the soil, soon took on the
shade and texture of Virginia tobacco — ceased to offer tenure
to the foreign born, and was able to call itself a university.

Around this time I was invited to Osier twice, to deliver a
guest lecture on Talleyrand and to receive an honorary degree.
On the second occasion, Lapwing, wearing the maroon gown
Osier had adopted in a further essay at smartening up, prodded
my arm with his knuckle and whispered, "We both made it, eh,
Burnet?"

To Lapwing I was simply an Easterner, Anglo-Quebec — a

permanent indictment. Like many English-Canadians brought up to consider French an inferior dialect, visited on hotel maids and unprincipled politicians, he had taken up the cause of Quebec after nationalism became a vanguard idea and moved over from right to left. His loyalties, once he defined them, traveled easily: I remember a year when he and his wife would not eat lettuce grown in Ontario because agricultural workers in California were on strike. With the same constancy, he now dismissed as a racist any Easterner from as far down the seaboard as Maryland whose birth and surroundings caused him to speak English.

Our wives were friends; that was what threw us into each other's company for a year, in France. Some of the external, convivial life of men fades when they get married, except in places like Saudi Arabia. I can think of no friendship I could have maintained where another woman, the friend's wife or girlfriend, was uncongenial to Lily. Lapwing and I were both graduate students, stretching out grants and scholarships, for the first time in our lives responsible for someone else. That was what we had in common, and it was not enough. Left to ourselves, we could not have discussed a book or a movie or a civil war. He thought I was supercilious and rich; thought it when I was in my early twenties, and hard up for money, and unsure about most things. What I thought about him I probably never brought into focus, until the day I felt overburdened by dislike. I had been raised by my widowed aunt, cautioned to find in myself opinions that could be repeated without embarrassing anyone; that were not displeasing to God; on the whole, that saved wear.

In France, once we started to know people, we were often invited all four together, as a social unit. We went to dinner in rooms where there were eight layers of wallpaper, and for tea and drinks around cracked ornamental pools (Rivebelle had been badly shelled only a few years before), and Lapwing told strangers the story of his life; rather, what he thought about his life. He had been born into a tough-minded, hard-working, well-educated family. Saying so, he brought all other conversation to a standstill. It was like being stalled in an open, snowy plain, with nothing left to remind you of culture and its advantages but legends of the Lapwings — how they had studied and struggled, with what ease they had passed exams in medicine and law, how Dr. Porter Lapwing had discovered a cheap and ready antidote for wasp venom. (He blew cigar smoke on the sting.)

We met a novelist, Watt Chadwick, who invited us, all four, to a concert. None of us had known a writer before, and we observed him at first uneasily — wondering if he was going to store up detractory stuff about us — then with interest, trying to surmise if he wrote in longhand or on a typewriter, worked in the morning or the afternoon, and where he got his ideas. At the back of our wondering was the notion that writing novels was not a job for a man — a prejudice from which we had to exclude Dickens and others, and which we presently overcame. The conflict was more grueling for Lapwing, whose aim was to teach literature at a university. Mr. Chadwick's family had built a villa in Rivebelle in the eighteen-eighties which he still occupied much of the year. He was regarded highly in the local British colony, where his books were lent and passed around until the bindings collapsed. Newcomers are always disposed to enter into local snobberies: the invitation delighted and flattered us.

"He finds us good-looking and interesting," Lily said to me, seriously, when we talked it over. Lapwing must have risen as an exception in her mind, because she added, "And Harry has lots to say."

Rivebelle was a sleepy place that woke up once a year for a festival of chamber music. The concerts were held in a square overlooking the harbor, a whole side of it open to a view of the sea. The entire coastal strip as far as the other side of Nice had been annexed to Italy, until about a year prior to the shelling I've mentioned, and the military commander of the region had shown more aptitude for improving the town than for fortifying its beaches. No one remembers his name or knows what became of him: his memorial is the Rivebelle square. He had the medieval houses on its south boundary torn down (their inhabitants were quartered God knows where) and set his engineering corps to build a curving staircase of stone, mosaic, and stucco, with a pattern of Vs for Viva and Ms for Mussolini, to link the square

and the harbor. In the meantime children went down to the
shore and paddled in shallow water, careful not to catch their
feet in a few strands of barbed wire. The commander did not
believe an attack could come from that direction. Perhaps he
thought it would never come at all.

On concert nights Lily and I often leaned on the low wall that
replaced the vanished houses and watched, as they drifted up
and down the steps and trod on the *V*s, visitors in evening dress.
They did not look rich, as we understood the word, but indefin-
ably beyond that. Their French, English, German, and Italian
were not quite the same as the languages we heard on the
beaches, spoken by tourists who smacked their children and
buried the remains of pizzas in the sand. To me they looked a
bit like extras in prewar films about Paris or Vienna, but Lily
studied their clothes and manner. There was a difference between pulling out a mauled pack of cigarettes and opening a
heavy cigarette case: the movement of hand and wrist was not
the same. She noticed all that. She once said, leaning on the
wall, that there was something unfinished about us, the Burnets
and Lapwings. We had packed for our year abroad as if the
world were a lakeside summer cottage. I still couldn't see myself
removing my squashed Camels to a heavy case and snapping it
open, like a gigolo.

"You've never seen a gigolo," said Lily. And, almost regret-
fully, "Neither have I."

She dressed with particular attention to detail for Mr. Chadwick's evening, in clothes I had never noticed before. Edie gave
her a silk blouse that had got too tight. Lily wore it the way
Italian girls did, with the collar raised and the sleeves pushed
up and the buttons undone as far as she dared. I wondered
about the crinoline skirt and the heart-shaped locket on a gold
chain.

"They're from Mrs. Biesel," Lily said. "She went to a lot of
trouble. She even shortened the skirt." The Biesels were an
American couple who had rented a house that Queen Alexan-
dra was supposed to have stayed in, seeking relief from her
chronic rheumatism and the presence of Edward VII. Mr. Biesel, a former naval officer who had lost an arm in the North
Africa landings, was known locally as the Admiral, though I

don't think it was his rank. Mr. Chadwick always said, "Admiral Bessel." He often had trouble with names, probably because he had to make up so many.

The Biesels attracted gossip and rumors, simply by being American: if twenty British residents made up a colony, two Americans were a mysterious invasion. Some people believed the Admiral reported to Washington on Rivebelle affairs: there were a couple of diplomats' widows and an ex–military man who had run a tin-pot regiment for a sheikh or an emir. Others knew for certain that Americans who cooperated with the Central Intelligence Agency were let off paying income tax. Mr. Chadwick often dined and played bridge at Villa Delizia, but he had said to Lily and me, "I'm careful what I say. With Admiral Bessel, you never can tell."

He had invited a fifth guest to the concert — David Ogdoad, his part-time gardener, aged about nineteen, a student of music and an early drifter. His working agreement with Mr. Chadwick allowed him to use the piano, providing Mr. Chadwick was not at the same moment trying to write a novel upstairs. The piano was an ancient Pleyel that had belonged to Mr. Chadwick's mother; it was kept in a room called the winter salon, which jutted like a promontory from the rest of the house, with shuttered windows along two sides and a pair of French doors that were always locked. No one knew, and perhaps Mr. Chadwick had forgotten, if he kept the shutters closed because his mother had liked to play the piano in the dark or if he did not want sunlight further to fade and mar the old sofas and rugs. Here, from time to time, when Mr. Chadwick was out to lunch or dinner, or, for the time being, did not know what to do next with "Guy" and "Roderick" and "Marie-Louise," David would sit among a small woodland of deprived rubber plants and labor at getting the notes right. He was surprisingly painstaking for someone said to have a restless nature but badly in need of a teacher and a better instrument: the Pleyel had not been tuned since before the war.

Now, of course Mr. Chadwick could have managed all this differently. He could have made David an allowance instead of paying token wages; introduced David to his friends as an equal; found him a teacher, had the piano restored, or bought a new one; built a music studio in the garden. Why not? Male couples abounded on this part of the coast. There were distinguished precedents, who let themselves be photographed and interviewed. Mr. Maugham lived not far away. But Mr. Chadwick was smaller literary stuff, and he didn't want the gossip. The concert outing was a social trial balloon. Any of Mr. Chadwick's friends, seeing the six of us, were supposed to say, "Watt has invited a party of young people," and not the fatal, the final, "Watt has started going out with his gardener."

Mr. Chadwick had not been able to book six seats together, which was all to the good: it meant there was no chance of my having to sit next to Lapwing. He was opposed on principle to the performance of music and liked to say so while it was going on, and his habit of punching one in the arm to underscore his opinions always made me feel angry and helpless. I sat with Lily in the second row, with the Lapwings and Mr. Chadwick and his gardener just behind. The front row was kept for honored guests. Mr. Chadwick pointed them out to Edie: the local mayor, and Jean Cocteau, and some elderly Bavarian princesses.

People applauded as Cocteau was shown to his seat. He was all in white, with bright quick eyes. The Bavarians were stout and dignified, in blue or pink satin, with white fur stoles.

"How do you get to be a Bavarian princess?" I heard Edie say.

"You could be born one," said Mr. Chadwick. He kept his voice low, like a radio announcer describing an opera. "Or you could marry a Bavarian prince."

"What about the fantastic-looking Italians?" said Edie. "At the end of the row. The earrings! Those diamonds are diamonds."

Mr. Chadwick was willing to give the wearer of the earrings a niche in Italian nobility.

"Big money from Milan," said Lapwing, as if he knew all about both. "Cheese exporters." His tone became suspicious, accusing almost: "Do you actually know Cocteau?"

"I have met M. Cocteau," said Mr. Chadwick. "I make a distinction between meeting and knowing, particularly with someone so celebrated."

"That applause for him just now — was it ironic?"

I could imagine Lapwing holding his glasses on his blob of a nose, pressing his knuckle between his eyes. I felt responsible, the way you always do when a compatriot is making a fool of himself.

Of course not, Mr. Chadwick replied. Cocteau was adored in Rivebelle, where he had decorated an abandoned chapel, now used for weddings. It made everyone happy to know he was here, the guest of the town, and that the violinist Christian Ferras would soon emerge from the church, and that the weather could be trusted — no mistral, no tramontane to carry the notes away, no threat of rain.

I think he said some of this for David, so that David would be appreciative even if he could not be content, showing David he had reason upon reason for staying with Mr. Chadwick; for at any moment David might say he had had enough and was going home. Not home to Mr. Chadwick's villa, where he was said to occupy a wretched room — a nineteenth-century servant's room — but home to England. And here was the start of Mr. Chadwick's dilemma — his riddle that went round and round and came back to the same point: What if David stopped playing gardener and was moved into the best spare bedroom — the room with Monet-like water lilies on three walls? What would be his claim on the room? What could he be called? Mr. Chadwick's adopted nephew? His gifted young friend? And how to explain the shift from watering the agapanthus to spending the morning at the piano and the afternoon on the beach?

"Do you know who the three most attractive men in the world are?" said Edie all of a sudden. "I'll tell you. Cary Grant, Ali Khan, and Prince Philip."

None of the three looked even remotely like Lapwing. I glanced at Lily, expecting a flash of complicity.

Instead she said softly, "Pablo Picasso, Isaac Stern, Juan Fangio."

"What about them?"

"The most attractive."

"Who's Fangio? You mean the racing driver? Have you ever seen him?"

"Just his pictures."

"I can't see what they've got in common."

"Great, dark eyes," said Lily.

I suppressed the mention that I did not have great, dark eyes, and decided that what she really must have meant was nerve and genius. I knew by now that nerve comes and goes, with no relation to circumstance; as for genius, I had never been near it. Probably genius grew stately and fat or gaunt and haunted, lost its hair, married the wrong person, died in its sleep. David Ogdoad, of whom I was still barely aware except as a problem belonging to Mr. Chadwick, had been described — by Mr. Chadwick, of course — as a potential genius. (I never heard his name again after that year.) He had small, gray eyes, and with his mouth shut looked like a whippet — something about the way he stretched his neck.

A string orchestra filed onstage, to grateful applause (the musicians were half an hour late), and an eerie hush settled over the square. For the next hour or so, both Lapwings held still.

At intermission Mr. Chadwick tried to persuade us to remain in our seats; he seemed afraid of losing us — or perhaps just of losing David — in the shuffling crowd. Some people were making for a bar across the square, others struggled in the opposite direction, toward the church. I imagined Christian Ferras and the other musicians at bay in the vestry, their hands cramped from signing programs. David was already in the aisle, next to Lily.

"The intermission lasts a whole hour," said Lapwing, lifting his glasses and bringing the program close to his face. "Why don't we just say we'll meet at the bar?"

"And I'll look after Mr. Chadwick," said Edie, taking him by the arm. But it was not Edie he wanted.

Lily turned to David, smiling. She loved being carried along by this crowd of players from old black-and-white movies, hearing the different languages mingling and overlapping.

"Glorious, isn't he?" said David, about Ferras.

Lily answered something I could not hear but took to be more enthusiastic small talk, and slipped a hand under her collar, fingering the gold chain. As we edged past the cheaper seats, she said, "This is where Steve and I usually sit. It's so far back that you don't see the musicians. We're very grateful to Mr. Chadwick for tonight." No one could say she had undermined

David's sense of thankfulness; he had been given a spring and summer in the South, and it hadn't cost him a centime. I thought we should not discuss Mr. Chadwick with David at all, but my reasons were confused and obscure. I believed David liked Lily because she took him seriously as a musician and not as someone's gardener. I thought the constant company of an older, nervous man must be stifling, even though I could not imagine him with a young one: he wanted to be looked after and to be rebellious, all at once. The natural companion for David was someone like Lily — attractive, and charming, and married to another man. I knew he was restless and had talked to her about London. That was all I thought I knew.

At the grocery store that served as theater bar, wine and French gin and whiskey and soft drinks were being dispensed, at triple price. The wine was sour and undrinkable. David asked for tonic; Lily and I usually had Cokes. The French she had learned in her Catholic boarding school allowed her to negotiate this, timidly. She liked ordering, enjoyed taking over sometimes, but Mr. Chadwick had corrected her Canadian accent and made her shy. David, merely impressed, asked if she had been educated in Switzerland.

The possibility of becoming a different person must have occurred to her. She picked up the bottle of tonic, as if she had never heard of Coca-Cola, still less ordered it, and demanded a glass. No more straws; no more drinking from bottles. She then handed David a tepid Coke, and he was too struck by love to do anything but swallow it down.

Lapwing in only a few minutes had managed to summon and consume large quantities of wine. His private reasoning had Mr. Chadwick paying for everything: after all, he had brought Lapwing up here to be belabored by Mozart. Edie, who had somehow lost Mr. Chadwick, was drinking wine, too. I noticed that Lily wanted me to foot the bill: the small wave of her hand was an imperial gesture. Distancing herself from me, the graduate of a Swiss finishing school forgot we had no money, or nearly none. I fished a wad of francs out of my pocket and dropped them on the counter. Lapwing punched me twice on the shoulder, perhaps his way of showing thanks.

"I don't know about you," he said, "but I'm one of those

people for whom music is wave after wave of disjointed noise."
He made "those people" sound like a superior selection.

Mr. Chadwick, last to arrive, looked crumpled and mortified,
as if he had been put through some indignity. All I could do
was offer him a drink. He looked silently and rather desperately
at the grocery shelves, the cans of green peas, the cartons leaking sugar, the French gin with the false label.

"It's very kind of you," he said.

Lily and Edie linked arms and started back toward the
church. They wanted to see the musicians at close quarters. Mr.
Chadwick had recaptured David, which left me saddled with
Lapwing.

"I don't have primitive anti-Catholic feelings," said Lapwing.
"Edie was a Catholic, of course, being a Pole. A middle-class
Pole. I encouraged her to keep it up. A woman should have a
moral basis, especially if she doesn't have an intellectual one. Is
Lily still Catholic?"

"It's her business." We had been over this ground before.

"And you?"

"I'm not anything."

"You must have started out as something. We all do."

"My parents are Anglican missionaries," I said. "I'm nothing
in particular."

"I'm sorry to hear that," Lapwing said.

"Why?"

I hoped he would say he didn't know, which would have
raised him a notch. Instead he drank the wine left in Edie's glass
and hurried after the two women.

In the bright church, where every light had been turned on
and banks of votive candles blazed, our wives wandered from
saint to saint. Edie had tied a bolero jacket around her head.
The two were behaving like little girls, laughing and giggling,
displaying ex-Catholic behavior of a particular kind, making it
known that they took nothing in this place seriously but that
they were perfectly at home. Lapwing responded with Protes-
tant prudence and gravity, making the remark that Lily should
cover her hair. I looked around and saw no red glow, no Presence. For the sake of the concert the church had been turned
into a public hall; in any case, what Lily chose to do was her

business. Either God existed and was not offended by women
and their hair or He did not; it came to the same thing.

Mr. Chadwick was telling David about design and decoration.
He pointed to the ceiling and to the floor. I heard him say some
interesting things about the original pagan site, the Roman
shrine, the early Christian chapel, and the present rickety Ba-
roque — a piece of nonsense, he said. Lapwing and I, stranded
under a nineteenth-century portrayal of Saint Paul, given the
face of a hanging judge, kept up an exchange that to an outsider
might have resembled conversation. I was so hard up for something to say that I translated the inscription under the picture:
"Saint Paul, Apostle to the Gentiles, put to death as a martyr in
Rome, A.D. 67."

"I've been working on him," Lapwing said. "I've written a lot
of stuff." He tipped his head to look at the portrait, frowning.
"Saul is the name, of course. The whole thing is a fake. The
whole story."

"What do you mean? He never existed?"

"Oh, he existed, all right. Saul existed. But that seizure on the
road to Damascus can be explained in medical terms of our
time." Lapwing paused, and then said rather formally, "I've got
doctors in the family. I've read the books. There's a condition
called eclampsia. Toxemia of pregnancy, in other words. Say
Lily was pregnant — say she was carrying the bacteria of diph-
theria, or typhoid, or even tetanus . . ."

"Why couldn't it be Edie?"

"O.K., then, Edie. I'm not superstitious. I don't imagine the
gods are up there listening, waiting for me to make a slip. Say
it's Edie. Well, she could have these seizures, she could halluci-
nate. I'm not saying it's a common condition. I'm not saying it
often happens in the civilized world. I'm saying it could have
happened in very early A.D."

"Only if Paul was a pregnant woman."

"Men show female symptoms. It's been known to happen —
the male equivalent of hysterical pregnancy. Oh, not deliberately. I'm not saying it's common behavior. I don't want you to
misquote me, if you decide to research my topic. I'm only saying that Saul, Paul, was on his way to Damascus, probably to
be treated by a renowned physician, and he had this convul-

sion. He heard a voice. You know the voice I mean." Lapwing
dropped his tone, as though nothing to do with Christianity
should ever be mentioned in a church. "He hallucinated. It was
a mystical hallucination. In other words, he did a Joan of Arc."

It was impossible to say if Lapwing was trying to be funny. I
thought it safer to follow along: "If it's true, it could account for
his hostility to women. He had to share a condition he wasn't
born to."

"I've gone into that. If you ever research my premise, remember I've gone into everything. I think I may drop it, actually. It
won't get me far. There's no demand."

"I don't see the complete field," I said. That sounded all right
— inoffensive.

"Well, literature. But I may have strayed. I may be over the
line." He dropped his gaze from the portrait to me, but still had
to look up. "I don't really want to say more."

I think he was afraid I might encroach on his idea, try to pick
his brain. I assured him that I was committed to French history
and politics, but even that may have seemed too close, and he
turned away to look for Edie, to find out for certain what she
was doing, and ask her to stop.

Mr. Chadwick had found the evening so successful that he decided on a bolder social move: David must give a piano recital
in the villa, with a distinguished audience in attendance. A re-
ception would follow — white-wine cup, petits fours — after
which some of us would be taken to a restaurant, as Mr. Chadwick's guests, for a dinner in David's honor. The event was
meant to be a long jump in his progress from gardener to fa-
vored house guest.

He was let off gardening duty and spent much of his time
now at the Biesels', where they offered him a cool room with a
piano in it and left him in peace. Meanwhile the winter salon
was torn apart and cleaned, dust covers were removed from the
sofas, the windows and shutters opened and washed and sealed
tight again. The expert brought in from Nice to restore the
Pleyel had a hard time putting it to rights, and asked for an
extra fee. Mr. Chadwick would not give it, and for a time it
looked as if there would be no recital at all.

Mrs. Biesel quietly intervened and paid the difference. Mr. Chadwick never knew. One result of the conflict and its solution, apart from the piano's having been fixed, was that Mr. Chadwick began to tell stories about how he had, in the past, showed great firmness with workmen and tradesmen. They were boring stories, but, as Lily said, it was better than hearing the stories about his mother.

It seemed to me that the recital could end in nothing but disgrace and ridicule. I wondered why David went along with the idea.

"Amateurs have a lot of self-confidence," said Mrs. Biesel, when I asked what she thought. "A professional would be scared." I had come round to her house to call for Lily: she was spending a lot of time there, too, encouraging David.

Mrs. Biesel had a soft Southern voice and was not always easy to understand. (I was amazed when I discovered that to Mr. Chadwick all North Americans sounded alike.) I recall Mrs. Biesel with her head to one side, poised to listen, and her curved way of sitting, as if she were too tall and too thin for most chairs. I could say she was like a Modigliani, but it's too easy, and I am not sure I had heard of Modigliani then. The Biesels were rich, by which I mean that they had always lived with money, and when they spent any they always gave themselves a moral excuse. The day Lily decided she wanted to go to London without me, the Biesels paid her way. They saw morality on that occasion as a matter of happiness, Lily's in particular. Any suggestion that they might have conspired to harm and deceive was below their view of human nature. Conversation on the subject soon became like a long talk in a dream, with no words remembered, just an impression of things intended.

Mr. Chadwick pored over stacks of yellowed sheet music his mother had kept in a rosewood Canterbury. He wanted David to play short pieces with frequent changes in mood. "None of your all-Schubert," he said. "It just puts people to sleep."

Mrs. Biesel supplied printed programs on thick ivory paper. We were supposed to keep them as souvenirs, but the printer had left off the date. She apologized to Mr. Chadwick, as though it were her own fault. (It is curious how David was overlooked; the recital seemed to have become a social arrangement between

Mrs. Biesel and Mr. Chadwick.) Mr. Chadwick ran his eye down the page and said, "But he's not doing the Debussy. He's doing the Ravel."

"It's a long, hard program," said Mrs. Biesel, in just above a whisper. "It might have been easier if he had simply worked up some Bach."

At three o'clock on one of the hottest afternoons since the start of recorded temperatures, David sat down to the restored Pleyel. On the end wall behind him was a large Helleu drawing of Mr. Chadwick's mother playing the piano, with her head thrown back and a bunch of violets tied to her wrist. The winter carpets, rolled up and stacked next to the fireplace, smelled of old dust and moth repellent. Still Mr. Chadwick would not let the room be aired. To open the windows meant letting in heat. "You must all sit very still," he announced, as David got ready to start. "It's moving about, stirring up the atmosphere, that makes one feel warm."

Who was there? Mr. Chadwick's friends and neighbors, and a number of people I suspect he brought in on short acquaintance. I remember his doctor, a dour Alsatian who had the complete confidence of the British colony; he had acquired a few reassuring expressions in English, such as "It's just a little chill on the liver" and "Port's the thing." People liked that. When I think of the Canadians in the winter salon — the Lapwings, and Lily and me, and Fergus Bray, and an acquaintance of Lapwing's called Michael Hagen-Beck — it occurs to me that abroad, outside embassy premises or official functions, I never saw that many in one room again. Hagen-Beck was an elderly-looking undergraduate of nineteen or twenty, dressed in scant European-style shorts, a khaki shirt, knee socks, and gym shoes. Near the end of the recital, he walked out of the house and did not come back.

Lily mooned at David, as she had at Christian Ferras. I supposed it must be her way of contemplating musicians. There was nothing wrong with it; I had just never thought of her as a mooner of any kind. Once she sprang from her chair and pushed open a shutter: the room was so dim that David had to strain to read the music. Mr. Chadwick left the shutter ajar, but latched the window once more, murmuring again his objection to stirring up the atmosphere.

During the Chopin Edie went to sleep, wearing one of those triangular smiles that convey infinite secret satisfaction. Her husband wiped his forehead with a cotton scarf he took out of her handbag and returned carefully, without waking her up. I had the feeling they got along better when one of them was unconscious. He adjusted his glasses and frowned at a gilt Buddha sitting in front of the cold fireplace, as if he were trying to assess its place in Mr. Chadwick's spiritual universe. During the pause between the Chopin and the Albéniz, he unlocked the French doors, left them wide, and went out to the baking terrace, half covered by the branches of a jacaranda; into the hot shade of the tree he dragged a wrought-iron chair and a chintz-covered pillow (the chair looked as if it had not been moved since the reign of Edward VII), making a great scraping sound over the flagstones. The scraping blended with the first bars of the Albéniz; those of us in the salon who were still awake pretended not to hear.

I envied Lapwing, settled comfortably in iron and chintz, in the path of a breeze, however tepid, with trumpet-shaped blue flowers falling on his neck and shoulders. He seemed to be sizing up over the chalkier blue of a plumbago hedge the private beach and white umbrellas of the Pratincole, Rivebelle's only smart hotel — surviving evidence that this part of the coast had been fashionable before the war. In an open court couples were dancing to a windup gramophone, as they did every day at this hour. We could hear one of those tinny French voices, all vivacity, but with an important ingredient missing — true vitality, I think — singing an old American show tune with sentimental French lyrics: *pour toi, pour moi, pour toujours.* It reminded me of home, all but the words, and finally I recognized a song my aunt had on a record, with "She Didn't Say 'Yes' " on the other side. Perhaps she used to dance to it, before she decided to save her energy for bringing me up. I remembered just some of the words: "new luck, new love." I wondered if there was any sense to them — if luck and love ever changed course after moving on. Mr. Chadwick was old enough to know, but it wasn't a thing I could ask.

Lapwing sat between two currents of music. Perhaps he didn't hear: the Pratincole had his whole attention. Our wives longed to dance, just once, in that open court, under the great white

awning, among the lemon trees in tubs, and to drink champagne mixed with something at the white and chromium bar,
but we could not afford so much as a Pratincole drink of water.
I don't know how, but Lapwing had gained the impression that
Mr. Chadwick was taking us for dinner there. He sat at his ease
under the jacaranda, choosing his table. (A later review of
events had Lapwing urging Hagen-Beck to join us for dinner,
even though his share of the day was supposed to end with the
petits fours: a story that Lapwing continued to evoke years after
in order to deny it.)

The rest of us sat indoors, silent and sweating. We seemed to
be suffocating under layers of dark green gauze, what with the
closed shutters, and the vines pressing on them, and the verd-
antique incrustation in the ancient bronze ornaments and
candelabra. The air that came in from the terrace, now that
Lapwing had opened the French doors, was like the emanation
from a furnace, and the sealed windows cut off any hope of a
cross-breeze. Mrs. Biesel fanned herself with a program, when
she was not using it to beat time. Fergus Bray slid from his sofa
to the marble floor and lay stretched, propped on an elbow.
I noticed he had concealed under the sofa a full tumbler of
whiskey, which he quietly sipped. Once, sinking into a deep
sleep and pulling myself up just in time, I caught sight of Lapwing leaning into the room, with his eyes and glasses glittering,
looking — in memory — like the jealous husband he was about
to become.

If a flash of prophecy could occur to two men who have no
use for each other, he and I would have shared the revelation
that our wives were soon to travel — his to Madrid with one of
that day's guests, mine to London on the same train as our host's
gardener and friend. (It was Mrs. Biesel's opinion that Lily had
just wanted company on the train.) Mentioning two capital cities
makes their adventure sound remote, tinged with fiction, like so
many shabby events that occur in foreign parts. If I could say
that Lily had skipped to Detroit and Edie to Moose Jaw, leaving
Lapwing and me stranded in a motel, we would come out of it
like a couple of gulls. But "Madrid," and "London," and "the
Mediterranean," and a musician, a playwright, a novelist, a recital in a winter salon, lend us an alien glow. We seem to belong

to a generation before our own time. Lapwing and I come on as actors in a film. The opening shot of a lively morning street and a jaunty pastiche of circus tunes set the tone, and all the rest is expected to unfold to the same pulse, with the same nostalgia. In fact, there was nothing to unfold except men's humiliation, which is bleached and toneless.

The compliments and applause David received at the end of the recital were not only an expression of release and relief. We admired his stamina and courage. The varied program, and David's dogged and reliable style, made me think of an anthology of fragments from world literature translated so as to make it seem that everyone writes in the same way. Between fleeting naps, we had listened and had found no jarring mistakes, and Mr. Chadwick was close to tears of the humblest kind of happiness.

David looked drawn and distant, and very young — an exhausted sixteen. I felt sorry for him, because so much that was impossible was expected from him; although his habitual manner, at once sulky and superior, and his floppy English haircut got on my nerves. He resembled the English poets of about ten years before, already ensconced as archetypes of a class and a kind. Lily liked him; but, then, she had been nice to Hagen-Beck, even smiling at him kindly as he walked out. I decided that to try to guess what attracted women, or to devise some rule from temporary evidence, was a waste of time. On the whole, Hagen-Beck — oaf and clodhopper — was somehow easier to place. I could imagine him against a setting where he looked like everybody else, whereas David seemed to me everywhere and forever out of joint.

Late in the evening, Mr. Chadwick's dinner guests, chosen by David, climbed the Mussolini staircase to the square, now cleared of stage and chairs, and half filled with a wash of restaurant tables. A few children wheeled round on bikes. Old people and lovers sat on the church steps and along the low wall. Over the dark of the sky, just above the church, was the faintest lingering trace of pink.

The party was not proceeding as it should: Mr. Chadwick had particularly asked to be given a round table, and the one reserved for us was definitely oblong. "A round table is better for conversation," he kept saying, "and there is less trouble about the seating."

"It doesn't matter, Mr. Chadwick," said Edie, in the appeasing tone she often used with her husband. "This one is fine." She stroked the pink and white tablecloth, as if to show that it was harmless.

"They promised the round table. I shall never come here again."

At the table Mr. Chadwick wanted, a well-dressed Italian in his fifties was entertaining his daughter and her four small children. The eldest child might have been seven; the youngest had a large table napkin tied around his neck, and was eating morsels of Parma ham and melon with his fingers. But presently I saw that the striking good looks of the children were drawn from both adults equally, and that the young mother was the wife of that much older man. The charm and intelligence of the children had somehow overshot that of the parents, as if they had arrived at a degree of bloom that was not likely to vary for a long time, leaving the adults at some intermediate stage. I kept this observation to myself. English-speaking people do not as a rule remark on the physical grace of children, although points are allowed for cooperative behavior. There is, or used to be, a belief that beauty is something that has to be paid for and that a lovely child may live to regret.

A whole generation between two parents was new to me. Mr. Chadwick, I supposed, could still marry a young wife. It seemed unlikely; and yet he was shot through with parental anguish. His desire to educate David, to raise his station, to show him off, had a paternal tone. At the recital he had been like a father hoping for the finest sort of accomplishment but not quite expecting it.

We continued to stand while he counted chairs and place settings. "Ten," he said. "I told them we'd be nine."

"Hagen-Beck may turn up," said Lapwing. "I think he went to the wrong place."

"He was not invited," said Mr. Chadwick. "At least, not by me."

"He wasn't anywhere around to be invited," said Mrs. Biesel. "He left before the Ravel."

"I told him where we were going," said Edie. "I'm sorry. I thought David had asked him."

"What are you sorry about?" said Lapwing. "He didn't hear what you said, that's all."

"Mr. Chadwick," said Lily. "Where do you want us to sit?"

The Italian had taken his youngest child on his lap. He wore a look of alert and careful indulgence, from which all anxiety had been drained. Anxiety had once been there; you could see the imprint. Mr. Chadwick could not glance at David without filling up with mistrust. Perhaps, for an older man, it was easier to live with a young wife and several infants than to try to hold on to one restless boy.

"Sit wherever you like," said Mr. Chadwick. "Perhaps David would like to sit here," indicating the chair on his left. (Lapwing had already occupied the one on the right.) Protocol would have given him Mrs. Biesel and Edie. Lily and the Biesels moved to the far end of the table. Edie started to sit down next to David, but he put his hand on the chair, as if he were keeping it for someone else. She settled one place over, without fuss; she was endlessly good-tempered, taking rudeness to be a mishap, toughened by her husband's slights and snubs.

"It's going to be all English again," she said, looking around, smiling. I remember her round, cheerful face and slightly slanted blue eyes. "Doesn't anyone know any French people? Here I am in France, forgetting all my French."

"There was that French doctor this afternoon," said Mrs. Biesel. "You could have said something to him."

"No, she couldn't," said Lapwing. "She was sound asleep."

"You would be obliged to go a long way from here to hear proper French," said Mr. Chadwick. "Perhaps as far as Lyons. Every second person in Rivebelle is from Sicily."

Lapwing leaned into the conversation, as if drawn by the weight of his own head. "Edie doesn't have to hear proper French," he said. "She can read it. She's been reading a French classic all summer — *Forever Amber*."

I glanced at Lily. It was the only time that evening I was able to catch her eye. Yes, I know, he's humiliating her, she signaled back.

"There are the Spann-Monticules," said Mr. Chadwick to Edie. "They have French blood, and they can chatter away in

French, when they want to. They never come down here except
at Easter. The villa is shut the rest of the year. Sometimes they
let the mayor use it for garden parties. Hugo Spann-Monticule's
great-great-grandmother was the daughter of Arnaud Monticule, who was said to have sacked the Bologna library for Na-
poleon. Monticule kept a number of priceless treasures for
himself, and decided he would be safer in England. He married
a Miss Spann. The Spanns had important wool interests, and
the family have continued to prosper. Some of the Bologna loot
is still in their hands. Lately, because of Labour, they have
started smuggling some things back into France."

"Museum pieces belong in museums, where people can see
them," said Lapwing.

"They shouldn't be kept in an empty house," said the Admiral.

Lapwing was so unused to having anyone agree with him that
he looked offended. "I wouldn't mind seeing some of the collection," he said. "They might let one person in. I don't mean a
whole crowd."

"The day France goes Communist they'll be sorry they ever
brought anything here," said Mrs. Biesel.

"France will never go Communist," said her husband. "Stalin
doesn't want it. A Communist France would be too independent
for the Kremlin. The last thing Stalin wants is another Tito on
his hands."

I was surprised to hear four sentences from the Admiral. As
a rule he drank quietly and said very little, like Fergus Bray. He
gave me the impression that he did not care where he lived or
what might happen next. He still drove a car, and seemed to
have great strength in his remaining arm, but a number of
things had to be done for him. He had sounded just now as if
he knew what he was talking about. I remembered the rumor
that he was here for an undergroud purpose, but it was hard to
see what it might be, in this seedy border resort. According to
Lily, his wife had wanted to live abroad for a while. So perhaps
it really was as simple as that.

"You're right," Mrs. Biesel said. "Even French Communists
must know what the Russians did in Berlin."

"Liberated the Berliners, you mean?" said Lapwing, getting
pink in the face.

"Our neighbors are all French," said Edie, speaking to Mr. Chadwick across David and the empty chair. "They aren't Sicilians. I've never met a Sicilian. I'm not even sure where they come from. I was really thinking of a different kind of French person — someone Harry might want to talk to. He gets bored sometimes. There's nobody around here on his level. Those Spanns you mentioned — couldn't we meet them? I think Harry might enjoy them."

"They never meet anyone," said Mr. Chadwick. "Although if you stay until next Easter you might see them driving to church. They drive to Saint George's on Easter Sunday."

"We don't go to church, except to look at the art," said Edie. "I just gradually gave it up. Harry started life as a Baptist. Can you believe it? He was fully immersed, with a new suit on."

"In France, it's best to mix either with peasants or the very top level," said Mrs. Biesel. "Nothing in between." Her expression suggested that she had been offered and had turned down a wide variety of native French.

I sat between Fergus Bray and the Admiral. Edie, across the table, was midway between Fergus and me, so that we formed a triangle, unlikely and ill assorted. To mention Fergus Bray now sounds like a cheap form of name-dropping. His work has somehow been preserved from decay. There always seems to be something, somewhere, about to go into production. But in those days he was no one in particular, and he was there. He had been silent since the start of the concert and had taken his place at table without a word, and was now working through a bottle of white wine intended for at least three of us. He began to slide down in his chair, stretching his legs. I saw that he was trying to capture Edie's attention, perhaps her foot. She looked across sharply, first at me. When his eyes were level with hers, he said, "Do you want to spend the rest of your life with that shrimp?"

I think no one but me could hear. Lapwing, on the far side of Fergus, was calling some new argument to the Biesels; Mr. Chadwick was busy with a waiter; and David was lost in his private climate of drizzle and mist.

"What shrimp?" said Edie. "You mean Harry?"

"If I say 'the rest of your life,' I must mean your husband."

"We're not really married," Edie said. "I'm his common-law

wife, but only in places where they recognize common law. Like, I can have 'Lapwing' in my passport, but I couldn't be a Lapwing in Quebec. That's because in Quebec they just have civil law. I'm still married to Morrie Ringer there. Legally, I mean. You've never heard of him? You're a Canadian, and you've never heard of Morrie Ringer? The radio personality? *The Ringer Singalong*? That's his most famous program. They even pick it up in Cleveland. Well, he can't live with me, can't forget me, won't divorce me. Anyway, the three of us put together haven't got enough money for a real divorce. You can't get a divorce in Quebec. You have to do some complicated, expensive thing. When you break up one marriage and set up another, it takes money. It's expensive to live by the rules — I don't care what you say." So far, he had said scarcely anything, and not about that. "In a way, it's as if I was Morrie's girl and Harry's wife. Morrie could never stand having meals in the house. We ate out. I lived for about two years on smoked meat and pickles. With Harry, I've been more the wife type. It's all twisted around."

"That's not what you're like," said Fergus.

"Twisted around?"

"Wife type. I've been married. I never could stand them. Wife types." He made a scooping movement with his hand and spread his palm flat.

In the falsetto men assume when they try to imitate a woman's voice, he addressed a miniature captive husband: "From now on, you've got to work for me, and no more girlfriends."

"Some women are like that," said Edie. "I'm not."

"Does the shrimp work for you?"

"We don't think that way. He works for himself. In a sense, for me. He wants me to have my own intellectual life. I've been studying. I've studied a few things." She looked past him, like a cat.

"What few things?"

"Well . . . I learned a few things about the Cistercians. There was a book in a room Harry and I rented in London. Someone left it behind. So, I know a few things."

"Just keep those few things to yourself, whatever they may be. Was your father one?"

"A monk? You must be a Catholic, or you wouldn't make that

sort of a joke. My father — I hardly know what to think about him. He won't have anything to do with me. Morrie was Jewish, and my father didn't like that. Then I left Morrie for a sort of Baptist Communist. That was even worse. He used to invite Morrie for Christmas dinner, but he won't have Harry in the house. I can't help what my father feels. You can't live on someone else's idea of what's right."

"You say all those things as though they were simple," he said. "Look, can you get away?"

She glanced once round the table; her eyes swept past me. She looked back at Fergus and said, "I'll try." She lifted her hair with both hands. "I'll tell Harry the truth. I'll say I want to show you the inside of the church. We were in it the other night. That's the truth."

"I didn't mean that. I meant, leave him and come to me."

"Leave Harry?"

"You aren't married to him," Fergus said. "I'm not talking about a few minutes or a week or a vacation. I mean, leave him and come to Spain and live with me."

"Whereabouts in Spain?" she said.

"Madrid. I've got a place. You'll be all right."

"As what? Wife or girlfriend?"

"Anything you want."

She let go her hair, and laughed, and said, "I was just kidding. I don't know you. I've already left somebody. You can't keep doing that, on and on. Besides, Harry loves me."

We were joined now by Michael Hagen-Beck. The stir caused by his arrival may have seemed welcoming, but it was merely surprise. On the way to the restaurant Mrs. Biesel had set forth considerable disapproval of the way he had left the concert before the Ravel. Lily had defended him (she believed he had gone to look for a bathroom and felt too shy to come back), but Lapwing had said gravely, "I'm afraid Hagen-Beck will have to be wiped off the board," and I had pictured him turning in a badge of some kind and slinking out of class.

He nodded in the curt way that is supposed to conceal diffidence but that usually means a sour nature, removed the empty chair next to David, dragged it to the far end of the table, and wedged it between Mrs. Biesel and Lily.

"Hey, there's Hagen-Beck," said Lapwing, as if he were astonished to find him this side of the Atlantic.

"I'm afraid he is too late for the soup," said Mr. Chadwick.

"He won't care," said Lapwing. "He'd sooner talk than eat.
He's brilliant. He's going to show us all up, one day. Well, he
may show some people up. Not everybody."

Lily sat listening to Hagen-Beck, her cheek on her hand. In
the dying light her hair looked silvery. I could hear him telling
her that he had been somewhere around the North Sea, to the
home of his ancestors, a fishing village of superior poverty. He
spoke of herrings — how many are caught and sold in a year,
how many devoured by seagulls. Beauty is in the economics of
Nature, he said. Nowhere else.

"But isn't what people build beautiful, too?" said Lily, pleading for the cracked and faded church.

A waiter brought candles, deepening the color of the night
and altering the shade and tone of the women's skin and hair.

"This calls for champagne," Mr. Chadwick said, in a despair-
ing voice.

David had not touched the fish soup or the fresh langouste
especially ordered for him. He stared at his plate, and sometimes down the table to the wall of candlelight, behind which
Lily and Hagen-Beck sat talking quietly. Mr. Chadwick looked
where David was looking. I saw that he had just made a complex
and understandable mistake; he thought that David was watching Hagen-Beck, that it was for Hagen-Beck he had tried to
keep the empty chair.

"Great idea, champagne," said Lapwing, once he had made
certain Mr. Chadwick was paying for it. "We haven't toasted
David's wonderful performance this afternoon." From a man
who detested the very idea of music, this was a remarkable sign
of good will.

Hagen-Beck would not drink wine, probably because it had
been unknown to his ancestors. Summoning a waiter, who had
better things to do, he asked for water — not false, bottled water
but the real kind, God's kind, out of a tap. It was brought to
him, in a wine-stained carafe. Two buckets of ice containing
champagne had meanwhile been placed on the table, one of
them fatally close to Fergus. The wine was opened and poured.

Hagen-Beck swallowed water. Mr. Chadwick struck his glass with a knife: he was about to estrange David still further by making a speech.

Fergus and Edie, deep in some exchange, failed to hear the call for silence. In the sudden hush at our table Edie said distinctly, "When I was a kid, we made our own Christmas garlands and decorations. We'd start in November, the whole family. We made birds out of colored paper, and tied them to branches, and hung the branches all over the house. We spent our evenings that way, making these things. Now my father won't even open my Christmas cards. My mother writes to me, and she sends me money. I wouldn't have anything to wear if she didn't. My father doesn't know. Harry doesn't know. I've never told it to anybody, until now."

She must have meant "to any man," because she had told it to Lily.

"It's boring," said Fergus. "That's why you don't tell it. Nobody cares. If you were playing an old woman, slopping on in a bathrobe and some old slippers, it might work. But here you are — golden hair, golden skin. You looked carved in butter. The dress is too tight for you, though. I wouldn't let you wear it if I had any say. And those god-awful earrings — where do they come from?"

"London, Woolworth's."

"Well, get rid of them. And your hair should be longer. And nobody cares about your bloody garlands. Don't talk. Just be golden, be quiet."

I suppose the others thought he had insulted her. I was the only one who knew what had gone on before, and how easily she had said, "Wife or girlfriend?" Lapwing merely looked interested. Another man might have challenged Fergus, or, thinking he was drunk, drawn his attention away from Edie and let it die. But Lapwing squeaked, "That's what I keep telling her, Bray. Nobody cares! Nobody cares! Be quiet! Be quiet!"

I saw Lapwing's heavy head bowing and lifting, and Edie's slow expression of shock, and Fergus pouring himself, and nobody else, champagne. This time there surely must have been a flash of telepathy between two people with nothing in common. Fergus and I must have shared at least one thought: Lapwing had just opened his palm, revealing a miniature golden wife, and handed her over.

Then Edie looked at Fergus, and Fergus at Edie, and I watched her make up her mind. The spirit of William Morris surrounded the new lovers, evading his most hard-working academic snoop. Lapwing ought to have stood and quoted, "Fear shall not alter these lips and these eyes of the loved and the lover," but he seemed to see nothing, notice nothing; or like Mr. Chadwick he continued to see and notice the wrong things.

Three of the future delinquents at our table were ex-Catholics. They took it for granted that the universe was eternal and they could gamble their lives. Whatever thin faith they still had was in endless renewal — new luck, new love. Nothing worked out for them, but even now I can see what they were after. Remembering Edie at the split second when she came to a decision, I can find it in me to envy them. The rest of us were born knowing better, which means we were stuck. When I finally looked away from her it was at another pool of candlelight, and the glowing, blooming children. I wonder now if there was anything about us for the children to remember, if they ever later on reminded one another: There was that long table of English-speaking people, still in bud.

DOUGLAS GLOVER

Why I Decide to Kill Myself and Other Jokes

FROM TRANSLATION

THE PLAN BEGINS to fall apart the instant Professor Rainbolt, Hugo's graduate advisor, spots me slipping out of the lab at eleven P.M. on a Sunday. Right away he is suspicious (I am not a student; the lab is supposed to be locked). But, like a gentleman, he doesn't raise a stink. He just nods and watches me lug my bulging (incriminating) purse through the fire doors at the end of the corridor.

Problems. Problems. Professor Rainbolt knows I'm Hugo's girl. He's seen us around together. Now he's observed me sneaking out of the lab at eleven P.M. (on a Sunday). He's probably already checked to see if, by chance, Hugo had come in to do some late-night catch-up work on his research project. Hugo will not be there; the lights will be out; and Hugo will be in shit for letting me have his lab key (I stole it).

Now, I didn't plan this to get Hugo into trouble. At least, not this kind of trouble. Other kinds of trouble, maybe. Guilt, for example. But now, when they find my corpse and detect the distinctive almond odor of the cyanide, they will know exactly where the stuff came from, whose lab key I used, and Hugo will lose his fellowship, not to mention his career (such as it is). Let me tell you, Hugo is not going to lay this trip on me after I am dead.

Also, the whole Rainbolt thing raises the question of timing. Let us say that a person wants, in general, to kill herself. She has a nice little supply of cyanide (obtained illegally from a university research lab — plants, not animals), which she intends to hoard for use when the occasion arises. For example, she might prefer to check out on a particularly nice day, after a walk with her dogs along the bank of the River Speed, perhaps after sex with Hugo, and a bottle of Beaujolais, in bed by herself (Hugo exiting the picture; forget where he goes, probably a bar somewhere, with his guitar, flicking his long hair — grow up, Hugo — to attract the adoration of coeds), her Victorian nightie with the lace bodice fanning out from her legs and a rose, symbol of solidarity with the plant world, in her hand.

But now she has to factor in Professor Rainbolt and the thought that her little escapade into the realm of break, enter and theft will soon be common knowledge on the faculty grapevine, the campus police alerted, the town police on the lookout (slender blonde, five ten, twenty-six years old, with blue eyes and no scars — outside — answers to the name Willa), and that Hugo will be, well, livid and break something (once he broke his own finger, ha ha).

A girl decides to kill herself and life suddenly becomes a cesspit of complications. Isn't that the way it always is? I think, suddenly reminded of my dad, who, coincidentally, was waylaid and disarmed on his way to the garden with the family 12-gauge one afternoon after kissing Mom with unusual and suspicious fervor because (he claimed) of her spectacular pot roast (why he kissed her, not why he was going out the door with the gun — target practice, he said). Can you guess that it was me who wrestled that gun out of his pathetically weakened hands (well, you know, he was already far gone with cancer, in his brain and other places — trying to sneak into the garden was the last sane thing he did)? That I spent the next six months carrying him from room to room, feeding him mush, wiping his ass? That in my wallet I still carry a Polaroid of Dad in his coffin (along with other photographic memorabilia)?

Let me pause to point out certain similarities, parallels, or spiritual ratios. Gardens play a role in both these stories. That lab is really an experimental garden full of flats choked with green shoots. Hugo breeds them, harvests them, pulverizes them, whirls them, refrigerates them, distills them, micro-in-spects them — in short, he is a plant vivisectionist. (It is a question of certain enzymes, I am told, their presence or absence being absolutely crucial to something something, I forget.) We have made love here amongst the plants — me bent over a cen-trifuge with my ass in the air and my pants around my ankles, which did not seem seriously outré at the time. (On this or another occasion I noticed the cyanide on the shelf above, clearly marked with a skull-and-crossbones insignia.)

Gardens and suicide run in the family. Failed suicides, I am now forced to conjecture. Clearly, one did not foresee the myr-iad difficulties or that fate would place Dr. Rainbolt at the door as I left the lab/garden, feeling sorry for the plants, making analogies with animal experiments (I have heard that African violets scream), thinking why, why can't they just leave well enough alone? The time factor is crucial. I do not admire being rushed. But when will I have another chance? Also, quite suddenly, I realize I have forgotten to find out if cyanide poison-ing is painful. I have a brief, blinding vision of blue me writh-ing in the Victorian nightie, frothing vomit and beshitting my-self. Someone would have to wipe my butt, and I (like my father) never wanted that. Never, never, never.

I have made some mistakes, I will be the first to admit. Once I was crossing Bloor Street at Varsity Stadium, being a cool, sexy lady without any underpants, when the wind lifted my skirt and showed my pussy to eighty-five strange men. And once I con-fessed to Hugo's mother about my affair with a lead guitarist named Chuck Madalone — the rest of the history on Chuck is that he subsequently became drunk on Southern Comfort and fell out a second-story bathroom window, breaking both wrists.

(I see I have reached my car, our car, Hugo's and mine, a wine-colored Pinto with an exploding gas tank — we both like to live cheaply and dangerously — and am greeted with preens, wriggles and barks of delight by Bismarck the Doberman and Jake the mutt, whose smudged nose prints and muddy paw marks blur the back and side windows. It is a relief to be among friends.)

Hugo called this affair with Chuck an "affair" on a technical-ity. In my opinion Hugo and I were not (a) officially going together, (b) in love (I was in love; Hugo was in doubt, which is not the same thing). In my opinion my tryst, fling, whatever, with Chuck (the innocent in all this) was pre-Hugo. Hugo said we had "had sex" (his words — Hugo, like many men, appears to believe that ejaculation is a form of territorial marking, like dogs peeing on hydrants; I say it washes off).

How was I to know, as Hugo claims, that he was in love, though in a kind of doubtful, nonverbal way, or that he would follow us home that night and spy through the window in a hideous state of guilt, rage and titillation. Hugo says "affair"; I say meanings migrate like lemmings and words kill. In this way, we are always hurting, thwarting, destroying others, splashing paint (blue) over the spacious artworks of their imaginations — sleeping with Chuck was (my guilt is infinite) like twisting the 12-gauge out of Dad's hands.

The dogs sniff at my purse, where I often carry treats, rawhide bones or doggy biscuits or rubber balls. This time we have cyanide, which I ponder while the car warms up (the winter outside corresponds to the winter of my spirit, which is a dry cold wind, or the snow crystals on the windshield remind me of the poison crystals in the jar — what is clear is that when one is living intensely everything is significant and reminds you of everything else).

Here we have, I say to myself, a jar of cyanide which, as we who live with guitar-playing scientists know, is a simple compound of cyanogen with a metal or organic radical, as in potassium cyanide (KCN). Cyanogen is dark blue mineral named for its entering into the composition of Prussian blue, which I think is rather nice, giving my death an aesthetic dimension. The cyanide (in this case KCN) will also turn me blue, as in cyanosis, a lividness of the skin owing to the circulation of imperfectly oxygenated blood (something like drowning — inward shudder).

The time factor, as I say, is crucial. I do not wish to die in this Pinto with my dogs looking on. Life will be sad enough for them afterward. With dogs, as with women, Hugo has a certain winning enthusiasm that charms you at the beginning but which soon wears off as he develops new interests. But, I console myself, dogs are born to a life of waiting and abasement (as are women). Myself, I must use guile and cunning; I must be Penelope weaving and unraveling. The trick will be to secrete enough of this snowy, crystalline substance (which turns people blue) in, say, yes, a plastic cassette box, which when filed in Hugo's cassette tray will resemble in external particulars every other (nonlethal) cassette box, and then surrender the jar to Hugo for return to Dr. Rainbolt with beaucoup d'apologies. I will look like an ass but this is not new.

I carefully pour out what I consider to be the minimum lethal dose, then double it (oops, we spill a little — I flick it off the seat covers with a glove).

I dread facing Hugo, but without actually using the cyanide (in unseemly and undignified haste) there seems no way out. We are going to have a scene, no doubt about it. Hugo loves production numbers. He invariably assumes an attitude of righteous indignation, believing himself to be a morally superior being. This has something to do with his being a vegetarian (though a smoker — consistency is the hobgoblin of other minds) and my "affair." Which reminds me about his mother, that particular production.

How we arrived there for my first visit in the midst of a vicious quarrel over Chuck — Hugo threatening to leave me (now he was in love with me though doubtful if I was worth keeping). I was in tears or in and out of them. We separated on gender lines — I went upstairs to his bedroom with his mother trailing me, all feminine concern and sisterliness, Hugo stayed with his father in the living room. His mother soothed me, comforted me, said she understood Hugo was a difficult boy (he is twenty-nine), and that we have to keep smiling, put a bright face on things.

Gullible Willa fell for this and confessed all, thinking his mother would understand and perhaps explain to Hugo that a tryst before we were actually together should not be regarded as high treason. Well, you could tell the mention of sex before Hugo upset her. Right away I could sense I'd made the biggest mistake of my life (next to taking the gun from Dad's shaking fingers, that look of helpless appeal). She continued to stroke and console but we did not pursue the conversation.

Presently Hugo, having had an argument with his father,

came bounding up the stairs. "Are you two talking about?" he
shouted (hysterical). "Are you two talking about me?" His
mother was frightened or (this is my opinion) pretended to be
frightened and hurried downstairs. Thus goaded, Hugo fell to
raving about his parents, treating me as a friend, a co-conspira-
tor against the previous generation. He did his usual fist-smash-
ing and book-throwing routine. (At the peak of his performance
he will try to destroy even himself, beating his chest or thighs or
temples with clenched fists — it is amazing to see, and clear
evidence of simian genes in that family.)

Downstairs his mother was busy telling his father everything
I had revealed to her in confidence, woman to woman, my sor-
did and nymphomaniacal sex life. (Chuck and I did it once,
though I suppose it seems worse because Hugo actually saw it
— I did not tell his mother this.) When I went downstairs to the
bathroom before going to bed (dinner was out of the question
now), I passed his father, who said one word in a low but distinct
voice: "Slut." Clearly Hugo had ruined any chance of my being
accepted into this family as his wife. Or I had ruined it. Living
with Hugo, one begins to suspect one's own motives, actions,
and inactions in a vertiginous and infinite regress of second
guesses.

Perhaps I had engineered the whole thing. I confessed, and
I confess I was too trusting. Or is trust just another moment of
aggression? (Very early in our relationship, Hugo said, "I don't
want to feel responsible"; his theory of psychology goes like this:
behind the mind there is another mind which is "out to get
you.") In this way, time gradually masks one's true personality,
replacing it with a sense of failure, a history of failures, like
coral building up its house of sediment; and when the coral dies
(as I have died) only the sediment remains. (Sometimes it is clear
to me that I wanted Dad to live those extra six painful, humiliating, semiconscious months — my soul is shot with evil.)

The dogs cavort and make peepee as I climb the icy steps to our
apartment, lugging my suicidal burden (now ever so slightly
lightened). I compose my face into an expression of shock and
remorse. "What have I done? What have I done?" I keep saying
to myself (though I don't particularly feel any of this, Hugo will
expect it).

I walk into the kitchen, where he studies, with my jar of KCN and place it on the table in front of him

"Hugo," I say, "I wanted to kill myself. I stole this from the lab. I would have gone through with it but Professor Rainbolt saw me and I didn't want to get you into trouble."

His handsome face wears an expression of irritation. I have disturbed his concentration; I have created a situation which he will have to deal with; a situation to be dealt with is a crisis; his world implodes, crumples, disintegrates.

He says, "It's my fault. It's all my fault."

I am ready for this. When we were first together, I found it endearing the way Hugo thought everything was his fault, his willingness to take blame, to confess his failings. Now, after some years of familiarization, I realize that this is a ploy to diffuse (not defuse) the issue. By taking the blame for everything, Hugo takes the blame for nothing (apparently this tactic proved effective with his parents for many years, still does). Also he expects you to console him for being such a fuck-up. And sometimes you do, if he catches you on the wrong foot.

This time he doesn't catch me on the wrong foot, mainly because I have a secret agenda and cannot be bothered.

I say, "Okay, well, Professor Rainbolt saw me so you'd better take it back. If you take it back, then nothing will be missing and you can just say you sent me to pick up a book."

"I can't lie about a thing like this," he says.

Of course he can't. If he tells the truth, it puts me further in the wrong. I've stolen his key, broken into the university lab, and burgled chemicals with which I intend to kill myself. Not since he watched me "having sex" with Chuck has Hugo possessed such damning evidence of my inadequacy as a human being (and this time without the embarrassing question of what he was doing outside my bedroom window watching).

The phone rings. Rainbolt or Mama Hugo.

"Mom," says Hugo excitedly. "I can't talk. I'm in a jam. Willa tried to kill herself. She's all right now but she stole some cyanide from the lab and I have to put it back somehow before she's charged —"

Charged! — now this is interesting. Hugo intends to bring the full weight of the law to bear in his incessant battle to prove that he's right and I am wrong. (I have often wondered what he would do if he ever proved it, actually satisfied himself that it was true, because I think he needs this war of words to keep his energy up, this dialogue with me, with a woman, that's what I believe — he gets his élan, his charm with other people, from the struggle to prove himself.) But it doesn't really matter, and I drift down the hall to the bathroom and run water in the tub and pour bath salts (resembling cyanide), depressed and indolent. The problem is if I love Hugo he slays me and if I don't love him it proves what he's been saying all along (just as I cannot bring back Dad or the moment when I wrestled him for the shotgun), that I never mean what I say, that I loved Chuck to humiliate him. It's a battle of words (dialogue, duet, duel) to the death.

Presently, as I soak and pretend that I am already dead (reminiscing lightheartedly about my little stash of KCN), Hugo pushes through the bathroom door, urgent, worried, self-important. He is somewhat disappointed to find me taking a bath. Hanging from the shower head with my wrists slashed would have been better.

He says, "Rainbolt called." (I had heard the phone ring a second time.) He kneels on the floor beside the tub. "I told him what happened. It's amazing. He understands completely — his wife has been trying to kill herself for years. She's been hospitalized three times."

This is an intriguing turn of events, I think to myself, recalling a wan but gaily (bravely) dressed individual evanescing through one or two student-faculty get-togethers. Now I feel I should have paid more attention to her (me with my punk hair and skin-tight jeans and silk blouse open to my breasts), for we have something in common (and in common with Dad).

"Does Professor Rainbolt play the guitar?" I ask, watching my nipples float above the iridescent soapy water like twin island paradises (swim to my little island homes, Hugo; he is looking at them, but they do not distract him; rather, he seems to be thinking he has seen them too often).

I shut my eyes and slide beneath the surface of the bath water, feel my hair wave gently like water weeds, sense a bubble tickling the end of my nose, relax. Everything is dark and warm, and a sensuous pressure (pleasure) enfolds my body (except for my knees, which are above the water and feel a little chilly). I have rather hoped that death will be like this but suspect I am mistaken. And if I were dead I wouldn't be able to hear Hugo's voice hectoring me in the distance, echoing through the tub and the aqueous elements.

It is pleasant, and there is a sense in which I even nod off. Which gives me time to tell that I am a photographer whom no one recognizes as such. (The Polaroid snapshot of Dad in his coffin was my first inspiration and the ideal of compositional clarity toward which I have journeyed ever since. Every artist is thus involved in a quest to reinvent her own first, best impulse, the germ of creation which preceded the sad and cloying process of learning "the craft." Every artist is thus also involved in moving further and further from that first impulse — it is a tragic aspect of the vocation.) For money I wait on tables at a chicken restaurant. Because I can't get anyone to look at my photographs and I work in a chicken restaurant (patronized by undergraduates), Hugo often slips into the error of believing I want to be a chicken waitress and not an artist.

"— counseling," he says, plunging his arm into the bath water and hooking me up by the shoulders. I am mildly irritated at the interruption of my meditation but truthfully cannot tell how long I have been under the water, years maybe (he looks exasperated yet faintly self-righteous; he has just saved a chicken waitress from possible drowning).

"For heaven's sake," I say. "I don't need counseling. I do not want to turn into Mrs. Rainbolt. Evanescence is not my preferred mode of existence."

Hugo pounds the lip of the tub with his palm, a preliminary to chest-thumping. He doesn't like it when I carry on conversations like this, jumping ahead, bringing in thoughts I have had on my own. He will never understand my intuition about Mrs. Rainbolt. I have only seen her briefly and at the most once or twice (and perhaps I am thinking of an entirely different woman, though that has nothing to do with what I know I know about her). But Hugo lives in a world of progressive rock, vegetables and plant molecules — he loves rules; every riff, every experiment, is controlled and conventionalized, though clearly he believes he is, and the world sees him as, a person on the cutting edge of — choose one and fill in the blank: chaos, nature, knowledge, genius, protein deficiency.

Bismarck runs into the bathroom, making a dog face when he tries to drink from the tub. For a dog (Doberman) with such a killer reputation, he is timid and a clown. I giggle and splash him a little and he slides on the tile floor trying to escape. Hugo loses his temper and rips his shirt open, popping buttons into my bath. Then we adjourn (after I pause for drying) to the bedroom, where he lies on the bed staring at the ceiling. He says nothing while I dress, won't even look at my body (too familiar, functional). We maintain our silence as we throw on our coats and head toward the car with the jar of cyanide and a warm avalanche of dog on the stairs behind us.

Hugo drives. He usually drives when we're together. It's all the same to me and now especially he feels it's his prerogative. A woman who commits crimes and tries to kill herself automatically loses her ability (ever shaky at the best of times) to perform simple, everyday tasks like, say, driving a car. The dogs, now sensing a fight, cower in the rear, pretending to sleep. I try to remember the exact shade of blue Prussian blue is and wonder if I would look good that color. Perhaps I should dye my hair.

We are about halfway to the university when Hugo suddenly pulls into a Wendy's parking lot and stops the car. For a while he stares over the steering wheel into the snow, which is beginning to pile up and melt on the warm metal above the engine. Clearly he has thought of something to say, and I wait patiently, as I know I am supposed to.

"Is this all of it?" he asks, enunciating carefully, without looking at me.

"Sure," I say. "I may like the stuff once in a while, but I'm not an addict."

Hugo smashes his fist down on the dash and a cassette ejects from the player. This kind of humor is subversive and he doesn't like it (male humor is based on the stupidity of women). But I have to grab my ribs beneath my coat to keep from laughing as Bismarck sniffs the cassette between the seats.

Actually I don't feel like laughing but my nerves are frayed and I am tired. My bath had not been a success. And, though I

affect stoicism vis-à-vis Hugo's temper, his violence, his impre-
cations, I am quivering inside. I have failed at the simplest of
human activities, dying. It seems proof of a deep-grained and
amazing incompetence on my part, an incompetence reinforced
by my lack of artistic success and the chicken-waitressing (all
emblems, signs or icons of my earlier lack of shrewdness and
foresight when I stopped Dad from killing himself).

I am not actually surprised that Hugo suspects me of hiding
a portion of the KCN for future use. He is used to sifting possibilities in a rational (some would say irrational) manner, used
to making lists of might-have-beens. (What might we have become if four things had gone right: if I hadn't prevented Dad
from killing himself, if I hadn't misunderstood Hugo's doubt, if
I hadn't slept with Chuck, if I hadn't told Hugo's mother?) And
he thinks I am devious (right from the start — sneaking off with
Chuck — though we didn't sneak, it was a date).

The worst thing is that I am now wondering if I am doing
this all myself, manipulating Hugo into a position that is an
analogue of my own ten years earlier. Or, have I simply become
my father in order to punish myself? I seem to be drifting into
a phantasmagoria of analogies or substitutions (or myth or psychology) where only the verbs remain constant and the subjects
and predicates are interchangeable (for Hugo, I am clearly
often his mother, or previous girlfriends; we fall in love, I think
sometimes, in order to get even).

My sense of guilt increases as I recall how much I love Hugo,
when I remember the gentle, loving man he wishes to be, when
I think of his multiple talents and his struggle to be a musician
(the scientist/musician thing induces a kind of schizophrenia in
Hugo, a doubleness with its own hierarchy of substitutions).
There are times when in confusion he lets you see this and then
you want to rush up and hold him and let your pity wash over
him. When we are at our best, Hugo and I, we share this sense
of dismemberment or dis(re)memberment, a sense that the
beauty and magic are gone. (This is my explanation of Original
Sin. Men have invented whole religions to divert themselves
from this germ of self-doubt; they are an amazingly industrious
sex.)

Just at this moment Hugo makes one of those intuitive connections which he is so good at but which he distrusts in me. He's been eyeing the cassette which has just popped out of the player, thinking. Suddenly he looks at me, surprised that he knows what he knows. Then he begins rifling through the cassette boxes till he finds the one that doesn't rattle when he shakes it.

"No," I shout, but it is too late. The cyanide (KCN — stands for 12-gauge shotgun) scatters in the air like snowflakes. It is as if we are inside one of those glass globe shake-ups, a winter scene, couple with dogs, but the snow smells like almonds.

This is funny and scary at the same time. I stop breathing, shout "Get out!" and scream at the dogs (who lift their noses interrogatively). Hugo watches the cyanide with his mouth gaping open, a somewhat suicidal attitude, I think. It rattles against the seat covers like tiny balls of hail or spilled salt.

Suddenly we are both fumbling for door handles, heaving ourselves into the open air. I am a split second ahead of Hugo because I know what is going on. I race to the hatchback to release the dogs, screaming at them to jump out. This dramatic and violent behavior on my part intimidates Bismarck, who refuses to leave the car until I grab his collar and drag him out, whimpering and choking.

Hugo stands at the open driver's door, staring into the Pinto with disbelief. Snow sifts through the open doors and mixes with the white crystals, starting to melt almost as soon as it touches the vinyl. Perhaps he is thinking of possible headlines (AREA COUPLE KILLS DOGS IN BIZARRE DEATH PACT) or of his own near brush with extinction.

The Wendy's parking lot is silent. Though the lights blaze from the interior and there is a constant shushing sound of cars along the street, these seem not to impinge upon our little world. The dogs sit and shiver nervously, plainly confused, frightened.

"Are you all right?" asks Hugo. "Do you feel okay?"

He looks straight at me, into my eyes, as if to read me. I am a book he usually doesn't care to take off the shelf. Unaccountably and somewhat infuriatingly, I begin to cry.

"No, I'm not all right. No, I don't feel okay. Okay?"

I turn away and the dogs follow me.

"Where are you going?"

"Home. I'm tired of this."

And I am tired. In the past few hours, I have broken several laws, had a fight with Hugo, and failed to kill myself, not to mention thinking many desperate and ingenious thoughts to pass the time. Now, for all I know, we will never be able to drive the Pinto again. How will I get to work? How will Hugo drive to Toronto for rehearsals? What is the resale value of a cyanide-filled Pinto with an exploding gas tank? They probably won't even take it for junk. My life is a sorry and pathetic mess and all I want to do is go home and crawl into bed and pull a pillow over my face.

Hugo runs after me and takes me in his arms. Either he thinks a hug will improve my outlook or near-death has made him horny. His cheek is cold and stubbly, rubbing against mine. Bismarck whines thinly. My nose begins to drip. I begin to lose my balance. I wish Hugo would let go because we are making a scene for people coming out of the restaurant. Suddenly I am aware that he is crying; Hugo wants *me* to comfort *him*. Who just tried to kill herself? I ask myself, a little nonplused. Jake chases Bismarck in a tight circle around the parking lot.

I pull away and walk back to the Pinto. With my gloves I begin to dust the snow and cyanide off the seats and out the door (I keep my scarf over my mouth and nose; listen, I don't want to die in a Wendy's parking lot either). After watching for a while, Hugo walks into the restaurant, returning with paper napkins, which we damp in the melting snow and use to wash down the inside of the car. It is cold, dirty work and my hands and lips turn blue (as do Hugo's — not an effect of cyanide; this is because the body directs the blood to the major organs, the heart and brain, for example, to keep them warm). We are all cold and wet and miserable.

At length we get back into the car and drive with the windows open to the lab (basement rec room), where I wait with the dogs while Hugo (Willa) returns the jar of cyanide (shotgun) to its glass-doored shelf (deer-antler rack). He seems to take an exceptionally long time, and I imagine (we are creatures of each other's imagination) him lost in thought, surprised and troubled, amongst the whispering plants, arrested, as it were, by the thunderous echoing whispers of things which daily he compels with his thoughts. (Momentarily, he understands, as I and my father did, what it means to finish the sentence.)

Home again, we shake our clothes outside and wash the dogs in the tub (the evening has turned into a complete horror show for Bismarck) and then take turns holding the shower attachment over each other. I keep my eyes and mouth shut tight while Hugo gently and carefully hoses my face, my neck and ears and hair. I do the same for him and have to bite my lip seeing him with his eyes closed, naked, blind and trusting.

It is after two A.M. when we finally go to bed. We're both exhausted. Hugo curls up with his back to me and begins to snore. Bismarck's nails click nervously up and down the hallway outside our door, then he goes and curls up beside his friend under the kitchen table.

I lie awake thinking, thinking about what happened to Hugo back there by the car, what made him run after me, embrace me and weep — some inkling, I think, some intuition of the truth, that I am leaving, a truth that only now begins to spread like imperfectly oxygenated blood through my arteries and capillaries, turning my limbs leaden and my skin blue.

BARBARA GOWDY

Disneyland

FROM THE NORTH AMERICAN REVIEW

THE CHRISTMAS that Louise and Linda were twelve and Sandy
was eleven, there was only one gift under the tree for each of
them. Viewmasters for the twins and a beatnik doll with a string
that you pulled to make it talk for Sandy. The three girls wept.

Their father let them go at it for a while, and then he sprang
the surprise; he was taking them to Disneyland in a top-of-the-
line trailer that slept five.

"When, Daddy? When?" the girls cried.

"The summer. Maybe take a couple of extra weeks off work
and drive down to Me-hi-co while we're at it. Eh, señorita?" He
pulled the string on Sandy's doll.

"I'm hip, like uh, you know, beatnik," the doll said.

That was Christmas nineteen-sixty, and it was the next month
that air-raid drills started in Glenn Mills Public School for when
the Russians dropped the bomb. The principal made a speech
in the gymnasium to all the students. If it ever suddenly got
very light, he said, like a huge flashbulb going off in the sky,
you were to cover your eyes with your hands and crouch under
your desks until the teacher said it was safe to come out. Then,
two by two, you were to file down to the cellar. You were not to
try to run home.

"The hell with that," their father said when they told him.
"You run home." He had decided to build a fallout shelter. He
had a pamphlet that he'd sent away for called "Pioneers of Self-
Defense" on how to do it.

As soon as the ground was soft enough, about the end of

April, he had a man with a bulldozer dig a hole in the back yard. The next day another man in a truck delivered a pile of concrete blocks, and some pipes and boards and sheets of metal, and their father went right to work.

It took a month. Every minute that their father wasn't sleeping or working he was down in that hole; he even ate his meals there. He let Louise help, and she got pretty good at mixing mortar and hammering nails in the floorboards, as long as he didn't yell at her that she was doing it all wrong, which, if he stood over her shoulder, she did. But if he left her alone, she seemed to have a knack. In the morning she woke up yearning for the feel of the hammer in her hand, she dreamed about hammering all day at school. She wished she could do it when he wasn't around, and yet sometimes, when he wasn't mad or tired, she liked the fact that they worked as a team: she mixing the mortar, he setting the blocks; he sawing the boards, she nailing them down. He had to have everything perfect, and the longer she helped him the more she wanted everything to be perfect, too, the more she couldn't blame him for his tantrums. She wondered if he wished her brother was alive so he could help instead of her.

When the outside was done, the man came back with the bulldozer to shovel the earth back on the roof. Inside, Louise and her father built shelves and fold-up bunks and painted the walls canary-yellow, which was supposed to add a note of cheerfulness. Even though Louise said that she and her sisters never played hopscotch anymore, her father painted a hopscotch on the floor because the pamphlet said you should if you had kids.

He bought two weeks' worth of canned food, jugs for the water, candles, lanterns, paper plates, a chemical toilet, canned heat, a fire extinguisher and a camping stove. The rest of what the pamphlet said he should buy — bedding, Band-Aids, a transistor radio, a flashlight, batteries, board games, a shovel in case they had to dig themselves out from the house falling on top of them — they already had. A small library of books on nature and American history would prove useful and inspirational, the pamphlet said, but he said, did they know how much a book cost nowadays, and he carried down a box of his old *Life* magazines. He also brought down two cases of Canadian Club whiskey for their mother, and his World War Two gun.

Every three days the girls had to empty the water jugs and refill them using the hose, so that the supply would always be fresh. Their father started to have drills, but they were nothing like the ones at school, where the important thing was to stay calm. He would blow a whistle, sometimes in the middle of the night, and they all had to run like crazy to do their assigned tasks: Linda, shut and latch the windows and lock the front door; Louise, unscrew all the fuses in the fuse box and turn off the valve to the water heater; Sandy, shut off the furnace switch; their mother, just get herself to the cellar landing. Meanwhile he went on blowing the whistle and shouting, "Move it!" Then they charged out the back door to the shelter, which they entered in order of size, Sandy first, him last to pull the hatch shut. Down inside he shone the flashlight on his stopwatch and announced how long it had taken. He shone the light in their faces and told them how they could shave off those precious seconds. It was cold down there, and they shivered, especially at night in their pajamas and bare feet, or if it had been raining. Their mother asked how many more drills they had to do, and he said they had to keep at it until the bomb dropped — they had to be in top form.

"Well," she said. "Let's just hope it drops before winter. We'll catch our deaths, running out here all the time in the snow."

He slept in the shelter. He put in an electric outlet so he could listen to his Judy Garland records down there. The girls imagined him dancing with the shovel, smooching it: "How's about a little kiss, baby." They loved him being out of the house in the evenings. They could change the channels, say whatever they felt like, go to bed late. As long as their mother's coffee mug was filled with Canadian Club whiskey, she didn't care what happened.

The drills didn't stop though. The girls could go through them in their sleep, and sometimes did, waking up in the morning barely recalling that a few hours before they'd been flying around the house and out into the night. Often their mother didn't bother coming back up. She just fell onto one of the bunks and stayed there until morning. The girls could have too, their father said so. But they never would. When the light was off it was so black it was like being dead. Also there was a weird smell, which they thought came from where they'd buried

Checkers, their puppy that hung itself one night trying to get in the basement window out of the cold, not knowing it couldn't jump in unless one of the girls had unhooked its chain, not knowing that they could only unhook its chain and cry, "Jump, Checkers!" when their father wasn't home.

At breakfast, the Saturday before the last week of school, their father announced that they were going down the bomb shelter for two weeks.

They didn't get it. Did he mean, have a drill every day for two weeks? No, he meant stay down for two weeks. Sleep there? they asked. Sleep there, he said, eat there, not come out for two whole weeks.

"Oh, my lord," their mother said quietly, dropping her spoon in her cereal.

"Watch TV down there?" Louise asked.

"No TV. We'll be living as if the bomb's dropped and all electricity is out."

"What if the phone rings?" Sandy asked.

"We'll tell everyone where we are beforehand."

"But won't you have to go to work?" Linda asked.

"Nope. I've got two weeks coming."

They still didn't get it. "Two *more* weeks?" Louise asked.

"Two weeks," he said. "Two weeks is two weeks." He clapped his hands. "Okay, we'll be going down a week from today. So this Friday I want the sheets and blankets out on the line for an airing. I want the water changed. I want you all to have baths."

"But when are we going to Disneyland?" Linda asked.

"We're not," he said.

They weren't down the shelter an hour when Louise got her first period. It started after breakfast with cramps; gas pains is what she thought they were and she thought she must have to go number two, but she didn't want to smell up the place and didn't want them all listening. After a few minutes, though, she felt like she couldn't hold it — she sure couldn't hold it for two weeks — so she went behind the plywood partition and sat on the toilet.

In the shadowy lantern light her white underpants were dark. She touched them, felt wetness and held her fingers in front of her, toward the light in the corner. Her fingers were red.

A sound like someone yelling far away came out of her mouth. She was outside the shelter, in the yard, listening to herself calling under the lawn.

"What's the matter?" It was her father, standing in front of her. Linda and Sandy were behind him.

Louise pulled her pants up to her thighs. "Daddy," she said, frightened and shamed. She was on the toilet.

"What the hell are you making that noise for?" he said.

Linda came around him and blocked his view. "What's the matter?" she asked.

"I'm bleeding," Louise said, barely a whisper, but Linda heard.

"It's okay," Linda said to their father.

"What's the matter?" Sandy asked.

"She's just having a hard time going to the bathroom," Linda said, pushing Sandy away.

"Well, let's try to keep this kind of thing down," their father said, walking off. "We don't need a big production."

"I'm dying," Louise whispered to Linda.

"You moron," Linda whispered. "It's the curse."

"What?"

"Menstruation. You know."

"How do you know?"

"Well, what else? What a moron."

"Do you have it?"

"No," Linda said, as if she wouldn't be caught dead.

"How do you know then?"

"Because everybody knows. When you start bleeding down there, that's what it is."

Louise looked at the dark stain on her underpants. She was dripping blood into the toilet now. "What am I going to do?"

"Well, you use Kotex. But I guess there isn't any down here." She scanned the shelf beside the toilet. Band-Aids, toilet paper, Tums. "Just a sec." She poked her head around the end of the partition. "Mommy? Can you come here?"

"What's going on?" their father asked.

"Nothing. Mommy?"

Their mother's slippers flapped as she walked across the floor.

"Louise is menstruating," Linda whispered.

Their mother covered her mouth with both hands.

"Do we have any Kotex down here?" Linda asked.

Their mother shook her head. She turned around. "Jim," she said. "I'm just popping up to the house."

"What are you talking about?" he said. "There's radiation out there."

"Well, there isn't really."

"Yeah, but we have to act like there is or we ruin the whole exercise."

"Louise has started her period."

Silence. Louise shut her eyes.

"Jesus Christ," their father said.

"So I have to get her some napkins."

"She's really bleeding?" he asked.

"Well, yes."

"All right," he said. "We tear up a sheet." He took one off the shelf where the linen was and ripped it in half. "What d'ya think the pioneers did?" he said.

The rest of the morning Louise was allowed to lie on the bunk with her mother, who drank whiskey from her coffee mug and smoked. Louise curled up on her side with her head on her mother's shoulder. Her mother's neck smelled of Evening in Paris perfume. When her father wasn't looking, her mother let her have sips from her mug to ease the cramps. Her mother patted her head and said, "You're a young lady now," about every fifteen minutes.

Linda and Sandy had to stick to "The Regime." This was a chart that their father had written out on a piece of yellow Bristol board and nailed to the wall. The time of day was down one side, and what they were supposed to do was down the other. "Eight o'clock — rise; eight o'clock to eight fifteen — use toilet in the following order: Dad, Mom, Louise, Linda, Sandy." Et cetera. In front of some of the things they had to do were the initials "l.o." standing for "lights out" to save on candles and fuel. For instance, the singsong and afternoon exercises had an l.o. in front of them.

Ten-thirty to eleven-thirty in the morning was exercises with the lights on. For the first part, their father led Linda and Sandy in a march around and around the shelter, hollering, "Hup two three four! Left! Left!" By the end they both had to go to the bathroom. It seemed like one of the five of them was always on the toilet. And since you couldn't flush, there was no way of drowning out the noise. When their father had a pee before breakfast, it sounded like Niagara Falls.

The next exercise, after they used the toilet, was touching their toes twenty-five times. Then they had to do pushups. The floor was cold on their hands, and Linda and Sandy could only do a couple before their arms gave out.

"Five! Six! Seven!" their father went on counting. He clapped between each of his pushups, holding himself in the air for a second. His face darkened. He glared out of the corners of his eyes for the girls to keep on going. They did a few more, but it was just too hard.

He went on to fifty. Then he bounced up like a jack-in-the-box and shouted, "Stride jumps!"

They jumped facing him, stepping on each other's toes and hitting each other's hands because there wasn't enough room. His mouth was open in a circle and he gusted coffee-smelling breath at them. His eyes bulged, sweat streamed down his face. If they had seen a man on the street looking like he was, they'd have run away.

"Okay, play hopscotch," he said after the stride jumps.

"We need stones," Linda said.

"Play without 'em." He went over to the shelves and poured himself a glass of water. Linda asked if she could have one, she was dying of thirst.

"Wait till lunch," he said. "We have to ration."

"Come here," her mother whispered, crooking her finger, and when Linda went over she snuck her a sip from her mug. "We'll never get through this otherwise," she whispered.

Sandy came over for a sip, too. She'd tried it before, she knew it burned going down your throat and she didn't like it. But she liked this — sneaking drinks behind his back. Them against him.

"Come on," their father said, cranking the blower for fresh air. "Hopscotch!" So they returned to the middle of the floor and jumped up and down the squares. It was dumb playing without stones. It was dumb anyway, a kid's game.

He lay down on a bottom bunk and had a smoke. He kept

checking the time, and after about a quarter of an hour announced that it was eleven-thirty and they could stop. Now what they had to do was sit at the foot of the one chair in the shelter — a pink-painted wooden chair that used to be in Linda and Louise's bedroom — while he went around putting out all the lights except for one candle, which he carried back to the chair. He sat down and blew the candle out. Sandy shut her eyes, opened them. There was no difference. She felt for Linda's hand.

"All right," he said. "What do you want to sing?" His voice seemed to come from all directions.

"Um," Linda said, but couldn't think of anything. "Um," she said again to hear her thin voice, like a pin of light in the black.

"It's a long way to Tipperary," he started singing. "Come on! Everybody! Sally, Louise."

"It's a long way to go," their mother sang from the bunk in her high shaky voice.

The girls joined in, softly at first, then louder and louder because he was yelling at them to.

Sandy squeezed Linda's fingers. She smelled Checkers. Every time the lights went out she suddenly smelled him. He was buried at the bottom of the yard. Was that behind her, where the air vent was? Down here she had no sense of direction, but the smell was so strong she thought the air vent must be right next to where he was. But why did he give off a smell only when it was pitch dark? She remembered that rhyme: "The worms crawl in, the worms crawl out, up your brain, and out your snout."

They sang "The British Grenadiers," "The Battle Hymn of the Republic," "Marching to Pretoria" and "You're a Sap Mister Jap," all at the top of their lungs. Then they switched to songs from Judy Garland movies, singing these quietly. Dulcet tones was what their father demanded for Judy Garland songs, even for "Ballin' the Jack" and "The Trolley Bus Song." They ended with "Somewhere over the Rainbow." Their father had a really good voice — it sounded even better in the dark, not seeing him singing — and at the last line of "Somewhere over the Rainbow," the line that goes, "Why oh why can't I?" where the girls and their mother knew to slow right down, his voice rose clear and smooth as a boy's before their softer, higher voices, making a sound in the blackness so sweet and beautiful that it surprised them all and they were quiet for a moment afterward.

Linda spoke first. "We're like stars," she said softly. She meant the stars in the sky.

"Look out, Broadway," their father said. He struck a match, lit the candle and looked at his watch. "Twelve on the dot. Lunch time."

He heated up two cans of spaghetti on the camping stove while Linda mixed up the powdered milk and spread margarine on slices of bread. They ate sitting on the edge of the bottom bunks. After one mouthful, Louise found she wasn't hungry. She gave her plate back to her father and went to the toilet to see if her rag needed changing.

It sure did. How could so much blood be coming out of her and she was still alive, she wondered. Her stomach didn't hurt any longer, but she was dizzy. Maybe that was the whiskey, though. What if it wasn't, what if she really was bleeding to death? He wouldn't believe her.

She unpinned the old rag, wrapped it in toilet paper and pinned on another from the ones on the shelf above the toilet. On the way back to the bed she opened the lid of the garbage pail and dropped the balled-up rag in. The pail was lined with polyethylene and there was a container of disinfectant on the floor for sprinkling inside. If she died, would he keep her down here for two weeks?

In the shelter the girls had jobs, even Sandy, who never did anything up in the house. Her job was washing the dishes. Their father said that she had to use the same dishwater for two days, so when she went to wash the lunch things, there were soggy Cheerios and Frosted Flakes swimming around. Now there were white snakes of spaghetti. She held the plates by the rim and tried to keep her hands out of the water.

The Regime said lunch and cleanup were to take one hour, but Sandy was done by twelve-forty.

"What'll we do until one?" Linda asked, sneaking a sip of her mother's whiskey. One o'clock to three o'clock was cards and board games.

Their father tapped his watch, frowning. "Well, I guess we can start the games early," he said. "But tomorrow we stretch lunch out. Eat slower. Talk. I want you all to think up topics of conversation."

He spread a blanket on the floor over the hopscotch and they sat in a circle. Their mother came over, too, although she never played games in the house. She said that she just couldn't get used to no TV. It was like losing one of your senses, she said, like not being able to see or hear. Their father reached across the floor for the Canadian Club and topped up her glass.

First they played cards. Rummy. Usually the girls hated playing cards with him. He yelled at them to hurry up and discard and then said, "Are you kidding?" when they did. He yelled at them to hold their cards up — they were showing everyone their hand. He said they were lucky when they won, but when he won he said that it was 80 percent skill, 20 percent luck. He swore at his cards, he swore at them if they picked up a card he had been planning to. "It's only a game," he told them when they got upset or excited, but he would shout "Yes, Momma!" and slap his cards down. He would pace and swear. How the games usually ended was with him either sending them to bed or storming out of the house.

Today, though, maybe because their mother was playing or maybe because he couldn't storm out, he was nicer. He used his nice voice. It made the girls giggle. Everything he said and did, just picking up a card and looking at it, struck them as really funny.

Their mother smiled at them over the perfect fan of her cards. She kept winning, a surprise to the girls but not to her, and they realized that rummy must be something else, like sewing and tap dancing, that she was secretly good at.

"Mommy!" they cried, hugging her when she laid down her cards in neat rows, catching them all with mittfuls.

"Well, well," their father said, his smile stopping at the edges of his mouth. The girls laughed. "Settle down," he said nicely.

They were having a great time. It was fun down here. It was like being in a fort. They played hearts next, and their mother went on winning, going for all the cards twice and getting them.

Their father started pacing between deals. "There's something going on," he said, wagging his cigarette at the girls. "This is a trick on your old dad."

"No!" They laughed.

But he didn't believe them. He said that he wanted to play Scrabble, a game of every man for himself. Except that only four could play, so Sandy and their mother were a team. While he was getting the game off the shelf the girls had another sip of whiskey.

Their father went first and made the word "bounce." That broke them up. Their mother and Sandy made "tinkle," which was even funnier. Louise used the *b* to make "bust." They shrieked with laughter. Linda did "fuse" and they couldn't stand it, it seemed so funny.

"Settle down," their father said again. They saw the vein in his forehead come out and throb, a danger sign, but they couldn't stop laughing.

It was his turn. Using the *k*, he made "kidny."

"Okay," he said enthusiastically, starting to add up his score. "Double word —"

"What is it?" Linda asked.

"Kidney," he said. "An organ. Also a bean."

"But kidney's got an *e!*" she cried.

He frowned at the board. "No it doesn't."

"Well, it does," their mother said. "K-i-d-n-*e*-y."

"That's the British spelling," he said. "I'm using the American."

Their mother shook her head. "I think there's only the one way to spell it, Jim."

"Daddy, you can't spell," Sandy said tenderly. She couldn't spell either.

"Hey, you can make 'dinky'!" Linda said, rearranging his letters.

"Dinky!" Louise cried. They all three burst out laughing.

He hit Linda with a backhand across her mouth. She fell sideways, screaming. Louise and Sandy leaped up and ran to the wall. Their mother leaned over to get the whiskey bottle, and held it tight on the floor. He stood. He kicked the Scrabble board. It went shooting straight up, scattering letters, bent at the crease down the middle as if it would fly, then fell back to the floor, flat.

Linda, on her feet now, was making jumps at the roof, trying to grab the stairs, which you pulled down.

"The hatch is locked," their father said matter-of-factly.

"Let me out!" Linda screamed.

He looked at his watch. "Nap time," he said, and began putting out the lights.

Linda threw herself back on the floor. She cried that she was never going to get up. He stepped over her.

The others went to the bunks. There were two bunks on the end wall, which were Linda's and Louise's; one along the same wall as the toilet was, which was Sandy's; and two on the wall across from that — their mother's and father's. Their father took a candle to his bunk, and after he'd climbed up and set the alarm he blew it out. Black. And then that smell. Linda imagined it was coming from under the shelter, beneath where she was lying. She started to shiver. The floor was cold and hard, and suddenly she was so tired. She began crawling to the end of the room, knowing where she was by her father's snores. She waved her hand in front of her. When it hit the bottom bunk, she laid her head on the edge, too weary to climb to the top or even to climb in with Louise. She fell into a dead sleep.

Louise was aware of her sister crawling across the floor. She felt the mattress go down — Linda's foot, she thought, but it didn't move. She touched it and felt hair.

"Linda," she whispered.

No answer.

"Get up." She shook Linda's head a little, then remembered her face might be sore. She laid her palm gently on Linda's mouth for a minute. She put her other hand under the covers, down her pants, to see if her rag was leaking. She couldn't tell. It felt kind of damp, though. If she leaked all over the bed, he'd kill her. But he'd kill her if she got up and lit a candle to see. She had meant to put on a new rag after the games. Her head throbbed. Also she felt sick to her stomach. Was that the curse? Why did she have the curse and Linda didn't? What if boys tried to get her pregnant? Boys smelled the blood. Boys stared at her. She saw them staring at her chest, and it frightened her how childish their faces went, as if they hadn't learned any rules or manners yet. Even on hot days she wore two undershirts and a sweater. She slept on her stomach so she wouldn't grow any bigger. She couldn't do that now because of feeling like she was going to bring up. How was anyone supposed to sleep down here anyway, with their father snoring his head off?

Under the covers, pressing the place where the sound came out of the mattress, Sandy pulled the doll's string over and over. She didn't like this doll. It had black straight hair, and she was too old for dolls. The only reason she'd brought it down was that their father said she could, so she thought she had to. It was stuck, saying, "Hey cool cat, let's jive." She didn't care what it said, as long as it kept talking. But when she pulled the string, in the second when it wasn't talking, the smell crept in. The smell was the worms eating. The way Checkers's head had flopped, like a puppet's, had made her think that that's what it was hanging there. A Checkers puppet that somebody had hung in the window. She had screamed, then laughed, then gone closer and screamed. She was afraid to ask their father to leave the candle burning. She was afraid to make him mad. "What's the matter with you?" he asked after he hit Louise or Linda, and she was the one who couldn't stop crying. He never hit her. She thought it was because she was the prettiest.

For some reason the alarm went off at ten after four instead of four o'clock, cutting into their exercise hour. He gave them only a minute each to use the toilet, Louise two minutes to change her rag. The blood hadn't leaked onto her sheets, but it had gone through to her underpants and made a spot on her blue corduroy pants. She would have to wear them like that all week. There was no laundry detergent down here, let alone extra water or a time on The Regime for doing a wash, and they had only been allowed to bring down one change of clothing, which they weren't supposed to put on until next Saturday.

Sandy begged for a drink of water and he let her have a sip. Linda wouldn't ask, but she drank a whole glass when he was peeing. She said she had a headache, and Sandy and Louise said, "Same here." Their mother let them have more whiskey.

Louise got out of exercises again by saying her stomach hurt. In the dark (afternoon exercises were lights out), she and her mother passed the mug back and forth, and pretty soon Louise's headache was gone.

Sandy clung to Linda's hand as they marched, and Linda only pretended to lift her knees and swing her free arm. She let Sandy go on holding her hand during touching toes, where the two of them only touched their knees, and during pushups, where they just lay on their stomachs making grunting and panting noises. During stride jumps they jumped up and down holding hands. Their father's sweat rained on them.

The next hour, "Pep Talk," was him telling stories of his hardships in the war: marching for three days on a broken ankle, eating a can of moldy peach halves, saving a wounded buddy under a barrage of Jerry fire — stories they'd heard a thousand times. Then there was supper and dishes, then two hours of "Free Time," which was either playing games quietly or reading. The girls played hearts with their mother and took a couple of sips from her mug. Linda also snuck puffs of her cigarette. Louise conked out on the floor. Their father lay on his bunk, smoking and reading his *Life* magazines, mostly aloud, making them stop their game and listen. At nine o'clock Louise had to wake up, and they changed into their pajamas, facing their bunks. He went behind the partition to change. Then they climbed into their beds and said, "Now I lay me down to sleep," all together. Then he blew the candle out. Instantly he started snoring. They smelled Checkers. Sandy wept.

"What is it, honey?" their mother said.

"I smell worms eating Checkers," she whimpered.

"That's just Daddy."

"No, it's a rotten smell," Louise said. "Don't you smell it?"

"It happens in the dark," Sandy said.

Their mother got up and lit the lantern in the corner by the toilet. "There," she said. The smell disappeared and they went to sleep. An hour or so later, when the alarm rang for their father to crank the blower, he wanted to know who had lit the lantern. Their mother said she had. The dark gave her that nightmare, she said. He turned around and looked at her. What nightmare? the girls wondered. He went back to bed, leaving the lantern burning. Every few hours the alarm went off for him to get up and crank the blower. One of the times, the lantern was out, and he put in more fuel and lit it again.

LINDA HOGAN

Aunt Moon's Young Man

FROM THE MISSOURI REVIEW

THAT AUTUMN when the young man came to town, there was a
deep blue sky. On their way to the fair, the wagons creaked into
town. One buckboard, driven by cloudy white horses, carried a
grunting pig inside its wooden slats. Another had cages of chickens. In the heat, the chickens did not flap their wings. They
sounded tired and old, and their shoulders drooped like old
men.

There was tension in the air. Those people who still believed
in omens would turn to go home, I thought, white chicken
feathers caught on the wire cages they brought, reminding us
all that the cotton was poor that year and that very little of it
would line the big trailers outside the gins.

A storm was brewing over the plains, and beneath its clouds
a few people from the city drove dusty black motorcars through
town, angling around the statue of General Pickens on Main
Street. They refrained from honking at the wagons and the
white, pink-eyed horses. The cars contained no animal life, just
neatly folded stacks of quilts, jellies, and tomato relish, large
yellow gourds, and pumpkins that looked like the round faces
of children through half-closed windows.

"The biting flies aren't swarming today," my mother said. She
had her hair done up in rollers. It was almost dry. She was
leaning against the window frame, looking at the ink-blue trees
outside. I could see Bess Evening's house through the glass,
appearing to sit like a small, hand-built model upon my mother's shoulder. My mother was a dreamer, standing at the window with her green dress curved over her hip.

Her dress was hemmed slightly shorter on one side than on the other. I decided not to mention it. The way she leaned, with her abdomen tilted out, was her natural way of standing. She still had good legs, despite the spidery blue veins she said came from carrying the weight of us kids inside her for nine months each. She also blamed us for her few gray hairs.

She mumbled something about "the silence before the storm" as I joined her at the window.

She must have been looking at the young man for a long time, pretending to watch the sky. He was standing by the bushes and the cockscombs. There was a flour sack on the ground beside him. I thought at first it might be filled with something he brought for the fair, but the way his hat sat on it and a pair of black boots stood beside it, I could tell it held his clothing, and that he was passing through Pickens on his way to or from some city.

"It's mighty quiet for the first day of fair," my mother said. She sounded far away. Her eyes were on the young stranger. She unrolled a curler and checked a strand of hair.

We talked about the weather and the sky, but we both watched the young man. In the deep blue of sky his white shirt stood out like a light. The low hills were fire-gold and leaden.

One of my mother's hands was limp against her thigh. The other moved down from the rollers and touched the green cloth at her chest, playing with a flaw in the fabric.

"Maybe it was the tornado," I said about the stillness in the air. The tornado had passed through a few days ago, touching down here and there. It exploded my cousin's house trailer, but it left his motorcycle standing beside it, untouched. "Tornadoes have no sense of value," my mother had said. "They are always taking away the saints and leaving behind the devils."

The young man stood in that semi-slumped, half-straight manner of fullblood Indians. Our blood was mixed like Heinz 57, and I always thought of purebloods as better than us. While my mother eyed his plain moccasins, she patted her rolled hair as if to put it in order. I was counting the small brown flowers in the blistered wallpaper, the way I counted ceiling tiles in the new school, and counted each step when I walked.

I pictured Aunt Moon inside her house up on my mother's

shoulder. I imagined her dark face above the yellow oilcloth, her hands reflecting the yellow as they separated dried plants. She would rise slowly, as I'd seen her do, take a good long time to brush out her hair, and braid it once again. She would pet her dog, Mister, with long slow strokes while she prepared herself for the fair.

My mother moved aside, leaving the house suspended in the middle of the window, where it rested on a mound of land. My mother followed my gaze. She always wanted to know what I was thinking or doing. "I wonder," she said, "why in tarnation Bess's father built that house up there. It gets all the heat and wind."

I stuck up for Aunt Moon. "She can see everything from there, the whole town and everything."

"Sure, and everything can see her. A wonder she doesn't have ghosts."

I wondered what she meant by that, everything seeing Aunt Moon. I guessed by her lazy voice that she meant nothing. There was no cutting edge to her words.

"And don't call her Aunt Moon." My mother was reading my mind again, one of her many tricks. "I know what you're thinking," she would say when I thought I looked expressionless. "You are thinking about finding Mrs. Mark's ring and holding it for a reward."

I would look horrified and tell her that she wasn't even lukewarm, but the truth was that I'd been thinking exactly those thoughts. I resented my mother for guessing my innermost secrets. She was like God, everywhere at once knowing everything. I tried to concentrate on something innocent. I thought about pickles. I was safe; she didn't say a word about dills or sweets.

Bess, Aunt Moon, wasn't really my aunt. She was a woman who lived alone and had befriended me. I liked Aunt Moon and the way she moved, slowly, taking up as much space as she wanted and doing it with ease. She had wide lips and straight eyelashes.

Aunt Moon dried medicine herbs in the manner of her parents. She knew about plants, both the helpful ones and the ones that were poisonous in all but the smallest of doses. And she knew how to cut wood and how to read the planets. She told me why I was stubborn. It had to do with my being born in May. I believed her because my father was born a few days after me, and he was stubborn as all get out, even compared to me.

Aunt Moon was special. She had life in her. The rest of the women in town were cold in the eye and fretted over their husbands. I didn't want to be like them. They condemned the men for drinking and gambling, but even after the loudest quarrels, ones we'd overhear, they never failed to cook for their men. They'd cook platters of lard-fried chicken, bowls of mashed potatoes, and pitchers of creamy flour gravy.

Bess called those meals "sure death by murder."

Our town was full of large and nervous women with red spots on their thin-skinned necks, and we had single women who lived with brothers and sisters or took care of an elderly parent. Bess had comments on all of these: "They have eaten their anger and grown large," she would say. And there were the sullen ones who took care of men broken by the war, women who were hurt by the men's stories of death and glory but never told them to get on with living, like I would have done.

Bessie's own brother, J.D., had gone to the war and returned with softened, weepy eyes. He lived at the veterans hospital and he did office work there on his good days. I met him once and knew by the sweetness of his eyes that he had never killed anyone, but something about him reminded me of the lonely old shacks out on cotton farming land. His eyes were broken windows.

"Where do you think that young man is headed?" my mother asked.

Something in her voice was wistful and lonely. I looked at her face, looked out the window at the dark man, and looked back at my mother again. I had never thought about her from inside the skin. She was the mind reader in the family, but suddenly I knew how she did it. The inner workings of the mind were clear in her face, like words in a book. I could even feel her thoughts in the pit of my stomach. I was feeling embarrassed at what my mother was thinking when the stranger crossed the street. In front of him an open truck full of prisoners passed by. They wore large white shirts and pants, like immigrants from Mexico. I began to count the flowers in the wallpaper again, and the truckful of prisoners passed by, and when it was gone, the young man had also vanished into thin air.

Besides the young man, another thing I remember about the fair that year was the man in the bathroom. On the first day of the fair, the prisoners were bending over like great white sails, their black and brown hands stuffing trash in canvas bags. Around them the children washed and brushed their cows and raked fresh straw about their pigs. My friend Elaine and I escaped the dust-laden air and went into the women's public toilets, where we shared a stolen cigarette. We heard someone open the door, and we fanned the smoke. Elaine stood on the toilet seat so her sisters wouldn't recognize her shoes. Then it was silent, so we opened the stall and stepped out. At first the round dark man, standing by the door, looked like a woman, but then I noticed the day's growth of beard at his jawline. He wore a blue work shirt and a little straw hat. He leaned against the wall, his hand moving inside his pants. I grabbed Elaine, who was putting lipstick on her cheeks like rouge, and pulled her outside the door, the tube of red lipstick still in her hand.

Outside, we nearly collapsed by a trash can, laughing. "Did you see that? It was a man! A man! In the women's bathroom." She smacked me on the back.

We knew nothing of men's hands inside their pants, so we began to follow him like store detectives, but as we rounded a corner behind his shadow, I saw Aunt Moon walking away from the pigeon cages. She was moving slowly with her cane, through the path's sawdust, feathers, and sand.

"Aunt Moon, there was a man in the bathroom," I said, and then remembered the chickens I wanted to tell her about. Elaine ran off. I didn't know if she was still following the man or not, but I'd lost interest when I saw Aunt Moon.

"Did you see those chickens that lay the green eggs?" I asked Aunt Moon.

She wagged her head no, so I grabbed her free elbow and guided her past the pigeons with curly feathers and the turkeys with red wattles, right up to the chickens.

"They came all the way from South America. They sell for five dollars, can you imagine?" Five dollars was a lot for chickens when we were still recovering from the Great Depression, men

were still talking about what they'd done with the CCC, and
children still got summer complaint and had to be carried
around crippled for months.

She peered into the cage. The eggs were smooth and resting
in the straw. "I'll be" was all she said.

I studied her face for a clue as to why she was so quiet, thinking she was mad or something. I wanted to read her thoughts
as easily as I'd read my mother's. In the strange light of the sky,
her eyes slanted a bit more than usual. I watched her carefully.
I looked at the downward curve of her nose and saw the young
man reflected in her eyes. I turned around.

On the other side of the cage that held the chickens from
Araucania was the man my mother had watched. Bess pretended to be looking at the little Jersey cattle in the distance,
but I could tell she was seeing that man. He had a calm look on
his face and his dark chest was smooth as oil where his shirt was
opened. His eyes were large and black. They were fixed on Bess
like he was a hypnotist or something magnetic that tried to pull
Bess Evening toward it, even though her body stepped back.
She did step back, I remember that, but even so, everything in
her went forward, right up to him.

I didn't know if it was just me or if his presence charged the
air, but suddenly the oxygen was gone. It was like the fire at the
Fisher Hardware when all the air was drawn into the flame.
Even the chickens clucked softly, as if suffocating, and the cattle
were more silent in the straw. The pulse in everything changed.

I don't know what would have happened if the rooster hadn't
crowed just then, but he did, and everything returned to normal. The rooster strutted and we turned to watch him.

Bessie started walking away and I went with her. We walked
past the men and boys who were shooting craps in a cleared
circle. One of them rubbed the dice between his hands as we
were leaving, his eyes closed, his body's tight muscles willing a
winning throw. He called me Lady Luck as we walked by. He
said, "There goes Lady Luck," and he tossed the dice.

At dinner that evening we could hear the dance band tuning
up in the makeshift beer garden, playing a few practice songs
to the empty tables with their red cloths. They played "The
Tennessee Waltz." For a while, my mother sang along with it.

She had brushed her hair one hundred strokes and now she was talking and regretting talking all at the same time. "He was such a handsome man," she said. My father wiped his face with a handkerchief and rested his elbows on the table. He chewed and looked at nothing in particular. "For the longest time he stood there by the juniper bushes."

My father drank some coffee and picked up the newspaper. Mother cleared the table, one dish at a time and not in stacks like usual. "His clothes were neat. He must not have come from very far away." She moved the salt shaker from the end of the table to the center, then back again.

"I'll wash," I volunteered.

Mother said, "Bless you," and touched herself absently near the waist, as if to remove an apron. "I'll go get ready for the dance," she said.

My father turned a page of the paper.

The truth was, my mother was already fixed up for the dance. Her hair looked soft and beautiful. She had slipped into her new dress early in the day, "to break it in," she said. She wore nylons and she was barefoot and likely to get a runner. I would have warned her, but it seemed out of place, my warning. Her face was softer than usual, her lips painted to look full, and her eyebrows were much darker than usual.

"Do you reckon that young man came here for the rodeo?" She hollered in from the living room, where she powdered her nose. Normally she made up in front of the bathroom mirror, but the cabinet had been slammed and broken mysteriously one night during an argument so we had all taken to grooming ourselves in the small framed mirror in the living room.

I could not put my finger on it, but all the women at the dance that night were looking at the young man. It wasn't exactly that he was handsome. There was something else. He was alive in his whole body while the other men walked with great effort and stiffness, even those who did little work and were still young. Their male bodies had no language of their own in the way that his did. The women themselves seemed confused and lonely in the presence of the young man, and they were ridiculous in their behavior, laughing too loud, blushing like schoolgirls, or casting him a flirting eye. Even the older women were brighter than usual. Mrs. Tubby, whose face was usually as grim as the statue of General Pickens, the Cherokee hater, played with her necklace until her neck had red lines from the chain. Mrs. Tens twisted a strand of her hair over and over. Her sister tripped over a chair because she'd forgotten to watch where she was going.

The men, sneaking drinks from bottles in paper bags, did not notice any of the fuss.

Maybe it was his hands. His hands were strong and dark.

I stayed late, even after wives pulled their husbands away from their ball game talk and insisted they dance.

My mother and father were dancing. My mother smiled up into my father's face as he turned her this way and that. Her uneven skirt swirled a little around her legs. She had a run in her nylons, as I predicted. My father, who was called Peso by the townspeople, wore his old clothes. He had his usual look about him, and I noticed that faraway, unfocused gaze on the other men too. They were either distant or they were present but rowdy, embarrassing the women around them with the loud talk of male things: work and hunting, fights, this or that pretty girl. Occasionally they told a joke, like, "Did you hear the one about the traveling salesman?"

The dancers whirled around the floor, some tapping their feet, some shuffling, the women in new dresses and dark hair all curled up like in movie magazines, the men with new leather boots and crew cuts. My dad's rear stuck out in back, the way he danced. His hand clutched my mother's waist.

That night, Bessie arrived late. She was wearing a white dress with a full gathered skirt. The print was faded and I could just make out the little blue stars on the cloth. She carried a yellow shawl over her arm. Her long hair was braided as usual in the manner of the older Chickasaw women, like a wreath on her head. She was different from the others with her bright shawls. Sometimes she wore a heavy shell necklace or a collection of bracelets on her arm. They jangled when she talked with me, waving her hands to make a point. Like the time she told me that the soul is a small woman inside the eye who leaves at night to wander new places.

No one had ever known her to dance before, but that night

the young man and Aunt Moon danced together among the
artificial geraniums and plastic carnations. They held each other
gently like two breakable vases. They didn't look at each other
or smile the way the other dancers did; that's how I knew they
liked each other. His large dark hand was on the small of her
back. Her hand rested tenderly on his shoulder. The other
dancers moved away from them and there was empty space all
around them.

My father went out into the dark to smoke and to play a hand
or two of poker. My mother went to sit with some of the other
women, all of them pulling their damp hair away from their
necks and letting it fall back again, or furtively putting on lipstick, fanning themselves, and sipping their beers.

"He puts me in the mind of a man I once knew," said Mrs.
Tubby.

"Look at them," said Mrs. Tens. "Don't you think he's young
enough to be her son?"

With my elbows on my knees and my chin in my hands, I
watched Aunt Moon step and square when my mother loomed
up like a shadow over the bleachers where I sat.

"Young lady," she said in a scolding voice. "You were supposed to go home and put the children to bed."

I looked from her stern face to my sister Susan, who was like
a chubby angel sleeping beside me. Peso Junior had run off to
the gambling game, where he was pushing another little boy
around. My mother followed my gaze and looked at Junior. She
put her hands on her hips and said, "Boys!"

My sister Roberta, who was twelve, had stayed close to the
women all night, listening to their talk about the fullblood who
had come to town for a rodeo or something and who danced so
far away from Bessie that they didn't look friendly at all except
for the fact that the music had stopped and they were still waltzing.

Margaret Tubby won the prize money that year for the biggest pumpkin. It was 220.4 centimeters in circumference and
weighed 190 pounds and had to be carried on a stretcher by the
volunteer firemen. Mrs. Tubby was the town's chief social justice. She sat most days on the bench outside the grocery store.

Sitting there like a full-chested hawk on a fence, she held court. She had watched Bess Evening for years with her sharp gold eyes. "This is the year I saw it coming," she told my mother, as if she'd just been dying for Bess to go wrong. It showed up in the way Bess walked, she said, that the woman was coming to a no good end just like the rest of her family had done.

"When do you think she had time to grow that pumpkin?" Mother asked as we escaped Margaret Tubby's court on our way to the store. I knew what she meant, that Mrs. Tubby did more time with gossip than with her garden.

Margaret was even more pious than usual at that time of year when the green tent revival followed on the heels of the fair, when the pink-faced men in white shirts arrived and, really, every single one of them was a preacher. Still, Margaret Tubby kept her prize money to herself and didn't give a tithe to any church.

With Bess Evening carrying on with a stranger young enough to be her son, Mrs. Tubby succeeded in turning the church women against her once and for all. When Bessie walked down the busy street, one of the oldest dances of women took place, for women in those days turned against each other easily, never thinking they might have other enemies. When Bess appeared, the women stepped away. They vanished from the very face of earth that was named Comanche Street. They disappeared into the Oklahoma redstone shops like swallows swooping into their small clay nests. The women would look at the new bolts of red cloth in Terwilligers with feigned interest, although they would never have worn red, even to a dog fight. They'd purchase another box of face powder in the five and dime, or drink cherry phosphates at the pharmacy without so much as tasting the flavor.

But Bessie was unruffled. She walked on in the empty mirage of heat, the sound of her cane blending in with horse hooves and the rhythmic pumping of oil wells out east.

At the store, my mother bought corn meal, molasses, and milk. I bought penny candy for my younger sisters and for Peso Junior with the money I earned by helping Aunt Moon with her remedies. When we passed Margaret Tubby on the way out, my mother nodded at her, but said to me, "That pumpkin grew fat on gossip. I'll bet she fed it with nothing but all-night rumors."

I thought about the twenty-five-dollar prize money and decided
to grow pumpkins next year.

My mother said, "Now don't you get any ideas about growing
pumpkins, young lady. We don't have room enough. They'd
crowd out the cucumbers and tomatoes."

My mother and father won a prize that year, too. For dancing.
They won a horse lamp for the living room. "We didn't even
know it was a contest," my mother said, free from the sin of
competition. Her face was rosy with pleasure and pride. She
had the life snapping out of her like hot grease, though sometimes I saw that life turn to a slow and restless longing, like
when she daydreamed out the window where the young man
had stood that day.

Passing Margaret's post and giving up on growing a two-
hundred-pound pumpkin, I remembered all the things good
Indian women were not supposed to do. We were not supposed
to look into the faces of men. Or laugh too loud. We were not
supposed to learn too much from books because that kind of
knowledge was a burden to the soul. Not only that, it always
took us away from our loved ones. I was jealous of the white
girls who laughed as loud as they wanted and never had rules.
Also, my mother wanted me to go to college no matter what
anyone else said or thought. She said I was too smart to stay
home and live a life like hers, even if the other people thought
book learning would ruin my life.

Aunt Moon with her second sight and heavy breasts managed
to break all the rules. She threw back her head and laughed out
loud, showing off the worn edges of her teeth. She didn't go to
church. She did a man's work, cared for animals, and chopped
her own wood. The gossiping women said it was a wonder Bessie Evening was healthy at all and didn't have female problems
— meaning with her body, I figured.

The small woman inside her eye was full and lonely at the
same time.

Bess made tonics, remedies, and cures. The church women,
even those who gossiped, slipped over to buy Bessie's potions at
night and in secret. They'd never admit they swallowed the
"snake medicine," as they called it. They'd say to Bess, "What
have you got to put the life back in a man? My sister has that
trouble, you know." Or they'd say, "I have a friend who needs a

cure for the sadness." They bought remedies for fever and for coughing fits, for sore muscles and for sleepless nights.

Aunt Moon had learned the cures from her parents, who were said to have visited their own sins upon their children, both of whom were born out of wedlock from the love of an old Chickasaw man and a young woman from one of those tribes up north. Maybe a Navajo or something, the people thought.

But Aunt Moon had numerous talents and I respected them. She could pull cotton, pull watermelons, and pull babies with equal grace. She even delivered those scrub cattle, bred with Holsteins too big for them, caesarean. In addition to that, she told me the ways of the world and not just about the zodiac or fortune cards. "The United States is in love with death," she would say. "They sleep with it better than with lovers. They celebrate it on holidays, the Fourth of July, even in spring when they praise the loss of a good man's body."

She would tend her garden while I'd ask questions. What do you think about heaven? I wanted to know. She'd look up and then get back to pulling the weeds. "You and I both would just grump around up there with all those righteous people. Women like us weren't meant to live on golden streets. We're Indians," she'd say as she cleared out the space around a bean plant. "We're like these beans. We grew up from mud." And then she'd tell me how the people emerged right along with the craw-dads from the muddy female swamps of the land. "And what is gold anyway? Just something else that comes from mud. Look at the conquistadors." She pulled a squash by accident. "And look at the sad women of this town, old already and all because of gold." She poked a hole in the ground and replanted the roots of the squash. "Their men make money, but not love. They give the women gold rings, gold-rimmed glasses, gold teeth, but their skin dries up for lack of love. Their hearts are little withered raisins." I was embarrassed by the mention of making love, but I listened to her words.

This is how I came to call Bessie Evening by the name of Aunt Moon: She'd been teaching me that animals and all life should be greeted properly as our kinfolk. "Good day, Uncle," I learned to say to the longhorn as I passed by on the road. "Good

morning, cousins. Is there something you need?" I'd say to the
sparrows. And one night when the moon was passing over Bessie's house, I said, "Hello, Aunt Moon. I see you are full of silver
again tonight." It was so much like Bess Evening, I began to
think, that I named her after the moon. She was sometimes full
and happy, sometimes small and weak. I began saying it right
to her ears: "Auntie Moon, do you need some help today?"

She seemed both older and younger than thirty-nine to me.
For one thing, she walked with a cane. She had developed some
secret ailment after her young daughter died. My mother said
she needed the cane because she had no mortal human to hold
her up in life, like the rest of us did.

But the other thing was that she was full of mystery and she
laughed right out loud, like a Gypsy, my mother said, pointing
out Bessie's blue-painted walls, bright clothes and necklaces,
and all the things she kept hanging from her ceiling. She decorated outside her house, too, with bits of blue glass hanging
from the trees, and little polished quartz crystals that reflected
rainbows across the dry hills.

Aunt Moon had solid feet, a light step, and a face that clouded
over with emotion and despair one moment and brightened up
like light the next. She'd beam and say to me, "Sassafras will
turn your hair red," and throw back her head to laugh, knowing
full well that I would rinse my dull hair with sassafras that very
night, ruining my mother's pans.

I sat in Aunt Moon's kitchen while she brewed herbals in
white enamel pans on the woodstove. The insides of the pans
were black from sassafras and burdock and other plants she
picked. The kitchen smelled rich and earthy. Some days it was
hard to breathe from the combination of woodstove heat and
pollen from the plants, but she kept at it and her medicine for
cramps was popular with the women in town.

Aunt Moon made me proud of my womanhood, giving me
bags of herbs and an old eagle feather that had been doctored
by her father back when people used to pray instead of going
to church. "The body divines everything," she told me, and
sometimes when I was with her, I knew the older Indian world
was still here and I'd feel it in my skin and hear the night sounds
speak to me, hear the voice of water tell stories about people

who lived here before, and the deep songs came out from the hills.

One day I found Aunt Moon sitting at her table in front of a plate of untouched toast and wild plum jam. She was weeping. I was young and didn't know what to say, but she told me more than I could ever understand. "Ever since my daughter died," she told me, "my body aches to touch her. All the mourning has gone into my bones." Her long hair was loose that day and it fell down her back like a waterfall, almost to the floor.

After that I had excuses on the days I saw her hair loose. "I'm putting up new wallpaper today," I'd say, or "I have to help Mom can peaches," which was the truth.

"Sure," she said, and I saw the tinge of sorrow around her eyes even though she smiled and nodded at me.

Canning the peaches, I asked my mother what it was that happened to Aunt Moon's daughter.

"First of all," my mother set me straight, "her name is Bess, not Aunt Moon." Then she'd tell the story of Willow Evening. "That pretty child was the light of that woman's eye," my mother said. "It was all so fast. She was playing one minute and the next she was gone. She was hanging on to that wooden planter and pulled it right down onto her little chest."

My mother touched her chest. "I saw Bessie lift it like it weighed less than a pound — did I already tell you that part?"

All I had seen that day was Aunt Moon holding Willow's thin body. The little girl's face was already gone to ashes and Aunt Moon blew gently on her daughter's skin, even though she was dead, as if she could breathe the life back into her one more time. She blew on her skin the way I later knew that women blow sweat from lovers' faces, cooling them. But I knew nothing of any kind of passion then.

The planter remained on the dry grassy mound of Aunt Moon's yard, and even though she had lifted it, no one else, not even my father, could move it. It was still full of earth and dead geraniums, like a monument to the child.

"That girl was all she had," my mother said through the steam of boiling water. "Hand me the ladle, will you?"

The peaches were suspended in sweet juice in their clear jars. I thought of our lives — so short, the skin so soft around us that we could be gone any second from our living — thought I saw

Willow's golden brown face suspended behind glass in one of the jars.

The men first noticed the stranger, Isaac, when he cleaned them out in the poker game that night at the fair. My father, who had been drinking, handed over the money he'd saved for the new bathroom mirror and took a drunken swing at the young man, missing him by a foot and falling on his bad knee. Mr. Tubby told his wife he lost all he'd saved for the barber shop business, even though everyone in town knew he drank it up long before the week of the fair. Mr. Tens lost his Mexican silver ring. It showed up later on Aunt Moon's hand.

Losing to one another was one thing. Losing to Isaac Cade meant the dark young man was a card sharp and an outlaw. Even the women who had watched the stranger all that night were sure he was full of demons.

The next time I saw Aunt Moon, it was the fallow season of autumn, but she seemed new and fresh as spring. Her skin had new light. Gathering plants, she smiled at me. Her cane moved aside the long dry grasses to reveal what grew underneath. Mullein was still growing, and holly.

I sat at the table while Aunt Moon ground yellow ochre in a mortar. Isaac came in from fixing the roof. He touched her arm so softly I wasn't sure she felt it. I had never seen a man touch a woman that way.

He said hello to me and he said, "You know those fairgrounds? That's where the three tribes used to hold sings." He drummed on the table, looking at me, and sang one of the songs. I said I recognized it, a song I sometimes dreamed I heard from the hill.

A red handprint appeared on his face, like one of those birthmarks that only show up in the heat or under the strain of work or feeling.

"How'd you know about the fairgrounds?" I asked him.

"My father was from here." He sat still, as if thinking himself into another time. He stared out the window at the distances that were in between the blue curtains.

I went back to Aunt Moon's the next day. Isaac wasn't there, so Aunt Moon and I tied sage in bundles with twine. I asked her about love.

"It comes up from the ground just like corn," she said. She pulled a knot tighter with her teeth.

Later, when I left, I was still thinking about love. Outside where Bess had been planting, black beetles were digging themselves under the turned soil, and red ants had grown wings and were starting to fly.

When I returned home, my mother was sitting outside the house on a chair. She pointed at Bess Evening's house. "With the man there," she said, "I think it best you don't go over to Bessie's house anymore."

I started to protest, but she interrupted. "There are no ands, ifs, or buts about it."

I knew it was my father who made the decision. My mother had probably argued my point and lost to him again, and lost some of her life as well. She was slowed down to a slumberous pace. Later that night as I stood by my window looking toward Aunt Moon's house, I heard my mother say, "God damn them all and this whole damned town."

"There now," my father said. "There now."

"She's as dark and stained as those old black pans she uses," Margaret Tubby said about Bess Evening one day. She had come to pick up a cake from Mother for the church bake sale. I was angered by her words. I gave her one of those "looks could kill" faces, but I said nothing. We all looked out the window at Aunt Moon. She was standing near Isaac, looking at a tree. It leapt into my mind suddenly, like lightning, that Mrs. Tubby knew about the blackened pans. That would mean she had bought cures from Aunt Moon. I was smug about this discovery.

Across the way, Aunt Moon stood with her hand outstretched, palm up. It was filled with roots or leaves. She was probably teaching Isaac about the remedies. I knew Isaac would teach her things also, older things, like squirrel sickness and porcupine disease that I'd heard about from grandparents.

Listening to Mrs. Tubby, I began to understand why, right after the fair, Aunt Moon had told me I would have to fight hard to keep my life in this town. Mrs. Tubby said, "Living out of wedlock! Just like her parents." She went on, "History repeats itself."

I wanted to tell Mrs. Tubby a thing or two myself. "History, my eye," I wanted to say. "You're just jealous about the young man." But Margaret Tubby was still angry that her husband had lost his money to the stranger, and also because she probably still felt bad about playing with her necklace like a young girl that night at the fair. My mother said nothing, just covered the big caramel cake and handed it over to Mrs. Tubby. My mother looked like she was tired of fools and that included me. She looked like the woman inside her eye had just wandered off.

I began to see the women in Pickens as ghosts. I'd see them in the library looking at the stereopticons, and in the ice cream parlor. The more full Aunt Moon grew, the more drawn and pinched they became.

The church women echoed Margaret. "She's as stained as her pans," they'd say, and they began buying their medicines at the pharmacy. It didn't matter that their coughs returned and that their children developed more fevers. It didn't matter that some of them could not get pregnant when they wanted to or that Mrs. Tens grew thin and pale and bent. They wouldn't dream of lowering themselves to buy Bessie's medicines.

My mother ran hot water into the tub and emptied one of her packages of bubble powder in it. "Take a bath," she told me. "It will steady your nerves."

I was still crying, standing at the window, looking out at Aunt Moon's house through the rain.

The heavy air had been broken by an electrical storm earlier that day. In a sudden crash, the leaves flew off their trees, the sky exploded with lightning, and thunder rumbled the earth. People went to their doors to watch. It scared me. The clouds turned green and it began to hail and clatter.

That was when Aunt Moon's old dog, Mister, ran off, went running like crazy through the town. Some of the older men saw him on the street. They thought he was hurt and dying because of the way he ran and twitched. He butted right into a tree and the men thought maybe he had rabies or something. They meant to put him out of his pain. One of them took aim with a gun and shot him, and when the storm died down and

the streets misted over, everything returned to heavy stillness
and old Mister was lying on the edge of the Smiths' lawn. I
picked him up and carried his heavy body up to Aunt Moon's
porch. I covered him with sage, like she would have done.

Bess and Isaac had gone over to Alexander that day to sell
remedies. They missed the rain, and when they returned, they
were happy about bringing home bags of beans, ground corn,
and flour.

I guess it was my mother who told Aunt Moon about her dog.

That evening I heard her wailing. I could hear her from my
window and I looked out and saw her with her hair all down
around her shoulders like a black shawl. Isaac smoothed back
her hair and held her. I guessed that all the mourning was back
in her bones again, even for her little girl, Willow.

That night my mother sat by my bed. "Sometimes the world
is a sad place," she said and kissed my hot forehead. I began to
cry again.

"Well, she still has the burro," my mother said, neglecting to
mention Isaac.

I began to worry about the burro and to look after it. I went
over to Aunt Moon's against my mother's wishes, and took car-
rots and sugar to the gray burro. I scratched his big ears.

By this time, most of the younger and healthier men had
signed up to go to Korea and fight for their country. Most of
the residents of Pickens were mixed-blood Indians and they
were even more patriotic than white men. I guess they wanted
to prove that they were good Americans. My father left and we
saw him off at the depot. I admit I missed him saying to me,
"The trouble with you is you think too much." Old Peso, always
telling people what their problems were. Margaret Tubby's lazy
son had enlisted because, as his mother had said, "It would
make a man of him," and when he was killed in action, the
townspeople resented Isaac, Bess Evening's young man, even
more since he did not have his heart set on fighting the war.

Aunt Moon was pregnant the next year when the fair came
around again, and she was just beginning to show. Margaret
Tubby had remarked that Bess was visiting all those family sins
on another poor child.

This time I was older. I fixed Mrs. Tubby in my eyes and I

said, "Miss Tubby, you are just like history, always repeating yourself."

She pulled her head back into her neck like a turtle. My mother said, "Hush, Sis. Get inside the house." She put her hands on her hips. "I'll deal with you later." She almost added, "Just wait till your father gets home."

Later, I felt bad, talking that way to Margaret Tubby so soon after she lost her son.

Shortly after the fair, we heard that the young man inside Aunt Moon's eye was gone. A week passed and he didn't return. I watched her house from the window and I knew, if anyone stood behind me, the little house was resting up on my shoulder.

Mother took a nap and I grabbed the biscuits off the table and snuck out.

"I didn't hear you come in," Aunt Moon said to me.

"I didn't knock," I told her. "My mom just fell asleep. I thought it'd wake her up."

Aunt Moon's hair was down. Her hands were on her lap. A breeze came in the window. She must not have been sleeping and her eyes looked tired. I gave her the biscuits I had taken off the table. I lied and told her my mother had sent them over. We ate one.

Shortly after Isaac was gone, Bess Evening again became the focus of the town's women. Mrs. Tubby said, "Bessie would give you the shirt off her back. She never deserved a no good man who would treat her like dirt and then run off." Mrs. Tubby went over to Bess Evening's and bought enough cramp remedy from the pregnant woman to last her and her daughters for the next two years.

Mrs. Tens lost her pallor. She went to Bessie's with a basket of jellies and fruits, hoping in secret that Bess would return Mr. Tens's Mexican silver ring now that the young man was gone.

The women were going to stick by her; you could see it in their squared shoulders. They no longer hid their purchases of herbs. They forgot how they'd looked at Isaac's black eyes and lively body with longing that night of the dance. If they'd had dowsing rods, the split willow branches would have flown up to the sky, so much had they twisted around the truth of things and even their own natures. Isaac was the worst of men. Their husbands, who were absent, were saints who loved them. Every morning when my mother said her prayers and forgot she'd damned the town and everybody in it, I heard her ask for peace for Bessie Evening, but she never joined in with the other women who seemed happy over Bessie's tragedy.

Isaac was doubly condemned in his absence. Mrs. Tubby said, "What kind of fool goes off to leave a woman who knows about tea leaves and cures for diseases of the body and the mind alike? I'll tell you what kind, a card shark, that's what."

Someone corrected her. "Card *sharp,* dearie, not *shark.*"

Who goes off and leaves a woman whose trees are hung with charming stones, relics, and broken glass, a woman who hangs sage and herbs to dry on her walls and whose front porch is full of fresh-cut wood? Those women, how they wanted to comfort her, but Bess Evening would only go to the door, leave them standing outside on the steps, and hand their herbs to them through the screen.

My cousins from Denver came for the fair. I was going to leave with them and get a job in the city for a year or so, then go on to school. My mother insisted she could handle the little ones alone now that they were bigger, and that I ought to go. It was best I made some money and learned what I could, she said.

"Are you sure?" I asked while my mother washed her hair in the kitchen sink.

"I'm sure as the night's going to fall." She sounded light-hearted, but her hands stopped moving and rested on her head until the soap lather began to disappear. "Besides, your dad will probably be home any day now."

I said, "Okay then, I'll go. I'll write you all the time." I was all full of emotion, but I didn't cry.

"Don't make promises you can't keep," my mother said, wrapping a towel around her head.

I went to the dance that night with my cousins, and out in the trees I let Jim Tens kiss me and promised him that I would be back. "I'll wait for you," he said. "And keep away from those city boys."

I meant it when I said, "I will."

He walked me home, holding my hand. My cousins were still at the dance. Mom would complain about their late city hours. Once she even told us that city people eat supper as late as eight o'clock P.M. We didn't believe her.

After Jim kissed me at the door, I watched him walk down the street. I was surprised that I didn't feel sad.

I decided to go to see Aunt Moon one last time. I was leaving at six in the morning and was already packed and I had taken one of each herb sample I'd learned from Aunt Moon, just in case I ever needed them.

I scratched the burro's gray face at the lot and walked up toward the house. The window was gold and filled with lamplight. I heard an owl hooting in the distance and stopped to listen.

I glanced in the window and stopped in my tracks. The young man, Isaac, was there. He was speaking close to Bessie's face. He put his finger under her chin and lifted her face up to his. He was looking at her with soft eyes and I could tell there were many men and women living inside their eyes that moment. He held her cane across the back of her hips. With it, he pulled her close to him and held her tight, his hands on the cane pressing her body against his. And he kissed her. Her hair was down around her back and shoulders and she put her arms around his neck. I turned to go. I felt dishonest and guilty for looking in at them. I began to run.

I ran into the bathroom and bent over the sink to wash my face. I wiped Jim Tens's cold kiss from my lips. I glanced up to look at myself in the mirror, but my face was nothing, just shelves of medicine bottles and aspirin. I had forgotten the mirror was broken.

From the bathroom door I heard my mother saying her prayers, fervently, and louder than usual. She said, "Bless Sis's Aunt Moon and bless Isaac, who got arrested for trading illegal medicine for corn, and forgive him for escaping from jail."

She said this so loud, I thought she was talking to me. Maybe she was. Now how did she read my mind again? It made me smile, and I guessed I was reading hers.

All the next morning, driving through the deep blue sky, I thought how all the women had gold teeth and hearts like withered raisins. I hoped Jim Tens would marry one of the Tubby girls. I didn't know if I'd ever go home or not. I had Aunt Moon's herbs in my bag, and the eagle feather wrapped safe in a scarf. And I had a small, beautiful woman in my eye.

DAVID WONG LOUIE

Displacement

FROM PLOUGHSHARES

Mrs. Chow heard the widow. She tried reading faster but kept stumbling over the same lines. She thought perhaps she was misreading them: "There comes, then, finally, the prospect of atomic war. If the war is ever to be carried to China, common sense tells us only atomic weapons could promise maximum loss with minimum damage."

When she heard the widow's wheelchair she tossed the copy of *Life* down on the couch, afraid she might be found out. The year was 1952.

Outside the kitchen, Chow was lathering the windows. He worked a soft brush in a circular motion. Inside, the widow was accusing Mrs. Chow of stealing her cookies. The widow had a handful of them clutched to her chest and brought one down hard against the table. She was counting. Chow waved, but Mrs. Chow only shook her head. He soaped up the last pane and disappeared.

Standing accused, Mrs. Chow wondered if this was what it was like when her parents faced the liberators who had come to reclaim her family's property in the name of the People. She imagined her mother's response to them: What people? All of my servants are clothed and decently fed.

The widow swept the cookies off the table as if they were a canasta trick won. She started counting again. Mrs. Chow and the widow had played out this scene many times before. As on other occasions, she didn't give the old woman the satisfaction of a plea, guilty or otherwise.

Mrs. Chow ignored the widow's busy blue hands. She fixed her gaze on the woman's milky eyes instead. Sight resided at the peripheries. Mornings, before she prepared the tub, emptied the pisspot, or fried the breakfast meat, Mrs. Chow cradled the widow's oily scalp and applied the yellow drops that preserved what vision was left in the cold, heaven-directed eyes.

"Is she watching?" said the widow. She tilted her big gray head sideways; a few degrees in any direction Mrs. Chow became a blur. In happier days Mrs. Chow might have positioned herself just right or left of center, neatly within a line of sight.

Mrs. Chow was thirty-five years old. After a decade-long separation from her husband she finally had entered the United States in 1950 under the joint auspices of the War Brides and Refugee Relief acts. She would agree she was a bride, but not a refugee, even though the Red Army had confiscated her home and turned it into a technical school. During the trouble she was away, safely studying in Hong Kong. Her parents, with all their wealth, could've easily escaped, but they were confident a few well-placed bribes among the Red hooligans would put an end to the foolishness. Mrs. Chow assumed her parents now were dead. She had seen pictures in *Life* of minor landlords tried and executed for lesser crimes against the People.

The widow's fondness for calling Mrs. Chow a thief began soon after the old woman broke her hip. At first Mrs. Chow blamed the widow's madness on pain displacement. She had read in a textbook that a malady in one part of the body could show up as a pain in another locale — sick kidneys, for instance, might surface as a mouthful of sore gums. The bad hip had weakened the widow's brain funtion. Mrs. Chow wanted to believe the crazy spells weren't the widow's fault, just as a baby soiling its diapers can't be blamed. But even a mother grows weary of changing them.

"I live with a thief under my roof," the widow said to the kitchen. "I could yell at her, but why waste my breath?"

When the widow was released from the hospital she returned to the house with a live-in nurse. Soon afterward her daughter paid a visit, and the widow told her she didn't want the nurse around anymore. "She can do me," the widow said, pointing in

Mrs. Chow's direction. "She won't cost a cent. Besides, I don't like being touched that way by a person who knows what she's touching," she said of the nurse.

Nobody knew, but Mrs. Chow spoke a passable though highly accented English she had learned in British schools. Her teachers in Hong Kong always said that if she had the language when she came to the States she'd be treated better than other immigrants. Chow couldn't have agreed more. Once she arrived he started to teach her everything he knew in English. But that amounted to very little, considering he had been here for more than ten years. And what he had mastered came out crudely and strangely twisted. His phrases, built from a vocabulary of deference and accommodation, irritated Mrs. Chow for the way they resembled the obsequious blabber of her servants back home.

The Chows had been hired ostensibly to drive the widow to her canasta club, to clean the house, to do the shopping, and since the bad hip, to oversee her personal hygiene. In return they lived rent-free upstairs in the children's rooms, three bedrooms and a large bath. Plenty of space, it would seem, except the widow wouldn't allow them to remove any of the toys and things from her children's cluttered rooms.

On weekends and Tuesday afternoons Chow borrowed the widow's tools and gardened for spending money. Friday nights, after they dropped the widow off at the canasta club, the Chows dined at Ming's and then went to the amusement park at the beach boardwalk. First and last, they got in line to ride the Milky Way. On the day the immigration authorities finally let Mrs. Chow go, before she even saw her new home, Chow took his bride to the boardwalk. He wanted to impress her with her new country. All that machinery, brainwork, and labor done for the sake of fun. He never tried the roller coaster before she arrived; he saved it for her. After that very first time he realized he was much happier with his feet on the ground. But not Mrs. Chow: Oh, this speed, this thrust at the sky, this UP! Oh, this raging, clattering, pushy country! So big! And since that first ride she looked forward to Friday nights and the wind whipping through her hair, stinging her eyes, blowing away the top layers of dailiness. On the longest, most dangerous descent her dry mouth would open to a silent O and she would thrust up her arms, as if she could fly away.

Some nights as the Chows waited in line, a gang of toughs out on a strut, trussed in denim and combs, would stop and visit: MacArthur, they said, will drain the Pacific; the H-bomb will wipe Korea clean of Commies; the Chows were to blame for Pearl Harbor; the Chows, they claimed, were Red Chinese spies. On occasion, overextending his skimpy English, Chow mounted a defense; he had served in the U.S. Army; his citizenship was blessed by the Department of War; he was a member of the American Legion. The toughs would laugh at the way he talked. Mrs. Chow cringed at his habit of addressing them as "sirs."

"Get out, get out," the widow hissed. She brought her fist down on the table. Cookies broke, fell to the floor.

"Yes, Missus," said Mrs. Chow, thinking how she'd have to clean up the mess.

The widow, whose great-great-great-grandfather had been a central figure within the faction advocating Washington's coronation, was eighty-six years old. Each day Mrs. Chow dispensed medications that kept her alive. At times, though, Mrs. Chow wondered if the widow would notice if she were handed an extra blue pill or one less red.

Mrs. Chow filled an enamel-coated washbasin with warm water from the tap. "What's she doing?" said the widow. "Stealing my water now, is she?" Since Mrs. Chow first came into her service, the widow, with the exception of her hip, had avoided serious illness. But how she had aged: her ears were enlarged; the opalescence in her eyes had spread; her hands worked as if they were chipped from glass. Some nights, awake in their twin-size bed, Mrs. Chow would imagine old age as green liquid that seeped into a person's cells, where it coagulated and, with time, crumbled, caving in the cheeks and the breasts it had once supported. In the dark she fretted that fluids from the widow's old body had taken refuge in her youthful cells. On such nights she reached for Chow, touched him through the cool top sheet, and was comforted by the fit of her fingers in the shallows between his ribs.

Mrs. Chow knelt at the foot of the wheelchair and set the washbasin on the floor. The widow laughed. "Where did my little thief go?" She laughed again, her eyes closing, her head dropping to her shoulder. "Now she's after my water. Better see if the tap's still there." Mrs. Chow abruptly swung aside the wheelchair's footrests and slipped off the widow's matted cloth slippers and dunked her puffy blue feet into the water. It was the widow's nap time, and before she could be put to bed, her physician prescribed a warm foot bath to stimulate circulation; otherwise, in her sleep, her blood might settle comfortably in her toes.

Chow was talking long distance to the widow's daughter in Texas. Earlier the widow had told the daughter that the Chows were threatening again to leave. She apologized for her mother's latest spell of wildness. "Humor her," the daughter said. "She must've had another one of her little strokes."

Later Mrs. Chow told her husband she wanted to leave the widow. "My fingers," she said, snapping off the rubber gloves the magazine ads claimed would guarantee her beautiful hands into the next century. "I wasn't made for such work."

As a girl her parents had sent her to a Christian school for training in Western-style art. The authorities agreed she was talented. As expected she excelled there. Her portrait of the King was chosen to hang in the school cafeteria. When the colonial Minister of Education on a tour of the school saw her painting he requested a sitting with the gifted young artist.

A date was set. The rumors said a successful sitting would bring her the ultimate fame: a trip to London to paint the royal family. But a month before the great day she refused to do the Minister's portrait. She gave no reason why; in fact, she stopped talking. The school administration was embarrassed, and her parents were furious. It was a great scandal; a mere child from a country at the edge of revolution but medieval in its affection for authority had snubbed the mighty British colonizers. She was sent home. Her parents first appealed to family pride, then they scolded and threatened her. She hid from them in a wardrobe, where her mother found her holding her fingers over lighted matches.

The great day came and went, no more momentous than the hundreds that had preceded it. That night her father apolo-

gized to the world for raising such a child. With a bamboo cane
he struck her outstretched hand — heaven help her if she let it
fall one inch — and as her bones were young and still pliant,
they didn't fracture or break, thus multiplying the blows she
had to endure.

"Who'd want you now?" her mother said. Her parents sent
her to live with a servant family. She could return home when
she was invited. On those rare occasions she refused to go. Many
years passed before she met Chow, who had come to the estate
seeking work. They were married on the condition he take her
far away. He left for America, promising to send for her when
he had saved enough money for her passage. She returned to
Hong Kong and worked as a secretary. Later she studied at the
university.

Now as she talked about leaving the widow, it wasn't the
chores or the old woman that she gave as the reason, though in
the past she had complained the widow was a nuisance, an in-
fantile brat born of an unwelcomed union. This time she said
she had a project in mind, a great canvas of a yet undetermined
subject. But that would come. Her imagination would return,
she said, once she was away from that house.

It was the morning of a late spring day. A silvery light filtered
through the wall of eucalyptus and warmed the dew on the
widow's roof, striking the plums and acacia, irises and lilies, in
such a way that, blended with the heavy air and the noise of a
thousand birds, one sensed the universe wasn't so vast, so cold,
or so angry, and even Mrs. Chow suspected that it was a loving
thing.

Mrs. Chow had finished her morning chores. She was in the
bathroom rinsing the smell of bacon from her hands. She
couldn't wash deep enough, however, to rid her fingertips of
perfumes from the widow's lotions and creams, which, over the
course of months, had seeped indelibly into the whorls. But
today her failure was less maddening. Today she was confident
the odors would eventually fade. She could affort to be patient.
They were going to interview for an apartment of their very
own.

"Is that new?" Chow asked, pointing to the blouse his wife

had on. He adjusted his necktie against the starched collar of a white short-sleeved shirt, which billowed out from baggy, pin-striped slacks. His hair was slicked back with fragrant pomade.

"I think it's the daughter's," said Mrs. Chow. "She won't miss it." Mrs. Chow smoothed the silk undershirt against her stomach. She guessed the shirt was as old as she was; the daughter probably had worn it in her teens. Narrow at the hips and the bust, it fit Mrs. Chow nicely. Such a slight figure, she believed, wasn't fit for labor.

Chow saw no reason to leave the estate. He had found his wife what he thought was the ideal home, certainly not as grand as her parents' place, but one she'd feel comfortable in. Why move, he argued, when there were no approaching armies, no floods, no one telling them to go? Mrs. Chow understood. It was just that he was very Chinese, and very peasant. Sometimes she would tease him. If the early Chinese sojourners who came to America were all Chows, she would say, the railroad wouldn't have been constructed, and Ohio would be all we know of California.

The Chows were riding in the widow's green Buick. As they approached the apartment building Mrs. Chow reapplied lipstick to her mouth.

It was a modern two-story stucco building, painted pink, surrounded by asphalt, with aluminum windows and a flat roof that met the sky like an engineer's level. Because their friends lived in the apartment in question, the Chows were already familiar with its layout. They went to the manager's house at the rear of the property. Here the grounds were also asphalt. Very contemporary, no greenery anywhere. The closest things to trees were the clothesline's posts and crossbars.

The manager's house was a tiny replica of the main building. Chow knocked on the screen door. A radio was on and the smell of baking rushed past the wire mesh. A cat came to the door, followed by a girl. "I'm Velvet," she said. "This is High Noon." She gave the cat's orange tail a tug. "She did this to me," said Velvet, throwing a wicked look at the room behind her. She picked at her hair, ragged as tossed salad; someone apparently had cut it while the girl was in motion. She had gray, almost colorless eyes, which, taken with her hair, gave her the appearance of agitated smoke.

A large woman emerged from the back room carrying a basket of laundry. She wasn't fat, but large in the way horses are
large. Her face was round and pink, with fierce little eyes and
hair the color of olive oil and dripping wet. Her arms were thick
and white, like soft tusks of ivory.

"It's the people from China," Velvet said.

The big woman nodded. "Open her up," she told the girl.
"It's okay."

The front room was a mess, cluttered with evidence of frantic
living. This was, perhaps, entropy in its final stages. The Chows
sat on the couch. From all around her Mrs. Chow sensed a slow
creep: the low ceiling seemed to be sinking, cat hairs clung to
clothing, a fine spray from the fish tank moistened her bare
arm.

No one said anything. It was as if they were sitting in a hospital waiting room. The girl watched the Chows. The large
woman stared at a green radio at her elbow broadcasting news
about the war. Every so often she looked suspiciously up at the
Chows. "You know me," she said abruptly. "I'm Remora Cass."

On her left, suspended in a swing, was the biggest, ugliest
baby Mrs. Chow had ever seen. It was dozing, arms dangling,
great melon head flung so far back that it appeared to be all
nostrils and chins. "A pig-boy," Mrs. Chow said in Chinese.
Velvet jabbed two fingers into the baby's rubbery cheeks. Then
she sprang back from the swing and executed a feral dance, all
elbows and knees. She seemed incapable of holding her body
still.

She caught Mrs. Chow's eye. "This is Ed," she said. "He has
no hair."

Mrs. Chow nodded.

"Quit," said Remora Cass, swatting at the girl as if she were a
fly. Then the big woman looked Mrs. Chow in the eyes and said,
"I know what you're thinking, and you're right. There's not a
baby in the state bigger than Ed; eight pounds, twelve ounces at
birth and he doubled that inside a month." She stopped, bringing her palms heavily down on her knees, and shook her wet
head. "You don't understand me, do you?"

Mrs. Chow was watching Velvet.

"Quit that!" Remora Cass slapped the girl's hand away from
the baby's face.

"Times like this I'd say it's a blessing my Aunt Eleanor's deaf," said Remora Cass. "I've gotten pretty good with sign language." From her overstuffed chair she repeated in pantomime what she had said about the baby.

Velvet mimicked her mother's generous, sweeping movements. When Remora Cass caught sight of her she added a left jab to the girl's head to her repertoire of gestures. Velvet slipped the punch with practiced ease. But the blow struck the swing set. Everyone tensed. Ed flapped his arms and went on sleeping. "Leave us alone," said Remora Cass, "before I really get mad."

The girl chased down the cat and skipped toward the door. "I'm bored anyway," she said.

Remora Cass asked the Chows questions, first about jobs and pets. Then she moved on to matters of politics and patriotism. "What's your feeling about the Red Chinese in Korea?"

A standard question. "Terrible," said Chow, giving his standard answer. "I'm sorry. Too much trouble."

Mrs. Chow sat by quietly. She admired Chow's effort. She had studied the language, but he did the talking; she wanted to move, but he had to plead their case; it was his kin back home who benefited from the new regime, but he had to badmouth it.

Remora Cass asked about children.

"No, no, no," Chow said, answering as his friend Bok had coached him. His face was slightly flushed from the question. Chow wanted children, many children. But whenever he discussed the matter with his wife, she answered that she already had one, meaning the old woman, of course, and that she was enough.

"Tell your wife later," the manager said, "what I'm about to tell you now. I don't care what jobs you do, just so long as you have them. What I say goes for the landlady. I'm willing to take a risk on you. Be nice to have nice quiet folks up there like Rikki and Bok. Rent paid up, I can live with anyone. Besides, I'm real partial to Chinese take-out. I know we'll do just right."

The baby moaned, rolling its head from side to side. His mother stared at him as if in all the world there were just the two of them.

Velvet came in holding a beach ball. She returned to her place beside the swing and started to hop, alternating legs, with the beach ball held to her head. "She must be in some kind of pain," Mrs. Chow said to her husband.

The girl mimicked the Chinese she heard. Mrs. Chow glared at Velvet, as if she were the widow during one of her spells. The look froze the girl, standing on one leg. Then she said, "Can Ed come out to play?"

Chow took hold of his wife's hand and squeezed it, as he did to brace himself before the roller coaster's forward plunge. Then in a single, well-rehearsed motion Remora Cass swept off her slipper and punched at the girl. Velvet masterfully side-stepped the slipper and let the beach ball fly. The slipper caught the swing set; the beach ball bounced off Ed's lap.

The collisions released charged particles into the air that seemed to hold everyone in a momentary state of paralysis. The baby's eyes peeled open, and he blinked at the ceiling. Soon his distended belly started rippling. He cried until he turned pur-ple, then devoted his energy to maintaining that hue. Mrs. Chow had never heard anything as harrowing. She visualized his cry as large cubes forcing their way into her ears.

Remora Cass picked Ed up and bounced on the balls of her feet. "You better start running," she said to Velvet, who was already on her way out the door.

Remora Cass half smiled at the Chows over the baby's shoul-der. "He'll quiet down sooner or later," she said.

Growing up, Mrs. Chow was the youngest of five girls. She had to endure the mothering of her sisters, who, at an early age, were already in training for their future roles. Each married in her teens, plucked in turn by a Portuguese, a German, a Brit, and a New Yorker. They had many babies. But Mrs. Chow thought little of her sisters' example. Even when her parents made life unbearable she never indulged in the hope that a man — foreign or domestic — or a child could save her from her unhappiness.

From the kitchen Remora Cass called Mrs. Chow. The big woman was busy with her baking. The baby was slung over her shoulder. "Let's try something," she said as she transferred the screaming Ed into Mrs. Chow's arms.

Ed was a difficult package. Not only was he heavy and hot

and sweaty but he spat and squirmed like a sack of kittens. She tried to think of how it was done. She tried to think of how a baby was held. She remembered Romanesque Madonnas cradling their gentlemanly babies in art history textbooks. If she could get his head up by hers, that would be a start.

Remora Cass told Mrs. Chow to try bouncing and showed her what she meant. "Makes him think he's still inside," she said. Ed emitted a long, sustained wail, then settled into a bout of hiccups. "You have a nice touch with him. He won't do that for just anyone."

As the baby quieted, a pain rolled from the heel of Mrs. Chow's brain, down through her pelvis, to a southern terminus at the backs of her knees. She couldn't blame the baby entirely for her discomfort. He wanted only to escape; animal instinct told him to leap from danger.

She was the one better equipped to escape. She imagined invading soldiers murdering livestock and planting flags in the soil of her ancestral estate, as if it were itself a little nation; they make history by the slaughter of generations of her family; they discover her in the wardrobe, striking matches; they ask where she has hidden her children, and she tells them there are none; they say, good, they'll save ammunition, but also too bad, so young and never to know the pleasure of children (even if they'd have to murder them). Perhaps this would be the subject of her painting, a nonrepresentational canvas that hinted at a world without light. Perhaps —

Ed interrupted her thought. He had developed a new trick. "Woop, woop, woop," he went, thrusting his pelvis against her sternum in the manner of an adult male in the act of mating. She called for Chow.

Remora Cass slid a cookie sheet into the oven and then stuck a bottle of baby formula into Ed's mouth. He drained it instantly. "You do have a way with him," said Remora Cass.

They walked into the front room. The baby was sleepy and dripping curds on his mother's shoulder. Under the swing High Noon, the cat, was licking the nipple of an abandoned bottle. "Scat!" she said. "Now where's my wash gone to?" she asked the room. "What's she up to now?" She scanned the little room, big feet planted in the deep, brown shag carpet, hands on her beefy hips, baby slung over her shoulder like a pelt. "Velvet —" she started. That was all. Her jaw locked, her gums gleamed, her eyes rolled into her skull. Her head flopped backwards, as if at the back of her neck there was a great hinge. Then she yawned, and the walls seemed to shake.

Remora Cass rubbed her eyes. "I'm bushed," she said.

Mrs. Chow went over to the screen door. Chow and the girl were at the clothesline. Except for their hands and legs, they were hidden behind a bed sheet. The girl's feet were in constant motion. From the basket her hands picked up pieces of laundry which Chow's hands then clipped to the line.

"Her daddy's hardly ever here," Remora Cass said. "Works all hours, he does. Has to." She patted Ed on the back, then rubbed her eyes again. "Looks like Velvet's found a friend. She won't do that with anyone. You two are naturals with my two. You should get you some of your own." She looked over at Mrs. Chow and laughed. "Maybe it's best you didn't get that. Here." She set the baby on Mrs. Chow's shoulder. "This is what it's like when they're sleeping."

Before leaving, the Chows went to look at Rikki and Bok's apartment. They climbed up the stairs. No one was home. Rikki and Bok had barely started to pack. Bok's naked man, surrounded by an assortment of spears and arrows, was still hanging on the living room wall. Bok had paid good money for the photograph: an aboriginal gent stares into the camera, he's smiling, his teeth are good and large, and in his palms he's holding his sex out like a prize eel.

Mrs. Chow looked at the photograph for as long as it was discreetly possible before she averted her eyes and made her usual remark about Bok's tastes. Beyond the building's edge she saw the manager's cottage, bleached white in the sun. Outside the front door Remora Cass sat in a folding chair, her eyes shut, her pie-tin face turned up to catch the rays, while Velvet, her feet anchored to the asphalt, rolled her mother's hair in pink curlers. Between the big woman's legs the baby lay in a wicker basket. He was quietly rocking from side to side. Remora Cass's chest rose and fell in the rhythm of sleep.

Driving home, they passed the boardwalk, and Mrs. Chow asked if they might stop.

Chow refused to ride the roller coaster in the daytime, no

matter how much Mrs. Chow teased. It was hard enough at night, when the heights from which the cars fell were lit by a few rows of bulbs. As he handed her an orange ticket, Chow said, "A drunk doesn't look in mirrors."

The Milky Way clattered into the terminus. After she boarded the ride, she watched Chow, who had wandered from the loading platform and was standing beside a popcorn wagon, looking up at a billboard. His hands were deep in the pockets of his trousers, his legs crossed at the shins. That had been his pose, the brim of his hat low on his brow, as he waited for her finally to pass through the gates of Immigration.

"Go on," an old woman said. "You'll be glad you did." The old woman nudged her young charge toward the empty seat in Mrs. Chow's car. "Go on, she won't bite." The girl looked back at the old woman. "Grand-muth-ther!" she said, and then reluctantly climbed in beside Mrs. Chow.

Once the attendant strapped the girl in, she turned from her grandmother and stared at her new companion. The machine jerked away from the platform. They were climbing the first ascent when Mrs. Chow snuck a look at the girl. She was met by the clearest eyes she had ever known, eyes that didn't shy from the encounter. The girl's pupils, despite the bright sun, were fully dilated, stretched with fear. Now that she had Mrs. Chow's attention she turned her gaze slowly toward the vertical track ahead. Mrs. Chow looked beyond the summit to the empty blue sky.

Within seconds they tumbled through that plane and plunged downward, the cars flung suddenly left and right, centrifugal force throwing Mrs. Chow against the girl's rigid body. She was surprised by Chow's absence.

It's gravity that makes the stomach fly, that causes the liver to flutter; it's the body catching up with the speed of falling. Until today, she had never known such sensations. Today there was a weightiness at her core, like a hard, concentrated pull inward, as if an incision has been made and a fist-sized magnet embedded.

Her arms flew up, two weak wings cutting the rush of wind. But it wasn't the old sensation this time, not the familiar embrace of the whole fleeting continent, but a grasp at something once there, now lost.

Chow had moved into position to see the riders' faces as they careened down the steepest stretch of track. Whenever he was up there with her, his eyes were clenched and his scream so wild and his grip on his life so tenuous that he never noticed her expression. At the top of the rise the cars seemed to stop momentarily, but then up and over, tumbling down, at what appeared, from his safe vantage point, a surprisingly slow speed. Arms shot up, the machine whooshed past him, preceded a split second earlier by the riders' collective scream. And for the first time Chow thought he heard her, she who loved this torture so, scream too.

As she was whipped skyward once more, her arms were wrapped around the little girl. Not in flight, not soaring, but anchored by another's being, as her parents stood against the liberators to protect their land.

Some curves, a gentle dip, one last sharp bend, and the ride rumbled to rest. The girl's breath was warm against Mrs. Chow's neck. For a moment longer she held on to the girl, whose small ribs were as thin as paintbrushes.

The Chows walked to the edge of the platform. He looked up at the billboard he had noticed earlier. It was a picture of an American woman with bright red hair, large red lips, and a slightly upturned nose; a fur was draped around her neck, pearls cut across her throat.

"What do you suppose they're selling?" he asked.

His wife pointed at the billboard. She read aloud what was printed there: "No other home permanent wave looks, feels, behaves so much like naturally curly hair."

She then gave a quick translation and asked what he thought of her curling her hair.

He made no reply. For some time now he couldn't lift his eyes from her.

"I won't do it," she said, "but what do you say?"

She turned away from him and stared a long time at the face on the billboard and then at the beach on the other side of the boardwalk and at the ocean, the Pacific Ocean, and at the horizon where all lines of sight converge, before she realized the land on the other side wouldn't come into view.

BHARATI MUKHERJEE

The Management of Grief

FROM FICTION NETWORK

A WOMAN I don't know is boiling tea the Indian way in my
kitchen. There are a lot of women I don't know in my kitchen,
whispering and moving tactfully. They open doors, rummage
through the pantry, and try not to ask me where things are
kept. They remind me of when my sons were small, on Mother's
Day or when Vikram and I were tired, and they would make
big, sloppy omelets. I would lie in bed pretending I didn't hear
them.

Dr. Sharma, the treasurer of the Indo-Canada Society, pulls
me into the hallway. He wants to know if I am worried about
money. His wife, who has just come up from the basement with
a tray of empty cups and glasses, scolds him. "Don't bother Mrs.
Bhave with mundane details." She looks so monstrously pregnant her baby must be days overdue. I tell her she shouldn't be
carrying heavy things. "Shaila," she says, smiling, "this is the
fifth." Then she grabs a teenager by his shirttails. He slips his
Walkman off his head. He has to be one of her four children;
they have the same domed and dented foreheads. "What's the
official word now?" she demands. The boy slips the headphones
back on. "They're acting evasive, Ma. They're saying it could be
an accident or a terrorist bomb."

All morning, the boys have been muttering, Sikh bomb, Sikh
bomb. The men, not using the word, bow their heads in agreement. Mrs. Sharma touches her forehead at such a word. At
least they've stopped talking about space debris and Russian
lasers.

Two radios are going in the dining room. They are tuned to different stations. Someone must have brought the radios down from my boys' bedrooms. I haven't gone into their rooms since Kusum came running across the front lawn in her bathrobe. She looked so funny, I was laughing when I opened the door.

The big TV in the den is being whizzed through American networks and cable channels.

"Damn!" some man swears bitterly. "How can these preachers carry on like nothing's happened?" I want to tell him we're not that important. You look at the audience, and at the preacher in his blue robe with his beautiful white hair, the potted palm trees under a blue sky, and you know they care about nothing.

The phone rings and rings. Dr. Sharma's taken charge. "We're with her," he keeps saying. "Yes, yes, the doctor has given calming pills. Yes, yes, pills are having necessary effect." I wonder if pills alone explain this calm. Not peace, just a deadening quiet. I was always controlled, but never repressed. Sound can reach me, but my body is tensed, ready to scream. I hear their voices all around me. I hear my boys and Vikram cry, "Mommy, Shaila!" and their screams insulate me, like headphones.

The woman boiling water tells her story again and again. "I got the news first. My cousin called from Halifax before six A.M., can you imagine? He'd gotten up for prayers and his son was studying for medical exams and he heard on a rock channel that something had happened to a plane. They said first it had disappeared from the radar, like a giant eraser just reached out. His father called me, so I said to him, what do you mean, 'something bad'? You mean a hijacking? And he said, *Behn*, there is no confirmation of anything yet, but check with your neighbors because a lot of them must be on that plane. So I called poor Kusum straight-away. I knew Kusum's husband and daughter were booked to go yesterday."

Kusum lives across the street from me. She and Satish had moved in less than a month ago. They said they needed a bigger place. All these people, the Sharmas and friends from the Indo-Canada Society, had been there for the housewarming. Satish and Kusum made tandoori on their big gas grill and even the white neighbors piled their plates high with that luridly red, charred, juicy chicken. Their younger daughter had danced, and even our boys had broken away from the Stanley Cup telecast to put in a reluctant appearance. Everyone took pictures for their albums and for the community newspapers — another of our families had made it big in Toronto — and now I wonder how many of those happy faces are gone. "Why does God give us so much if all along He intends to take it away?" Kusum asks me.

I nod. We sit on carpeted stairs, holding hands like children. "I never once told him that I loved him," I say. I was too much the well-brought-up woman. I was so well brought up I never felt comfortable calling my husband by his first name.

"It's all right," Kusum says. "He knew. My husband knew. They felt it. Modern young girls have to say it because what they feel is fake."

Kusum's daughter Pam runs in with an overnight case. Pam's in her McDonald's uniform. "Mummy! You have to get dressed!" Panic makes her cranky. "A reporter's on his way here."

"Why?"

"You want to talk to him in your bathrobe?" She starts to brush her mother's long hair. She's the daughter who's always in trouble. She dates Canadian boys and hangs out in the mall, shopping for tight sweaters. The younger one, the goody-goody one according to Pam, the one with a voice so sweet that when she sang *bhajans* for Ethiopian relief even a frugal man like my husband wrote out a hundred-dollar check, *she* was on that plane. *She* was going to spend July and August with grandparents because Pam wouldn't go. Pam said she'd rather waitress at McDonald's. "If it's a choice between Bombay and Wonderland, I'm picking Wonderland," she'd said.

"Leave me alone," Kusum yells. "You know what I want to do? If I didn't have to look after you now, I'd hang myself."

Pam's young face goes blotchy with pain. "Thanks," she says, "don't let me stop you."

"Hush," pregnant Mrs. Sharma scolds Pam. "Leave your mother alone. Mr. Sharma will tackle the reporters and fill out the forms. He'll say what has to be said."

Pam stands her ground. "You think I don't know what Mummy's thinking? *Why her?* That's what. That's sick! Mummy wishes my little sister were alive and I were dead."

Kusum's hand in mine is trembly hot. We continue to sit on the stairs.

She calls before she arrives, wondering if there's anything I need. Her name is Judith Templeton and she's an appointee of the provincial government. "Multiculturalism?" I ask, and she says "partially," but that her mandate is bigger. "I've been told you knew many of the people on the flight," she says. "Perhaps if you'd agree to help us reach the others . . . ?"

She gives me time at least to put on tea water and pick up the mess in the front room. I have a few *samosas* from Kusum's housewarming that I could fry up, but then I think, why prolong this visit?

Judith Templeton is much younger than she sounded. She wears a blue suit with a white blouse and a polka-dot tie. Her blond hair is cut short, her only jewelry is pearl-drop earrings. Her briefcase is new and expensive looking, a gleaming cordovan leather. She sits with it across her lap. When she looks out the front windows onto the street, her contact lenses seem to float in front of her light blue eyes.

"What sort of help do you want from me?" I ask. She has refused the tea, out of politeness, but I insist, along with some slightly stale biscuits.

"I have no experience," she admits. "That is, I have an M.S.W. and I've worked in liaison with accident victims, but I mean I have no experience with a tragedy of this scale —"

"Who could?" I ask.

"— and with the complications of culture, language, and customs. Someone mentioned that Mrs. Bhave is a pillar — because you've taken it more calmly."

At this, perhaps, I frown, for she reaches forward, almost to take my hand. "I hope you understand my meaning, Mrs. Bhave. There are hundreds of people in Metro directly affected, like you, and some of them speak no English. There are some widows who've never handled money or gone on a bus, and there are old parents who still haven't eaten or gone outside their bedrooms. Some houses and apartments have been looted.

Some wives are still hysterical. Some husbands are in shock and
profound depression. We want to help, but our hands are tied
in so many ways. We have to distribute money to some people,
and there are legal documents — these things can be done. We
have interpreters, but we don't always have the human touch,
or maybe the right human touch. We don't want to make mistakes, Mrs. Bhave, and that's why we'd like to ask you to help
us."

"More mistakes, you mean," I say.

"Police matters are not in my hands," she answers.

"Nothing I can do will make any difference," I say. "We must
all grieve in our own way."

"But you are coping very well. All the people said, Mrs. Bhave
is the strongest person of all. Perhaps if the others could see
you, talk with you, it would help them."

"By the standards of the people you call hysterical, I am behaving very oddly and very badly, Miss Templeton." I want to
say to her, *I wish I could scream, starve, walk into Lake Ontario, jump
from a bridge.* "They would not see me as a model. I do not see
myself as a model."

I am a freak. No one who has ever known me would think of
me reacting this way. This terrible calm will not go away.

She asks me if she may call again, after I get back from a long
trip that we all must make. "Of course," I say. "Feel free to call,
anytime."

Four days later, I find Kusum squatting on a rock overlooking
a bay in Ireland. It isn't a big rock, but it juts sharply out over
water. This is as close as we'll ever get to them. June breezes
balloon out her sari and unpin her knee-length hair. She has
the bewildered look of a sea creature whom the tides have
stranded.

It's been one hundred hours since Kusum came stumbling
and screaming across my lawn. Waiting around the hospital,
we've heard many stories. The police, the diplomats, they tell us
things thinking that we're strong, that knowledge is helpful to
the grieving, and maybe it is. Some, I know, prefer ignorance,
or their own versions. The plane broke into two, they say. Un-
consciousness was instantaneous. No one suffered. My boys

must have just finished their breakfasts. They loved eating on planes, they loved the smallness of plates, knives, and forks. Last year they saved the airline salt and pepper shakers. Half an hour more and they would have made it to Heathrow.

Kusum says that we can't escape our fate. She says that all those people — our husbands, my boys, her girl with the nightingale voice, all those Hindus, Christians, Sikhs, Muslims, Parsis, and atheists on that plane — were fated to die together off this beautiful bay. She learned this from a swami in Toronto.

I have my Valium.

Six of us "relatives" — two widows and four widowers — chose to spend the day today by the waters instead of sitting in a hospital room and scanning photographs of the dead. That's what they call us now: relatives. I've looked through twenty-seven photos in two days. They're very kind to us, the Irish are very understanding. Sometimes understanding means freeing a tourist bus for this trip to the bay, so we can pretend to spy our loved ones through the glassiness of waves or in sun-speckled cloud shapes.

I could die here, too, and be content.

"What is that, out there?" She's standing and flapping her hands, and for a moment I see a head shape bobbing in the waves. She's standing in the water, I on the boulder. The tide is low, and a round, black, head-sized rock has just risen from the waves. She returns, her sari end dripping and ruined, and her face is a twisted remnant of hope, the way mine was a hundred hours ago, still laughing but inwardly knowing that nothing but the ultimate tragedy could bring two women together at six o'clock on a Sunday morning. I watch her face sag into blankness.

"That water felt warm, Shaila," she says at length.

"You can't," I say. "We have to wait for our turn to come."

I haven't eaten in four days, haven't brushed my teeth.

"I know," she says. "I tell myself I have no right to grieve. They are in a better place than we are. My swami says depression is a sign of our selfishness."

Maybe I'm selfish. Selfishly I break away from Kusum and run, sandals slapping against stones, to the water's edge. What if my boys aren't lying pinned under the debris? What if they aren't stuck a mile below that innocent blue chop? What if, given the strong currents . . .

Now I've ruined my sari, one of my best. Kusum has joined me, knee deep in water that feels to me like a swimming pool. I could settle in the water, and my husband would take my hand and the boys would slap water in my face just to see me scream.

"Do you remember what good swimmers my boys were, Kusum?"

"I saw the medals," she says.

One of the widowers, Dr. Ranganathan from Montreal, walks out to us, carrying his shoes in one hand. He's an electrical engineer. Someone at the hotel mentioned his work is famous around the world, something about the place where physics and electricity come together. He has lost a huge family, something indescribable. "With some luck," Dr. Ranganathan suggests to me, "a good swimmer could make it safely to some island. It is quite possible that there may be many, many microscopic islets scattered around."

"You're not just saying that?" I tell Dr. Ranganathan about Vinod, my elder son. Last year he took diving as well.

"It's a parent's duty to hope," he says. "It is foolish to rule out possibilities that have not been tested. I myself have not surrendered hope."

Kusum is sobbing once again. "Dear lady," he says, laying his free hand on her arm, and she calms down.

"Vinod is how old?" he asks me. He's very careful, as we all are. *Is*, not was.

"Fourteen. Yesterday he was fourteen. His father and uncle were going to take him down to the Taj and give him a big birthday party. I couldn't go with them because I couldn't get two weeks off from my stupid job in June." I process bills for a travel agent. June is a big travel month.

Dr. Ranganathan whips the pockets of his suit jacket inside out. Squashed roses, in darkening shades of pink, float on the water. He tore the roses off creepers in somebody's garden. He didn't ask anyone if he could pluck the roses, but now there's been an article about it in the local papers. When you see an Indian person, it says, please give them flowers.

"A strong youth of fourteen," he says, "can very likely pull to safety a younger one."

My sons, though four years apart, were very close. Vinod wouldn't let Mithun drown. *Electrical engineering*, I think, foolishly perhaps: this man knows important secrets of the universe, things closed to me. Relief spins me lightheaded. No wonder my boys' photographs haven't turned up in the gallery of photos of the recovered dead. "Such pretty roses," I say.

"My wife loved pink roses. Every Friday I had to bring a bunch home. I used to say, Why? After twenty-odd years of marriage you're still needing proof positive of my love?" He has identified his wife and three of his children. Then others from Montreal, the lucky ones, intact families with no survivors. He chuckles as he wades back to shore. Then he swings around to ask me a question. "Mrs. Bhave, you are wanting to throw in some roses for your loved ones? I have two big ones left."

But I have other things to float: Vinod's pocket calculator; a half-painted model B-52 for my Mithun. They'd want them on their island. And for my husband? For him I let fall into the calm, glassy waters a poem I wrote in the hospital yesterday. Finally he'll know my feelings for him.

"Don't tumble, the rocks are slippery," Dr. Ranganathan cautions. He holds out a hand for me to grab.

Then it's time to get back on the bus, time to rush back to our waiting posts on hospital benches.

Kusum is one of the lucky ones. The lucky ones flew here, identified in multiplicate their loved ones, then will fly to India with the bodies for proper ceremonies. Satish is one of the few males who surfaced. The photos of faces we saw on the walls in an office at Heathrow and here in the hospital are mostly of women. Women have more body fat, a nun said to me matter-of-factly. They float better.

Today I was stopped by a young sailor on the street. He had loaded bodies, he'd gone into the water when — he checks my face for signs of strength — when the sharks were first spotted. I don't blush, and he breaks down. "It's all right," I say. "Thank you." I heard about the sharks from Dr. Ranganathan. In his orderly mind, science brings understanding, it holds no terror. It is the shark's duty. For every deer there is a hunter, for every fish a fisherman.

The Irish are not shy; they rush to me and give me hugs and

some are crying. I cannot imagine reactions like that on the streets of Toronto. Just strangers, and I am touched. Some carry flowers with them and give them to any Indian they see.

After lunch, a policeman I have gotten to know quite well catches hold of me. He says he thinks he has a match for Vinod. I explain what a good swimmer Vinod is.

"You want me with you when you look at photos?" Dr. Ranganathan walks ahead of me into the picture gallery. In these matters, he is a scientist, and I am grateful. It is a new perspective. "They have performed miracles," he says. "We are indebted to them."

The first day or two the policemen showed us relatives only one picture at a time; now they're in a hurry, they're eager to lay out the possibles, and even the probables.

The face on the photo is of a boy much like Vinod; the same intelligent eyes, the same thick brows dipping into a V. But this boy's features, even his cheeks, are puffier, wider, mushier.

"No." My gaze is pulled by other pictures. There are five other boys who look like Vinod.

The nun assigned to console me rubs the first picture with a fingertip. "When they've been in the water for a while, love, they look a little heavier." The bones under the skin are broken, they said on the first day — try to adjust your memories. It's important.

"It's not him. I'm his mother. I'd know."

"I know this one!" Dr. Ranganathan cries out, and suddenly, from the back of the gallery, "And this one!" I think he senses that I don't want to find my boys. "They are the Kutty brothers. They were also from Montreal." I don't mean to be crying. On the contrary, I am ecstatic. My suitcase in the hotel is packed heavy with dry clothes for my boys.

The policeman starts to cry. "I am so sorry, I am so sorry, ma'am. I really thought we had a match."

With the nun ahead of us and the policeman behind, we, the unlucky ones without our children's bodies, file out of the makeshift gallery.

From Ireland most of us go on to India. Kusum and I take the same direct flight to Bombay, so I can help her clear customs quickly. But we have to argue with a man in uniform. He has large boils on his face. The boils swell and glow with sweat as we argue with him. He wants Kusum to wait in line and he refuses to take authority because his boss is on a tea break. But Kusum won't let her coffins out of sight, and I shan't desert her though I know that my parents, elderly and diabetic, must be waiting in a stuffy car in a scorching lot.

"You bastard!" I scream at the man with the popping boils. Other passengers press closer. "You think we're smuggling contraband in those coffins!"

Once upon a time we were well-brought-up women; we were dutiful wives who kept our heads veiled, our voices shy and sweet.

In India, I become, once again, an only child of rich, ailing parents. Old friends of the family come to pay their respects. Some are Sikh, and inwardly, involuntarily, I cringe. My parents are progressive people; they do not blame communities for a few individuals.

In Canada it is a different story now.

"Stay longer," my mother pleads. "Canada is a cold place. Why would you want to be by yourself?" I stay.

Three months pass. Then another.

"Vikram wouldn't have wanted you to give up things!" they protest. They call my husband by the name he was born with. In Toronto he'd changed to Vik so the men he worked with at his office would find his name as easy as Rod or Chris. "You know, the dead aren't cut off from us!"

My grandmother, the spoiled daughter of a rich zamindar, shaved her head with rusty razor blades when she was widowed at sixteen. My grandfather died of childhood diabetes when he was nineteen, and she saw herself as the harbinger of bad luck. My mother grew up without parents, raised indifferently by an uncle, while her true mother slept in a hut behind the main estate house and took her food with the servants. She grew up a rationalist. My parents abhor mindless mortification.

The zamindar's daughter kept stubborn faith in Vedic rituals; my parents rebelled. I am trapped between two modes of knowledge. At thirty-six, I am too old to start over and too young to give up. Like my husband's spirit, I flutter between worlds.

*

Courting aphasia, we travel. We travel with our phalanx of servants and poor relatives. To hill stations and to beach resorts.
We play contract bridge in dusty gymkhana clubs. We ride
stubby ponies up crumbly mountain trails. At tea dances, we let
ourselves be twirled twice round the ballroom. We hit the holy
spots we hadn't made time for before. In Varanasi, Kalighat,
Rishikesh, Hardwar, astrologers and palmists seek me out and
for a fee offer me cosmic consolations.

Already the widowers among us are being shown new bride
candidates. They cannot resist the call of custom, the authority
of their parents and older brothers. They must marry; it is the
duty of a man to look after a wife. The new wives will be young
widows with children, destitute but of good family. They will
make loving wives, but the men will shun them. I've had calls
from the men over crackling Indian telephone lines. "Save me,"
they say, these substantial, educated, successful men of forty.
"My parents are arranging a marriage for me." In a month they
will have buried one family and returned to Canada with a new
bride and partial family.

I am comparatively lucky. No one here thinks of arranging a
husband for an unlucky widow.

Then, on the third day of the sixth month into this odyssey,
in an abandoned temple in a tiny Himalayan village, as I make
my offering of flowers and sweetmeats to the god of a tribe of
animists, my husband descends to me. He is squatting next to a
scrawny sadhu in moth-eaten robes. Vikram wears the vanilla
suit he wore the last time I hugged him. The sadhu tosses petals
on a butter-fed flame, reciting Sanskrit mantras, and sweeps his
face of flies. My husband takes my hands in his.

You're beautiful, he starts. Then, *What are you doing here?*

Shall I stay? I ask. He only smiles, but already the image is
fading. *You must finish alone what we started together.* No sea-
weed wreathes his mouth. He speaks too fast, just as he used to
when we were an envied family in our pink split-level. He is
gone.

In the windowless altar room, smoky with joss sticks and clar-
ified butter lamps, a sweaty hand gropes for my blouse. I do not
shriek. The sadhu arranges his robe. The lamps hiss and sputter
out.

When we come out of the temple, my mother says, "Did you feel something weird in there?"

My mother has no patience with ghosts, prophetic dreams, holy men, and cults.

"No," I lie. "Nothing."

But she knows that she's lost me. She knows that in days I shall be leaving.

Kusum's put up her house for sale. She wants to live in an ashram in Hardwar. Moving to Hardwar was her swami's idea. Her swami runs two ashrams, the one in Hardwar and another here in Toronto.

"Don't run away," I tell her.

"I'm not running away," she says. "I'm pursuing inner peace. You think you or that Ranganathan fellow are better off?"

Pam's left for California. She wants to do some modeling, she says. She says when she comes into her share of the insurance money she'll open a yoga-cum-aerobics studio in Hollywood. She sends me postcards so naughty I daren't leave them on the coffee table. Her mother has withdrawn from her and the world.

The rest of us don't lose touch, that's the point. Talk is all we have, says Dr. Ranganathan, who has also resisted his relatives and returned to Montreal and to his job, alone. He says, Whom better to talk with than other relatives? We've been melted down and recast as a new tribe.

He calls me twice a week from Montreal. Every Wednesday night and every Saturday afternoon. He is changing jobs, going to Ottawa. But Ottawa is over a hundred miles away, and he is forced to drive two hundred and twenty miles a day from his home in Montreal. He can't bring himself to sell his house. The house is a temple, he says; the king-sized bed in the master bedroom is a shrine. He sleeps on a folding cot. A devotee.

There are still some hysterical relatives. Judith Templeton's list of those needing help and those who've "accepted" is in nearly perfect balance. Acceptance means you speak of your family in the past tense and you make active plans for moving ahead with your life. There are courses at Seneca and Ryerson we could be taking. Her gleaming leather briefcase is full of college catalogues and lists of cultural societies that need our help. She has done impressive work, I tell her.

"In the textbooks on grief management," she replies — I am her confidante, I realize, one of the few whose grief has not sprung bizarre obsessions — "there are stages to pass through: rejection, depression, acceptance, reconstruction." She has compiled a chart and finds that six months after the tragedy, none of us still rejects reality, but only a handful are reconstructing. "Depressed acceptance" is the plateau we've reached. Remarriage is a major step in reconstruction (though she's a little surprised, even shocked, over *how* quickly some of the men have taken on new families). Selling one's house and changing jobs and cities is healthy.

How to tell Judith Templeton that my family surrounds me, and that like creatures in epics, they've changed shapes? She sees me as calm and accepting but worries that I have no job, no career. My closest friends are worse off than I. I cannot tell her my days, even my nights, are thrilling.

She asks me to help with families she can't reach at all. An elderly couple in Agincourt whose sons were killed just weeks after they had brought their parents over from a village in Punjab. From their names, I know they are Sikh. Judith Templeton and a translator have visited them twice with offers of money for airfare to Ireland, with bank forms, power-of-attorney forms, but they have refused to sign, or to leave their tiny apartment. Their sons' money is frozen in the bank. Their sons' investment apartments have been trashed by tenants, the furnishings sold off. The parents fear that anything they sign or any money they receive will end the company's or the country's obligations to them. They fear they are selling their sons for two airline tickets to a place they've never seen.

The high-rise apartment is a tower of Indians and West Indians, with a sprinkling of Orientals. The nearest bus-stop kiosk is lined with women in saris. Boys practice cricket in the parking lot. Inside the building, even I wince a bit from the ferocity of onion fumes, the distinctive and immediate Indianness of frying ghee, but Judith Templeton maintains a steady flow of information. These poor old people are in imminent danger of losing their place and all their services.

I say to her, "They are Sikh. They will not open up to a Hindu woman." And what I want to add is, as much as I try not to, I stiffen now at the sight of beards and turbans. I remember a time when we all trusted each other in this new country, it was only the new country we worried about.

The two rooms are dark and stuffy. The lights are off, and an oil lamp sputters on the coffee table. The bent old lady has let us in, and her husband is wrapping a white turban over his oiled, hip-length hair. She immediately goes to the kitchen, and I hear the most familiar sound of an Indian home, tap water hitting and filling a teapot.

They have not paid their utility bills, out of fear and inability to write a check. The telephone is gone; electricity and gas and water are soon to follow. They have told Judith their sons will provide. They are good boys, and they have always earned and looked after their parents.

We converse a bit in Hindi. They do not ask about the crash and I wonder if I should bring it up. If they think I am here merely as a translator, then they may feel insulted. There are thousands of Punjabi speakers, Sikhs, in Toronto to do a better job. And so I say to the old lady, "I too have lost my sons, and my husband, in the crash."

Her eyes immediately fill with tears. The man mutters a few words which sound like a blessing. "God provides and God takes away," he says.

I want to say, But only men destroy and give back nothing. "My boys and my husband are not coming back," I say. "We have to understand that."

Now the old woman responds. "But who is to say? Man alone does not decide these things." To this her husband adds his agreement.

Judith asks about the bank papers, the release forms. With a stroke of the pen, they will have a provincial trustee to pay their bills, invest their money, send them a monthly pension.

"Do you know this woman?" I ask them.

The man raises his hand from the table, turns it over, and

seems to regard each finger separately before he answers. "This young lady is always coming here, we make tea for her, and she leaves papers for us to sign." His eyes scan a pile of papers in the corner of the room. "Soon we will be out of tea, then will she go away?"

The old lady adds, "I have asked my neighbors and no one else gets *angrezi* visitors. What have we done?"

"It's her job," I try to explain. "The government is worried. Soon you will have no place to stay, no lights, no gas, no water."

"Government will get its money. Tell her not to worry, we are honorable people."

I try to explain the government wishes to give money, not take. He raises his hand. "Let them take," he says. "We are accustomed to that. That is no problem."

"We are strong people," says the wife. "Tell her that."

"Who needs all this machinery?" demands the husband. "It is unhealthy, the bright lights, the cold air on a hot day, the cold food, the four gas rings. God will provide, not government."

"When our boys return," the mother says.

Her husband sucks his teeth. "Enough talk," he says.

Judith breaks in. "Have you convinced them?" The snaps on her cordovan briefcase go off like firecrackers in that quiet apartment. She lays the sheaf of legal papers on the coffee table. "If they can't write their names, an X will do — I've told them that."

Now the old lady has shuffled to the kitchen and soon emerges with a pot of tea and two cups. "I think my bladder will go first on a job like this," Judith says to me, smiling. "If only there was some way of reaching them. Please thank her for the tea. Tell her she's very kind."

I nod in Judith's direction and tell them in Hindi, "She thanks you for the tea. She thinks you are being very hospitable but she doesn't have the slightest idea what it means."

I want to say, Humor her. I want to say, My boys and my husband are with me too, more than ever. I look in the old man's eyes and I can read his stubborn, peasant's message: *I have protected this woman as best I can. She is the only person I have left. Give to me or take from me what you will, but I will not sign for it. I will not pretend that I accept.*

In the car, Judith says, "You see what I'm up against? I'm
sure they're lovely people, but their stubbornness and ignorance
are driving me crazy. They think signing a paper is signing their
sons' death warrants, don't they?"

I am looking out the window. I want to say, *In our culture, it is
a parent's duty to hope.*

"Now Shaila, this next woman is a real mess. She cries day
and night, and she refuses all medical help. We may have to —"

"Let me out at the subway," I say.

"I beg your pardon?" I can feel those blue eyes staring at me.

It would not be like her to disobey. She merely disapproves,
and slows at a corner to let me out. Her voice is plaintive. "Is
there anything I said? Anything I did?"

I could answer her suddenly in a dozen ways, but I choose
not to. "Shaila? Let's talk about it," I hear, then slam the door.

A wife and mother begins her new life in a new country, and
that life is cut short. Yet her husband tells her, Complete what
we have started. We, who stayed out of politics and came halfway around the world to avoid religious and political feuding,
have been the first in the New World to die from it. I no longer
know what we started, nor how to complete it. I write letters to
the editors of local papers and to members of Parliament. Now
at least they admit it was a bomb. One MP answers back, with
sympathy, but with a challenge. You want to make a difference?
Work on a campaign. Work on mine. Politicize the Indian voter.

My husband's old lawyer helps me set up a trust. Vikram was
a saver and a careful investor. He had saved the boys' boarding
school and college fees. I sell the pink house at four times what
we paid for it and take a small apartment downtown. I am
looking for a charity to support.

We are deep in the Toronto winter, gray skies, icy pavements. I
stay indoors, watching television. I have tried to assess my situation, how best to live my life, to complete what we began so
many years ago. Kusum has written me from Hardwar that her
life is now serene. She has seen Satish and has heard her daughter sing again. Kusum was on a pilgrimage, passing through a
village, when she heard a young girl's voice, singing one of her

daughter's favorite *bhajans*. She followed the music through the squalor of a Himalayan village, to a hut where a young girl, an exact replica of her daughter, was fanning coals under the kitchen fire. When she appeared, the girl cried out, "Ma!" and ran away. What did I think of that?

I think I can only envy her.

Pam didn't make it to California, but writes me from Vancouver. She works in a department store, giving makeup hints to Indian and Oriental girls. Dr. Ranganathan has given up his commute, given up his house and job, and accepted an academic position in Texas, where no one knows his story and he has vowed not to tell it. He calls me now once a week.

I wait, I listen and I pray, but Vikram has not returned to me. The voices and the shapes and the nights filled with visions ended abruptly several weeks ago.

I take it as a sign.

One rare, beautiful, sunny day last week, returning from a small errand on Yonge Street, I was walking through the park from the subway to my apartment. I live equidistant from the Ontario Houses of Parliament and the University of Toronto. The day was not cold, but something in the bare trees caught my attention. I looked up from the gravel, into the branches and the clear blue sky beyond. I thought I heard the rustling of larger forms, and I waited a moment for voices. Nothing.

"What?" I asked.

Then as I stood in the path looking north to Queen's Park and west to the university, I heard the voices of my family one last time. *Your time has come*, they said. *Go, be brave.*

I do not know where this voyage I have begun will end. I do not know which direction I will take. I dropped the package on a park bench and started walking.

ALICE MUNRO

Meneseteung

FROM THE NEW YORKER

I

Columbine, bloodroot,
And wild bergamot,
Gathering armfuls,
Giddily we go.

OFFERINGS, the book is called. Gold lettering on a dull-blue
cover. The author's full name underneath: Almeda Joynt Roth.
The local paper, the *Vidette*, referred to her as "our poetess."
There seems to be a mixture of respect and contempt, both for
her calling and for her sex — or for their predictable conjunc-
ture. In the front of the book is a photograph, with the photographer's name in one corner, and the date: 1865. The book was
published later, in 1873.

The poetess has a long face; a rather long nose; full, somber
dark eyes, which seem ready to roll down her cheeks like giant
tears; a lot of dark hair gathered around her face in droopy
rolls and curtains. A streak of gray hair plain to see, although
she is, in this picture, only twenty-five. Not a pretty girl but the
sort of woman who may age well, who probably won't get fat.
She wears a tucked and braid-trimmed dark dress or jacket, with
a lacy, floppy arrangement of white material — frills or a bow
— filling the deep V at the neck. She also wears a hat, which
might be made of velvet, in a dark color to match the dress. It's
the untrimmed, shapeless hat, something like a soft beret, that

makes me see artistic intentions, or at least a shy and stubborn eccentricity, in this young woman, whose long neck and forward-inclining head indicate as well that she is tall and slender and somewhat awkward. From the waist up, she looks like a young nobleman of another century. But perhaps it was the fashion.

"In 1854," she writes in the preface to her book, "my father brought us — my mother, my sister Catherine, my brother William, and me — to the wilds of Canada West (as it then was). My father was a harness-maker by trade, but a cultivated man who could quote by heart from the Bible, Shakespeare, and the writings of Edmund Burke. He prospered in this newly opened land and was able to set up a harness and leather-goods store, and after a year to build the comfortable house in which I live (alone) today. I was fourteen years old, the eldest of the children, when we came into this country from Kingston, a town whose handsome streets I have not seen again but often remember. My sister was eleven and my brother nine. The third summer that we lived here, my brother and sister were taken ill of a prevalent fever and died within a few days of each other. My dear mother did not regain her spirits after this blow to our family. Her health declined, and after another three years she died. I then became housekeeper to my father and was happy to make his home for twelve years, until he died suddenly one morning at his shop.

"From my earliest years I have delighted in verse and I have occupied myself — and sometimes allayed my griefs, which have been no more, I know, than any sojourner on earth must encounter — with many floundering efforts at its composition. My fingers, indeed, were always too clumsy for crochetwork, and those dazzling productions of embroidery which one sees often today — the overflowing fruit and flower baskets, the little Dutch boys, the bonneted maidens with their watering cans — have likewise proved to be beyond my skill. So I offer instead, as the product of my leisure hours, these rude posies, these ballads, couplets, reflections."

Titles of some of the poems: "Children at Their Games," "The Gypsy Fair," "A Visit to My Family," "Angels in the Snow," "Champlain at the Mouth of the Meneseteung," "The Passing of the Old Forest," and "A Garden Medley." There are some other, shorter poems, about birds and wildflowers and snowstorms. There is some comically intentioned doggerel about what people are thinking about as they listen to the sermon in church.

"Children at Their Games": The writer, a child, is playing with her brother and sister — one of those games in which children on different sides try to entice and catch each other. She plays on in the deepening twilight, until she realizes that she is alone, and much older. Still she hears the (ghostly) voices of her brother and sister calling. *Come over, come over, let Meda come over.* (Perhaps Almeda was called Meda in the family, or perhaps she shortened her name to fit the poem.)

"The Gypsy Fair": The Gypsies have an encampment near the town, a "fair," where they sell cloth and trinkets, and the writer as a child is afraid that she may be stolen by them, taken away from her family. Instead, her family has been taken away from her, stolen by Gypsies she can't locate or bargain with.

"A Visit to My Family": A visit to the cemetery, a one-sided conversation.

"Angels in the Snow": The writer once taught her brother and sister to make "angels" by lying down in the snow and moving their arms to create wing shapes. Her brother always jumped up carelessly, leaving an angel with a crippled wing. Will this be made perfect in Heaven, or will he be flying with his own makeshift, in circles?

"Champlain at the Mouth of the Meneseteung": This poem celebrates the popular, untrue belief that the explorer sailed down the eastern shore of Lake Huron and landed at the mouth of the major river.

"The Passing of the Old Forest": A list of all the trees — their names, appearance, and uses — that were cut down in the original forest, with a general description of the bears, wolves, eagles, deer, waterfowl.

"A Garden Medley": Perhaps planned as a companion to the forest poem. Catalogue of plants brought from European countries, with bits of history and legend attached, and final Canadianness resulting from this mixture.

The poems are written in quatrains or couplets. There are a

couple of attempts at sonnets, but mostly the rhyme scheme is simple — *abab* or *abcb*. The rhyme used is what was once called "masculine" ("shore"/"before"), though once in a while it is "feminine" ("quiver"/"river"). Are those terms familiar anymore? No poem is unrhymed.

II

> White roses cold as snow
> Bloom where those "angels" lie.
> Do they but rest below
> Or, in God's wonder, fly?

In 1879, Almeda Roth was still living in the house at the corner of Pearl and Dufferin streets, the house her father had built for his family. The house is there today: the manager of the liquor store lives in it. It's covered with aluminum siding; a closed-in porch has replaced the veranda. The woodshed, the fence, the gates, the privy, the barn — all these are gone. A photograph taken in the eighteen-eighties shows them all in place. The house and fence look a little shabby, in need of paint, but perhaps that is just because of the bleached-out look of the brownish photograph. The lace-curtained windows look like white eyes. No big shade tree is in sight, and, in fact, the tall elms that overshadowed the town until the nineteen-fifties, as well as the maples that shade it now, are skinny young trees with rough fences around them to protect them from the cows. Without the shelter of those trees, there is a great exposure — back yards, clotheslines, woodpiles, patchy sheds and barns and privies — all bare, exposed, provisional looking. Few houses would have anything like a lawn, just a patch of plantains and anthills and raked dirt. Perhaps petunias growing on top of a stump, in a round box. Only the main street is graveled; the other streets are dirt roads, muddy or dusty according to season. Yards must be fenced to keep animals out. Cows are tethered in vacant lots or pastured in back yards, but sometimes they get loose. Pigs get loose, too, and dogs roam free or nap in a lordly way on the boardwalks. The town has taken root, it's not going to vanish,

yet it still has some of the look of an encampment. And, like an
encampment, it's busy all the time — full of people, who, within
the town, usually walk wherever they're going; full of animals,
which leave horse buns, cowpats, dog turds, that ladies have to
hitch up their skirts for; full of the noise of building and of
drivers shouting at their horses and of the trains that come in
several times a day.

I read about that life in the *Vidette*.

The population is younger than it is now, than it will ever be
again. People past fifty usually don't come to a raw, new place.
There are quite a few people in the cemetery already, but most
of them died young, in accidents or childbirth or epidemics.
It's youth that's in evidence in town. Children — boys — rove
through the streets in gangs. School is compulsory for only four
months a year, and there are lots of occasional jobs that even a
child of eight or nine can do — pulling flax, holding horses,
delivering groceries, sweeping the boardwalk in front of stores.
A good deal of time they spend looking for adventures. One
day they follow an old woman, a drunk nicknamed Queen
Aggie. They get her into a wheelbarrow and trundle her all
over town, then dump her into a ditch to sober her up. They
also spend a lot of time around the railway station. They jump
on shunting cars and dart between them and dare each other to
take chances, which once in a while result in their getting
maimed or killed. And they keep an eye out for any strangers
coming into town. They follow them, offer to carry their bags,
and direct them (for a five-cent piece) to a hotel. Strangers who
don't look so prosperous are taunted and tormented. Speculation surrounds all of them — it's like a cloud of flies. Are they
coming to town to start up a new business, to persuade people
to invest in some scheme, to sell cures or gimmicks, to preach
on the street corners? All these things are possible any day of
the week. Be on your guard, the *Vidette* tells people. These are
times of opportunity and danger. Tramps, confidence men,
hucksters, shysters, plain thieves, are traveling the roads, and
particularly the railroads. Thefts are announced: money in-
vested and never seen again, a pair of trousers taken from the
clothesline, wood from the woodpile, eggs from the henhouse.
Such incidents increase in the hot weather.

Hot weather brings accidents, too. More horses run wild then, upsetting buggies. Hands caught in the wringer while doing the washing, a man lopped in two at the sawmill, a leaping boy killed in a fall of lumber at the lumberyard. Nobody sleeps well. Babies wither with summer complaint, and fat people can't catch their breath. Bodies must be buried in a hurry. One day a man goes through the streets ringing a cowbell and calling "Repent! Repent!" It's not a stranger this time, it's a young man who works at the butcher shop. Take him home, wrap him in cold wet cloths, give him some nerve medicine, keep him in bed, pray for his wits. If he doesn't recover, he must go to the asylum.

Almeda Roth's house faces on Dufferin Street, which is a street of considerable respectability. On this street merchants, a mill owner, an operator of salt wells, have their houses. But Pearl Street, which her back windows overlook and her back gate opens onto, is another story. Workmen's houses are adjacent to hers. Small but decent row houses — that is all right. Things deteriorate toward the end of the block, and the next, last one becomes dismal. Nobody but the poorest people, the unrespectable and undeserving poor, would live there at the edge of a boghole (drained since then), called the Pearl Street Swamp. Bushy and luxuriant weeds grow there, makeshift shacks have been put up, there are piles of refuse and debris and crowds of runty children, slops are flung from doorways. The town tries to compel these people to build privies, but they would just as soon go in the bushes. If a gang of boys goes down there in search of adventure, it's likely they'll get more than they bargained for. It is said that even the town constable won't go down Pearl Street on a Saturday night. Almeda Roth has never walked past the row housing. In one of those houses lives the young girl Annie, who helps her with her housecleaning. That young girl herself, being a decent girl, has never walked down to the last block or the swamp. No decent woman ever would.

But that same swamp, lying to the east of Almeda Roth's house, presents a fine sight at dawn. Almeda sleeps at the back of the house. She keeps to the same bedroom she once shared with her sister Catherine — she would not think of moving to the larger front bedroom, where her mother used to lie in bed all day, and which was later the solitary domain of her father.

From her window she can see the sun rising, the swamp mist filling with light, the bulky, nearest trees floating against that mist and the trees behind turning transparent. Swamp oaks, soft maples, tamarack, bitternut.

III

Here where the river meets the inland sea,
Spreading her blue skirts from the solemn wood,
I think of birds and beasts and vanished men,
Whose pointed dwellings on these pale sands stood.

One of the strangers who arrived at the railway station a few years ago was Jarvis Poulter, who now occupies the house next to Almeda Roth's — separated from hers by a vacant lot, which he has bought, on Dufferin Street. The house is plainer than the Roth house and has no fruit trees or flowers planted around it. It is understood that this is a natural result of Jarvis Poulter's being a widower and living alone. A man may keep his house decent, but he will never — if he is a proper man — do much to decorate it. Marriage forces him to live with more ornament as well as sentiment, and it protects him, also, from the extremities of his own nature — from a frigid parsimony or a luxuriant sloth, from squalor, and from excessive sleeping, drinking, smoking, or freethinking.

In the interests of economy, it is believed, a certain estimable gentleman of our town persists in fetching water from the public tap and supplementing his fuel supply by picking up the loose coal along the railway track. Does he think to repay the town or the railway company with a supply of free salt?

This is the *Vidette*, full of shy jokes, innuendo, plain accusation, that no newspaper would get away with today. It's Jarvis Poulter they're talking about — though in other passages he is spoken of with great respect, as a civil magistrate, an employer, a churchman. He is close, that's all. An eccentric, to a degree.

All of which may be a result of his single condition, his widower's life. Even carrying his water from the town tap and filling his coal pail along the railway track. This is a decent citizen, prosperous: a tall — slightly paunchy? — man in a dark suit with polished boots. A beard? Black hair streaked with gray. A severe and self-possessed air, and a large pale wart among the bushy hairs of one eyebrow? People talk about a young, pretty, beloved wife, dead in childbirth or some horrible accident, like a house fire or a railway disaster. There is no ground for this, but it adds interest. All he has told them is that his wife is dead.

He came to this part of the country looking for oil. The first oil well in the world was sunk in Lambton County, south of here, in the eighteen-fifties. Drilling for oil, Jarvis Poulter discovered salt. He set to work to make the most of that. When he walks home from church with Almeda Roth, he tells her about his salt wells. They are twelve hundred feet deep. Heated water is pumped down into them, and that dissolves the salt. Then the brine is pumped to the surface. It is poured into great evaporator pans over slow, steady fires, so that the water is steamed off and the pure, excellent salt remains. A commodity for which the demand will never fail.

"The salt of the earth," Almeda says.

"Yes," he says, frowning. He may think this disrespectful. She did not intend it so. He speaks of competitors in other towns who are following his lead and trying to hog the market. Fortunately, their wells are not drilled so deep, or their evaporating is not done so efficiently. There is salt everywhere under this land, but it is not so easy to come by as some people think.

Does that not mean, Almeda says, that there was once a great sea?

Very likely, Jarvis Poulter says. Very likely. He goes on to tell her about other enterprises of his — a brickyard, a lime kiln. And he explains to her how this operates, and where the good clay is found. He also owns two farms, whose woodlots supply the fuel for his operations.

Among the couples strolling home from church on a recent, sunny Sabbath morning we noted a certain salty gentleman and literary lady, not perhaps in their first youth but by no means blighted by the frosts of age. May we surmise?

This kind of thing pops up in the *Vidette* all the time.

May they surmise, and is this courting? Almeda Roth has a bit of money, which her father left her, and she has her house. She is not too old to have a couple of children. She is a good enough housekeeper, with the tendency toward fancy iced cakes and decorated tarts which is seen fairly often in old maids. (Honorable mention at the Fall Fair.) There is nothing wrong with her looks, and naturally she is in better shape than most married women of her age, not having been loaded down with work and children. But why was she passed over in her earlier, more marriageable years, in a place that needs women to be partnered and fruitful? She was a rather gloomy girl — that may have been the trouble. The deaths of her brother and sister and then of her mother, who lost her reason, in fact, a year before she died, and lay in her bed talking nonsense — those weighed on her, so she was not lively company. And all that reading and poetry — it seemed more of a drawback, a barrier, an obsession, in the young girl than in the middle-aged woman, who needed something, after all, to fill her time. Anyway, it's five years since her book was published, so perhaps she has got over that. Perhaps it was the proud, bookish father, encouraging her?

Everyone takes it for granted that Almeda Roth is thinking of Jarvis Poulter as a husband and would say yes if he asked her. And she is thinking of him. She doesn't want to get her hopes up too much, she doesn't want to make a fool of herself. She would like a signal. If he attended church on Sunday evenings, there would be a chance, during some months of the year, to walk home after dark. He would carry a lantern. (There is as yet no street lighting in town.) He would swing the lantern to light the way in front of the lady's feet and observe their narrow and delicate shape. He might catch her arm as they step off the boardwalk. But he does not go to church at night.

Nor does he call for her, and walk with her *to* church on Sunday mornings. That would be a declaration. He walks her home, past his gate as far as hers; he lifts his hat then and leaves her. She does not invite him to come in — a woman living alone could never do such a thing. As soon as a man and woman of almost any age are alone together within four walls, it is assumed that anything may happen. Spontaneous combustion, instant fornication, an attack of passion. Brute instinct, triumph of the senses. What possibilities men and women must see in each other to infer such dangers. Or, believing in the dangers, how often they must think about the possibilities.

When they walk side by side she can smell his shaving soap, the barber's oil, his pipe tobacco, the wool and linen and leather smell of his manly clothes. The correct, orderly, heavy clothes are like those she used to brush and starch and iron for her father. She misses that job — her father's appreciation, his dark, kind authority. Jarvis Poulter's garments, his smell, his movement, all cause the skin on the side of her body next to him to tingle hopefully, and a meek shiver raises the hairs on her arms. Is this to be taken as a sign of love? She thinks of him coming into her — *their* — bedroom in his long underwear and his hat. She knows this outfit is ridiculous, but in her mind he does not look so; he has the solemn effrontery of a figure in a dream. He comes into the room and lies down on the bed beside her, preparing to take her in his arms. Surely he removes his hat? She doesn't know, for at this point a fit of welcome and submission overtakes her, a buried gasp. He would be her husband.

One thing she has noticed about married women, and that is how many of them have to go about creating their husbands. They have to start ascribing preferences, opinions, dictatorial ways. Oh, yes, they say, my husband is very particular. He won't touch turnips. He won't eat fried meat. (Or he will only eat fried meat.) He likes me to wear blue (brown) all the time. He can't stand organ music. He hates to see a woman go out bareheaded. He would kill me if I took one puff of tobacco. This way, bewildered, sidelong-looking men are made over, made into husbands, head of households. Almeda Roth cannot imagine herself doing that. She wants a man who doesn't have to be made, who is firm already and determined and mysterious to her. She does not look for companionship. Men — except for her father — seem to her deprived in some way, incurious. No doubt that is necessary, so that they will do what they have to do. Would she herself, knowing that there was salt in the earth, discover how to get it out and sell it? Not likely. She would be thinking about the ancient sea. That kind of speculation is what Jarvis Poulter has, quite properly, no time for.

Instead of calling for her and walking her to church, Jarvis

Poulter might make another, more venturesome declaration. He could hire a horse and take her for a drive out to the country. If he did this, she would be both glad and sorry. Glad to be beside him, driven by him, receiving this attention from him in front of the world. And sorry to have the countryside removed for her — filmed over, in a way, by his talk and preoccupations. The countryside that she has written about in her poems actually takes diligence and determination to see. Some things must be disregarded. Manure piles, of course, and boggy fields full of high, charred stumps, and great heaps of brush waiting for a good day for burning. The meandering creeks have been straightened, turned into ditches with high, muddy banks. Some of the crop fields and pasture fields are fenced with big, clumsy uprooted stumps, others are held in a crude stitchery of rail fences. The trees have all been cleared back to the woodlots. And the woodlots are all second growth. No trees along the roads or lanes or around the farmhouses, except a few that are newly planted, young and weedy looking. Clusters of log barns — the grand barns that are to dominate the countryside for the next hundred years are just beginning to be built — and mean-looking log houses, and every four or five miles a ragged little settlement with a church and school and store and a blacksmith shop. A raw countryside just wrenched from the forest, but swarming with people. Every hundred acres is a farm, every farm has a family, most families have ten or twelve children. (This is the country that will send out wave after wave of settlers — it's already starting to send them — to northern Ontario and the West.) It's true that you can gather wildflowers in spring in the woodlots, but you'd have to walk through herds of horned cows to get to them.

IV

The Gypsies have departed.
Their camping-ground is bare.
Oh, boldly would I bargain now
At the Gypsy Fair.

Almeda suffers a good deal from sleeplessness, and the doctor has given her bromides and nerve medicine. She takes the bromides, but the drops gave her dreams that were too vivid and disturbing, so she has put the bottle by for an emergency. She told the doctor her eyeballs felt dry, like hot glass, and her joints ached. Don't read so much, he said, don't study; get yourself good and tired out with housework, take exercise. He believes that her troubles would clear up if she got married. He believes this in spite of the fact that most of his nerve medicine is prescribed for married women.

So Almeda cleans house and helps clean the church, she lends a hand to friends who are wallpapering or getting ready for a wedding, she bakes one of her famous cakes for the Sunday-school picnic. On a hot Saturday in August she decides to make some grape jelly. Little jars of grape jelly will make fine Christmas presents, or offerings to the sick. But she started late in the day and the jelly is not made by nightfall. In fact, the hot pulp has just been dumped into the cheesecloth bag, to strain out the juice. Almeda drinks some tea and eats a slice of cake with butter (a childish indulgence of hers), and that's all she wants for supper. She washes her hair at the sink and sponges off her body, to be clean for Sunday. She doesn't light a lamp. She lies down on the bed with the window wide open and a sheet just up to her waist, and she does feel wonderfully tired. She can even feel a little breeze.

When she wakes up, the night seems fiery hot and full of threats. She lies sweating on her bed, and she has the impression that the noises she hears are knives and saws and axes — all angry implements chopping and jabbing and boring within her head. But it isn't true. As she comes further awake she recognizes the sounds that she has heard sometimes before — the fracas of a summer Saturday night on Pearl Street. Usually the noise centers on a fight. People are drunk, there is a lot of protest and encouragement concerning the fight, somebody will scream "Murder!" Once, there was a murder. But it didn't happen in a fight. An old man was stabbed to death in his shack, perhaps for a few dollars he kept in the mattress.

She gets out of bed and goes to the window. The night sky is clear, with no moon and with bright stars. Pegasus hangs

straight ahead, over the swamp. Her father taught her that
constellation — automatically, she counts its stars. Now she can
make out distinct voices, individual contributions to the row.
Some people, like herself, have evidently been wakened from
sleep. "Shut up!" they are yelling. "Shut up that caterwauling or
I'm going to come down and tan the arse off yez!"

But nobody shuts up. It's as if there were a ball of fire rolling
up Pearl Street, shooting off sparks — only the fire is noise, it's
yells and laughter and shrieks and curses, and the sparks are
voices that shoot off alone. Two voices gradually distinguish
themselves — a rising and falling howling cry and a steady
throbbing, low-pitched stream of abuse that contains all those
words which Almeda associates with danger and depravity and
foul smells and disgusting sights. Someone — the person crying out, "Kill me! Kill me now!" — is being beaten. A woman
is being beaten. She keeps crying, "Kill me! Kill me!" and
sometimes her mouth seems choked with blood. Yet there is
something taunting and triumphant about her cry. There is
something theatrical about it. And the people around are calling
out, "Stop it! Stop that!" or "Kill her! Kill her!" in a frenzy, as if
at the theater or a sporting match or a prizefight. Yes, thinks
Almeda, she has noticed that before — it is always partly a cha-
rade with these people; there is a clumsy sort of parody, an
exaggeration, a missed connection. As if anything they did —
even a murder — might be something they didn't quite believe
but were powerless to stop.

Now there is the sound of something thrown — a chair, a
plank? — and of a woodpile or part of a fence giving way. A lot
of newly surprised cries, the sound of running, people getting
out of the way, and the commotion has come much closer. Almeda can see a figure in a light dress, bent over and running.
That will be the woman. She has got hold of something like a
stick of wood or a shingle, and she turns and flings it at the
darker figure running after her.

"Ah, go get her!" the voices cry. "Go baste her one!"

Many fall back now; just the two figures come on and grapple,
and break loose again, and finally fall down against Almeda's
fence. The sound they make becomes very confused — gagging,
vomiting, grunting, pounding. Then a long, vibrating, choking

sound of pain and self-abasement, self-abandonment, which could come from either or both of them.

Almeda has backed away from the window and sat down on the bed. Is that the sound of murder she has heard? What is to be done, what is she to do? She must light a lantern, she must go downstairs and light a lantern — she must go out into the yard, she must go downstairs. Into the yard. The lantern. She falls over on her bed and pulls the pillow to her face. In a minute. The stairs, the lantern. She sees herself already down there, in the back hall, drawing the bolt of the back door. She falls asleep.

She wakes, startled, in the early light. She thinks there is a big crow sitting on her windowsill, talking in a disapproving but unsurprised way about the events of the night before. "Wake up and move the wheelbarrow!" it says to her, scolding, and she understands that it means something else by "wheelbarrow" — something foul and sorrowful. Then she is awake and sees that there is no such bird. She gets up at once and looks out the window.

Down against her fence there is a pale lump pressed — a body.

Wheelbarrow.

She puts a wrapper over her nightdress and goes downstairs. The front rooms are still shadowy, the blinds down in the kitchen. Something goes *plop*, *plup*, in a leisurely, censorious way, reminding her of the conversation of the crow. It's just the grape juice, straining overnight. She pulls the bolt and goes out the back door. Spiders have draped their webs over the doorway in the night, and the hollyhocks are drooping, heavy with dew. By the fence, she parts the sticky hollyhocks and looks down and she can see.

A woman's body heaped up there, turned on her side with her face squashed down into the earth. Almeda can't see her face. But there is a bare breast let loose, brown nipple pulled long like a cow's teat, and a bare haunch and leg, the haunch bearing a bruise as big as a sunflower. The unbruised skin is grayish, like a plucked, raw drumstick. Some kind of nightgown or all-purpose dress she has on. Smelling of vomit. Urine, drink, vomit.

Barefoot, in her nightgown and flimsy wrapper, Almeda runs

away. She runs around the side of her house between the apple trees and the veranda; she opens the front gate and flees down Dufferin Street to Jarvis Poulter's house, which is the nearest to hers. She slaps the flat of her hand many times against the door.

"There is the body of a woman," she says when Jarvis Poulter appears at last. He is in his dark trousers, held up with braces, and his shirt is half unbuttoned, his face unshaven, his hair standing up on his head. "Mr. Poulter, excuse me. A body of a woman. At my back gate."

He looks at her fiercely. "Is she dead?"

His breath is dank, his face creased, his eyes bloodshot.

"Yes. I think murdered," says Almeda. She can see a little of his cheerless front hall. His hat on a chair. "In the night I woke up. I heard a racket down on Pearl Street," she says, struggling to keep her voice low and sensible. "I could hear this — pair. I could hear a man and a woman fighting."

He picks up his hat and puts it on his head. He closes and locks the front door, and puts the key in his pocket. They walk along the boardwalk and she sees that she is in her bare feet. She holds back what she feels a need to say next — that she is responsible, she could have run out with a lantern, she could have screamed (but who needed more screams?), she could have beat the man off. She could have run for help then, not now.

They turn down Pearl Street, instead of entering the Roth yard. Of course the body is still there. Hunched up, half bare, the same as before.

Jarvis Poulter doesn't hurry or halt. He walks straight over to the body and looks down at it, nudges the leg with the toe of his boot, just as you'd nudge a dog or a sow.

"You," he says, not too loudly but firmly, and nudges again.

Almeda tastes bile at the back of her throat.

"Alive," says Jarvis Poulter, and the woman confirms this. She stirs, she grunts weakly.

Almeda says, "I will get the doctor." If she had touched the woman, if she had forced herself to touch her, she would not have made such a mistake.

"Wait," says Jarvis Poulter. "Wait. Let's see if she can get up."

"Get up, now," he says to the woman. "Come on. Up, now. Up."

Now a startling thing happens. The body heaves itself onto

all fours, the head is lifted — the hair all matted with blood and vomit — and the woman begins to bang this head, hard and rhythmically, against Almeda Roth's picket fence. As she bangs her head she finds her voice, and lets out an open-mouthed yowl, full of strength and what sounds like an anguished pleasure.

"Far from dead," says Jarvis Poulter. "And I wouldn't bother the doctor."

"There's blood," says Almeda as the woman turns her smeared face.

"From her nose," he says. "Not fresh." He bends down and catches the horrid hair close to the scalp to stop the head banging.

"You stop that now," he says. "Stop it. Gwan home now. Gwan home, where you belong." The sound coming out of the woman's mouth has stopped. He shakes her head slightly, warning her, before he lets go of her hair. "Gwan home!"

Released, the woman lunges forward, pulls herself to her feet. She can walk. She weaves and stumbles down the street, making intermittent, cautious noises of protest. Jarvis Poulter watches her for a moment to make sure that she's on her way. Then he finds a large burdock leaf, on which he wipes his hand. He says, "There goes your dead body!"

The back gate being locked, they walk around to the front. The front gate stands open. Almeda still feels sick. Her abdomen is bloated; she is hot and dizzy.

"The front door is locked," she says faintly. "I came out by the kitchen." If only he would leave her, she could go straight to the privy. But he follows. He follows her as far as the back door and into the back hall. He speaks to her in a tone of harsh joviality that she has never before heard from him. "No need for alarm," he says. "It's only the consequences of drink. A lady oughtn't to be living alone so close to a bad neighborhood." He takes hold of her arm just above the elbow. She can't open her mouth to speak to him, to say thank you. If she opened her mouth she would retch.

What Jarvis Poulter feels for Almeda Roth at this moment is just what he has not felt during all those circumspect walks and all his own solitary calculations of her probable worth, undoubted respectability, adequate comeliness. He has not been able to imagine her as a wife. Now that is possible. He is sufficiently stirred by her loosened hair — prematurely gray but thick and soft — her flushed face, her light clothing, which nobody but a husband should see. And by her indiscretion, her agitation, her foolishness, her need?

"I will call on you later," he says to her. "I will walk with you to church."

At the corner of Pearl and Dufferin streets last Sunday morning there was discovered, by a lady resident there, the body of a certain woman of Pearl Street, thought to be dead but only, as it turned out, dead drunk. She was roused from her heavenly — or otherwise — stupor by the firm persuasion of Mr. Poulter, a neighbour and a Civil Magistrate, who had been summoned by the lady resident. Incidents of this sort, unseemly, troublesome, and disgraceful to our town, have of late become all too common.

V

I sit at the bottom of sleep,
As on the floor of the sea.
And fanciful Citizens of the Deep
Are graciously greeting me.

As soon as Jarvis Poulter has gone and she has heard her front gate close, Almeda rushes to the privy. Her relief is not complete, however, and she realizes that the pain and fullness in her lower body come from an accumulation of menstrual blood that has not yet started to flow. She closes and locks the back door. Then, remembering Jarvis Poulter's words about church, she writes on a piece of paper, "I am not well, and wish to rest today." She sticks this firmly into the outside frame of the little window in the front door. She locks that door, too. She is trembling, as if from a great shock or danger. But she builds a fire, so that she can make tea. She boils water, measures the tea leaves, makes a large pot of tea, whose steam and smell sicken her further. She pours out a cup while the tea is still quite weak and adds to it several dark drops of nerve medicine. She sits to drink it without raising the kitchen blind. There, in the middle of the floor, is the cheesecloth bag hanging on its broom handle between the two chair backs. The grape pulp and juice has stained the swollen cloth a dark purple. *Plop, plup* into the basin beneath. She can't sit and look at such a thing. She takes her cup, the teapot, and the bottle of medicine into the dining room.

She is still sitting there when the horses start to go by on the way to church, stirring up clouds of dust. The roads will be getting hot as ashes. She is there when the gate is opened and a man's confident steps sound on her veranda. Her hearing is so sharp she seems to hear the paper taken out of the frame and unfolded — she can almost hear him reading it, hear the words in his mind. Then the footsteps go the other way, down the steps. The gate closes. An image comes to her of tombstones — it makes her laugh. Tombstones are marching down the street on their little booted feet, their long bodies inclined forward, their expressions preoccupied and severe. The church bells are ringing.

Then the clock in the hall strikes twelve and an hour has passed.

The house is getting hot. She drinks more tea and adds more medicine. She knows that the medicine is affecting her. It is responsible for her extraordinary languor, her perfect immobility, her unresisting surrender to her surroundings. That is all right. It seems necessary.

Her surroundings — some of her surroundings — in the dining room are these: walls covered with dark green garlanded wallpaper, lace curtains and mulberry velvet curtains on the windows, a table with a crocheted cloth and a bowl of wax fruit, a pinkish-gray carpet with nosegays of blue and pink roses, a sideboard spread with embroidered runners and holding various patterned plates and jugs and the silver tea things. A lot of things to watch. For every one of these patterns, decorations, seems charged with life, ready to move and flow and alter. Or possibly to explode. Almeda Roth's occupation throughout the day is to keep an eye on them. Not to prevent their alteration so much as to catch them at it — to understand it, to be a part of it. So much is going on in this room that there is no need to leave it. There is not even the thought of leaving it.

Of course, Almeda in her observations cannot escape words. She may think she can, but she can't. Soon this glowing and swelling begins to suggest words — not specific words but a flow of words somewhere, just about ready to make themselves known to her. Poems, even. Yes, again, poems. Or one poem. Isn't that the idea — one very great poem that will contain everything and, oh, that will make all the other poems, the poems she has written, inconsequential, mere trial and error, mere rags? Stars and flowers and birds and trees and angels in the snow and dead children at twilight — that is not the half of it. You have to get in the obscene racket on Pearl Street and the polished toe of Jarvis Poulter's boot and the plucked-chicken haunch with its blue-black flower. Almeda is a long way now from human sympathies or fears or cozy household considerations. She doesn't think about what could be done for that woman or about keeping Jarvis Poulter's dinner warm and hanging his long underwear on the line. The basin of grape juice has overflowed and is running over her kitchen floor, staining the boards of the floor, and the stain will never come out.

She has to think of so many things at once — Champlain and the naked Indians and the salt deep in the earth but as well as the salt the money, the money-making intent brewing forever in heads like Jarvis Poulter's. Also, the brutal storms of winter and the clumsy and benighted deeds on Pearl Street. The changes of climate are often violent, and if you think about it there is no peace even in the stars. All this can be borne only if it is channeled into a poem, and the word "channeled" is appropriate, because the name of the poem will be — it *is* — "The Meneseteung." The name of the poem is the name of the river. No, in fact it is the river, the Meneseteung, that is the poem — with its deep holes and rapids and blissful pools under the summer trees and its grinding blocks of ice thrown up at the end of winter and its desolating spring floods. Almeda looks deep, deep into the river of her mind and into the tablecloth, and she sees the crocheted roses floating. They look bunchy and foolish, her mother's crocheted roses — they don't look much like real flowers. But their effort, their floating independence, their pleasure in their silly selves, does seem to her so admirable. A hopeful sign. *Meneseteung.*

She doesn't leave the room until dusk, when she goes out to the privy again and discovers that she is bleeding, her flow has started. She will have to get a towel, strap it on, bandage herself up. Never before, in health, has she passed a whole day in her nightdress. She doesn't feel any particular anxiety about this. On her way through the kitchen she walks through the pool of grape juice. She knows that she will have to mop it up, but not yet, and she walks upstairs leaving purple footprints and smelling her escaping blood and the sweat of her body that has sat all day in the closed hot room.

No need for alarm.

For she hasn't thought that crocheted roses could float away or that tombstones could hurry down the street. She doesn't mistake that for reality, and neither does she mistake anything else for reality, and that is how she knows that she is sane.

VI

I dream of you by night,
I visit you by day.
Father, Mother,
Sister, Brother,
Have you no word to say?

April 22, 1903. At her residence, on Tuesday last, between three and four o'clock in the afternoon, there passed away a lady of talent and refinement whose pen, in days gone by, enriched our local literature with a volume of sensitive, eloquent verse. It is a sad misfortune that in later years the mind of this fine person had become somewhat clouded and her behaviour, in consequence, somewhat rash and unusual. Her attention to decorum and to the care and adornment of her person had suffered, to the degree that she had become, in the eyes of those unmindful of her former pride and daintiness, a familiar eccentric, or even, sadly, a figure of fun. But now all such lapses pass from memory and what is recalled is her excellent published verse, her labours in former days in the Sunday school, her dutiful care of her parents, her noble womanly nature, charitable concerns, and unfailing religious faith. Her last illness was of mercifully short duration. She caught cold, after having become thoroughly wet from a ramble in the Pearl Street bog. (It has been said that some urchins chased her into the water, and such is the boldness and cruelty of some of our youth, and their observed persecution of this lady, that the tale cannot be entirely discounted.) The cold developed into pneumonia, and she died, attended at the last by a former neighbour, Mrs. Bert (Annie) Friels, who witnessed her calm and faithful end.

January, 1904. One of the founders of our community, an early maker and shaker of this town, was abruptly removed from our midst on Monday morning last, whilst attending to his correspondence in the office of his company. Mr. Jarvis Poulter possessed a keen and lively commercial spirit, which was instrumental in the creation of not one but several local enterprises, bringing the benefits of industry, productivity, and employment to our town.

I looked for Almeda Roth in the graveyard. I found the family stone. There was just one name on it — Roth. Then I noticed two flat stones in the ground, a distance of a few feet — six feet? — from the upright stone. One of these said "Papa," the other "Mama." Farther out from these I found two other flat stones, with the names William and Catherine on them. I had to clear away some overgrowing grass and dirt to see the full name of Catherine. No birth or death dates for anybody, nothing about being dearly beloved. It was a private sort of memorializing, not for the world. There were no roses, either — no sign of a rosebush. But perhaps it was taken out. The grounds keeper doesn't like such things, they are a nuisance to the lawnmower, and if there is nobody left to object he will pull them out.

I thought that Almeda must have been buried somewhere else. When this plot was bought — at the time of the two children's deaths — she would still have been expected to marry, and to lie finally beside her husband. They might not have left room for her here. Then I saw that the stones in the ground fanned out from the upright stone. First the two for the parents, then the two for the children, but these were placed in such a way that there was room for a third, to complete the fan. I paced out from "Catherine" the same number of steps that it took to get from "Catherine" to "William," and at this spot I began pulling grass and scrabbling in the dirt with my bare hands. Soon I felt the stone and knew that I was right. I worked away and got the whole stone clear and I read the name "Meda." There it was with the others, staring at the sky.

I made sure I had got to the edge of the stone. That was all

the name there was — Meda. So it was true that she was called
by that name in the family. Not just in the poem. Or perhaps
she chose her name from the poem, to be written on her stone.

I thought that there wasn't anybody alive in the world but me
who would know this, who would make the connection. And I
would be the last person to do so. But perhaps this isn't so.
People are curious. A few people are. They will be driven to
find things out, even trivial things. They will put things together, knowing all along that they may be mistaken. You see
them going around with notebooks, scraping the dirt off grave-
stones, reading microfilm, just in the hope of seeing this trickle
in time, making a connection, rescuing one thing from the rub-
bish.

DALE RAY PHILLIPS

What Men Love For

FROM THE ATLANTIC

WHEN I was twelve, my father called on weeknights to convince my mother that he would return safely that weekend and to assure himself that his house was still in order. The phone's ringing always startled my mother from what she was doing — blowing smoke rings through the window screen, or, when she was extremely melancholy, cutting her face out of old pictures of herself. The calls sent her swiftly to the bathroom, where she locked the door and gargled. She had returned home that spring after a nervous breakdown, and she believed that each ring meant my father had driven off some mountainside or had abandoned us because she was a manic-depressive. Her worst fear was that he was calling from a pay phone somewhere past the Appalachians, to say he was on his way to sunny and golden California.

"Richard," my father said one night. "You keeping the home motor tuned and purring for your old man?" Our weekend hobby was restoring motorcycles. "How's the chrome tank on that Harley coming along? You got the rust spots off yet?"

"Everything's as shiny as a new dime," I said.

"And your mother. You would tell me if something was wrong again?"

"Old Buck's got everything under control," I said. Buck Rogers was my father's childhood hero, and he trusted me when I called myself that. This was the summer of the moon shot; I suspect almost every father wanted his son to be an astronaut.

"You can count on old Buck." My mother picked up the bedroom extension. My father explained to her that when he came home that weekend, we would grill steaks and make ice cream.

"By God, we might even break out the old Satchmo records and some wine, and dance in the kitchen. Have us a cozy little party with the lights turned low."

My father addressed me, on the kitchen extension. "Hey, Richard. They called your old man Fleet Foot back in the days when dancing was dancing." There on the kitchen table my mother had carefully aligned the cut-out faces in one row and the pictures in another. And then my father was rambling again, saying that he was up for a promotion, which would mean less traveling. "After Labor Day, I should be home two days a week, plus weekends. Two or three years of that and who knows?" His dream was to quit traveling through North Carolina, where we lived, and Virginia. He presented my mother with a version of how life would be once he got the right breaks and became the owner of his own hospital-supply company. "I'd be home every night. The business would be shaky at first, but hell, all businesses are. Ours would be a family enterprise that *worked*. We'd all take an interest in it, make decisions together, things like that."

"You can count old Buck in," I said.

"What about now?" my mother asked.

"Labor Day," my father said. "Let me snag that promotion and I'll be home more. Is that too much to ask?"

"I suppose not." My mother hung up her exension. I said the good-byes for us both. I put the faces and the pictures they'd come from into the photograph box, and then I retrieved a sleeping pill from the supply I kept hidden. I went to where my mother lay in bed, gave her one, and turned the fan on low.

"You have to stop doing this," I said.

"It helps when I feel bad." I had a difficult time understanding what had happened to the woman who had once laughed and clapped as I walked around the kitchen on my hands, saying to her, "This is how they walk in China — upside down," the change tumbling from my pockets. She had been glum and anxious since coming back. "Please don't tell," she had said when I first caught her cutting her face from the pictures. She held the photograph to her face, looking at me through an image of herself, eye blinking and peering where her face had been. At the time I was afraid that my father would guess that her nervousness had returned, and that they would take her away again. These secrets from my father held us together.

"Can we do cat's cradle?" she asked. She had folded her robe over a chair beside the bed, and she took the string from its pocket. I sat beside her and played cat's cradle. The twine slipped from her hands to mine and then back, each exchange making a different configuration. As she slipped into sleep, I made Jacob's ladder, weaving a narrow net of string twisted taut between my fingers. We were strings of a fragile ladder, working in collusion with and against each other.

The cool portion of each morning, I set up a ladder before the dew had evaporated, when no one was stirring on our street except the milkman and husbands taking out the garbage before leaving for work. My job was to reglaze a third-floor window. I learned the simple but universal law that craftsmen somehow know — that working with your hands is a pleasure, especially work so mindless that everything you need to forget becomes absorbed by the sash to be mended. This law's implication is that in routing out a bad strip of glazing, in sanding the sash carefully, protecting the glass pane from the paper's grains with a fingertip, in the decisions made on each of the window's sixteen panes, something small is set straight that affects the universe. Window glazing requires a dangerous angling of your body if the putty lines are to be drawn straight and true. Everything sits arranged on the sill — hammer, sandpaper, primer, points, and putty. The dissonant parts of yourself hang divided in the graph made by the window sash. To fall inward toward your reflection would be as disastrous as falling backward, to the ground. This tension feels natural, good. The morning smelled of sweat and of the linseed oil rubbed into the wood yesterday to revive its vigor. Vigor is also in the worker. Women sense this, and they are pleased.

"I made you some coffee," my mother said one morning. She stood at the ladder's bottom in her robe and slippers. I came down the ladder for the coffee.

"It's going to be a *good* day, isn't it?" A good day meant she would not need crying or the pictures.

"It's going to be a *great* day," I said.

We shared a cigarette. She allowed me to smoke on certain mornings like this. Often she talked to me about the way she felt.

"The problem, Richard, is that everything makes me so sad. It's like Christmas, with all those presents. Most people look at the gifts and think of all the nice things inside. But ever since I was a small girl, I've worried about tearing the wrappers open and finding something inside I didn't want. The wrappers were so pretty, but I was always afraid they were hiding something awful. Is it like that for you? Are you afraid of finding something inside that you don't want?"

I told her that almost anything but long underwear suited me fine.

"You're like your father. You're lucky you're easy to please. Any other man would probably have left me, I know. I get mad at him for *not* leaving, Richard. Then I get mad when he isn't here. Isn't it strange, the way you feel sometimes?"

"It'll be a good day," I said. "Don't worry."

My mother went inside, and I stood for a moment admiring my work and the sun held tightly in the window. The ladder sagged as I climbed back up. As I passed my mother's room, I stopped to watch her in her bathroom before the mirror. She was brushing her hair, and I was startled when her hair held static and a few strands reached up to grab at the brush. She stroked, stopped to scrutinize something in her face, resumed. The awkwardness of being outside and not able to affect her settled in my stomach. She saw me for an instant and waved and went back to her reflection. The wave was one of those waves you see from someone on a porch when he suddenly notices a passing car and gives in to the urge to establish some kind of human contact.

Saturday afternoons my father said things like "See how this chain fits itself into the teeth of the sprocket?" Home from a week's traveling, he tinkered with motorcycles until dusk. He wore khakis and a sleeveless T-shirt. He bought the motorcycles second hand — usually from someone who had taken a spill — and restored them. When we had renovated one to mint condition, he sold it, and we began renovating another. Frames hung

from the garage's rafters like carcasses. When we got a motorcycle whose rider had been killed, we salvaged the parts. My
father wouldn't rebuild those particular motorcycles, nor would
he sell to a man with a family. He thought motorcycles were too
dangerous for any family man besides himself. His favorite customers were men who had just enlisted. He would tell them to
be very careful driving to Fort Bragg and would often talk to
them about his own service days. He had been a Navy man, had
almost reenlisted. Before he closed each deal, he gave the buyer
a list of maintenance tips and tune-up instructions that he made
him promise to follow.

"And what about you?" one of them asked. "You still ride?"
We had just sold a Triumph to a recruit. When the man toyed
with the clutch, the machine jerked forward in a spasm.

"No. I don't really ride anymore." My father pointed at me
and the house where my mother was emerging with tea. "I can't
afford the chance of taking a spill." He considered our midnight
rides not really riding but something else entirely.

My mother brought us tea in Mason jars; the man wobbled
down the driveway and missed second gear. My parents had
argued that morning over the promotion my father was to get
after Labor Day. She had said that two months was a long time
to wait for someone in her condition.

"Condition?" he had asked.

"I missed my period," she had said.

"Here comes the new mother now," my father said. "Here."
He helped her with the tray. He said that she should be careful
carrying things, especially with two strong men around who
could do things for her. All morning she had basked in my
father's unexpected attention. My father set down the tea and
cornered her and gave her a hug and a nip at her ear.

"Baby money." He presented her with a wad of cash. "What
say I get some fat porterhouses and a bottle of wine. French
stuff."

"This isn't a substitute for your being here, you know." Then
she seemed to understand that she had spoiled the moment,
and she rushed back inside the house.

"Pregnant women," my father said. He gave me a wink.

"Should I put some potatoes on?" my mother asked.

"The biggest you've got," my father yelled. He looked down the driveway at something the recruit had dropped. My father went and picked up his handwritten instructions.

"He'll probably forget to put oil in the crankcase, and seize it up," he said as we walked to the back yard. My father poured charcoal briquettes into the grill, and I stacked them into a pyramid. "Stand back," he said, and after dousing the charcoal with lighter fluid, he lit the fire. Leaning against the sides of the garage and the fence, scattered like giant cicada husks, were more motorcycles that my father's hands would set into motion. My father got a sad pleasure from selling mint-condition motorcycles to people who, he feared, would ruin them.

Late one Saturday night we stretched out on a blanket in the back yard. My mother sat at the blanket's edge and swayed to the music playing loudly in the kitchen. Louis Armstrong was ejecting lonesome notes from his horn. A box of light spilled out the door and held a portion of my mother. My father pointed out the constellations and gave them names.

"How about a dance?" he said, and gathered my mother up into his arms. When he dipped her, she giggled and hugged the back of his neck. They were two shadows, keeping cadence to Armstrong's melody. Now and then my father stopped and looked up into the night sky. "We could travel to China, Richard, with that night sky and a little luck." They resumed their sleepy dance, and I thought, If you dug down past the roots and the fossils and the dead, you'd hit another world. The idea that our disturbances were a small part of something as immense as the world was dizzying. Men had walked in space a few years before, floating dangerously out to rope's length and then hauling themselves back, their feet searching for firm footing and balance in a realm where none could be found. This was how we were that summer.

"Do my back and shoulders," my mother said. She had tired of dancing, and she sat where the light verged into shadows and darkness. My father loosened her blouse's top button. He kneaded her muscles and called her his "girl." She rubbed and stretched herself against his hands. Soon she fell asleep, and he carried her up the steps. "How about a ride?" he whispered to me as he stepped inside. When he came back out, he stood in the box of light and stretched. Now he said to me again, "How about a ride?" We pushed his Harley to the driveway's edge, so as not to awaken her. The Harley grumbled and came to life with a kick.

My father coaxed the engine gently through the gears. We slid through the night like a snake through slick growth. My father eased into the turns with a knowing motion. He said once that you never really ride a motorcycle; instead you let it take you where it wants to go. We traveled for several hours, retracing the same tired path. We rode until the darkness eased into a notion that dawn would come. That night we circled wide of our sorrows.

"Here we go, Buck." The home stretch of a quarter of a mile was straight and streetlighted. My father turned off the headlight.

To ride a motorcycle at night is a simple thing: you become one with the darkness. The engine's motion works up through your crotch and settles in your chest. You feel caught up in the exhilaration of blind motion. I wore no helmet, and I had conversations with my father that occurred only in my mind.

I warned my father that my mother was doing the best she could but that he might lose her if he was not careful. I explained that people are different from motorcycles; you can't make them into what you want. I felt giddy being a father to my father. I assured him that we were all doing the best we could. I couldn't tell my father what I had learned that summer — that trying might not be enough. I understood that for a long time my mother had suspected this — that trying might not be enough — and had it been in her power to do so, she would have protected me from this sad knowledge. Instead I told him the biggest thing I knew — that my mother, by being at home safe and sleeping, was somehow giving me shelter from the sadness of motorcycles on a summer night. The two of us rushed into the road ahead like two sleepers riding the back of a dream.

"Hell, let's just ride to China," my father always said at our driveway. He slapped his pants pocket, claiming that with his change and a few bills we could make it. He was very proud of his motorcycle's gas mileage. "We *could* get there." *There* covered all the possibilities of where we might be headed.

Sunday morning I often joined my parents in their room. My father snored while my mother read romances. Reading comforted her in much the same way that blowing smoke rings at the screen seemed to comfort her. She was trying to hold things together, warding off depression by intoxicating herself with books whose endings were not surprises. She read romance after romance, all of whose white covers pictured forlorn women about to be saved by gentlemen striding confidently out of the background. As she read to me, I watched my father sleep, wondering if she were somehow interpreting his dreams. When he awoke, he scratched his chest and propped himself on a pillow while she gave us a synopsis of this or that book.

"This promising and beautiful young woman is engaged to a doctor. She really loves a poor but honest young butler. He is a servant in the aging doctor's household. It turns out the young butler is the only living heir to a diamond fortune. Mr. Chadworth, a trusted aide to the dying diamond magnate, is commanded to find the last living heir. He successfully locates the butler. She and the butler marry and have a happy life."

"Sounds nice," my father said. "I like to hear you tell us stories." He was up and choosing clothes for his suitcase. "Too bad things are often different."

"Too bad, isn't it." I heard an edge in my mother's voice.

During the week, my mother left the house only at night. We took her car after dark and bought groceries at a grocery store open until ten. My mother drove with the window up, though the air conditioner was broken. She stopped at each intersection and then proceeded in screeching spurts. Once past an intersection, she drove slowly, to avoid any possibility of an accident.

We talked on these rides to the store, my mother usually fretting over my father's absence.

"Just let him get his promotion," I said.

"I'm not worried," my mother said. "Another baby will make him stay at home, I bet."

I said it probably would.

"Do I ruin things when he's at home?"

"Not that I know of."

"It's been a good few weeks, hasn't it?"

"Very good," I said.

"It's too early for me to start showing. You understand that, don't you?"

Another time, she said, "I hear you on that motorcycle late Saturday nights. Whatever on earth do you do?"

"We just ride."

"Just ride?"

"Yeah. It's like all of us being on the bed when you tell a story. It's like early morning when we share a cigarette while I'm glazing."

The last Saturday of that month, while my mother visited her psychiatrist, my father and I hunted arrowheads. We took his Harley out to a field with a stone outcropping where the Indians had gotten flint for arrowheads. We parked the motorcycle beside a road sign that warned of low-flying airplanes. A mile away an airstrip for crop dusters had been cut from the tobacco fields and a tract of pine. The planes took off slowly and wobbled in low over the fields of tobacco, spraying them and then floating straight upward where the field gave way to the pines. We were far enough away for a lag to occur between the sight of the plane's rising and the sound of the pilot's gunning the motor. In the far distance cars on the interstate we had exited moved at a sleepy speed. My father and I spread out through the field and poked at the earth's raw redness. It had rained that morning, and humidity made the air seem as heavy as the mud on my shoes. We made several passes through the field, our paths slowly coiling to its center. When airplane shadows passed over me, I had the urge to run catch them and jump on them like a magic carpet. My father and I always met under a pine tree left for shade in the years when the field was planted with tobacco and the workers needed a spot to rest from the sun.

My father got excited when he found an unfinished arrowhead. "This old boy sure knew what he was doing." He showed me a tip with one side left unfinished.

"I think we can do it better," he said. He took out his pocket knife with the bone handle. He began pressure-flaking at what some Indian had abandoned three centuries earlier. My father squatted on his hams. His veins grew into a web as he tried to remove the flakes in exactly the right places. Now and then he struck the arrowhead a quick tap. Earlier that morning he had argued with my mother, accusing her of blaming him for things that were beyond his control. My father's knife *tick-tick-ticked*, and he seemed a child again, fumbling to make something whose exact shape he was still trying to discover.

Instead of a promotion they gave my father responsibility for half the state of Tennessee. This meant he would be gone even more. The whole Saturday morning of Labor Day weekend he refused to talk. Instead he cleaned and recleaned his Harley's spark plugs. Then he readjusted their gap. He cranked the engine again and again, listening to the cylinders' compression. Then he attached the plugs and laid them against the casing. He kicked the starter to watch their arc.

"It's my fault," my mother said. She came out from the bedroom to stand behind me where I stood at the kitchen door, watching. She had the box of photographs under her arm and a note in her hand. She told me to give the note to my father. Then she locked herself in the bedroom.

I read the note and then carried it to my father. The note said, "You've been doubting that you love me for some time now. If it's another mouth to feed that you're worried about, don't. I just made the baby up."

"Here," I said. He stuck it in his pocket. He had the plugs back in and was working degreaser into his hands.

"You might want to read it now."

He read it and threw down the rag with which he was cleaning away the loosened grease. When I got into the house, he was banging on the bedroom door.

"For God's sake, open up," my father said.

"Just leave," my mother said. "Love me or leave me, but the way things are now has to stop."

"Why did you claim to be *pregnant*? Just to trick me?"

"Didn't you notice how things changed when you thought I was pregnant?"

"Open up right now," my father said. "You hear me? Open up right this minute."

"I'm not coming out until you calm down," my mother said. "I might not even come out until this afternoon." She started slipping the faceless pictures of herself under the door.

"What in the hell is this supposed to mean?" he asked.

"It's how I feel. Have you spent so much time traveling that you don't understand *that*?"

"I understand one thing — it's time for a change. I'm taking my son with me, and I'm going to get drunk. D-R-U-N-K." He led me from the house to the Harley.

My father didn't get drunk that night, but by nightfall we had made the Appalachians. My father stopped at a tourist trap named Blowing Rock. It was near a road tunnel that fed through the mountains into Tennessee. We parked by an information sign that told of the legend of Blowing Rock. An Indian maiden jumped, and her lover, returning late from the hunt, saw her fall. He prayed so hard as she tumbled in the wind that God heard, and He blew her back up to the cliff's edge and safety.

"What the hell," my father said. "An Indian Lover's Leap." The sign said that this legend explained why anything thrown off Blowing Rock rose back up. On a windy day it could snow *upward* here.

My father stood near the guardrail and scratched his head. He pulled a cigar from his jacket and licked and puffed at it. He held himself to three a week. "This is the best way to taste a cigar," he said, and I didn't know if he would light it. Finally he did.

"Sometimes I believe she does everything in her power to drive me away. Richard, I never bargained for a crazy woman, even if I *do* love her. The hell of it is, I never once thought it would turn out this way." The cigar glowed and blinked at intervals. "There goes my own business," he said. "Tennessee." He pointed toward the darkness where the mountains, though invisible, could be felt.

"It's not like you've really been home a lot," I said.

"Well, they sure fixed that problem for me, didn't they? I

can't work for them after they throw me stinking Tennessee."
He looked at me with bewilderment. "Richard, what if your
mother and I *can't* make a go of it?"

My father reached into his pockets and gathered his change.
With his head making an arc of light, he motioned me to follow.
"Let's try this out, Buck." He leaned over the guardrail. He
pitched coin after coin off the mountain's edge, leaning as far
as he could to watch where they went. We felt no wind that
night, and of course they did not rise. After the coins he tried
rocks and sticks and even paper cups rummaged from the trash
bin. In the moonless night he was a shadow gathering pieces
and tossing them off. Each object was sucked from sight as it
fell. He stood there, a man tossing things off a mountainside,
caught in the human hope that they would rise again as promised. The night was as dark as I imagined the far side of the
moon might be. The thought occurred to me that though we
could, we wouldn't keep going west; we had gone as far as it was
possible to go and still turn back.

My father crushed the cigar near the motorcycle. "Climb
aboard, Buck." We drove to the main highway and turned toward home. I thought of how the road leading down from the
mountainside was steep and dangerous. Around one bend or
another would lie a blind curve whose far side held secret what
might or might not be. As we approached that curve there
would arise in us a steady drumming. Our chests would swell
and throb until our pulse beat in the quicks of our fingertips.
We were blood-full of the moment wherein, against all proba-
bilities, you lean into the curve and take your chances of making
it. You feel earthbound, not by the motorcycle but by your urge
to round that bend. Oil slick or happy ending, complete with a
hero's welcome, you ease into that snake of road whose other
side holds your future hidden. This moment is what men love
for. You are father and son, caught in a homeward motion.

"Hold on," my father said, and we went at that curve with all
the speed and hope that we could muster.

MARK RICHARD

Strays

FROM ESQUIRE

AT NIGHT stray dogs come up underneath our house to lick our leaking pipes. Beneath my brother and my's room we hear them coughing and growling, scratching their ratted backs against the boards beneath our beds. We lie awake listening, my brother thinking of names to name the one he is setting out to catch. Salute and Topboy are high on his list.

I tell my brother these dogs are wild and cowering. A bare-heeled stomp on the floor off our beds sends them scuttling spine-bowed out the crawl space beneath our open window. Sometimes when my brother is quick he leans out and touches one slipping away.

Our father has meant to put the screens back on the windows for spring. He has even hauled them out of the storage shed and stacked them in the drive. He lays them one by one over sawhorses to tack in the frames tighter and weave patches against mosquitoes. This is what he means to do, but our mother that morning pulls all the preserves off the shelves onto the floor, sticks my brother and my's Easter Sunday drawings in her mouth, and leaves the house on through the fields cleared the week before for corn.

Uncle Trash is our nearest relative with a car, and our mother has a good half-day head start on our father when Uncle Trash arrives. Uncle Trash runs his car up the drive in a big speed splitting all the screens stacked there from their frames. There is an exploded chicken in the grill of Uncle Trash's car. They don't even turn it off as Uncle Trash slides out and our father gets behind the wheel backing over the screens setting out in search of our mother.

Uncle Trash finds out that he has left his bottle under the seat of his car. He goes in our kitchen pulling out all the shelves our mother missed. Then he is in the towel box in the hall, looking, pulling out stuff in stacks. He is in our parents' room opening short doors. He is in the storage shed opening and sniffing a Mason jar of gasoline for the power mower. Uncle Trash comes up and asks, Which way is it to town for a drink? I point up the road and he sets off saying, Don't y'all burn the house down.

My brother and I hang out in the side yard doing handstands until dark. We catch handfuls of lightning bugs and smear bright yellow on our shirts. It is late. I wash our feet and put us to bed. We wait for somebody to come back home but nobody ever does. Lucky for me when my brother begins to whine for our mother the stray dogs show up under the house and he starts making up lists of new names for them, soothing himself to sleep.

Hungry, we wake up to something sounding in the kitchen not like our mother fixing us anything to eat. It is Uncle Trash throwing up and spitting blood into the pump-handled sink. I ask him did he have an accident and he sends my brother upstairs for Merthiolate and Q-Tips. His face is angled out from his head on one side, so that sided eye is shut. His good eye waters wiggling loose teeth with cut-up fingers. Uncle Trash says he had an accident all right. He says he was up in a card game and then he was real up in a card game, so he bet his car, accidentally forgetting that our father had driven off with it in search of our mother. Uncle Trash said the man who won the card game went ahead and beat up Uncle Trash on purpose anyway.

All day Uncle Trash sleeps in our parents' room. We can hear him snoring from the front yard where my brother and I dig in the dirt with spoons making roadbeds and highways for my tin-metal trucks. In the evening Uncle Trash comes down in one of our father's shirts, dirty, but cleaner than the one he had gotten beat up in. We then have banana sandwiches for supper and

Uncle Trash asks do we have a deck of cards in the house. He says he wants to see do his tooth-cut fingers still flex enough to work. I have to tell him how our mother disallows all card playing in the house but that my brother has a pack of Old Maid somewhere in the toy box. While my brother goes out to look I brag at how I always beat him out, leaving him the Old Maid, and Uncle Trash says, Oh yeah? and digs around in his pocket for a nickel he puts on the table. He says we'll play a nickel a game and I go into my brother and my's room to get the Band-Aid box of nickels and dimes I sometimes short from the collection plate on Sunday.

Uncle Trash is making painful faces flexing his red-painted fingers around the Old Maid deck of circus-star cards, but he still shuffles, cuts, and deals a three-way hand one-handed, and not much longer I lose my Band-Aid box of money and all the tin-metal trucks of mine out in the front yard. He makes me go out and get them and put them on his side of the table. My brother loses a set of bowling pins and a stuffed beagle. In two more hands we stack up our winter boots and coats with hoods on Uncle Trash's side of the table. In the last hand my brother and I step out of our shorts and underdrawers while Uncle Trash smiles and says, And now, gentlemen, if you please, the shirts off y'all's backs.

Uncle Trash rakes everything my brother and I own into the pillowcases off our beds and says let that be a lesson to me. He is off through the front porch leaving us buck naked across the table, his last words as he goes up the road shoulder-slinging his loot, Don't y'all burn the house down.

I am burning hot at Uncle Trash, then I am burning hot at our father for leaving us with him to look for our mother, and then I am burning hot at my mother for running off through the fields leaving me with my brother, and then I am burning hot at my brother who is starting to cry. There is only one thing left to do and that is to take all we still have left that we own and throw it at my brother, and I do, and Old Maid cards explode on his face setting him off on a really good red-face howl.

I tell my brother that making so much noise will keep the stray dogs away and he believes it, and then I start to believe it when it gets later than usual, past the crickets and into a long

moon over the trees, but they finally do come after my brother
finally falls asleep, so I just wait until I know there are several
beneath the bed boards scratching their rat-matted backs and
growling, and I stomp on the floor, what is my favorite part
about the dogs, watching them scatter in a hundred directions
and then seeing them one by one collect in a pack at the edge
of the field near the trees.

In the morning right off I recognize the bicycle coming wobble-
wheeling into the front yard. It's the one the boy outside Cuts
uses to run lunches and ice water to the pulpwood truck Mr.
Cuts has working cut-over timber on the edge of town. The
colored boy that usually drives it snaps bottle caps off his fingers
at my brother and I when we go to Cuts with our mother to
make groceries. We have to wait outside by the kerosene pump,
out by the papered-over lean-to shed, the pop-crate place where
the men sit around and Uncle Trash does his card work now.
White people generally don't go into Cuts unless they have to
buy on credit.
    We at school know Mr. and Mrs. Cuts come from a family
that eats children. There is a red metal tree with plastic-
wrapped toys in the window and a long candy counter case
inside to lure you in. Mr. and Mrs. Cuts have no children of
their own. They ate them during a hard winter and salted the
rest down for sandwiches the colored boy runs out to the pulpwood crew at noon. I count colored children going in to buy
some candy to see how many make it back out, but generally
our mother is ready to go home before I can tell. Our credit at
Cuts is short.
    The front tire catches in one of our tin-metal truck's under-
ground tunnel tracks and Uncle Trash takes a spill. The cut
crate bolted to the bicycle handlebars spills out brown paper
packages sealed with electrical tape into the yard along with a
case of Champale and a box of cigars. Uncle Trash is down
where he falls. He lays asleep all day under the tree in the yard
moving just to crawl back into the wandering shade.
    We have for supper sirloins, Champale, and cigars. Uncle
Trash teaches how to cross our legs up on the table after dinner
but says he'll go ahead and leave my brother and my's cigars
unlit. There is no outlook for our toys and my Band-Aid can of

nickels and dimes, checking all the packages, even checking twice again the cut crate bolted on the front of the bicycle. Uncle Trash shows us a headstand on the table drinking a bottle of Champale, then he stands in the sink and sings "Gather My Far-flung Thoughts Together." My brother and I chomp our cigars and clap, but in our hearts we are low and lonesome.

Don't y'all burn down the house, says Uncle Trash pedaling out the yard to Cuts. My brother leans out the window with a rope coil and scraps strung on strings. He is in a greasy-finger sleep when the strings slither like white snakes off our bed and over the sill into the fields out back.

There's July corn and no word from our parents. Uncle Trash doesn't remember the Fourth of July or the Fourth of July parade. Uncle Trash bunches cattails in the fenders of his bicy-cle and clips our Old Maid cards in the spokes and follows the fire engine through town with my brother and I in the front cut-out crate throwing penny candy to the crowds. What are you trying to be, the colored men at Cuts ask us when we end up there. I spot a tin-metal truck of mine broken by the Cutses' front step. Foolish, says Uncle Trash.

Uncle Trash doesn't remember winning Mrs. Cuts in a card game for a day to come out and clean the house for us in the bargain. She pushes the furniture around with a broom and calls us abominations. There's a bucket of soap to wash our heads and a jar of sour-smelling cream for our infected bites. Fleas from under the house and mosquitoes through the win-dows. The screens are rusty squares in the driveway dirt. Uncle Trash leaves her his razor opened as long as my arm. She comes after my brother and I with it to cut our hair, she says. We know better. My brother dives under the house and I am up a tree. Uncle Trash doesn't remember July, but when we tell him about it he says he thinks July was probably a good idea at the time.

It is August with the brown twisted corn in the fields next to the house. There is word from our parents. They are in the state capital. One of them has been in jail. I try to decide which. Uncle Trash is still promising screens. We get from Cuts bug spray instead.

I wake up in the middle of the night. My brother floats

through the window. Out in the yard he and a stray have each other on the end of a rope. He reels her in and I make the tackle. Already I feel the fleas leave her rag-matted coat and crawl over my arms and up my neck. We spray her down with a whole can of bug spray until her coat lathers like soap. My brother gets some matches to burn a tick like a grape out of her ear. The touch of the match covers her like a blue-flame sweater. She's a fireball shooting beneath the house. By the time Uncle Trash and the rest of town get there the fire warden says the house is Fully Involved.

In the morning our parents drive past where our house used to be. They go by again until they recognize the yard. Uncle Trash is trying to bring my brother out of the trance he is in by showing him how some card tricks work on the left-standing steps of the stoop. Uncle Trash shows Jack-Away, Queen in the Whorehouse, and No Money Down. Our father says for Uncle Trash to stand up so he can knock him down. Uncle Trash says he deserves that one. Our father knocks him down again and tells him not to get up. If you get up I'll kill you, our father says.

Uncle Trash crawls on all fours across our yard out to the road. Goodbye, men, Uncle Trash says. Don't y'all burn the house down, he says and I say, We won't.

During the knocking down nobody notices our mother. She is a flat-footed running rustle through the corn all burned up by the summer sun.

ARTHUR ROBINSON

The Boy on the Train

FROM THE NEW YORKER

IN 1891, at the age of five, Lewis Barber Fletcher traveled alone
from Jacksonville, Florida, to the little town of Camden, thirty-
one miles northwest of Utica, in upstate New York. Fifty years
later, his wife, children, and friends heard about his trip for the
first time when this item appeared on the editorial page of the
Utica Daily Press under a standing head, "50 Years Ago Today
in the Press": "Lewis B. Fletcher, 5, arrived in Utica yesterday
on a New York Central train on his way to join his mother in
Camden. He was traveling alone from Jacksonville, Florida." A
friend spotted the item and phoned Mrs. Fletcher, who called
her husband at his office and read it to him. She had to read it
twice before he got it straight; he was hard of hearing and even
with an amplifying device on his telephone often had trouble
understanding, mostly because he became tense when he had to
use it. When he understood what she had read him, he gave an
embarrassed "Ha!" and said he had forgotten about the trip.
There was no further discussion — he disliked talking about
personal matters at his office, possibly suspecting that all work
stopped while the help listened for material for gossip. When
he came home that evening, he had already read the item at
work, clipped it, stuck it in his billfold, and developed an attitude toward it — a sort of amused, self-conscious pride that
seemed to say yes, he had traveled nearly fourteen hundred
miles by himself when he was five, with two changes of train,
one of them involving a ferry from Jersey City to Manhattan,
and had managed the whole thing, as he had everything else in
his life, by strict application to business.

The item was a sort of one-day sensation. Two clippings were put away in a photograph album, and the subject was pretty much forgotten. Sarah, the youngest child, occasionally resurrected it when the family was together at Christmas or, in later years, during vacations at the elder Fletchers' place outside Utica. In the evening, when their parents had gone to bed and the children stayed up talking, Sarah might say in a reverential tone, "Can you imagine him traveling alone from Jacksonville to Camden when he was five?" The two others — Howard, the oldest, and Edward — would say they could imagine it, that it was the easiest thing in the world to imagine. The picture they'd then conjure up was of a five-year-old old man with white hair, steel-rimmed bifocals, and a hearing aid that he kept turned off to save the flat, half-pint-shaped battery. (Edward and Howard had never thought of him as anything but an old man, even when they were small and he was in his thirties.) He would have dickered, they'd say, with the railroad until it agreed to give him a ticket in exchange for some worn-out toys, and he would have worked a deal in the dining car for his food, perhaps agreeing to polish silver. He would have brought along candy, fruit, and tattered copies of old newspapers to sell on the train. When he wasn't busy selling, or polishing silver, he'd be doing his book-keeping. At every stop, he'd buy more stuff to sell, and at Jersey City he'd trade some of his inventory for the ferry ride to Manhattan. He'd be too busy to see the Hudson River or the Mohawk Valley, and when there was nothing else to do he'd make notes for the lectures he'd someday give his sons on How to Get Ahead and Be Somebody. "You don't get anything in this life without working . . . You'll never get anywhere until you learn to apply yourselves . . . How do you suppose we got this nice home? Nobody handed it to us. I worked hard for everything we've got . . . If you don't develop some get-up-and-go, you'll never amount to anything or have anything." He'd write a note to himself to mention the horrible example of Uncle Reggie, who was two at the time and showing unmistakable signs of having no get-up-and-go.

Edward did wonder that his father seemed to have forgotten about a trip that should have been a momentous experience for a five-year-old. He decided that his father may have felt there

was something shameful about it and the shame had caused him
to repress the memory. The children were dimly aware that
their paternal grandparents had separated in Jacksonville and
were later divorced, and that their grandmother had brought
up Lewis and Reginald in Camden, her home town, but they
didn't know any details; a divorce in a churchgoing family was
a matter of some embarrassment. What Edward learned later
was that right after the separation their grandmother had returned to Camden with Reginald, leaving Lewis with their
grandfather. The grandfather, who wasn't much good, had apparently decided that he didn't want Lewis and had put him on
a train for the two-day trip to his mother's. It was not an amus-
ing picture: a five-year-old had been left behind by his mother
and then sent off alone by his father — abandoned by one,
rejected by the other. Edward would try to imagine him without
white hair, hearing aid, or steel-rimmed bifocals, a small boy
with brown hair and a grave face, being taken to the train by his
father, so dumb with misery and fright that he couldn't cry,
knowing only that he was going somewhere out there into unknown space. A train would thunder into the station, all smoke
and steam. He had seen trains from a distance, and this one was
all the more terrifying for being seen from three feet above the
platform. His father would take him aboard and stow a bag in
the rack. After reminding him when to eat the food he had
brought along, his father would embrace him and leave, possibly waiting on the platform to gesture and smile until the train
moved, and then walking a few steps with it and waving. Lewis
would sit there, keeping a toy close to him, putting off as long
as he could going to the toilet, because so many people would
be watching him walk through the aisle and because he wouldn't
be sure he could undertake such a project without help. Maybe
two days of sitting there and sleeping in a berth, if his father
had bought him a Pullman ticket — long enough for the railroad car to become his world — and then Jersey City, the end
of the line. A conductor or Pullman porter who had been tipped
would take him across the river on a ferry to a horse-drawn cab
and instruct the driver to take Lewis to Grand Central and see
that someone put him on a train for Utica. Then the train out
of New York and up the Hudson and through the Mohawk

Valley. At Utica he would change trains for Camden. Edward supposed Lewis's mother would be at the Camden station to meet him.

Edward went over the trip from time to time, adding details, trying to get inside the boy to experience his anxiety and despair and very likely his distrust of people on the train, whose brief, unctuous kindnesses betrayed their fear of ending up with him on their hands.

This was the image of his father that could move Edward, and it seemed to bear no relation to the anxiety-ridden old man in his early forties who sat all evening with a *Saturday Evening Post* in his lap, his hands clasped over his stomach and his thumbs revolving first one way and then the other while he went over and over whatever was worrying him — whether his sons would turn out like Reggie or his own father, whether there'd be enough profit at the end of the year to enable him to meet his bank loan, whether the new Jewish family in the neighborhood meant more to come. In 1928, a pressing worry was whether a cocky Irish Catholic from New York City would defeat Herbert Hoover and succeed in destroying business and the country — Hoover, surpassed in wisdom and ability only by his great predecessor, Calvin Coolidge.

What upset their father as much as anything else was the attitude of his sons, particularly Howard's. They had done nothing to earn their good life, and yet they took it for granted, with never a word of gratitude or any acknowledgment of what he had done for them. He tried to teach them that it all came hard, that at eleven he supported his mother and Reggie by taking care of the fire in the Camden library stove, carrying the morning and evening Syracuse papers, delivering telegrams, shoveling walks in winter and doing yard work in summer, working in the hardware store on Saturdays, and pumping the organ in the Presbyterian church on Sundays. As he explained the importance and the rewards of work and the seriousness of life, Edward would stare past his head, glassy-eyed, and Howard would wear a bored smirk. At an age when their father was supporting his mother and Reggie, his sons were coasting on their Flexible Flyers, skating, building snowhouses and forts, riding bikes, exploring in a nearby woods, or playing baseball or football in vacant lots. He would come home to find the driveway unshoveled and be forced to park in the street, or the lawn unmowed, or the garage or attic uncleaned. There was always agitation for more things — for skis, pack baskets, hockey skates, hockey sticks, a double-bladed ax, new or more golf clubs, punching bag and rings for the attic, or a stay in the Adirondacks in summer. They were establishing attitudes that would be lifelong unless he succeeded in persuading them that life was more than play.

Dinnertime was lecture time. The speeches flowed right past both boys in a meaningless litany they knew by heart. Conversation at the table was on two levels: one, loud, between their parents, who were both slightly hard of hearing and left their hearing aids turned off to save the batteries, and the other among the children, who could carry on a protracted quarrel without their parents' knowledge until Sarah — it was usually Sarah — raised her voice to alert her parents that she was being picked on. Then both parents would set about adjusting their hearing aids to get tuned in. Sometimes, with heads bent, Howard and Edward would recite their father's speeches along with him, occasionally commenting on omissions ("He forgot money doesn't grow on trees"). Howard refined a talent for rephrasing their feisty mother's numerous sayings, turning them into nonsense. At the end of one of their father's speeches, Howard commented, "I always say you can lead a horse to drink but you can't make him water." All three children were convulsed; it was far and away Howard's most successful effort, and they were helpless with laughter. Their father, red-faced, demanded to know what was funny. Sarah, still shaking, said it was something Howard had said. Their father ordered Howard to tell him what it was. The thought of Howard's having to repeat the saying set them off again. Their mother, who loved a good laugh and was always on their side, joined them, although she didn't know what was funny. When Howard finally got it out, their mother gave a delighted shriek. Their father was left out of it altogether, a red-faced spoilsport.

"Reggie all over," he said.

"Don't be such a stick-in-the-mud," their mother said.

Their father's attitude toward Howard grew harsher and he often predicted Howard would amount to nothing, like Uncle Reggie, unless he changed. Howard, near tears, would fight back and was sometimes sent away from the table. Their mother, tears streaming down her face, would say their father was always picking on Howard. "I don't see why you can't leave him alone," she'd say.

"He thinks life's a joke. Well, it isn't, and it's time he learned it isn't. Believe me, I know what I'm talking about."

"Maybe you'd be better off if you loosened up a little."

"Loosen up. Loosen up. I like that."

He'd say Howard wasn't a Fletcher, he was a Davies. Their mother's name was Davies, and her father, a carpenter, had come from Wales. Her maternal forebears were farmers who had settled in central New York.

"Howard inherited a mean Welsh temper, just like your father's," he'd say.

He'd try to eat — he couldn't bear to waste food — but would have to give it up. He'd lay his napkin on the table, breathe deeply, and put his hand on his chest; these scenes brought on heartburn. A little later he'd mix a glass of Citrocarbonate, then sit in the living room with the *Saturday Evening Post* in his lap and a worried expression on his face.

Howard had a bagful of tricks with which to annoy his father. At the table he'd pour himself milk, starting with the pitcher close to the glass, then moving it higher and higher until it was a couple of feet in the air, all the time being careful not to spill. His expression throughout was one of intense concentration, as though he were performing some difficult but necessary task. It was a performance that Edward loved, partly because they both knew what was coming.

Their father would strike the table with the flat of his hand. "We're not going to have such goings on at our table," he'd say.

Howard would look incredulous. "You mean I can't drink milk?"

There'd be no reply.

"You can't do anything around here, Percival," Howard would say.

"Don't call me Percival," Edward would reply.

With the handle of his spoon, Howard would depress the tablecloth to form a crease where the pads under it came together; the crease marked a boundary between his and Edward's territories and was necessary, Howard insisted, because of Edward's habit of encroaching on Howard's territory with his elbow. It was really needed to annoy their father. By Howard's decree, territorial violations were punishable by a hit on the upper arm, administered with a flick of the wrist and the knuckle of the middle finger extended. Edward, who liked living on the brink, kept his elbow as close to the crease as he could and tried to find excuses for crossing. There were disputes in an undertone over whether his elbow had actually crossed and he had a hit coming. Howard always found him guilty and passed sentence, and for a few seconds, while Howard explained how sorry he was to have to do it, Edward tingled with suspense. Then Howard hit him. The pain was excruciating, and Edward would double over, laughing hysterically and weeping from pain.

Hearing aids came on. There were warnings, and their father would ask rhetorically if they couldn't have one dinner in peace. Edward carried a permanent bruise.

If everything else failed, Howard could often get things started by calling Edward Percival, or Archibald. Then he discovered a wonderful term, "poop deck," which sounded indecent but wasn't.

"Poopdeck, hand me the butter."

"What did you call him?" Sarah asked.

"Poopdeck."

Sarah, loud: "Howard used a nasty word."

Hearing aids were adjusted and there was debate about whether "poop deck" was a nasty word. Their mother didn't think so; she'd seen it in novels and, she thought, in the *Press* crossword. Their father said Howard wasn't to use it. Howard said he had a right to use it — it was part of a ship — and Edward didn't mind being called Poopdeck, did you, Poopdeck? Their father said Howard was only calling Edward *that* to get something started and he was not to call him *that* again at the table and that was final.

"Percival, the butter."

"Please."

"Poopdeck, you want your arm in a sling?"

Sarah, loud: "He's using that word again."

Howard was sent away from the table.

Their father seemed to get a new hearing aid every year or two as improved models came out. Their mother got the old one. They were bone-conducting devices, held in place behind one ear with a narrow band of spring steel that fitted over the head. A cord ran from the bone-conducting unit behind their father's ear down inside his collar and emerged from his shirtfront to connect with a microphone, which clipped to a vest pocket. Another cord led from the microphone to the battery pack in his hip pocket. A switch and volume control were on the microphone. Sometimes, after their father had fumbled with the control and still couldn't hear, Howard would suggest that maybe he was sitting on the cord. The possibility that current couldn't get through a wire because their father was sitting on it was one of their standing jokes. Whenever their father had trouble getting tuned in at the table, Howard would trot out the idea: "I think you're sitting on the cord." It amused them even more that their father would always reply, "What? What?" and feel around under him.

Their mother was self-conscious about having to wear a hearing aid and did her hair so as to conceal it; one had to look closely to see the cord that emerged from her hair at the back of her neck and disappeared into her dress. She didn't want anyone to know about the embarrassing gear she wore under her clothes. Doctors found nothing organically wrong with her hearing; her impairment, they said, was "sympathetic." The children referred to the hearing aids as speakers, and before saying anything to either parent would ask, "Is your speaker on?"

Edward — thin and small-boned — had more passive ways than Howard's of resisting their father. He was rarely hungry, and at dinner invariably became nauseated halfway through the meal. The nausea always came suddenly, usually when he had food in his mouth. He'd park it (a family expression) in a cheek and wait for the nausea to pass, meanwhile dangling his fork between two fingers and batting it between thumb and little finger, daydreaming. Their father was as distressed about seeing Edward's cheek packed with food he wasn't even chewing as he was about Howard's tricks — and it was food bought with his hard-earned money, the only kind of money he ever had.

"Chew," he'd exhort Edward. Edward would chew a couple of times experimentally and give up.

"Watch me chew," his father would say. He'd lean above Edward and solemnly chew. The sessions of chewing instruction were frequent, and Edward came to know every pore on the shiny plane at the tip of his father's nose. The image of his father's big face above him, his gray eyes peering down through steel-rimmed bifocals, was often what he remembered when he thought of his father, the jaw going in a slightly circular fashion, like a cow's. He was fully grown before he discovered pleasure in food, that things he thought he hated — peas, for example — were really rather good. He was never able to eat rice. It evoked a picture of his father at lunch, about to pour cream into a bowl of steaming rice mixed with brown sugar and butter, saying, "Oh, boy!" which was his way of expressing perfect contentment. Years later, Edward would feel the old nausea rising. He was surprised to discover that Howard, in his fifties, still became emotional on the subject of Boston baked beans. Their father, who adored them — their mother baked them all day until they were, as their father said, nutty — once forced Howard to eat them when he was very small. Howard threw up. Edward rather liked Boston baked beans.

Their father never merely liked or disliked something; he felt compelled to impose his opinions on his family. These opinions involved everything from his view of life to the food he ate, the Republican Party, the make of car he drove. Not eating the food that he believed in was subversive. Every meal that Edward couldn't finish represented a stalemate, or even a defeat, for his father.

In prepubescence, Edward gazed at his face in the mirror a great deal and studied the effects he could get with it. Once he discovered that a strip of toothpaste artfully placed just below a nostril produced an effect that could easily turn his father's queasy stomach. The result was more than he could have hoped for. He waited until everyone was at the table before joining them. Sarah, sitting opposite, was the first to notice. In a loud voice she announced that Edward was making her sick. Their father looked, and a few moments later rose, napkin over mouth, and left the room.

Curious about how he'd look without eyebrows, Edward shaved one off with his father's razor. His father was always conscious of the image that the family presented, and Edward could sense his discomfort at having to sit in church with a son who had only one eyebrow. After Howard persuaded Edward that the new eyebrow would grow in bushier than its mate, he shaved off the second one so that they'd match.

When Edward had become a conspicuously unsuccessful father, who quarreled with his children over their pot smoking, their rock music, their language, their clothes, until they had become alienated, he'd think with some respect and sympathy of his father's ability to survive, particularly as he and Howard grew older. Howard was addicted to strange projects, some of them involving firecrackers. When he was about thirteen, to see what would happen he dropped a lighted firecracker into an empty ink bottle and quickly put the stopper in the bottle. What he learned was that the bottle blows up and sprays the experimenter with bits of inky glass. For days, Howard's face was flecked with dark blue freckles. He and Edward decided Howard must have blinked at the instant of the explosion, since they could find no glass in his eyes and since he could still see. The walls of his room were speckled with the glass.

Impressed by a contortionist he had seen in vaudeville, Howard spent a few weeks trying to get a foot behind his head by tightening a belt that was looped around head and foot. He abandoned the project when he had a heel within a couple of inches of his forehead. He was strong, and proud of his muscles, and often scuffled with their ninety-five-pound mother, who had never quite grown up. Once, as they wrestled for some object — a ball, a report card — without intending to he tossed her over his hip. There was an audible crack as she hit the floor. "Howie," she said as she lay there, "I think you broke my ankle." She was on crutches for more than a month.

Howard had nearly perfect teeth, with one slight imperfection — a minute hole between the two upper front teeth, through which he could squirt a tiny water jet. He'd take a drink of water at the table and sit smiling, to uncover the hole. His mother, seeing him looking at her with a foolish grin and knowing what was coming, would say, "Howie, don't you dare!" At which he'd give her a small squirt. She'd no sooner get her glasses wiped off than he'd squirt her again. She'd laugh with delight. Howard would have enough water left to give Edward a shot or two on the ear. Their father, outnumbered as usual, would be silent. He may have thought it was funny.

There was a series of four or five automobile accidents that started when Howard was fourteen. His father had made the mistake of showing him how to drive. Edward was eager to have Howard teach him, and at the first opportunity, when their parents were out playing bridge, they pushed their father's car out of the garage and got in. Howard started the engine and they roared into the garage, crushing the Easy Washer against a laundry tub and knocking the tub off its supports. Howard made the first of the reports that came close to becoming a habit. He phoned the house where his parents were, asked for his father, and said, "Dad, I just had an accident." Accidents usually took place at night. They'd wake their father to break the news, and he'd sit on the edge of his bed, trying to comprehend through the fog of half sleep and saying in a singsong, "Oh, oh, oh, oh, oh, oh, ohhh." In the last and worst of them, in daylight, when he was through school and returning home from his first job, Edward collided at an intersection with an old Reo Speed Wagon, whose driver, a short bald man who worked on a W.P.A. project and was the father of four children, was pitched out the door on his head. He lay on his back in the roadway, dead.

Edward lived with a jumble of images of his father; some of them in time became moving, including that worried face hovering over him, showing him how to chew. Another was of his father sprawled flat on his face on Genesee Street, in New Hartford, while a car skidded to a stop a few feet from him. It was a Sunday, and the children wanted ice cream cones. Their father, of course, said they didn't need ice cream cones, but their mother shamed him, as she always shamed him: "Honest, Lewis, you're so tight you squeak." So he was crossing the street, red-faced and mad, to get cones for the children, who were waiting in the car with their mother. Seeing a car bearing down on him, he started to sprint. He tripped, or slipped, on a streetcar track and fell flat. They all watched, horrified. Their mother screamed. The driver managed to stop. Their father got up, picked up his glasses and cap, and completed his mission. He handed the children their cones and got into the car without a word. As they drove home, their mother wept quietly on the front seat and the children, in back, licked their ice cream without pleasure.

There was their father the golfer with the flossy waggle, and the skier with the strange posture. Occasionally, on a Sunday in winter, wrapped in blankets, the family drove in their 1922 Buick open touring car with isinglass curtains to the village of Sauquoit, south of Utica, where a farmer waited with a sleigh and a team of horses. They rode on straw under heavy blankets that smelled of a cow barn for the two miles uphill to the little house they owned overlooking the Sauquoit Valley. The unpaved road was snowed in, and the sleigh went through barnyards and across fields. They had a fire in the dining room stove and ate a hot meal that their mother had put up in aluminum containers that fitted into an insulated cylinder with a heated flat stone at the bottom — slices from a leg of lamb, mashed potatoes, gravy, and cauliflower. They used a privy inside a woodshed attached to the house. They skied through a planted pinewood to a snow-covered cornfield with a steep slope, and spent the afternoon there, their father standing straight up on his skis, feet together and arms extended from his sides like a tightrope walker. He said that was the correct form, and he liked to get the form right. (He had played high school football and baseball in Camden and church league baseball in Utica, and had a rather showy throwing motion; when they played catch with him, Howard and Edward called him, in an undertone, Joe Form.) Using their skis, they pushed up a mound of snow and compacted it to make a jump. The farmer returned with the sleigh in the late afternoon, lighted a lantern, hung it from a hook beside his raised seat, and jovially tucked them in — except for tireless Howard, who insisted on skiing down.

There was their father the competitor, who had to be taking on someone at something every day to keep his juices flowing. He always drove home for lunch to have a half hour of cards with their mother. For years the game was Russian bank, a two-handed form of solitaire; later, it was cribbage; still later, canasta; and, after he retired, Scrabble. He kept a running score in a little notebook, and could tell her at any time how many points he was ahead. There were often arguments over who was cheating whom, she joshing, he dead serious. He loved bridge — it challenged his ability to keep track of the cards played, and tested his ingenuity in making difficult contracts. He didn't like playing with people who took the game less seriously than he did, who talked and didn't pay attention, or, as he would say, didn't apply themselves. Howard, who didn't like to play when his father was in the game, was occasionally dragooned into making a fourth when no one else was available. His father may have suspected there was some justice in his wife's criticism that he was too hard on Howard. As Howard went about making himself comfortable, hauling up an easy chair and settling into it sideways to the table, his legs over an arm, his father would try to restrain himself, but several deep breaths gave him away. Howard kept up a silly chatter guaranteed to annoy his father, who couldn't abide silliness. Howard had become fond of the words "nicely" and "extremely," possibly from reading Damon Runyon stories in *Collier's*. "That's very nicely" and "That's extremely," he'd say, and sometimes he'd combine them: "That's extremely nicely." If the game lasted long enough, he might wind up with one leg on the back of the chair and his head almost under the table. He would finally succeed in provoking a confrontation. Once, his father told him sharply that he couldn't pass. "Your partner bid two no-trump," he said. "You have to say something."

Howard, not wanting to take a chance on getting stuck with the bid, stalled. "How do we get out of this, Poopdeck?" he said. "How about three no-spades?"

"What's your bid?" his father asked.

Loud, defiant: "Three no-spades."

His father threw down his cards. "Lord help us," he said. The game was over.

Howard raised his head and looked innocently around. "Something the matter, Poopdeck?"

As a lover, their father was unusual, and even playful. When courting their mother (both worked for a wholesale building-supply firm, she as a stenographer, he as a salesman), he'd call on her in the evening with a ball glove and ball, she once told the children, and they'd play catch in her parents' side yard, he gallantly letting her use the glove. Even in their sixties they'd occasionally chase each other out of the kitchen with a water pistol they kept there, laughing like schoolchildren. They became hysterical once when the hot-water bottle they were throwing at each other in their bedroom broke and soaked a bed. Another night, unable to restrain herself when she saw him praying on his knees beside his bed, she took the Bible, kept on a nightstand between their beds, and threw it, hitting him on the shoulder. He thought that was hilarious. Although for much of the time he carried the weight of the world on his shoulders, when mightily amused he went all out, laughing uncontrollably, tears streaming down his face. He'd pull himself together, blow his nose, and then have a second seizure.

Their father had given them a good life, a wonderful life, as the appreciative Sarah sometimes said; he worried about them, undoubtedly loved them, and tried to be just. And yet, it seemed to Edward, both sons had withheld affection and given him only grudging respect. Since Edward couldn't believe that he and Howard were mean by nature, he looked for the fault elsewhere. He always came back to the child on the train and the insecurity and despair he suspected the boy had experienced, possibly even before his trip to Camden, until an exaggerated sense of anxiety had become permanently established and was later inflicted on his sons. Almost too late, Edward pitied, if not loved, his father.

Edward wondered why his grandfather, a lawyer and member of a prosperous family, hadn't taken his son to Camden instead of sending him off by himself at age five. The answer seemed to be that he was monstrously irresponsible. He married two more times, left more children around the country, went on the gold rush to the Klondike, and died chasing a rumor of gold in British Honduras (now Belize), where he was buried. Why hadn't the boy's mother met him in New York, or even in Utica? Both parents seemed to have set him up for whatever might have happened to a small child making such a long journey alone.

It may have been inevitable that this touching child, this David Copperfield, metamorphosed into a ponderous apostle of get-up-and-go. His upbringing had taught him about the snares set for the unwary, a lesson made urgent by the example of his own father, and may have accounted for the harsh, bullying tone, for the implication that his sons would turn out like Uncle Reggie (he never mentioned his father) unless they shaped up. It was the implication and the tone that turned them off.

Contemplating his own disaster, Edward wondered why anyone who doesn't have to ever becomes a father. "There is no one right way to bring up children," a therapist once told him, to ease his guilt after he had poured out his own meanness as a father. There seemed to be only wrong ways. He had thought that all he needed to do was to avoid his father's example. No lectures on getting ahead and being somebody. Let the kid park all the food he wanted in his cheek or blow up ink bottles or spend his evenings trying to get his foot behind his head. Keep the hearing aid turned on, and keep smiling.

As it turned out, Edward was unprepared for the reality of the early seventies in southern Marin County. By the time he calmed down and began seeing a therapist, his seventeen-year-old son was living in a shack with a girl, and his fifteen-year-old daughter was scarcely speaking to him. He was shocked and depressed. On the day his son moved out of the house, Edward could barely contain his frustration. "How do you expect to have any kind of life?" he said. "Or have *anything*? Your mother and I work hard so we can live here, and you thumb your nose at what makes it possible — at the whole idea of making something of your life. Believe me, it doesn't come easy." Then he stopped. For a moment, he could hear Howard saying, in an undertone, "He forgot money doesn't grow on trees."

M. T. SHARIF

The Letter Writer

FROM THE AGNI REVIEW

For Mansoureh

A DERVISH who stopped in the town for a loaf of *barbari* saw
Haji the letter writer and proclaimed, "Mark my words. Today
that man inscribes cards and papers. Yet he will live in a seven-
columned house. And seven concubines will attend him. And
seven servants will obey his every wish." Saying this, he gathered
his bundle and disappeared.

Gossip spread faster in Rostam Abbad than lice on a donkey's
testicles; the dervish's words created a sensation. Drinking tea
in coffeehouses, people of different persuasions debated the
issue hotly. All referred to the one house of opulence they
knew, the Shah's summer mansion, Shady Palace. Though no
one approached it to peer through its gates, in this shady place
in the mountains, the informed assumed, there were many
rooms, many columns, many mirrored *darbars*. Here the consensus ended and arguments ensued. Some said, "Haji has eyes the
size of hubcaps, we tell you. Made for ogling over extrava-
gances, we tell you." Others said, "You propose that he will
occupy a home resembling the King's?" The local pundit said,
"Haji's a fool. He cannot tell a *mullah* from a mule." So the
rumors persisted and his future intrigued people.

Haji ignored the sudden interest in his affairs, muttering, "A
businessman has little time for chatter." Then he looked right
and left, and startled passers-by with a lusty call: "Hurry. Hurry.
Petitions. Affidavits. Money orders drafted here."

His professional apparatus consisted of a few pens and quills, some papers, a Koran, and colored pictures of the Prophet. Resorting to these pictures, citing the holy book, waving his material in the air, all day he accosted people. "*Agha*. Yes, you, chewing beet leaf. Are you deaf? Commission a card for your wife, children, or mother-in-law." He coaxed another, "Madame. Lady in the see-through veil. Are you married? Have you a father? What would he say if he saw you dressed like this? A postcard for your suitors?"

He scolded those who obstructed his view. He concocted, for a few *toomans*, a eulogy or a curse letter. He directed traffic. At all times he advertised an impressive array of services: "Hurry. Hurry. Checks. Wills. Notarized papers. By special arrangement, green cards and diary entries." Thus Haji held court in a corner of Cannon Square.

Salty skeptics watched him transacting business and said, "The man is a public nuisance. One cannot cross the square safely anymore." Haughty gossips said, "We hear that he consorts with all sorts of evil creatures." Cucumber-fingered cynics said, "God willing, rivals will trim that malicious tongue of his."

Indeed, Haji's was a competitive calling. In the narrow square professionals of all arts vied for attention. Vendors of bitter almonds, tire thieves, and junk sellers hawked their wares. Liver cooks and beet merchants praised their produce. Bankers, bakers, and butchers jostled one another. Also a typist hovered about, hiding in dark corners, ready to spring forth and set up shop the minute Haji averted his head.

Amidst this melee, Haji crouched, observing the bustle with that yearning look of a camel upon cotton seeds. If shoppers snubbed him, if regulars slighted him, if the typist snatched a customer and settled down to punch his machine, Haji appealed to the store owners directly. "Brother vendors. Neighbor businessmen. I ask of you, is there room for more than one author in this square? Instruct your patrons to frequent my establishment."

He raised prices and reduced them, he cursed and cajoled, he hurled unsolicited advice in the general direction of onlookers, until, cornering some hesitant customer, coercing the fellow to sit cross-legged on the ground, he said, "Enunciate properly. Who is to receive this letter?" This was just the first in a series of questions. For half an hour he interrogated his patron on the content and purpose of the piece, the desired tone, diction, style, and format. Then he licked his pen, raised his brow, blew *Allah Akbar* in the air, and wrote, "May I be your slave and servant, the carpet beneath your feet. Allow me to forward my salaam and prayers. My father forwards his salaam and prayers. My mother forwards her salaam and prayers. My other kith and kin forward their salaam and prayers." Later he ended a letter in a similar vein. "May your shadow never diminish. May I make a balcony from my head for your steps. This green leaf is from your slave and servant." Between these ceremonial introductions and conclusions, space permitting, he squeezed in a word or two uttered by the client.

Question the soul, however, who requested a slight alteration, abbreviation, or rephrasing. Pity the person who protested that he had no father or brother. Such impertinence angered Haji. He cast pen and paper aside and roared, "Why, sir, you know better? Take your business elsewhere. Find that typist. He has operated a grocery, dabbled in gynecology, proceeded to geographical astrology, and is now a writer of mail. Save for a few flowery maxims he is practically illiterate. But he will suit you better."

Now Haji neglected his customer. He chewed a *nabat* and gurgled. He cleaned his nails, scrubbed his feet. He napped; he drank a tumbler of tea. Now, abruptly, eyeing the letter seeker, he said, "Sir. You are still here? I ask of you, if a man lets his donkey to graze on the land of a friend and pays for this service, and it so happens that his donkey becomes pregnant, who, sir, does the offspring belong to — the owner of the animal or the proprietor of the land? You do not know? May I suggest to you, then, to leave important matters to your elders." With half a dozen riddles of this nature he thoroughly cowed the customer. Then he licked his pen, raised his brow, blew *Allah Akbar*, and said, "Tell me, who is this to be sent to and what do you propose to say?"

The inquisitive asked him, "Haji, why bother asking folks what they want said?"

"Your excellencies," he responded. "These are uneducated people. They tell me what they generally feel and I fashion that into acceptable prose."

His reasoning confounded friends, but it scarcely convinced foes. Arm-in-arm cucumber cynics and salty skeptics paced the square and said, "The blackguard robs simple, poor villagers. His whole family ought to find themselves honorable professions." Damning information had it that an elder brother of Haji's, a self-proclaimed ninety-nine-year-old chemist, palm reader, and beggar, led a flourishing practice in the main mosque feigning epileptic seizures.

Glib rumors of this sort pained him. "How do I know who goes where masquerading as my brother?" he remarked. "I have no kith or kin. Probably the man is cross-eyed and cannot see straight. Why else would he be sitting in a house of worship pleading for alms? I assure you, mosque beggars are the most suspicious personalities."

He marked the passage of time by the movement of schoolchildren. They passed him on their way to the Dabestan at eight, taunted him during recess, and raced home after four. By then he had exhausted his clientele, collected various copper coins, and stuffed them in his socks.

In due course the din of Cannon Square subsided. Shopkeepers closed their *megazehs*. Beggars, vendors, hired hands, went their separate ways. Haji followed suit, assembled his apparatus, and found shelter in the doorway of a house or the threshold of a shop.

No doubt he conducted a valuable service. No doubt he enjoyed wooing patrons, sparring with foes. No doubt he would have continued, to the hour when milk sprouts in the nipples of eunuchs.

One day, a day neither hot nor cold, at the most ordinary hour, the appointed hour, as the horizon resembled a sheet of charcoal dotted by camphor, Rostam Abbad discovered the Revolution. Word hummed down the dusty Tehran Road. Wise beards and white beards heard it. The local pundit heard it. In the shade of walnut trees, playing backgammon, reciting Ferdousi, men heard it. Soaking their hot feet in cool streams, children heard it.

Certain citizens feared the whole affair. Half a dozen sold their belongings and immigrated to Cleveland. Others appointed themselves Revolutionary Guards. They patrolled streets; they stopped cars; they searched houses. Also they liberated Shady Palace. This caused much commotion. Some folks organized an expedition and toured the property, noting watery gardens of *maryam* and narcissus, and many columns, and many rooms. They rushed home and said, "There are many things to see." The next day a larger crowd scaled the mountain and sought entry. An old officer wearing a new khaki stopped them at the gates and shouted, "Go back." For the guards had bolted the windows, wired the walls, inaugurating Rostam Abbad's Revolutionary Committee for Public Grievances.

Perched in his usual corner in Cannon Square, Haji witnessed the twists and turns of history. He wrote his letters. He kept to his own affairs.

A fortnight after that ordinary day, uniformed guards seized him and said, "Haji, Haji, what have you done?"

"What have I done, sirs?"

"Do not be coy with us, Haji. Your brother spied for the anti-Revolution."

"Brother? I have no brother."

"He painted all sorts of leaflets in the main mosque and God knows what else. Do you know him?"

"That beggar? I have heard of him. What of it? For the past fifteen years he has claimed kinship to me."

"Come with us."

"Why, sirs? Just because some rabble calls himself my relative? Besides, I never saw the man."

"Enough, Haji. Provide evidence and you will be freed."

Meekly he followed them. The palace brimmed with people. Guards ran to and fro. Relatives of detainees cried here and there. "Sit," the guards ordered. He sat and marveled, a finger of amazement in his mouth. Even the most exaggerated accounts left him ill prepared for this. A chandelier hung in every room. Oak doors connected room to room. While the authorities rushed back and forth, opening, shutting doors, Haji counted forty chandeliers above forty carpets smooth as a woman's mustache. These luxuries he saw on the first floor. Perhaps there was a second, he reasoned, a third and a fourth, since the winding staircase that linked floor to floor spiraled to the sky.

Hours later the guards returned and dragged him to a hall where thousands of books lay in glass shelves. There the authorities dared him. There they blamed him. Again and again he said, "I am no traitor. That man is not my brother." He spent the night in a cellar alongside Communists and pickpockets.

In the succeeding months he maintained his innocence. He cursed. He reeled. He swore. He petitioned the municipality, the different committees, the president of the republic. Each and every time the authorities informed him, "Your brother has confessed and is serving time in Tehran."

"That good for nothing character is not my brother."

"You are implicated in his affairs."

"Gentlemen, do not believe him. Mosque beggars are highly unreliable."

"Either admit to your crimes or show us proof."

"How am I to do that? Am I a biographer or a writer of birth certificates?"

"Take this fool away," they said.

Date-eyed and afraid, every day, handcuffed Loyalists, Royalists, and other assorted anti-Revolutionaries marched forth and met their colleagues in the cellars of Shady Palace. These suspects the authorities processed swiftly. A few were flogged. A few were freed. Crammed in trucks, the rest were forwarded to Tehran. None remained incarcerated longer than Haji. The authorities told him, "We have not harmed you, not sent you to the capital, where you could be tortured. Come. Come. Tell us what you know."

"I know nothing," he said. "Nothing." He clamored. He complained. A year or two passed. He said nothing. As the carpets wore thin, he said, "I know nothing." As the grass, *maryam*, and narcissus grew waist high in the untended garden, he said, "I know nothing." As the roof leaked and the tiled columns dulled, he said, "Nothing. Nothing." As the palace, trampled by numerous feet, prey to the dust and the wind, adapted a less splendorous look, he said, "That man is not my brother. I know nothing." And he clamored. And he complained.

The authorities sympathized with his predicament. "Haji," they said. "Stop this racket. There is no peace in this compound because of you." They transferred him to a spacious room on the second floor and said, "Now be content. You have your very own room, table, chair, and view of the garden."

"Pray, how long?" he asked. "How long?"

"It is not in our hands. Tehran demands a confession from all political prisoners. Ages ago you should have repented."

A friendly official hit upon an ingenious idea. He ordered a stack of magazines brought up to Haji's room from the library and said, "Haji, look here. There are pictures of women in these pages. American women. English women. They are misled, misinformed. Their hair is uncovered. They wear sleeveless shirts and low-cut dresses. Make good use of your time. Cover their nakedness. We plan to distribute these papers to the public."

"Am I a painter?" he retorted. But his days were long, his nights dreary. Presently he picked a pen, chose a magazine, and sat by the window. Glossy pictures filled this foreign text; not a word could he decipher. There were so many pictures, though. Most required prompt attention. From cover to cover he searched the paper, applying the ink at necessary junctures, draping exposed knees and bare arms. Something in the act soothed him. He moved to another text. When he had sorted through the whole bundle he called on the guards for a second supply.

Late spring the buffalo gazed westward, hiding one foot, hoping for rain. Midsummer the grape burned bright as a lamp; on strings spiders seemed too hot to hunt. Autumn arrived heavily, fattened like a persimmon, riper and riper, then retreated, ushering in the winter snow. Beyond the window panes the years breezed away and Haji worked.

He woke at dawn and toiled past dusk. To the authorities he said, "I have fallen behind. Do not expect to distribute these papers yet. I am working night and day to finish." He worked slowly. Each paper, each page, every photograph, posed a new problem, a fresh challenge.

He found women in a variety of positions, in all shapes and sizes. Some reclined on cars. Some rested on cushions. Some held objects and grinned. Some grimaced. Some were sweet as *halva*. Some sour as a saw. Some looked plump. Some looked thin. Some young. Some old. Some felt smooth to the touch. Some tough and taut.

Before tackling the task at hand, Haji examined his subjects, considered their flaws. Then he licked his pen and wove his veils. He clothed their sinewy legs and dyed nails. He blotted their necks. He covered their wrists and exposed chests. With the tip of his pen he stroked them, shaded their naked limbs from strange and shameless eyes. Those he liked he treated this way. But those whom he judged disreputable, he attacked and tore apart.

The authorities visited him once a month. Each and every time he shuddered and said, "I am yet to finish. I am a few weeks behind and am working night and day."

One day they told him, "Your brother has died."

"He was not my brother."

"Nevertheless, we will plead your case with Tehran." He nodded. They returned and said, "A recalcitrant lot. But do not despair. We have other means."

Nowadays he wandered around the palace freely. There were few prisoners left. The building was in desperate need of repair. Plaster flaked off the ceiling. Walls sagged. Columns cracked. "This place is uninhabitable," the authorities argued. They built a modern facility nearby and told Haji, "Tehran is adamant. They want a confession."

"Stranger things, I hear," Haji said. "I hear that typist fellow went out of business because masons, vendors, villagers, all have learned to read and write. Anyway I have much to do."

When the authorities prepared to evacuate the palace they explained, "We will contact them once more, Haji. Do not lose hope. In the meantime we will take you to our new facilities."

"Why, sirs? Are you dissatisfied with my performance? I will work harder. Only allow me to stay. The books, the papers, are here."

In this manner Haji and an old revolutionary guard became the sole occupants of Shady Palace. His jailer cooked for Haji, did his wash, and every morning hauled a bundle of magazines to the second floor. Pen in hand Haji greeted him and said, "Am I to go to the well and return thirsty again? If the authorities so inquire, inform them that I am working ceaselessly."

Snowy seasons, he toiled indoors. The yellowed, worm-eaten pages crumbled in his hands. The mold and dust irritated his eyes, itched his nails. He worked and worked. For after he clothed them, after he draped, after he veiled, traced their every curve, suddenly, their withered faces shone, their eyes loomed larger, and their lips quivered, promising perpetual enchantment.

Melon days and summer nights, his jailer placed a chair on one of the numerous balconies and there too Haji labored. Sometimes old salty skeptics and cucumber cynics saw him on these crumbling *eivans*, pointed him out to their grandchildren, and said, "During the Revolution, it is recorded, he was a spy and killed many. The Revolution, dear ones, have you heard of it? Do you know about that great turmoil?"

Contributors' Notes
*100 Other Distinguished
   Stories of 1988*
Editorial Addresses

Contributors' Notes

CHARLES BAXTER is the author of two books of stories and a novel, *First Light*, published by Viking Penguin. A book of his poems, *Imaginary Paintings*, will be published by Paris Review Editions this fall. He lives in Michigan.

• "This story, about an older generation more radical than a younger one, has its roots in a few distinct memories: of seeing a beggar in a restaurant in Detroit; skating at night in Minnesota; and reading, many years ago, a letter my aunt Helen Baxter was then writing to the Chilean dictator General Pinochet. She disapproved of his behavior and told him so. All her adult life she wrote such letters to tyrants. I did not think of her letter writing as eccentric, of course, but as admirable. I owe the *Workers' Vanguard* reference to my student Ira Livingston, who read it in freshman composition. Wisps and whiffs of various classes I have taught made their way into the story, but the dominant spirit in it is my aunt's, to whose memory the story is dedicated."

MADISON SMARTT BELL is the author of five novels, most recently *Soldier's Joy*. Born and raised in Tennessee, he has lived in New York and London and now lives in Baltimore. He has taught in various creative writing programs, including the Iowa Writers' Workshop, and currently teaches at Goucher College along with his wife, the poet Elizabeth Spires. His second collection of short stories, *Barking Man*, will be published by Ticknor & Fields in 1990.

• "Like a fair amount of my fiction, as I've lately come to realize, 'Customs of the Country' was born out of boredom. It began with a long car trip: my wife and I were driving from Nashville to Iowa City, with a stop in Circleville, Ohio, to visit her family. The route produced two very monotonous eight- or nine-hour drives. We were in separate cars, so there was no one to talk to, and I had nothing better to do than try to tell myself a story.

"The only song I liked on the radio that summer was Suzanne Vega's 'Luka.' It's an eerie little tune, and the first time I heard it, it got enough hold on my imagination to start me spinning the dial in hope of hitting it again. On subsequent listens, the song clicked with a memory and turned into a subplot. When Kim Kafka and I were graduate students at Hollins, we lived in the same housing cluster, and we used to cook together fairly often, in one apartment or the other. At her apartment, things would be interrupted now and again by the sound and shock of something soft and heavy slamming into the other side of her kitchen wall.

"Halfway up I-65, I began to toy with the idea of a story which would present the pots falling from the kitchen pegboard as a recurring background motif, and would end with somebody (I didn't yet know who) picking up that iron skillet and . . . In Circleville I made a few notes and little real progress. But as soon as I was back in the car for the second leg of the trip, I went back into the familiar autohypnotic torpor, and the main plot of the story spun itself out as a natural sequence of truths and consequences — or so they struck me at the time. The story was complete in my head by the time we got to Iowa City, all over but the writing.

"The only other thing I have to confess about this story is that I'm not sure what it means. I knew what was happening right along, but was seldom certain about what the narrator was thinking or why she was thinking it. And I have not yet quite made up my mind whether that means I have failed her in some way or if I just wasn't ever supposed to understand her perfectly. But it seemed to me she had something to say, and I reported it the best I could."

ROBERT BOSWELL has written two novels, *The Geography of Desire* and *Crooked Hearts*, and one collection of stories, *Dancing in the Movies*. He is married to the fiction writer Antonya Nelson, and they teach at New Mexico State University in Las Cruces. Mr. Boswell also teaches in the Warren Wilson MFA Program for Writers.

• "During the ten-day residences of the Warren Wilson MFA Program, I attend classes as well as teach them. It was after a day of classes led by Stuart Dybek and Stephen Dobyns and Francine Prose that I started seeing a particular and peculiar image — that of a man standing on a crossbeam and looking below at something that was going on down there. It was peculiar because I was drawn powerfully to the image although I couldn't make out exactly what was happening below. I used to work in construction, but none of the typical things one might see satisfied the image.

"A week or two later I was in Telluride, Colorado, where Toni and I spend our summers, and we were walking into town when we happened to witness a cat electrocuted on a transformer box. That moment of not knowing whether to go to my wife or the cat is the one truly autobiographical thing in the story. Eventually I tried to write about that moment and discovered that the image that had been haunting me since Warren Wilson also belonged in the story. One thing led to another and the story was born."

BLANCHE McCRARY BOYD's most recent book, *The Redneck Way of Knowledge*, was published by Knopf in 1981. Her stories and essays have appeared in the *Village Voice, Esquire, Vanity Fair, Vogue,* and numerous other publications. Her awards include a Wallace Stegner Fellowship from Stanford University and a Fiction Fellowship from the National Endowment for the Arts. She has been writer in residence at Connecticut College for the past six years.

▪ "I blame 'The Black Hand Girl' on my friend Lisa Alther, whom I was trying to impress in conversation. I admire Lisa's sense of humor and sense of story, so I said to her, 'I'm going to write a story about a girl trying to lose her virginity in a girdle.' Lisa didn't look impressed, so I added, 'And this boy catches his hand in it and sprains his wrist.' She laughed out loud.

"Of course it was several years before I actually wrote 'The Black Hand Girl,' and of course it went through many drafts. The girdle incident eventually became embedded in the larger context of a heroine who finds it necessary to deflower herself.

"People tend to think my stories are autobiographically accurate even if they're about elderly ladies or firebombings or are written from the viewpoints of men, and 'The Black Hand Girl,' like all the stories I'm doing lately, has an I-was-there-and-I'm-gonna-tell-you-something-amazing narrator, so I have been moving toward my problem rather than away from it, making a virtue out of a liability, making the best of it, as my mother would say.

"Still, 'The Black Hand Girl' is a hard story to take the rap for. I did go to Duke, and I once owned a wig, and I do *wish* I'd hypnotized the dean of students, but about the rest, I'm not sure. My fiction convinces me too, and I get confused. However, to the best of my knowledge, 'The Black Hand Girl' is an act of imagination, a piece of writing, some words strung together. I didn't do this, Momma, I swear I didn't."

LARRY BROWN lives in Yocona, Mississippi. His first collection of short stories, *Facing the Music*, won the 1989 Mississippi Institute of Arts and Letters Award for literature. He is a captain in the Oxford Fire Department, and his novel, *Dirty Work*, will appear this fall.

▪ "It would be nice if all stories arrived like bolts of lightning through the head, fully formed with a beginning and an ending. Usually I have to build them slowly, and worry over them, and be afraid they're no good while I'm working on them. But this one flowed like water from a barrel once these two sentences hit me: *Angel hear the back door slam. It Alan, in from work.*

"I knew a couple of things immediately when I wrote those first two sentences. I knew she was drinking, and I knew that door slamming was bad news, because I knew he wasn't going to be happy when he saw the glass she was holding. I knew she wasn't supposed to be drinking. There had been trouble with this in the past, and he wasn't going to have much patience with her. All that hit me, and then some other things hit me.

"What I'd written, those two sentences, was in a sort of dialect. Who was speaking these lines? Not Angel. She was sitting on the couch trying to decide whether to get up and hide the glass or not. Angel wasn't telling the story. Somebody else was. And who was that? That hit me, too. It was a young black girl. And she wasn't writing it so much as she was *telling* it, with all the inflections of her voice, in the immediacy of the present tense. The rest of the story, however it went, had to be true to the voice in the first two lines. It certainly wasn't me telling it, not Larry Brown. I didn't want my voice in it. I wanted to be submerged in somebody else's voice, somebody telling a story for the first time, her way. This black kid, this young writer, was going to make a name for herself, but not an American name. African. She needed one. Kubuku. I gave her one. It was her first story, first time out of the gate. 'Kubuku Rides.'

"Maybe I was afraid way down deep in my mind that nobody would get it, so maybe that's why I stuck the subtitle in. I know that's why I kept it around the house for nearly a year after I'd finished it, scared to send it out because I thought nobody would like it, or understand it. When I finally did send it out, to a major magazine, I believe the phrase that accompanied the rejection slip was 'boringly monotonous.' But fortunately, Jim Clark at *The Greensboro Review* didn't see it that way. He did call me up and ask me what the title meant. Jim, this is what it means: a bolt of lightning through the head."

FREDERICK BUSCH's most recent book is *Absent Friends*, a collection of short fiction published in May 1989 by Knopf.

• "When our son, Nick, was very small and very young, perhaps fourteen or fifteen years ago, I started telling him a bedtime story about his floating plastic yellow duck, whom one of us had named Ralph. Pink and dewy from his bath, Nick lay in bed and I sat or lay beside him and told him about a small duck who grew cold, and then comforted, then sleepy. Not only did the story always put him to sleep; he grew dependent on it and refused to sleep unless he heard Ralph's story first. When I had to travel to give a reading, I wrote the story out so that Judy could tell it to Nick with the required pauses and inflections; Nick wouldn't sleep unless 'Ralph' was right. Now that Nick is six foot three, I sometimes feel not only the profit in living with so much but the loss of holding what was once so little. I think that balance of loss and gain, and a need to talk on my pages both tough *and* soft in response, led to my writing 'Ralph the Duck,' which, as at first, is for Nick."

MICHAEL CUNNINGHAM's first novel, *Golden States*, appeared in 1984. He has had stories published in *The New Yorker*, *The Atlantic*, *Redbook*, and *The Paris Review*.
• " 'White Angel' is based, very loosely, on a tragedy that took place in my home town (nowhere near Cleveland) when I was thirteen. While the story is at least 90 percent invention, that other 10 percent — the raw fact of a kid running through a pane of glass at a party — has been stuck in my brain for more than thirty years.

"The story has now become part of something longer — a novel, *A Home at the End of the World*, to be published next year by Farrar, Straus and Giroux. Like the rest of the book, it resulted from an often uneasy marriage between design and intuition. I work in a slightly peculiar manner: I tend to get hold of a vivid mental image, and then follow the narrative backward and forward from there. The picture of a young boy running through plate glass was a starting point for the whole book, though for a long time it just banged around inside my head. Likewise, later on, I imagined a woman standing in an empty yard pulling at her own hair, and a man walking out into the desert with his father. Sometimes these images come straight from life, but more often they come from my unconscious, with all the illogic and inevitability of dreams. The intervening writing is an elaborate game of connect the dots, with extra challenges thrown in. The dots aren't numbered, and they rearrange themselves after each new line has been drawn."

RICK DEMARINIS teaches creative writing at the University of Texas at El Paso. A new novel, *The Year of the Zinc Penny*, is due out from Norton this fall. He is also working on a new collection of short stories.

▪ "I worked in the aerospace industry for a few years. It was a boring job and I didn't do very well at it. I never quite found out what the job was. They said I was an engineer. They paid me an engineer's salary for sitting behind a gray desk in a large room with a few hundred other people also sitting behind gray desks. We were building an ICBM, they said. I didn't ask anyone where it was. I never saw an ICBM. I paged through heavy documents all day because I wanted to feel that I had work to do. No one bothered me. When I lost my initial shyness, I asked people sitting near me what it was we were supposed to be doing. The wise ones winked. The novices shrugged. The pay was too good to get worked up about such things. Somehow, somewhere, ICBMs were getting built. I knew that because I saw them on TV.

"I believe thought processes are primitive. Logic and reason mask a dark topography rutted by glaciers of superstition. We prefer intuition over analysis. Reason tells me that smart men with blueprints and serious purpose create ICBMs. My limited experience and my intuition tell me something else. One of the results of this conviction is 'The Flowers of Boredom.' All this happened decades ago. It still astonishes me."

HARRIET DOERR is the author of *Stones for Ibarra* (Viking Penguin, 1984) and is working on a second novel set in Mexico.

▪ " 'Edie' began as a thirty-line poem written for a class, and turned, years later, into a story.

"Its events, scenes, and situations are entirely fictional, as are its characters, with one exception. Edie herself is true. She is someone I knew when I was young."

MAVIS GALLANT's most recent book is *In Transit* (Random House), a collection of short stories.

▪ "I can't pin down the origin of 'The Concert Party' exactly. I know that it started with images of Montreal and the old Riviera of forty years ago, and the rest followed naturally."

DOUGLAS GLOVER is the author of two story collections and two novels, the most recent of which, *The South Will Rise at Noon*, was published in the spring of 1989. He divides his time between Waterford, Ontario, and Saratoga Springs, New York.

▪ "Most of 'Why I Decide to Kill Myself and Other Jokes' comes from a place so personal, so intimate, and so painful that I cannot write about it except as fiction. The story's style, the chemical metaphor, the obsessive repetitions, the phantasmagoria of proliferating analogies and comparisons, are the things I learned reading the novels of the late great French Canadian writer Hubert Aquin, especially *Blackout* and

The Antiphonary. Nabokov lurks somewhere. And back of Nabokov the ghost of Viktor Shklovsky telling us to make things 'strange.' Tall, blond Willa, my narrator, is a friend who told me her story one hot August afternoon on the gravelly bank of a southwestern Ontario swimming hole after a long day's work on my family's tobacco farm. The stolen cyanide, the wind blowing her skirt over her head, the snapshot of her dead father — these are all real. The dogs are not real. Professor Rainbolt is not real. Hugo is mostly imaginary, and his strange laboratory full of whispering, suffering plants is a room that exists only in my mind, or is my mind."

BARBARA GOWDY is a full-time writer living in Grand Valley, Ontario. Her first novel was published in 1988 in the United States, Canada, and Great Britain. Her second novel, *Falling Angels*, will be published by Somerville House of Toronto in the fall of 1989.
▪ "I wrote 'Disneyland' because I wanted to write about growing up. For me that meant writing about post–Second World War suburban North America. It also meant writing about fear and desire, and thirty years ago two of the big generators of these emotions were the Bomb and Disneyland.

"Something else I wanted to deal with is the extreme point at which a thing turns into its opposite. Love turns into hate, attraction turns into repulsion, and so on. In the case of 'Disneyland' I chose the point at which safety becomes perilous. The protector changes into the bad guy.

"To research the story I read old *Life* magazines. There really was a pamphlet called 'Pioneers of Self-Defense,' and it really did recommend that you paint a hopscotch on the bomb shelter floor and that while you were down there you should keep your spirits up by reading books about American history. So here was another extreme point — the point at which an absolutely straight, bleak, unimaginative time loses its mind.

"Even before I started writing 'Disneyland,' I had it in the back of my head that I would develop the story into a novel, and eventually I did. 'Disneyland' became half a chapter in *Falling Angels*. Half a chapter because I realized that an up-in-the-air ending might be O.K. in a short story but that for a novel to go anywhere, I'd either have to get the family out of the bomb shelter or let them rot in there."

LINDA HOGAN's work has been widely published and anthologized. Her book *Seeing Through the Sun* won an American Book Award in 1985 from the Before Columbus Foundation. *Savings* was published by Coffee House Press in 1988, and her new novel, *Mean Spirit*, is due out from Knopf in 1990. She has received a National Endowment for the Arts award in fiction, a Minnesota State Arts Board grant, a Colorado Writer's Fellowship, and her stories have won awards such as the Pushcart Prize.

▪ "Like all of my stories, 'Aunt Moon,' also a film script, is a coming together of experience, people I know, and my own imagination. As a Chickasaw Indian writer, I remember my grandparents in 1950s and early 1960s Oklahoma. No automobiles; they used horses and wagons for transportation. I remember the sky and the land, and all of my work is a part of that early landscape and the influence it worked deep inside me. This story is set in that time, during the Korean War. It brings together the colors of the sky, the people, and the history. When my cousin John Frank read this story, he said, 'You wrote about me!' At first I was taken aback; I'd forgotten the incident about the tornado taking the house trailer and leaving the motorcycle was his own experience. I like my stories to speak about lives that are usually not found in American literature. I believe this speaking gives something back to the people whose lives have given me the energy and the need to write our stories. And I love Aunt Moon. For me, she is one of the courageous female heroes and adventurers I have seldom seen in stories."

DAVID WONG LOUIE has completed a collection of stories that have appeared individually in such magazines as *The Iowa Review*, *The Agni Review*, and *Ploughshares*. He is a recipient of a fellowship from the National Endowment for the Arts and teaches in the English Department at Vassar College in Poughkeepsie, New York.

▪ "At the time I wrote the first draft of 'Displacement,' my wife was pregnant with our son. We were living on the largest parcel of residentially zoned land in town, acreage golden with acacia, exotic with palms. Our home was the smallest of structures, a two-room, spider-infested cottage with ceilings designed low for Chinese or Mexican servants. The main house, a big red building, had a green roof that curved at the eaves like the pagodas I've seen on Chinese calendars. We cleaned after and chauffeured the house's lone occupant, a moody older woman who was a master bridge player. When we informed her of the baby, she said the cottage would be too small for the soon-to-be three of us and that we'd have to move.

"Experience, then, provided me with the basic plot: a couple forced by circumstance to relocate and start new lives. As the narrative developed, though, experience played a diminished role. Mrs. Chow and her husband took over. They are invention, and their story is an invented one. With my other stories I can easily remember how each part evolved in the writing, but the particulars of this story's origins escape memory. I cannot call back the clear-headed instant Mrs. Chow first walked across my imagination, nor the image or detail from which she bloomed. I don't remember a single crisis in the writing of the story, though I'm certain I suffered, as always, through many.

"I suspect this haziness of memory isn't a matter of forgetting at all, but has everything to do with having known the story, in some deep way, even before I wrote a single word of it. When the characters were new and strangers to me, when the story's events were still surprising, they were at the same time familiar. Nothing stands out about the story's writing because this familiarity won't allow it — in my memory the story wasn't revealed in steps, by a process, but was a piece that simply arrived, something had. The Chows' story is about refugees, people off balance, whose dislocation is not just spatial but cultural, psychic, and emotional; it is, as I understand things, the undefined, unarticulated unease I have known my whole life — my own displacement."

BHARATI MUKHERJEE's most recent work, *The Middleman and Other Stories*, received the 1989 National Book Critics Circle Award for fiction. Her seventh book, *Jasmine*, a novel, will be published by Grove Press in September 1989. She lives in New York City and is currently collaborating with her husband, Clark Blaise, on a screenplay.

▪ "I wish I could say, comfortingly, that the act of terrorism — the bombing of a passenger-loaded jumbo jet — that precedes the opening of 'The Management of Grief' is imagined, that it is a playful distortion on the scale of Salman Rushdie's in *The Satanic Verses*. In Rushdie's novel, the terrorists act with honor, letting go the women, children, and Sikhs; the protagonists survive the crash and go on to become better humans.

"But real life keeps proving itself more relentless, more monstrous, than any fantasist's fiction. 'The Management of Grief' is a story that exists *in* history and is *of* history. Early on the morning of June 23, 1985, an Air India Boeing 747 on its way from Toronto and Montreal to Delhi was blown up by a terrorist bomb off the coast of Ireland, killing all 329 passengers and crew members on board. In terms of body count, it is the bloodiest single terrorist incident to date. Over 90 percent of the passengers were Canadian citizens, mostly women and children on their way to India to visit relatives who had not chosen to make themselves new lives in the New World. I knew a few of the passengers. I might have been a passenger myself. Over many months, while co-authoring *The Sorrow and the Terror*, a nonfiction book on this

incident, I witnessed the grief of the bereaved relatives, mostly widowers who hour after hour thumbed through photo albums or played
home movies on VCRs. 'Grief' wrote itself in two long sittings in July
1987. It is a tribute to all who forget enough of their roots to start over
enthusiastically in a new land, but who also remember enough of those
roots to survive Fate's knockout punches."

ALICE MUNRO was born in Wingham, Ontario, and attended the University of Western Ontario. She has published several books of fiction,
two of which have received the Governor General's Literary Award in
Canada. Several of her stories have been selected to appear in *Best
American Short Stories*. Ms. Munro lives in Clinton, Ontario.
▪ "In the nineteenth century most of the raw, thriving small towns of
southwestern Ontario had a local 'poetess.' The town where I live had
a Miss Mountcastle, who sometimes signed her poems 'Carissima.'
Nearby Goderich, on Lake Huron, had someone known as 'the Sweet
Songstress of La Mer Douce.'
    "These women, who were taken notice of in the small-town papers
with an uneasy mingling of mockery and respect, seem to have been as
much a feature of town life as the hell-fire preacher, the social boss-
lady, the village idiot. They wrote poetry that was sometimes mediocre
and sometimes very bad, about Nature, Love, Childhood, Christianity,
the British Empire. They prattled in quatrains and couplets about an
innocence, an idyllic world, quite at variance with the one before their
eyes, and they were despised and quaintly exalted for this blinkered
exercise.
    "This was what people thought Poetry should be, and these women
were its lonesome practitioners out at the edge of Victorian civilization.
Reading their published poetry, reading what the papers said about
them, you get a sense of claustrophobia and waste. They are sometimes
jingoistic about the Empire and maudlin about Jesus, they indulge in
constant raptures about flowers, they are fussily virginal, conventional,
silly. Just the same, they're paying attention, they're making something.
Once in a while it can amount to more than the pansies painted on
china plates.
    "So I thought, What about imagining one of these women and giving
her some talent — not enough to make her any sort of Emily Dickinson, just enough to give her glimpses, stir her up? Then put her in one
of those towns and see what will happen. I didn't want her to be particularly odd. I wanted her to have choices. I wanted to see what she
would do about poetry, sex, and living, in that town, that time, when
so many sturdy notions were pushing up together — the boisterous
commercialism and austere hard-hearted religion, the tenacious gentil-

ity hungering for class distinction. I ended up with the poetess half mad but not, I thought, entirely unhappy in the midst of this."

DALE RAY PHILLIPS teaches at the University of Arkansas. He is married to the poet Elizabeth Ford, and they are expecting their first child. His stories have appeared in *The Atlantic, Intro 16*, and *The Greensboro Review*. He is working on a collection of stories titled *What It Costs Travelers*.

▪ " 'What Men Love For' came to me while I was fishing with two writers, Otto Selassi and Dixon Boyles. You can't fish without swapping lies and stories and bouncing ideas off each other. The next morning the idea still seemed a good one, so I began working on it.

"I built the story around an image I saw: a man and a boy riding a motorcycle around a bend on a mountain road. I invented relationships and people. I let these invented people walk around in my childhood in North Carolina. The original version had a grandmother, but I kicked her out of the story. Then I revised, and revised some more. The final version is a result of much luck and some sweat and certainly the fine editing of C. Michael Curtis.

"My theory of writing is a simple one: write to make the hair on the back of a reader's neck stand up. This can be accomplished with either plot or revelation. This story required revelation.

"I am one of those writers who should probably write and not talk about his work."

MARK RICHARD's stories have appeared in many magazines, including *Esquire, Shenandoah, The Quarterly, Antaeus*, and *Grand Street*. His first collection, *The Ice at the Bottom of the World*, was published this year by Knopf.

▪ "I was lucky. I had not written a word in weeks. Months. I had taken an attic room on the beach in Virginia Beach. It was summer. I would lay out and these words were in my brain: *At night, stray dogs come up underneath our house to lick our leaking pipes.* Over and over. I knew everything I needed was in that sentence but I would not sit down in front of the machine. My friends used to come by and throw pine bark and gravel through my window for me to go out at night. Richard, hey Richard, they used to yell. I would be lying below window level on a canvas cot I had found on the sidewalk in New York. Then they would get me out and I would drink some beers and stare at my bottle thinking: *At night, etc., etc.* My friends would say, Aw, he's just being moody again, or Aw, he's just being depressed again, or Aw, he's just missing Pam again. Often it was all three, but also often it was: *At night, etc., etc.*

"Then I heard there was a contest that paid money, and I was broke.

When I ate or drank, it was always my friends coming over and taking me out and paying for it. So I sat down one night after staring in the sand all day thinking: *At night, etc., etc.* And it all came down at once like I was just the radio, like it was just something in the air anybody else could have written if they had been tuned in to the same station. I sent it off titled 'Little Firebugs, Little Lightning Flies.' Originally it was longer. I won some money and some books (it was the Hemingway Short Story Contest in Key West), and the story got around. Rust Hills at *Esquire* called me up and said, Here is where the story ends. And he was right. I had overwritten. The rest was another story called 'This Is Us, Excellent.' So I got two stories out of that radio broadcast. One of those one-sitting deals that God gives you. I was very lucky."

ARTHUR ROBINSON has worked for newspapers in Herkimer and Albany, New York, and in Miami, Indianapolis, and Fort Lauderdale, and for a technical magazine in San Francisco. 'The Boy on the Train' is his first published story.

▪ " 'The Boy on the Train' grew out of an effort to understand a father for whom I failed to feel the affection that I thought I owed him. He was very decent, tried to be good and fair, had a sense of humor, and was as baffled by his sons as they were by him. My brother and I never really made an emotional connection with him, and in his heaviness he often seemed to us slightly comic.

"An item that appeared on the editorial page of the *Utica Daily Press* in 1941 eventually altered my view of him. Under a standing head, 'Fifty Years Ago Today in The Press,' it reported that he had arrived in Utica the day before on a New York Central train on his way to join his mother in Camden. He was five years old and was traveling alone from Jacksonville, Florida.

"I thought of his trip occasionally over the years, of what must have been the anguish and anxiety he suffered over the separation of his parents in Jacksonville, and of the complexities of his journey; he had to take a ferry from New Jersey to Manhattan (there was no railroad tunnel under the Hudson) and change trains again in Utica. Part of the wonder was that he remembered his trip only when the item about it appeared in the paper fifty years later. He seemed to be rather embarrassed.

"I had written a number of stories in the past. When *The New Yorker* returned them, I had taken their rejection as confirmation that they weren't much good. 'The Boy on the Train' was one of them. In retirement, I looked some of them over; 'The Boy on the Train' struck me as a pretty good story. I made some changes, retyped it, and sent it back.

"Karen Kaminsky at *The New Yorker* cut some of it and made several suggestions, including strengthening the ending. She was very good, and the operation went quickly and painlessly."

M. T. SHARIF's most recent story, "In the Kingdom of the Wise," will be published in *The Agni Review*.

▪ "For some months prior to the writing of Haji's story I had been fascinated by the current practice of 'veiling' foreign magazines. Then I came across a series of letters, applications for clemency or redress, drafted by professional letter writers and sent to the municipal authorities in early-twentieth-century Iran. The rest was a matter of rewriting, of bringing two images together."

100 Other Distinguished Stories of 1988

SELECTED BY SHANNON RAVENEL

MATYAS, CATHY
Signals. *The New Quarterly,* Winter.
MEINKE, PETER
Doubles. *The Virginia Quarterly Review,*
Spring.
MILLHAUSER, STEVEN
Rain. *The Paris Review,* No. 108.
MINUS, ED
The Birth and Death of Music. *The
Gettysburg Review,* Spring.
MOLNAR, JANE COLEMAN
Babysitter. *Carolina Quarterly,* Spring.
MORDDEN, ETHAN
I Read My Nephew Stories. *The New
Yorker,* August 29.
Talking Dog of the World. *The New
Yorker,* July 11.
MUNRO, ALICE
Five Points. *The New Yorker,* April 11.

NORDAN, LEWIS
The Family Oven. *Playgirl,* April.
A Hank of Hair, a Piece of Bone. *The
Southern Review,* Spring.

OATES, JOYCE CAROL
The Boy Friend. *The Massachusetts
Review,* Spring.
Getting to Know All About You. *The
Southern Review,* Summer.

PEREIRA, HELEN
Three for a Wedding. *The New
Quarterly,* Vol. 8, No. 1 (Spring).
PERROTTA, TOM
Wild Kingdom. *The Gettysburg Review,*
Autumn.
PFEIL, FRED
The Angel of Dad. *Witness,* Summer/
Fall.
PROSE, FRANCINE
Ghirlandaio. *Tikkun,* May/June.

RAYFIEL, THOMAS
Watch the Closing Doors. *Grand
Street,* Spring.

REED, DIANA
Bizarre Births. *The Georgia Review,*
Spring.
RHEINHEIMER, KURT
Homes. *Southern Magazine,* February.
ROFIHE, RICK
Father Must. *The New Yorker,*
October 10.
ROSS, VERONICA
Order in the Universe. *The New
Quarterly,* Spring.
RUSSO, RICHARD
The Further You Go. *Shenandoah,*
Vol. 38, No. 1.

SADOFF, IRA
Sorties. *The Seattle Review,* Fall/Winter
1988–1989.
SALTER, JAMES
American Express. *Esquire,* February.
Twenty Minutes. *Grand Street,* Winter.
SANDOR, MARJORIE
The Bonbon Man. *Shenandoah,* Vol.
38, No. 3.
SANFORD, ANNETTE
Six White Horses. *The Ohio Review,*
No. 40.
SCHUSTER, JOSEPH M.
Car Wash. *The Missouri Review,* Vol.
11, No. 1.
SCHWARTZ, ADAM
The Grammar of Love. *The New
Yorker,* July 18.
SEXSON, LYNDA
Deer Crossing. *Carolina Quarterly,*
Fall.
SHARP, PAULA
Hot Springs. *The Threepenny Review,*
Summer.
SINGER, ISAAC BASHEVIS
The Bitter Truth. *Playboy,* April.
SPEAK, DOROTHY
Caressing Mine Idol's Pillow. *Ontario
Review,* Fall/Winter.
STARK, SHARON SHEEHE
Leo. *The Atlantic,* May.

Editorial Addresses of American and Canadian Magazines Publishing Short Stories

When available, the annual subscription rate, the average number of stories published per year, and the name of the editor follow the address.

Agni Review
Creative Writing Department
Boston University
236 Bay State Road
Boston, MA 02115
$12, 15, Askold Melnyczuk

Alabama Literary Review
Troy State University, Smith 264
Troy, AL 36082
$4, Theron E. Montgomery

Alaska Quarterly Review
Department of English
University of Alaska
3221 Providence Drive
Anchorage, AK 99508
$8, 20, Ronald Spatz

Alfred Hitchcock's Mystery Magazine
Davis Publications
380 Lexington Avenue
New York, NY 10017
$19.50, 130, Cathleen Jordan

Ambergris
5521½ 12th Avenue NE
Seattle, WA 98105
$6, 4, Mark Kissling

Amelia
329 East Street
Bakersfield, CA 93304
$20, 10, Frederick A. Raborg, Jr.

American Book Review
Publications Center
English Department, Box 226
University of Colorado
Boulder, CO 80309

Analog Science Fiction/Science Fact
380 Lexington Avenue
New York, NY 10017
$19.50, 70, Stanley Schmidt

Antaeus
26 West 17th Street
New York, NY 10011
$10, 15, Daniel Halpern

Antietam Review
82 West Washington Street
Hagerstown, MD 21740
$5, 6, Ann B. Knox

Antioch Review
P.O. Box 148
Yellow Springs, OH 45387
$18, 20, Robert S. Fogarty

Apalachee Quarterly
P.O. Box 20106
Tallahassee, FL 32316
*$12, 10, Allen Woodman, Barbara
  Hanby, Monica Faeth*

Arizona Quarterly
University of Arizona
Tucson, AZ 85721
$5, 12, Albert F. Gegenheimer

Arts Journal
324 Charlotte Street
Asheville, NC 28801
$15, 5, Tom Patterson

Ascent
English Department
University of Illinois
608 South Wright Street
Urbana, IL 61801
$3, 20, Daniel Curley

Atlantic Monthly
745 Boylston Street
Boston, MA 02116
$14.95, 12, C. Michael Curtis

Aura Literary/Arts Review
P.O. Box University Center
University of Alabama
Birmingham, AL 35294
$6, 10, rotating editorship

Bellowing Ark
P.O. Box 45637
Seattle, WA 98145
$12, 5, Robert R. Ward

Beloit Fiction Journal
Beloit College, P.O. Box 11

Beloit, WI 53511
$9, 10, Clint McCown

Black Ice
P.O. Box 49
Belmont, MA 02178-0001
$6, 20, Dale Shank

Black Warrior Review
P.O. Box 2936
Tuscaloosa, AL 35487-2936
$6.50, 12, Amber Vogel

Boston Review
33 Harrison Avenue
Boston, MA 02111
$12, 6, Margaret Ann Roth

Boulevard
4 Washington Square Village, 9R
New York, NY 10012
$12, 10, David Brezovec

California Quarterly
100 Sproul Hall
University of California
Davis, CA 95616
$10, 4, Elliott L. Gilbert

Calyx
P.O. Box B
Corvallis, OR 97339
$10, 2, Margarita Donnelly

Canadian Fiction
Box 946, Station F
Toronto, Ontario
M4Y 2N9 Canada
$30, 16, Geoffrey Hancock

Capilano Review
Capilano College
2055 Purcell Way
North Vancouver
British Columbia
V7J 3H5 Canada
$12, 5, Crystal Hurdle

Carolina Quarterly
Greenlaw Hall 066A
University of North Carolina

Chapel Hill, NC 27514
$10, 20, rotating editorship

Chariton Review
Division of Language and Literature
Northeast Missouri State University
Kirksville, MO 63501
$7, 10, Jim Barnes

Chattahoochee Review
DeKalb Community College
2101 Womack Road
Dunwoody, GA 30338-4497
$15, 25, Lamar York

Chelsea
P.O. Box 5880
Grand Central Station
New York, NY 10163
$11, 6, Sonia Raiziss

Chicago Review
5801 South Kenwood
University of Chicago
Chicago, IL 60637
$18, 20, Elizabeth Arnold

Christopher Street
P.O. Box 1475
Church Street Station
New York, NY 10008
$27, 20, Tom Steele

Cimarron Review
205 Morrill Hall
Oklahoma State University
Stillwater, OK 74078-0135
$10, 15, John Kenny Crane

Clockwatch Review
737 Penbrook Way
Hartland, WI 53029
$6, 6, James Plath

Colorado Review
Department of English
360 Eddy Building
Colorado State University
Fort Collins, CO 80523
$9, 10, Bill Tremblay

Columbia
404 Dodge
Columbia University
New York, NY 10027
$4.50, 6, Jill Bird Sall, Peter B. Erdmann

Commentary
165 East 56th Street
New York, NY 10022
$36, 5, Norman Podhoretz

Concho River Review
English Department
Angelo State University
San Angelo, TX 76909
$12, 7, Terrence A. Dalrymple

Confrontation
English Department
C. W. Post College of Long Island University
Greenvale, NY 11548
$8, 25, Martin Tucker

Conjunctions
New Writing Foundation
866 Third Avenue
New York, NY 10022
$16, 6, Bradford Morrow

Cotton Boll/Atlanta Review
P.O. Box 76757, Sandy Springs
Atlanta, GA 30358-0703
$10, 12, Mary Hollingsworth

Crazyhorse
Department of English
University of Arkansas
Little Rock, AR 72204
$8, 10, David Jauss

Crescent Review
P.O. Box 15065
Winston-Salem, NC 27113
$7.50, 24, Dee Shneiderman

Crosscurrents
2200 Glastonbury Road
Westlake Village, CA 91361
$15, 36, Linda Brown Michelson

Cut Bank
Department of English
University of Montana
Missoula, MT 59812
$9, 10, rotating editorship

Denver Quarterly
University of Denver
Denver, CO 80208
$15, 27, David Milofsky

Descant
P.O. Box 314
Station P
Toronto, Ontario
M5S 2S8 Canada
$26, 20, Karen Mulhallen

Epoch
251 Goldwin Smith Hall
Cornell University
Ithaca, NY 14853-3201
$9.50, 36, C. S. Giscombe

Esquire
1790 Broadway
New York, NY 10019
$17.94, 15, Rust Hills

event
Douglas College
P.O. Box 2503
New Westminster
British Columbia
V3L 5B2 Canada
$9, 15, Maurice Hodgson

Fantasy & Science Fiction
Box 56
Cornwall, CT 06753
$17.50, 75, Edward L. Ferman

Farmer's Market
P.O. Box 1272
Galesburg, IL 61402
$7, 10, Jean C. Lee

Fiction
Fiction, Inc.
Department of English

The City College of New York
New York, NY 10031
$7, Mark Mirsky

Fiction International
Department of English &
    Comparative Literature
San Diego State University
San Diego, CA 92182
$14, 35, Roger Cunniff, Edwin Gordon

Fiction Network
P.O. Box 5651
San Francisco, CA 94101
$8, 25, Jay Schaefer

Fiction Review
P.O. Box 12268
Seattle, WA 98102
$15, 25, S. P. Stressman

Fiddlehead
Room 317, Old Arts Building
University of New Brunswick
Fredericton, New Brunswick
E3B 5A3 Canada
$14, 20, Kent Thompsen

Florida Review
Department of English, Box 25000
University of Central Florida
Orlando, FL 32816
$6, 16, Pat Rushin

Folio
Department of Literature
The American University
Washington, D.C. 20016
$8, 12, Carol Eron

Formations
P.O. Box 327
Wilmette, IL 60091
$15, 4, Jonathan and Frances Brent

Forum
Bay State University
Muncie, IN 47306
$15, 40, Bruce W. Hozeski

Four Quarters
LaSalle College
20th and Olney Avenues
Philadelphia, PA 19141
$8, 10, John J. Keenan

Gargoyle
Paycock Press
P.O. Box 30906
Bethesda, MD 20814
$15, 25, Richard Peabody

Georgia Review
University of Georgia
Athens, GA 30602
$12, 15, Stanley W. Lindberg

Gettysburg Review
Gettysburg College
Gettysburg, PA 17325
$12, 20, Peter Stitt

Good Housekeeping
959 Eighth Avenue
New York, NY 10019
$14.97, 24, Naomi Lewis

GQ
350 Madison Avenue
New York, NY 10017
$19.97, 12, Tom Jenks

Grain
Box 3986
Regina, Saskatchewan
S4P 3R9 Canada
$12, 20, Mick Burrs

Grand Street
50 Riverside Drive
New York, NY 10024
$20, 20, Ben Sonnenberg

Granta
250 West 57th Street, suite 1316
New York, NY 10107
$28, NY editor: Anne Kinard

Gray's Sporting Journal
205 Willow Street

South Hamilton, MA 01982
$26.50, 20, Edward E. Gray

Great River Review
211 West 7th
Winona, MN 55987
$9, 6, Ruth Forsyth

Greensboro Review
Department of English
University of North Carolina
Greensboro, NC 27412
$5, 16, Jim Clark

Harper's Magazine
666 Broadway
New York, NY 10012
$18, 15, Lewis H. Lapham

Hawaii Review
University of Hawaii
Department of English
1733 Donaghho Road
Honolulu, HI 96822
$6, 12, Jeannie Thompson

Helicon Nine
P.O. Box 22412
Kansas City, MO 64113
$18, 8, Gloria Vando Hickock

High Plains Literary Review
180 Adams Street, suite 250
Denver, CO 80206
$20, 10, Robert O. Greer, Jr.

Hudson Review
684 Park Avenue
New York, NY 10021
$18, 8, Paula Deitz, Frederick Morgan

Indiana Review
316 North Jordan Avenue
Bloomington, IN 47405
$10, 20, Elizabeth Dodd

In Earnest
P.O. Box 4177
James Madison University
Harrisonburg, VA 22807
6, Greg Barrett

Iowa Review
Department of English
University of Iowa, 308 EPB
Iowa City, IA 52242
$15, 10, David Hamilton

Iowa Woman
P.O. Box 680
Iowa City, IA 52244
$10, 12, Carolyn Hardesty

Isaac Asimov's Science Fiction
   Magazine
380 Lexington Avenue
New York, NY 10017
$19.50, 100, Gardner Dozois

Jewish Currents
22 East 17th Street
New York, NY 10003
$15, 20, editorial board

Jewish Monthly
1640 Rhode Island Avenue NW
Washington, DC 20036
$8, 3, Marc Silver

The Journal
Department of English
Ohio State University
164 West 17th Avenue
Columbus, OH 43210
$5, 2, David Citino

Kansas Quarterly
Department of English
Denison Hall
Kansas State University
Manhattan, KS 66506
$15, 20, Ben Nyberg

Karamu
English Department
Eastern Illinois University
Charleston, IL 61920
John Guzlowski

Kenyon Review
Kenyon College
Gambier, OH 43022

$15, 15, Philip D. Church, Galbraith M.
   Crump

Lilith
The Jewish Women's Magazine
250 West 57th Street
New York, NY 10107
$14, 5, Julia Wolf Mazow

Literary Review
Fairleigh Dickinson University
285 Madison Avenue
Madison, NJ 07940
$12, 25, Walter Cummins

Little Magazine
Dragon Press
P.O. Box 78
Pleasantville, NY 10570
$16, 5

McCall's
230 Park Avenue
New York, NY 10169
$13.95, 20, Helen DelMonte

Mademoiselle
350 Madison Avenue
New York, NY 10017
$15, 14, Eileen Schnurr

Madison Review
University of Wisconsin
Department of English
H. C. White Hall
600 North Park Street
Madison, WI 53706
$5, 8, Craig Alexander

Malahat Review
University of Victoria
P.O. Box 1700
Victoria, British Columbia
V8W 2Y2 Canada
$15, 25, Constance Rooke

Massachusetts Review
Memorial Hall
University of Massachusetts
Amherst, MA 01003
$12, 15, Mary Heath

Michigan Quarterly Review
3032 Rackham Building
University of Michigan
Ann Arbor, MI 48109
$13, 10, Laurence Goldstein

Mid-American Review
106 Hanna Hall
Department of English
Bowling Green State University
Bowling Green, OH 48109
$6, 10, Robert Early

Minnesota Review
Department of English
State University of New York
Stony Brook, NY 11794-5350
$7, Helen Cooper

Mississippi Review
University of Southern Mississippi
Southern Station, Box 5144
Hattiesburg, MS 39406-5144
$10, 25, Frederick Barthelme

Missouri Review
Department of English
231 Arts and Sciences
University of Missouri
Columbia, MO 65211
$12, 15, Speer Morgan

MSS
P.O. Box 530
State University of New York
Binghamton, NY 13901
$10, 30, L. M. Rosenberg

Nebraska Review
Writers' Workshop, ASH 212
University of Nebraska
Omaha, NE 68182-0324
$6, 10, Art Homer, Richard Duggin

Negative Capability
62 Ridgelawn Drive East
Mobile, AL 36605
$12, 15, Sue Walker

New Directions
New Directions Publishing

80 Eighth Avenue
New York, NY 10011
$11.95, 4, James Laughlin

New England Review and Bread Loaf
   Quarterly
Middlebury College
Middlebury, VT 05753
$12, 15, Sydney Lea

New Laurel Review
828 Lesseps Street
New Orleans, LA 70117
$8, 2, Lee Meitzer Grue

New Letters
University of Missouri
5216 Rockhill Road
Kansas City, MO 64110
$15, 10, Trish Reeves

New Mexico Humanities Review
P.O. Box A
New Mexico Tech
Socorro, NM 87801
$8, 15, John Rothfork

New Orleans Review
P.O. Box 195
Loyola University
New Orleans, LA 70118
$25, 4, John Biguenet, John Master

New Quarterly
English Language Proficiency
   Programme
University of Waterloo
Waterloo, Ontario
N2L 3G1 Canada
$13, 15, Peter Hinchcliffe

New Renaissance
9 Heath Road
Arlington, MA 02174
$11.50, 10, Louise T. Reynolds

New Virginia Review
1306 East Cary Street, 2A
Richmond, VA 23219
$13.50, 12, Mary Flinn

The New Yorker
25 West 43rd Street
New York, NY 10036
$32, 100

Nimrod
Arts and Humanities Council of
  Tulsa
2210 South Main Street
Tulsa, OK 74114
$10, 10, Francine Ringold

North American Review
University of Northern Iowa
Cedar Falls, IA 50614
$11, 35, Robley Wilson, Jr.

North Dakota Quarterly
University of North Dakota
P.O. Box 8237
Grand Forks, ND 58202
$10, 10, Robert W. Lewis

Northwest Review
369 PLC
University of Oregon
Eugene, OR 97403
$11, 10, John Witte

Oak Square
Box 1238
Allston, MA 02134
$10, 20, Anne E. Pluto

Ohio Journal
Department of English
Ohio State University
164 West 17th Avenue
Columbus, OH 43210
$5, 4, Don Citino

Ohio Review
Ellis Hall
Ohio University
Athens, OH 45701-2979
$12, 10, Wayne Dodd

Old Hickory Review
P.O. Box 1178
Jackson, TN 38301
$4, 5, Dorothy Starfill

Omni
1965 Broadway
New York, NY 10023-5965
$24, 20, Ellen Datlow

Ontario Review
9 Honey Brook Drive
Princeton, NJ 08540
$10, 8, Raymond J. Smith

Other Voices
820 Ridge Road
Highland Park, IL 60035
*$16, 30, Dolores Weinberg, Lois
  Hauselman*

Paris Review
541 East 72nd Street
New York, NY 10021
$20, 15, George Plimpton

Passages North
William Boniface Fine Arts Center
7th Street and 1st Avenue South
Escanaba, MI 49829
$2, 12, Elinor Benedict

Plainswoman
P.O. Box 8027
Grand Forks, ND 58202
$10, 10, Emily Johnson

Playboy
Playboy Building
919 North Michigan Avenue
Chicago, IL 60611
$24, 20, Alice K. Turner

Playgirl
Box 3710
Escondido, CA 92025
$35, 15, Mary Ellen Strote

Ploughshares
P.O. Box 529
Cambridge, MA 02139-0529
$15, 25, DeWitt Henry

Prairie Schooner
201 Andrews Hall
University of Nebraska

Lincoln, NE 68588-0334
$15, 20, Hugh J. Lake

Primavera
1212 East 59th Street
Chicago, IL 60637
$5, 10, Ann Gearen

Prism International
Department of Creative Writing
University of British Columbia
Vancouver, British Columbia
V6T 1W5 Canada
$12, 20, Jennifer Milton

Puerto del Sol
Department of English
New Mexico State University
Las Cruces, NM 88003
$7.75, 12, Kevin McIlvoy

Quarry Magazine
P.O. Box 1061
Kingston, Ontario
K7L 4Y5 Canada
$18, 20, Barry Grills

The Quarterly
Vintage Books
201 East 50th Street
New York, NY 10022
$28, 10, Bernie Wood

RE:AL
School of Liberal Arts
Stephen F. Austin State University
Nacogdoches, TX 75962
$4, 5, Neal B. Houston

River City Review
P.O. Box 34275
Louisville, KY 40232
$5, 10, Richard L. Neumayer

River Styx
Big River Association
14 South Euclid
St. Louis, MO 63108
$14, 10, Carol J. Pierman

A Room of One's Own
P.O. Box 46160
Station G
Vancouver, British Columbia
V6R 4G5 Canada
$11, 12, Gayla Reid

St. Andrews Review
St. Andrews Presbyterian College
Laurinsburg, NC 28352
$12, 10, Ronald H. Bayes

Salmagundi
Skidmore College
Saratoga Springs, NY 12866
$12, 2, Robert Boyers

San Jose Studies
English Department
San Jose State University
One Washington Square
San Jose, CA 95192
$12, 5, Fauneil J. Rinn

Santa Monica Review
Center for the Humanities
Santa Monica College
1900 Pico Boulevard
Santa Monica, CA 90405
$12, 16, Jim Krusoe

Saturday Night
511 King Street West, suite 100
Toronto, Ontario
M5V 2Z4 Canada
Robert Fulford

Seattle Review
Padelford Hall, GN-30
University of Washington
Seattle, WA 98195
$8, 10, Charles Johnson

Seventeen
850 Third Avenue
New York, NY 10022
$13.95, 12, Adrian Nicole LeBlanc

Sewanee Review
University of the South

Sewanee, TN 37375-4009
$18, 10, George Core

Shenandoah
Washington and Lee University
Box 722
Lexington, VA 24450
$11, 10, Dabney Stuart

Short Story Review
P.O. Box 882108
San Francisco, CA 94188-2108
$9, 8, Dwight Gabbard

Sinister Wisdom
P.O. Box 3252
Berkeley, CA 94703
$17, 25, Elana Dykewoman

Sonora Review
Department of English
University of Arizona
Tucson, AZ 85721
$5, 10, Tom Unger

South Carolina Review
Department of English
Clemson University
Clemson, SC 29634-1503
$5, 2, Richard J. Calhoun

South Dakota Review
University of South Dakota
P.O. Box 111 University Exchange
Vermillion, SD 57069
$10, 15, John R. Milton

Southern California Anthology
% Master of Professional Writing
   Program, WPH 404
University of Southern California
Los Angeles, CA 90089
$5.95, 6, Suzanne Harper

Southern Humanities Review
9088 Haley Center
Auburn University
Auburn, AL 36849
*$12, 5, Dan R. Latimer, Thomas L.
   Wright*

Southern Magazine
201 East Markham Street, suite 200
Little Rock, AR 72201
$15, 6, James Morgan

Southern Review
43 Allen Hall
Louisiana State University
Baton Rouge, LA 70803
$12, 20, Fred Hobson, James Olney

Southwest Review
Southern Methodist University
P.O. Box 4374
Dallas, TX 75275
$16, 15, Willard Spiegelman

Sou'wester
School of Humanities
Department of English
Southern Illinois University
Edwardsville, IL 62026-1438
$4, 10, Donald Gilbert

Special Edition, Fiction
Whittle Communications L.P.
505 Market Street
Knoxville, TN 37902
$14, 28, Elise Nakhnikian

Stories
14 Beacon Street
Boston, MA 02108
$16, 12, Amy R. Kaufman

Story Quarterly
P.O. Box 1416
Northbrook, IL 60065
$12, 20, Anne Brashler, Diane Williams

The Sun
412 Rosemary Street
Chapel Hill, NC 27514
$28, 12, Sy Safransky

Tampa Review
P.O. Box 19F
University of Tampa
401 West Kennedy Boulevard

Tampa, FL 33606-1490
$7, 12, Andy Solomon

Threepenny Review
P.O. Box 9131
Berkeley, CA 94709
$10, 10, Wendy Lesser

Tikkun
5100 Leona Street
Oakland, CA 94619
$30, 2, Rosellen Brown

Timbuktu
P.O. Box 469
Charlottesville, VA 22902
$6, 6, Molly Turner

TriQuarterly
2020 Ridge Avenue
Northwestern University
Evanston, IL 60208
$18, 15, Reginald Gibbons

Turnstile
175 Fifth Avenue, suite 2348
New York, NY 10010
$13, 12, Jill Benz

University of Windsor Review
Department of English
University of Windsor
Windsor, Ontario
N9B 3P4 Canada
$10, 6, Joseph A. Quinn

Virginia Quarterly Review
One West Range
Charlottesville, VA 22903
$15, 12, Staige D. Blackford

Voice Literary Supplement
842 Broadway
New York, NY 10003
$12, 8, M. Mark

Weber Studies
Weber State College
Ogden, UT 84408
$5, 2, Neila Seshachari

Webster Review
Webster University
470 East Lockwood
Webster Groves, MO 63119
$5, 5, Nancy Schapiro

West Branch
Department of English
Bucknell University
Lewisburg, PA 17837
$5, 10, Robert Love Taylor

Western Humanities Review
University of Utah
Salt Lake City, UT 84112
$15, 10, Barry Weller

William and Mary Review
College of William and Mary
Williamsburg, VA 23185
$4.50, 5, William Clark

Willow Springs
PUB P.O. Box 1063
Eastern Washington University
Cheney, WA 99004
$7, 8, Dennis Medina

Wind
RFD Route 1, P.O. Box 809K
Pikeville, KY 41501
$6, 20, Quentin R. Howard

Witness
31000 Northwestern Highway
P.O. Box 9079
Farmington Hills, MI 48333-9079
$16, 15, Peter Stine

Worcester Review
6 Chatham Street
Worcester, MA 01609
$10, 8, Rodger Martin

Writers Forum
University of Colorado
P.O. Box 7150
Colorado Springs, CO 80933-7150
$8.95, 15, Alexander Blackburn

Xavier Review
Xavier University
Box 110C
New Orleans, LA 70125
Rainulf A. Steizmann

Yale Review
1902A Yale Station
New Haven, CT 06520
$16, 12, Mr. Kai Erikson

Yankee
Yankee Publishing, Inc.
Dublin, NH 03444
$18, 10, Edie Clark

Yellow Silk
P.O. Box 6374
Albany, CA 94706
$15, 10, Lily Pond

Z Miscellaneous
P.O. Box 20041
New York, NY 10028
$9, 73, Charles Fabrizio

Zyzzyva
41 Sutter Street, suite 1400
San Francisco, CA 94104
$20, 12, Howard Junker